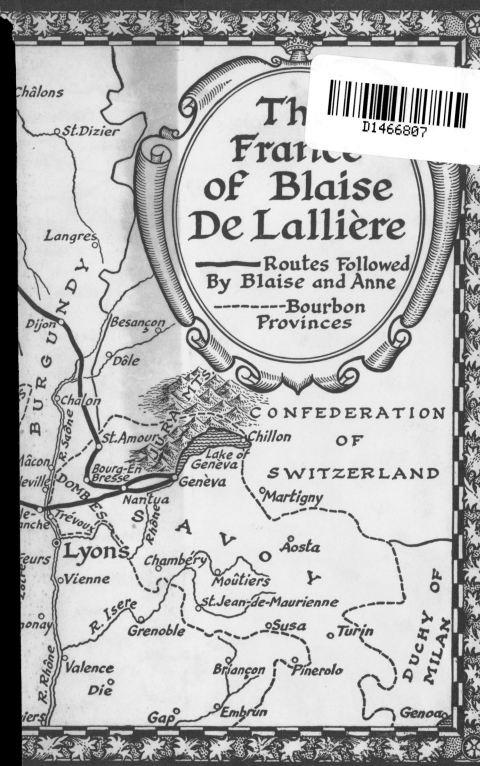

The
France
of Blaise
De Lallière

—— Routes Followed
By Blaise and Anne
- - - - - - - Bourbon
Provinces

Châlons

St.Dizier

Langres

BURGUNDY

Dijon

Besançon

Dôle

Chalon

R. Saône

St.Amour

JURA MTS

Chillon

CONFEDERATION

OF

Lake of
Geneva

Mâcon

Bourg-En-
Bresse

Genèva

Martigny

SWITZERLAND

DOMBES

leville

Nantua

Trévoux

le-
anche

R. Rhône

S

A

V

O

Feurs

Lyons

Chambéry

Aosta

Vienne

Moûtiers

Y

onay

R. Isere

St.Jean-de-Maurienne

DUCHY OF
MILAN

Grenoble

Susa

Turin

R. Rhône

Valence

Die

Briançon

Pinerolo

iers

Gap

Embrun

Genoa

THE KING'S
CAVALIER

THE KING'S
CAVALIER

by

SAMUEL SHELLABARGER

Little, Brown and Company   Boston

To my daughter Ingrid

THE KING'S
CAVALIER

PART ONE

Chapter 1

Old Clairon slept, if, indeed, a veteran wolfhound, conscious of his station and responsibilities, can ever be said to sleep. Clairon might close his eyes, but the other organs of sense remained awake. Out-stretched on the platform of the belvedere, an artificial mound which gave a commanding view both of the vast manor-house courtyard and of the highway beyond the walls, he was aware of relaxed contentment. Dozing, he could feel the comfortable warmth of the late July sun on his shaggy coat, tempered by a ruffling breeze off the mountains. Familiar sounds lulled his ears: clucking of poultry scattered over the three-acre courtyard; flutter and cooing of pigeons around the cone-shaped dovecote; grunting of swine from the sties, which, together with the stables, the chapel and other buildings, formed two projecting wings that flanked the body of the château; infinite hum of flies and bees; occasional traffic on the road below the walls, too usual for Clairon's attention. And, still more vivid, a feast of smells. The grandiose dung heap between cow barn and stables, the pond in the center of the court, the kitchen of the main building, the vegetable garden and fruit trees on the other side of the house, each furnished a part. More distant were odors from the adjacent village of Lallière, which lay close to the manor, with its circle of hay and grain fields. But most enchanting of all were scents from the pine-covered mountains, rich in promise of the chase. Altogether, a blending of delicious sensations.

Someone drew water from the well near the kitchen, sharpened a knife on the stone: a forecast of still remote supper . . .

Then suddenly Clairon's ears stiffened, his eyes opened. It was a sound and smell that deserved notice, the wisp of a sound and smell. He raised his head, considering it. He was no hothead but deliberate and discriminating. He saved his voice for important pronouncements; and, when Clairon spoke, the whole château listened. Was

3

this an occasion for report, the rapid thudding of horses' hoofs in the thick dust of the road from La Palisse, inaudible as yet to any ears save his? Not the thudding itself, perhaps, for many riders passed that way. But, coupled with this ghost of a scent on the wind that conveyed pleasant, vague associations . . .

He raised himself to his front legs and sat tense. Another puff of air. He sprang up, standing four feet high, gaunt, urgent. His tail, not often demonstrative, swung from side to side. He lifted his head and sounded the call which had given him his name. It reached every corner of the manor.

The dogs in the courtyard beneath scrambled to attention, took their cue, and furnished a chorus. The stabled horses pricked their ears and stamped. Ducks hurried into the pond. Hens cackled. People appeared at doors and windows.

"It's Clairon. . . ."

Upstairs in the circular tower bedroom, which looked out toward the east, Madame Constance de Lallière, erect, calm and inflexible, was instructing her daughter, Renée, a pretty girl of fifteen, in the finer points of civility. Guests were expected that evening, and this demanded a rehearsal in manners. Firm and poised, she sat on a bench at right angles to the casement, while Renée stood in front of her. If a string had been dropped from the back of Madame de Lallière's crescent-shaped headdress, it would have hung, like a plumb line, without encountering her shoulders. Educated at the strict court of Anne de Beaujeu, Duchess of Bourbon, she deplored the uncontrolled posture and general giddiness of modern girls, though a sense of humor tempered the disapproval. God knew that with Renée she had need both of humor and patience in full measure, for a more distracting flibbertigibbet never wore skirts. But a soft mother, it was said, made soft children; and she had no intention of neglecting her duty.

They had reached a point in the lesson where mildness would have been a sin.

"You know," said Madame de Lallière in a collected voice, "if you permit yourself to yawn once more — I say just once, m'amie — I shall box your ears. Do not imagine that I shall tolerate impertinence. I shudder to think of the consequence if I had yawned in the presence of my governess at the court of Madame de Bourbon. It would have been most unpleasant, I assure you. T'as compris?"

4

Renée tried to look contrite, but her piquant face succeeded only in looking mischievous.

"I pray you to pardon me, madame ma mère."

"That depends on your conduct. You have not yet answered the question I asked when that graceless yawn interrupted."

Renée stammered, "I hardly know . . ."

"You have forgot the question perhaps? It was not worthy of Mademoiselle's attention? You prefer to look at Cocorico."

Madame de Lallière glanced sternly at her daughter's toy spaniel, a jet-black, silken little creature, with long ears and expressive eyes, who sat blinking sympathetically at his mistress. Like Clairon, Cocorico had been named for his voice, which faintly resembled a rooster's. Under that masterful glance, he looked more apologetic than before and, rolling over on his back, folded his paws in deprecation.

"No, Mama" — Renée's voice had a rippling thrushlike tone that was irresistible — "but a thought crossed my mind while you were speaking, and I confess — "

"What thought?"

"About signs. I saw three spiders together this morning. Also the cat rubbed her ears with both paws at the same time. You see, like that. And I was wondering . . ."

"By Saint Catherine!" breathed her mother. "I shall go mad. Behold me laboring to teach you the manners of polite society, without which you can make no figure in the world nor please a husband if the good God mercifully sends you one, and you babble about spiders and cats!"

"But you believe in signs, madame. There's the horseshoe which I found yesterday on the highroad, its open end toward me. Sire François the Sorcerer himself happened to be passing. He congratulated me and said it meant a suitor within the week. Sire François told me to hang it up on a pink ribbon."

Constance de Lallière crossed herself. "A noted wolf-master and loup-garou, that fellow," she muttered. "He has the evil eye. I have forbidden you to speak with him. He will cast a spell on you; perhaps he already has."

"Then you won't let me hang it up?" Renée pleaded.

Her mother pretended to hesitate but then nodded. She saw here a heaven-sent opportunity. Besides, no one could deny that horseshoes brought luck. "I shall permit it," she declared, "on one condition: that you will give perfect attention to our lessons until this suitor arrives. If not, down it comes, for you will be unworthy of a suitor. Without manners, you would not be able to hold him and would disgrace our house. Is it a bargain?"

The strategy was sound. Renée's eyes sparkled. "I shall strive to learn."

"Good! We'll review the simpler points first. Suppose your suitor appears. He is a count or baron. He enters." She made a compelling gesture toward the door. "There he stands!"

Her imagination helping, Renée gazed speechless at the visionary gallant.

"Well," prompted her mother, "what now?"

Renée bobbed.

"Fie! What a dip! He would take you for a goosegirl. Again — and slow!"

This time Renée bent her knees, sinking gradually and gradually rising.

"Much better. And then? What will you call him? Even people of breeding are sometimes careless, but you should follow the rule."

"Monsieur."

"Perhaps. But more properly to a count or baron?"

"Monseigneur."

"Right. Of course, monsieur may be used in reference to anyone of birth, prince as well as gentleman — for example, Monsieur de Bourbon, Monsieur de Vendôme — but, when *addressing* a nobleman of rank, monseigneur is usual. And now, suppose your suitor a knight — you would say — ?"

"Messire."

"Yes. And to a simple gentleman like your father?"

Renée put in: "I should prefer a husband of that station, ma mère. I shouldn't care for a high and mighty lord. He would make me feel too small."

"You're not apt to get one," remarked her mother dryly. "But answer my question."

"To a gentleman, monsieur or messire."

"Good. And suppose him a doctor or advocate."

"No," said Renée.

"Of course not, but imagine."

The girl wrinkled her nose. "Maître."

"Bien, m'amie. We shall not afflict you with Sire Jean, the merchant, or Sire Jacques, the farmer. But now assume that you have

6

suitors of the different ranks we have mentioned, and assume (an absurdity, I grant) that they should all pay their respects to your father at the same time. How should they be received? How should they be seated in the main room? It is not so simple. . . ."

Clairon's call, though muffled by intervening walls, now reached them from the courtyard. Cocorico scrambled to his feet; Madame de Lallière broke off; Renée's dark eyes widened.

"Someone's coming," she whispered. "Clairon doesn't bark for nothing. He bayed like that when Monsieur de Norville rode in at noon. Only this sounds friendlier."

Her mother shrugged but looked thoughtful. "Business of the Duke's, I suppose, or about the meeting here tonight. War's in the wind, God save us! We're apt to have callers enough from now on. All the more reason," she added, "why you should learn manners. Well, then, as I was saying . . ."

Clairon's bark quickened. Renée's little slippers fidgeted, as if the tiled floor had turned hot.

"Ah, madame, let me only have one peep from the courtyard window. I'll return at once. A little moment."

The older woman yielded. Besides she was curious herself. "Very well," she said.

Renée and Cocorico had vanished. A flurry of skirts, a scampering across the big room beyond, a patter of footsteps down the spiral stairs of the southern turret.

"Set your bonnet to rights at least," called Madame de Lallière into emptiness. "It's on the back of your head. Vertu Dieu, what a grasshopper that girl is!"

With a smile, she rose from the bench and, unhurried as ever, crossed the adjacent room to a window overlooking the courtyard.

Behind closed doors in the main hall downstairs, three gentlemen were scanning a map. It was roughly drawn but it showed correctly enough the central and eastern provinces of France, with the Duchy of Savoy (which at that time included Geneva) beyond the eastern frontier. Chiefly it represented the immense estates of Charles, Duke of Bourbon and prince of the blood, who held also the supreme military rank of Constable. The thumb of the oldest gentleman pressed down hard here and there over this section, so hard that the nail whitened.

"Le Bourbonnais," he counted, "Le Forez, Auvergne, La Marche,

7

Beaujolais, Les Dombes, Gien, the mountains of Ardeche . . . What a domain! A kingdom within the kingdom. And Monseigneur the Duke is expected to hand this over to the King's mother on the strength of a barefaced, crooked lawsuit and a forced judgment! When, by every contract and decree, it has been established that no woman can inherit said domain! But the Duke knows that he has no chance against the royal interest."

The speaker thumped the map with his fist. His massive face looked a tint redder than usual. Framed between the lines of square-cut, iron-gray hair, which fell to his shoulders, it resembled some rudely carved, ancient effigy. And in most ways, Antoine de Lallière, Seigneur of Lallière, recalled the past, just as the grim, ill-lighted room, without ornament save for a scattering of old-fashioned arms on hooks along one side, recalled it. He, like most people, could have afforded a velvet cap of the latest mode; but he wore a stained old bonnet of homespun cloth forty years behind the times, such as Louis, the eleventh of that name, might have worn. The rest of his clothes, though not quite so antique, were aggressively out of date, almost to the point of affectation. For, indeed, conservatism was his code and his creed.

In striking contrast to him was the handsome gentleman at his right who nodded agreement to de Lallière's thumping. And yet *handsome*, as applied to the Duke of Bourbon's agent, Jean de Norville, ought to be considered an understatement. Rather, he was beautiful in a blond, angelic way, though with no feminine aftertaste. His close-cropped hair had only a touch of auburn, which was somewhat elaborated in his fashionable, youthful beard. According to the light, his eyes varied between sapphire and black; and the sapphire of his locket ring reflected their color. From the white plume of his cap to the slashes of his square-toed shoes, he represented perfection in feature and dress. The only discrepancy was certain lines about the mouth, which, though carefully controlled, seemed less angelic than the rest of him. He was a nobleman of Savoy and hence actually a foreigner; but he possessed large holdings in Forez, which he had inherited from his wife recently dead. To that extent, he became a vassal of Bourbon's, whom he now served in confidential matters. His charm and ability had raised him high in the Constable's favor.

"Of course the Duke knows it," he interrupted. "The Paris Parlement will hand down a decree against him next month. This fine

8

domain" (he flicked his hand toward the map) "will be seized by the King, who already demands La Marche and the Viscountcies of Carlat and Murat. There's no doubt possible. It's long live the House of Valois and farewell to the House of Bourbon, unless . . ."

He left the sentence hanging and smiled.

Antoine de Lallière burst out again. "Farewell to everything: justice, honor, the old way of life! Sirs, I have watched the trend in France for sixty years. Where now are the Duchies of Burgundy and Brittany? Absorbed by the Crown. Where now are the feudal rights of noblemen? Absorbed by the Crown. And now, in this year 1523, the last great fief, our Duchy of Bourbonnais, awaits the axe. I tell you, sirs, the day will come when we gentlemen of France are no more than slaves and lackeys of the King."

"Unless," repeated de Norville. "Monsieur, you attended the gathering of the Duke's nobles last week at Montbrison. You found plenty there who agree with you. Well then?"

A fanatical light crossed the older man's face. "The Duke can count on us. Eh, my son?"

Seated at his father's left, Guy de Lallière nodded. He was a man of few words. In this respect, as in appearance, people found that he resembled none other than Duke Charles of Bourbon himself, and he took no little pride in cultivating the impression. Like the Duke, he was tall and dark, had a full black beard, was dressed in complete black, and wore a tight-fitting coif under his cap. The suppressed passion in him gave an odd vibrancy to his speech.

"Monseigneur the Constable knows that he can count on us. We hold our land of him, and he has our oath. I served with his standard at Marignan and in Picardy. But it's time that he took us into his confidence. At Montbrison, there were rumors and gossip of an alliance with the Emperor, but nothing certain. Except this: we can't fight the rest of France alone. Or does he plan to fight at all? He should be open with us."

De Norville put in, "And for what other purpose do you think I'm here?" He lowered his voice. "Gentlemen, this is most secret. One word to the King of what has been hatched, and the whole scheme totters. I pray you to consider. The company at Montbrison was too large for confidences. Between ourselves, I can tell you frankly that on that very occasion the nobles of the Bourbonnais, the Forez, and Auvergne were not the only ones present. Closeted with the Duke in his private apartment was none other than Adrien de Croy, envoy

9

of the Emperor, who had been conducted there secretly from Bourg-en-Bresse in Savoy."

"Ha!" exclaimed Antoine de Lallière. "The Seigneur de Beaurain of Flanders. I knew him in Italy."

"The same," nodded the other. "And there a treaty was concluded between the Duke of Bourbon and the Emperor Charles V for their mutual defense and profit, to take effect shortly. But could the Duke announce *this* to so numerous a company? The King has spies everywhere. Besides, the vassals of Bourbon are not *all* ready to take up arms against the rest of France. For example your own family. Even you have a son in the King's service."

The Seigneur de Lallière boiled up. "By God, do you insinuate that, because my son Blaise is a man-at-arms in Monsieur de Bayard's company, we — his elder brother and I — are less than loyal to the Duke?"

De Norville met the other's glare. "If I doubted your loyalty, would I have spoken of that treaty with the Emperor? Still, it's a fact that your younger son, Blaise, was brought up in the household of his godfather, the Marquis de Vaulx, King Francis's chief schemer and agent."

"My old comrade," declared Antoine. "He was only Denis de Surcy then. If he has sold himself at court, does that reflect on me? Blaise entered the Marquis's household before the late King died. He left it when he was eighteen. As a younger son, he must make his own way. I hear he's done well enough in the army, madcap though he is; but I haven't seen him for three years. By all the devils, what are you hinting at?"

"Nothing at all." De Norville's limpid smile could not have been more artless. "I was only pointing out that, if you and Monsieur mon ami here, whom the Duke considers his truest friends, have a near relative in the enemy's camp, what could be said of a score of others at Montbrison, about whom Monseigneur knows too little? You task him with lack of confidence in you. Not at all. He prefers to deal privately with those he can trust and, therefore, sends me to represent him. You've seen his letters. The point is, can we trust the neighboring gentlemen you've called to meet here with us tonight?"

"Completely," said Guy de Lallière. "I'd pledge my life for them."

"Well, then, sirs, here in general is the plan. We'll take up the separate details later."

10

De Norville pointed out that no time was to be wasted in consolidating the Bourbonnais, the Forez, and Auvergne behind the Duke in readiness for the moment of rebellion. That would be due next month, or, at latest, in September, when the King had led his army across the mountains in the next effort to recover Lombardy. Then eastern France would blaze behind him; German mercenaries would pour in; the Emperor would attack from Spain; England would invade from the north; and the French monarchy, if it continued at all, would exist as a poor dependent on its neighbors. Charles de Bourbon would be proclaimed a sovereign prince and would receive the Emperor's sister in marriage. But the plan required secrecy. If any one of the gentlemen at tonight's meeting . . .

"I've told you," Guy interrupted, "that I pledge my life for them. What arrangements have been made with England?"

De Norville nodded. "I arrived from England two weeks ago and with good news. It's like this . . ." He broke off. "What a voice that dog of yours has! He belled me in this morning. Who's arriving now?"

"We'll have a look," returned the elder de Lallière, getting up. The others followed him out into the central corridor of the house and stood with him at the main door. Renée and Cocorico were already on the step below them.

Clairon's barking reached a climax. The galloping of perhaps a pair of horses could now be heard even by dull human ears. It slowed a little on the short ascent from the highway. Then one of the riders appeared between the gate turrets at the opposite end of the courtyard, reined in a moment to let his companion catch up with him, swung his cap in a circle above his head, and roared a halloo.

Pleasure and dismay crossed Antoine de Lallière's face. He gave a startled oath.

"Sainte Barbe! Speak of the devil! Here's Blaise himself!"

Chapter 2

The onlookers, who now included everybody in the château, were given no leisure to wonder at Blaise de Lallière's unexpected arrival. With the whoop of a cavalry charge and a "Come on!" to his companion, he headed full tilt down the courtyard toward the group in front of the main door.

Between the onrushing horse and them lay the small central pool or vivier, used as a fish tank and duckpond. It was irregularly about thirty feet long by eighteen wide. A shout of warning went up, as the rider, apparently forgetting this obstacle, dashed straight at it and picked up speed on the hard earth left uncobbled at the center of the court. "Thunder of God!" yelled Antoine de Lallière. "Fol enragé! Look out!" But with a *hura! ho!* the rider drove in his spurs, lifted his horse into the air, cleared the pool, came down within ten feet of the scattering spectators, slithered over the cobbled rim in front of the door, and, on the point of crashing into the house wall, masterfully brought his horse around, curbed him into a rear, and finished with a wide sweep of the cap. Then, almost on top of him, descended the next rider, who cleared the pool well enough but lost his stirrups and came to a jolting stop several yards away.

At the same moment, Blaise, swinging from the saddle, dropped to one knee in front of his father.

"God save you, monsieur mon père, and keep from harm this company!"

Still shaken by the impressions of the last few seconds — catapulting horses, crazy riders, shrieking servant girls, and whirlwind of terrified poultry swirling through the courtyard — Antoine de Lallière acknowledged his son's greeting with some heat.

"God save us, indeed, from fools like you! A thousand devils! Try to slaughter this company and wish 'em no harm in the same breath! Par le sang goy, you ought to be tied!" Then the hard lips cracked into a smile. "But I won't say it wasn't a stout jump and well managed." He folded Blaise in his arms, then held him away for inspection. "Welcome home! You've put on meat since I saw you last."

An eager group gathered around the newcomer. He was a broad-shouldered, well-knit young man of twenty-three, plentifully powdered with dust. His clean-shaven, tanned face radiated friendliness and good humor, with more than a trace of mischief. It was extremely wide between the two cheekbones; the remarkably alert eyes were set well apart; the nose, nicked on one side by a small scar, was straight and prominent. He had a big, whimsical mouth.

Standing in the background on the threshold of the main door, Jean de Norville, secretly cursing the embarrassment of this ill-timed arrival, watched the scene of welcome. Gradually he took some comfort in it. As far as appearances went, Blaise de Lallière was the typical lance, with more brawn than brains, to be found in any crack company of the royal troops. Those horsemen were reckless as the wind, high-spirited as schoolboys, and had the muscular grace of panthers; but they were easily led. De Norville noticed that Blaise's clothes looked worn; and his soft leather riding boots, which reached the middle of his thighs, showed several patches. His last haircut, administered by some amateur, had left his thick brown hair ragged at the edges. These last details suggested a limp purse which might be receptive to the Duke of Bourbon's gold. On the other hand, that he rode a good horse and carried a fine-hilted sword was rather perhaps to the credit of his captain, the famous Bayard, who would see to it that his men-at-arms were well mounted and equipped.

There was a possibility here, mused de Norville. A penniless soldier home on leave, probably keen for money and excitement, would be more than apt to stand with his family in the coming revolt. After all, Blaise's arrival might mean a recruit rather than a menace.

Meanwhile, with his two hands almost circling Renée's waist, while Cocorico growled at the impertinence, Blaise lifted her in the air and swung her around.

"Ha, m'amie la belle," he was saying, "you've grown a foot in these three years. As for looks, God have mercy on the poor hearts of men!"

He set her down to embrace his brother. "Congratulations to the beard, reverend sir! Stiff as Swiss pikes, vertu Dieu! I pity your bride on the wedding night. She'll get a present from me of a steel vizor. . . ."

Guy de Lallière met the joke with a cool look. He was proud of his beard and relished no lightness on the subject. But Blaise had turned away to shake hands with the servants and farm laborers.

"Philippe . . . Jean . . . André . . . Dame Alice!" He kissed a stout woman on both cheeks. "Isabeau Pernette! Married now, are you?"

His eyes wandered, then lightened, as Jean de Norville drew aside for Madame de Lallière, who came out of the house in more of a hurry than usual. For once, her schooled face was radiant.

13

"Blaise, mon petit! If I had known it was you, I should have been down . . ."

On one knee again, he kissed her hand and proffered the salutation that form required. But the next moment love brushed conventions aside, and he gathered her into his arms.

The watchful de Norville observed these proceedings with increased satisfaction. A popular fellow, he reflected, and devoted to his family. It shouldn't be difficult to win him over.

Last of all among the welcomers appeared Clairon, who, lifting himself upright, with his two paws on the young man's shoulders, licked Blaise's face.

The soldier laughed. "Why, old gossip! Vieux Clairon! I could hear your voice a quarter of a league off. Have done, have done! How's wolves? *Wolves,* Clairon?" The dog pricked up his ears. "That's it. We'll have a run together."

Then, disengaging himself, Blaise beckoned into the circle his companion, who had been standing at one side. "Messieurs-Dames, I have the honor to present the most promising young devil in Christendom, my archer, Pierre de la Barre."

The latter, a youth of eighteen, swept the cobblestones in an inclusive bow; but he contrived somehow to point it toward Renée, and, as he straightened up, his eyes lingered on her. He was erect as a lance and looked bold as a gamecock. In fact, he recalled that bird to such an extent that his fellows in the company had inevitably nicknamed him Le Coq. His short, crisp hair of a ruddy color, the upward tilt of his small, straight nose, his oval-shaped, hot-brown eyes, all expressed self-confidence and sparkle. He was fashionably dressed; wore a velvet cap with a gold token, a short, well-cut mantle, flawless boots and trunk hose, a gold-embroidered braguette. Fashionably, too, he carried his sword to the rear across his loins. No one needed to be told that he had recently served his time as page in some great house and was now, as the phrase went, making his first arms.

Self-consciously Renée gathered up Cocorico and played with his ears.

Antoine de Lallière asked, "Of the de la Barres of Beauce, monsieur?"

"No, of Poitou, honored sir, though nearly related. My father is Jean de la Barre, formerly of the King's guard, now residing near Saint-Maixent."

14

"I think I knew him. Yes! We were together at the assault of Genoa in 1507. A man of virtue."

"And let me tell you," put in Blaise, "that this Pierre of mine does not take after him. Women are his trouble, and he is theirs. A truelove by trade. So, be warned, Renée. Lock her up, Mama. He's only a third son and not interesting."

"Fie!" reproved Madame de Lallière. "How you run on! As if . . ."

"Though I'll say this for him," Blaise continued. "He had sense enough to accept an archer's rating in Captain de Bayard's company, when he might have been man-at-arms with Monseigneur d'Alençon."

De la Barre tilted his chin, if possible, higher than before. "And, may it please you, who wouldn't? An archer of ours ranks two men-at-arms in another company."

"Except for the pay, my friend."

Pierre snapped his fingers. "A fig for that! Even my good patroness, the Duchess herself, recommended Monsieur de Bayard. 'If you want honor,' she says, 'it's around him that things happen.'"

"What duchess, young sir?" asked Antoine de Lallière.

The other tried to sound modest. "D'Alençon, monsieur. I served as one of Her Grace's pages."

De Norville and Guy de Lallière exchanged glances. The Duchesse d'Alençon was the King's sister, Marguerite, a member of the royal trinity, whom Francis loved more dearly than anyone else except his mother, the all-powerful Louise de Savoie. Here was a pair of eyes and ears to be careful of. From the standpoint of the Bourbon rebels, Pierre de la Barre might just as well have belonged to the King's household.

"A great princess," said the older de Lallière dryly. He addressed Blaise. "You have not yet been presented to our guest, Monsieur de Norville, an officer and close friend of Monseigneur the Constable."

The two gentlemen bowed: de Norville with his sunniest smile, Blaise with obvious respect.

"Then certainly *my* friend, sir," declared the latter, "if I may make so bold. The Duke has no truer admirers than the men of our company. Yes, and our captain's among them. We're puzzled — shall I say? — by the King's stiffness with respect to my lord of Bourbon and feel that the Duke has had but a poor reward for his services to France. But the cloud will pass."

"Let us hope so," agreed de Norville, pleased that Blaise, without a word from him, had expressed sympathy for the cause. He

15

found the young man more promising with every moment; and, as the company now made its way into the house, he squeezed Guy de Lallière's arm. "Your brother will do, but we must keep young de la Barre out of the way."

"I'll attend to that," nodded the other.

It was naturally the kitchen, on the right of the central hall, which the family entered. Except on formal occasions, it served both as dining and living room. Like other French country gentlemen, who, save for noble rank and coats-of-arms, were essentially farmers, Antoine de Lallière sacrificed show for economy and comfort. He kept a personal eye on servants, livestock and larder. The kitchen was the focal point of the house. Together with the buttery and other offices, it comprised the whole right wing of the first floor, a big, raftered space black and savory with the cooking of generations, rich in pewter, iron and copper; on one side, the canopied fireplace and, on the other, a long table, with benches down the length of it and two armchairs for master and mistress at the upper end. Preparations for the entertainment that evening had already begun.

"A bait till supper," Antoine directed, "and something to wet your throats. The dust's a foot deep on the road this summer. Jacques, fetch the beef-joint to the table. Isabeau, draw me a pitcher from the Beaune cask. Set out the cups. We'll drink to the prodigal — eh, Blaise? — and to Monsieur de la Barre. Water in the basins there!"

Hands were washed; meat and bread were cut in generous slices. The newcomers emptied a half-tankard each.

"So, you're home on leave, my son, before the march to Italy?" asked Madame de Lallière. "How long can you give us?"

Blaise lowered his cup. "Save your grace, a night only and not on leave either, worse luck, but on the King's affairs. A recruiting mission to the Swiss cantons. His Majesty needs ten thousand pikemen for the coming war. Since Lallière's smack on the road from Paris, I snatched at the chance to stop off." He smiled at Renée and drank again. "To you, ma debonnaire!"

"But you're garrisoned in Grenoble, not Paris," his father objected.

Guy de Lallière put in, "And a mission like that isn't entrusted to a simple . . ."

"Wait!" Blaise speared a slice of meat with his knife. "I'll tell you the whole of it. The lord Bayard dispatched me to Paris with letters for the King. Somehow he fears to be left behind in the coming

16

campaign. Though the thought's ridiculous. Can you picture a French army beyond the mountains without his pennon! 'By God, monsieur,' I told him, 'spare your letters, for without them we'll get our marching orders.' But he shook his head. 'Nenni, it's not so sure . . .'"

Madame de Lallière sighed. Nothing was harder than to keep Blaise to the point. He was a born rattlebrain like Renée.

"You were dispatched to Paris with letters?" she prompted.

"So it was. And, of course, I took this rascal archer of mine along. If I'd left him behind, he'd have got into trouble, though the devil himself only knows what trouble he's caused me on the road . . ."

"We were speaking of Paris, my son."

"Saint John! In Paris, it was worse. What did he do but fall in love . . ."

"I mean, about your letters. God give us patience!"

"I beg pardon — Well, through the credit of my good patron, Monseigneur de Vaulx, I was able to deliver these letters into the King's own hands at his palace of Les Tournelles. And, of course, he laughed at them. He said, foi de gentilhomme, it would be a strange thing if he went to war and left his sword behind, meaning Monsieur de Bayard. So he took order at once to reassure the Captain by letter. Madame de Chateabriant herself was present. Have you heard the story of her in bed with Monsieur de Bonnivet, when who should knock at the door but His Majesty in mood for a . . ."

"Shsh!" cut in Madame de Lallière. "Remember your sister."

Blaise coughed. "But here's some news that the rats haven't eaten. It's being whispered at court that the star of Madame de Chateaubriant has faded, and that the King pays homage to a fresh young thing little older than Renée, one of the court girls . . ."

"Shsh!" Madame de Lallière repeated. "Can you talk nothing but ribaldry?"

"God pity France!" exclaimed her husband. "With a young whoremaster as king and ruled by skirts! Spending money like water on his palaces and shows. Robbing the people with his taxes and levies. Selling offices by the dozen. But all will not do. They tell me, he has even melted down the silver grating of Saint Martin at Tours, weighing seven thousand marcs, to spend on some new whim. By God, how different from our late King Louis, Father of the People! It's time that the gentry of France put a stop to this gallant."

17

De Norville, noting Blaise's surprise at his father's bitterness, intervened. "You haven't told us yet, sir, about this mission of yours to the Cantons."

"Aye, son, get on with your story," agreed Antoine.

"Well, the said ten thousand pikemen are necessary to stiffen our attack upon Milan. Until the time comes when our French foot soldiers are worth more than a mob of chickenhearted peasants, we must turn to the Swiss for infantry. A pox on them, too, for money-gouging, conceited rogues! . . . Pierre, stop making eyes at my sister."

Madame de Lallière spoke her mind. "I tell you straight, mon petit Blaise, that, if you were younger, I should take the birch to you. Will you never have done with your skips and give a plain answer to Monsieur de Norville's question?"

Blaise laughed. "To return, then, to this matter of the pikemen. The King, seeing me present and perceiving my merit at a glance, assigned me to said mission. There you are: the right man in the right place."

Guy de Lallière thrust out his black beard. "Pooh! Don't take us for idiots. I say again that an errand like that is entrusted to someone of station and not to a simple man-at-arms, much less to a scatterbrain like you."

"Why not, monsieur la barbe? Why not? I'll wager my brain against yours for a florin any time. But who said I was alone on the mission? Not I. The someone of station was appointed, and of high station at that." Blaise gathered in his audience with a glance. "Guess who?"

Antoine de Lallière shrugged. "Some court fop, I suppose — or one of the King's captains."

"No, sir." Blaise had the look of a man who has been holding back a pleasant surprise till the last moment. "No, sir. I have the pleasure of bringing you the best news you've had in a twelvemonth. The someone in question sent me ahead to announce him to you. He'll be here in a couple of hours."

De Norville's eyes quickened. Guy de Lallière stared at his brother. The thought of both was on tonight's meeting.

"One hundred thousand devils!" exploded Antoine. "Who is it then?"

"Sir, your old friend and comrade in arms and my good patron, Denis de Surcy, Marquis de Vaulx."

18

Blaise rolled out the name and looked around, beaming. But, expecting delight, he was faced by blank consternation.

"*Denis de Surcy?*" his father echoed. "*Here?*"

"Where else, sir? I knew it would surprise you. He bade me express his pleasure in the thought of seeing you again after better than twenty years."

"Sang Dieu!"

Blaise's face fell. "What's wrong?"

His question met shifting glances and cold silence, except that de Norville, suppressing a whistle, repeated, "The Marquis de Vaulx!"

Chapter 3

It was Constance de Lallière's tact that covered up the dismay caused by Blaise's announcement and gave the others time to follow her lead. Though, as a woman, she was permitted no share in the actual workings of the Bourbon plot, she knew well enough the point of that night's gathering and could understand the dilemma which the Marquis de Vaulx's arrival entailed. It would be impractical, if not impossible, to postpone the meeting. Antoine and Guy de Lallière had spent the last few days communicating with the people involved, many of whom lived at a considerable distance. These guests — some twenty of them — would be riding in from every direction, along every road. On the other hand, to refuse hospitality to an old friend like the Marquis would, aside from everything else, rouse the very suspicion which it was essential to avoid. Madame de Lallière, indeed, could see the faint dawn of it already behind Blaise's bewilderment. He might be a scatterbrain, but he was no fool.

"What an honor for you, my son," she declared, "to be attending so eminent a lord in business of such weight! And what honor for us to receive him! Tell the truth, now. I wager he asked the King for your services."

"Well, I admit he did." Blaise's glance wandered from his father to Guy, then to de Norville. "He needed an escort on the road, as well as someone to back him at the Swiss Diet in Lucerne. Seeing me at loose ends, he chose me. But it doesn't seem that . . ."

19

"We were startled," went on Madame de Lallière easily, "by the unexpected pleasure. And yet, alas, if he had only come yesterday or were coming tomorrow! That it should have to be this very day of all days! With a company tonight of twenty guests! Where shall we put him and his following? How to entertain him acceptably? I despair."

She was rewarded by seeing the doubt fade in Blaise's eyes. He exclaimed: "Twenty guests! Nom d'un nom! Lallière's looking up. Is it a betrothal, then? And no word to me! *Renée* . . . ?"

The girl shook her head and blushed. By this time, the gentlemen had recovered themselves. Guy de Lallière spoke. "No, brother. My lord of Bourbon is concerned that the ravages of a certain band of cutthroats, fit only for sack and cord, should not go unchecked in the mountains of the Forez. He has sent Monsieur de Norville to confer with the gentry hereabouts. We hope to take common action. Our meeting turns on that."

Nothing could have been more plausible. The bandit leader Guillaume de Montelon of Auvergne was at that moment awaiting execution in Paris. Gangs of disbanded soldiers and outlaws of all kinds infested the countryside and had long been the curse of France. It was one of the duties of the landed gentlemen to join with the provosts and other officials in suppressing them.

"Ah," said Blaise, "you'll have sport. There's been trouble with rogues of the same kind in Dauphiné. We fought a pitched battle against 'em two months ago near Vienne."

"And so," hinted Antoine de Lallière, "the Marquis will understand our embarrassment. He would be uncomfortable here. It's not overfar to Roanne, and *The Red Lion's* a good inn."

But craft was not the old gentleman's strong point. He hemmed so much over his words that Blaise stared at him again.

"Saints! Here's a famous to-do! This house can hold forty men, if we use the attic. My lord de Vaulx doesn't strain at trifles. He's an old campaigner and takes potluck. He wants to see you, and he'll be glad to meet the gentlemen. I don't understand. . . ."

De Norville shot a warning glance at Antoine and Guy. Short of a scandal, the Marquis had to be received; but, with good management, the original purpose of the meeting could still be carried out. Bourbon's agent had regained his usual poise and his winning smile.

"Speaking for myself," he put in, "I should grieve at missing the privilege of Monsieur de Vaulx's conversation, and so, too, I believe, would the other guests. It's seldom one has an occasion to talk with a man of his experience and knowledge of affairs. We should doubtless profit by his advice in this matter of the outlaws. If so, my lord of Bourbon would be indebted to him."

"We're only concerned for his comfort," said Antoine, puzzled by the other's game. "Of course, if he doesn't object . . ."

"We'll put him in the west turret bedroom," Madame de Lallière decided. "Blaise — "

"I should be glad of Monsieur Blaise's company in my own room," suggested de Norville, with the air of an accommodating guest; but an edge in his voice caught Madame de Lallière's attention.

"You're very good, sir; he'll be honored. Monsieur de la Barre, I'm afraid the attic must serve." She got up. "Gentlemen, we cumber the kitchen and distract our people from work. There's much to do."

The group separated. A solid brushing and combing improved the appearance of Blaise and his archer. Renée exclaimed at the lovely jet earrings, shaped like horns of plenty, that emerged from her brother's saddlebags, and at the hand mirror he had brought her from Paris. Alone with him for a moment in the small bedroom assigned to de Norville, she put both gifts to immediate use, while he changed from boots to shoes. As the youngest members of the family, they had always been close to each other.

"How beautiful!" she admired, shifting the mirror from side to side for a better look at the earrings.

"Like the wearer, m'amie. But they're becoming. Wait till young de la Barre sees them!"

She tossed her head. "As if I cared about *him!* The way he swaggers."

"Well, take him down a peg." Blaise pulled on a shoe and sat holding the other. "This de Norville's a pretty fellow."

"Yes." Renée's voice sounded flat.

Her brother smiled. "Married, eh?"

"No. I've heard that he *was* married to a rich heiress from the neighborhood of Feurs, a Mademoiselle de Chavan. But she died last spring."

"Too bad!"

Renée shrugged. "He takes it pretty well. They say he's engaged now to another heiress, an English milady."

"The devil!" Blaise stared. "How would he meet her? We're at war with England."

"He's been there this summer." Renée held out the hand mirror at arm's length and adjusted her small headdress. It always tended to slip backwards. De Norville did not interest her. "On the Duke's business," she added.

Blaise hummed some bars of a popular catch and drew on the other shoe, wriggling his toes beneath the comfortable, slashed velvet. "This meeting tonight?" he said casually.

But Renée was at the end of her Latin. If Madame de Lallière was left uninformed of the Bourbon projects, her daughter knew still less.

"Oh, the Duke's business," she answered vaguely. "Like they said."

Blaise put words to the tune he was humming:

> M'amour et m'amyette,
> Souvent je t'y regrette,
> Hé, par la vertu sainct Gris!

"Before I leave, I wish you'd sew me on these buttons of my doublet more stoutly. They're beginning to dangle."

"I'll do it now. Wait till I fetch my needle and thread."

She flitted off down the corridor, which ran the length of the house and gave access to the second-floor bedrooms; but Blaise could hear his mother's voice directing her to some task more urgent than sewing on buttons. He smiled: she would not be back so soon.

Then the smile faded out. He rubbed his hand over his hair, ruffling it up, an unconscious gesture with him when perplexed. Strolling over to the window, he stood looking out at the familiar landscape to the north, a crazy quilt of small fields farmed on shares by the peasants of the village, with a background of pasture and forest beyond. But his thought was not on the boyhood that this scene recalled. He felt an odd uneasiness, without any sufficient reason for it. Being one of the family, he knew by instinct that something was being concealed from him, something connected with that evening's assembly and which the Marquis's visit disturbed. His father had hung fire a second too long; his mother had sounded too bland. As for de Norville . . . This affair in England. The Duke's business. What business? No one who, like Blaise, had heard the wrongs of Charles de Bourbon hotly debated scores of times, could fail to hazard a guess.

The weak point of Bourbon's conspiracy was that the injustices he had suffered and his own stiff pride were of common knowledge. They made rebellion probable, if not inevitable. Blaise, like everybody else, remembered the Duke's unmerited recall from his successful government of Milan, which had since — and largely for that reason — been lost to France. Like most people, he knew that the salary due to Bourbon as Constable had been withheld; that the treasure he had spent for the King's service had never been repaid; that last year, in the Picardy campaign, he had been stripped of his command of the vanguard, a time-honored perquisite of his office. But, worse than that humiliation, and known everywhere, was this trumped-up lawsuit brought by the King's mother, Louise de Savoie, with the King's backing, which would deprive the Duke of the entire Bourbon succession and reduce him to insignificance. Being what he was, a great soldier prince with the pride of Lucifer, what could he do but rebel? The wonder was that he had swallowed so many affronts so long. No, de Norville's errand in England was not hard to understand.

But, as Blaise stood leaning against one side of the window recess, it gradually dawned on him that the reason for his uneasiness was an approaching personal issue, which he might have to meet. In full measure, he had the normal Frenchman's devotion to family, that inborn sense of clan which was a part of the national fiber. It matched religion as a keystone of life. He might be a younger son destined to fend for himself, but he remained a de Lallière with regard to anything which might affect the fortunes of his family. That was on one side. On the other side lay duty: all that was meant, in terms of association and loyalty, by his service as man-at-arms in one of the King's companies.

Not that Blaise analyzed this — he felt it, rather — but beneath the dash and devil-may-care, which were the most pronounced features of him, lay faculties of thought, largely unused, which a crisis could challenge. At the moment, the stirring of these depths made him uncomfortable, and he turned from the window to fidget absently about the room.

Then, as it happened, his vacant glance, drifting over some of de Norville's belongings on the bedside table, came to a stop. His mind

23

caught at the distraction, and he looked more closely. It was a miniature of a girl in an open leather case. As attention focused, he forgot his recent concern in favor of something so definite and arresting.

Sacristi, a pretty girl! But no, he reflected, not so much pretty as striking. She had fine, bold features; but the eyebrows were too straight and tilted for perfect beauty, and the firmly chiseled mouth was too large. An out-of-doors, boyish face at first glance, though feminine enough beneath the modish little headdress. Then he became aware of the eyes and after that saw nothing else. They were of an odd oval shape. He could not be sure of their color, gray or green; but the artist had given them a strange magnetism that was both mysterious and unrevealing. It seemed to Blaise that they expressed a contradiction of emotion: gaiety and daring, with an undercurrent of sadness.

Impulsively, he lifted the miniature from its case, turning it over in his hand. Two ovals of crystal glass inclosed the ivory disk and were held together by a plain gold rim. The crystal of the back covered a lock of russet-colored hair and displayed in gold lettering the initials A. R.

Warned by a footstep in the outer corridor, he had just time enough to replace the miniature; but his eyes were still on it when de Norville entered.

"Ha, monsieur mon ami — " began the latter, then paused, with a glance at the small table, before continuing. "I thank my good fortune that we're to be bedfellows tonight. Though it wasn't all luck, either. You saw how I snapped you up when Madame your mother left me an opening. What with the crowd of guests, I was apt to have a less agreeable sleeping companion. You don't look as if you snored, and I don't believe I do."

He seated himself on the bed, his eyes on Blaise; but his hand reached out to the case that held the miniature and closed it.

"We'll make a bet," returned Blaise in his usual vein — "the first snorer to pay a crown. That ought to keep me quiet. I may not win but I don't intend to lose."

They ran on with chitchat. Blaise had never met so engaging a cavalier. De Norville's handsome face and enchanting manner, the polish of him, gave a bouquet to conversation. With one knee clasped between his hands, he talked like a boon companion. They discovered tastes in common and mutual friends. They were soon at

24

a point of confidence where Blaise felt no scruple in remarking:

"My sister tells me that you were in England this summer."

And de Norville, without a flicker of embarrassment, replied that Monseigneur de Bourbon's affairs had compelled him to spend six weeks there. "A barbarous country in many ways, monsieur mon ami, but not without compensations. The climate is bad; the fare, atrocious; manners are crude. But some of the women, ma foi, are enchanting." He nodded toward the table. "I saw that you were looking at one of them, as I came in."

"A marvelous lady," said Blaise coloring. The miniature might be hidden, but the face lingered vividly before him. He remained conscious of it, as if a third person were in the room.

"And by no means a barbarian," de Norville added. "She has been trained at our court in Paris."

"You are betrothed perhaps?" It seemed indiscreet to quote Renée again.

"Yes, if affairs permit, we'll be married before long. We're to meet in Savoy as soon as the Duke of Bourbon's service gives me leisure. Even marriages must wait on politics."

"Is it permitted to ask her name?"

For some reason, de Norville winked. "Ah, monsieur, under the circumstances it would be *im*politic to reveal it. You will excuse me. Indeed, if it were anyone else but you, I should regret that Milady's portrait had been seen. . . . You know," he threw in, with a gust of feeling, "it's odd what a fancy I've taken to you on so short an acquaintance."

Blaise warmly confessed a like sentiment.

"And when I'm drawn to a man," de Norville went on, "I don't want to part with him. On second thought, why shouldn't we see more of each other? I mean thus. It happens that I stand well with Monseigneur de Bourbon, and I'm more than eager to serve you. Let me think." He pinched his chin. "I have it. What do you say to a command of thirty lances and the rank of captain in the Duke's guard? I mean, after your mission to the Cantons. Monseigneur pays well. I think I could promise you five hundred livres pension a year plus, of course, the usual twenty sous per lance per month. How does that strike you?"

"Saint John!" Blaise exclaimed. "Are you serious?"

He gaped at de Norville. The offer was magnificent: close to a thousand livres a year compared with his present pay of three hun-

25

dred, not to speak of rank and prestige. His imagination soared. *Monsieur le Capitaine!*

"Of course I'm serious."

"But my brother, Guy, has no such position."

"Don't be concerned for him. He'll have better than that."

"But will my lord of Bourbon — I mean, in view of the present coldness between him and the King . . ." It was unnecessary to finish the question.

De Norville's eyes narrowed. "Monsieur, you deserve frankness. I'll not deny that relations are strained between Monseigneur and the King. It may come to a break. In that case, the Duke will not offer his neck to the axe. Far from it. He'll look out for himself. And in that case, the position I offer you will depend on whether or not you take the side of justice, with your family and other noblemen, in defense of the right. . . . But I do you wrong even to suggest that you would not. You have already expressed your sympathy for my lord Constable. I count you as one of us." He embraced Blaise with a fraternal glance. "And, after all, why cross bridges? These princes may become reconciled. In any case, His Highness will give you the thirty lances on my petition. Come, sir, is it a bargain?"

Easily, as if caught in a deep, swift-flowing current, Blaise felt himself drawn along toward the issue he had dreaded. Even de Norville's charm did not lighten it. Indeed, that very charm, for the first time, ruffled him. It was too purposeful and too self-assured. This sudden devotion, these fine offers — why? A favorite saying of the Marquis de Vaulx's occurred to him, that it was not so much the hook and line which mattered, but the bait. Well, he refused to be hurried. The depths beneath his happy-go-lucky surface stirred again.

De Norville held out his hand. "Is it a bargain?" he repeated.

Blaise shook the proffered hand but smiled. "You're more than kind. Give me leave to consider."

"*Consider?*"

"Yes. One doesn't take a step of such importance as the one you propose without any more thought than cracking an egg. Of course I'm tempted."

The sound of horses and voices in the courtyard announced the arrival of guests. De Norville rose.

"Well, then, consider it. I'm sure you'll accept. Not a word, of course, to the Marquis de Vaulx."

26

Somewhat ashamed, Blaise nodded. In spite of anything he could do, the prongs of the issue were closing in.

"No. I understand."

Chapter 4

Denis de Surcy, Marquis de Vaulx, had spent last night in Moulins at the sign of *The Barbel* not far from the great Bourbon palace, where the Duke was reportedly lying ill with a quartan fever. As an officer of the King and an old acquaintance of Bourbon himself, he might easily have put up at the palace; but he had judged that this would be ill-advised. He would have learned nothing more of the Duke's intentions than he already knew through his secret agents; and, in the present ticklish state of affairs, his appearance at the château would have served only to cause irritation and alarm. So, he stopped at the inn and gave his people leave to speak freely of the embassy to the Swiss cantons. Then, after mass, at a convenient hour of the morning, he rode on south toward La Palisse and Lallière.

But, though careful to allay suspicions as to the reason of his journey through the Bourbonnais, he was too veteran an observer not to take note of things as he went along. In Moulins, he felt a certain tenseness and hush. He remarked too many lighted windows in the castle and that the candles behind them burned all night. On the roads today, he had encountered more than the usual number of couriers and horsemen. They rode fast and with set faces.

In short, everything he saw tallied with the reports of his informers. Rebellion was stirring. But, for the moment at least, his foreign mission relieved him of personal concern with it. Thanks largely to him, when the explosion came, it would, at least, not take the King unawares. Far more had been learned of their plot than the rebels had any notion of. But the situation was touch and go. De Surcy could only hope for the best. He must secure the Swiss pikemen without fail.

Riding south on his comfortable mule, with a train of servants behind him, the Marquis sighed more than once. What would he find on his return to France? He hated the futilities of war in any case;

but war coupled with civil strife — the arrests, torturing, executions and ravage between kinsmen — horrified him. If only that could be avoided! He secretly hoped to be still abroad when the tempest burst.

The court painter, Jean Clouet, often declared that no face had given him more trouble to interpret on canvas than Monseigneur de Vaulx's. It reflected a blending of many influences; it recorded a lifetime of such varied experience. But Clouet had finally chosen to emphasize, as fundamental to everything else, the Marquis's benevolence, the humane quality of him. Upon this foundation, cares and conflicts, political expediencies and personal sorrows, had etched their lines without obliterating it. The result was a thoughtful face, a little worldly, a little weary, but redeemed by kindness. From the finished portrait, which hung on the wall of the grand salon at Surcy-le-Château in Touraine, visitors gathered different impressions. To one, it portrayed the vigilant statesman, the untiring servant of the Crown; to another, the man of learning, the friend of Budé and Erasmus; to another, the urbane nobleman and courtier, disillusioned though without bitterness. But, however they viewed the portrait, all were affected in some way by the generosity, the warmth of heart, which it expressed.

During his many journeys, the Marquis had trained himself to make good use of time. The monotony of a long road supplied leisure for connected thought, and he had often developed policies of far-reaching consequence on muleback. His attendants — the physician, the secretary, pages and lackeys, who formed his retinue — were careful to keep well behind him, so that he usually rode alone and undisturbed.

Appropriately today the conflict of Charles de Bourbon with Francis the King furnished a topic for reflection. He reviewed it with pity and dread, but also realistically. He admired the Constable, as a brave man, a gifted soldier, and a distinguished person. He did not admire the King, who in spite of personal charm, seemed to him frivolous and superficial, a young gallant unable to grow up. As far as immediate justice went, the Duke was a victim of tyrannical, barefaced robbery. The Marquis could well understand his passionate revolt and the indignation of his followers. But the case had to be viewed from another level, the level of history, the level of the future.

The feudal order, which the Duke represented, was past; his principality in the center of France blocked national unity and might destroy it. Ironically the King, selfish and dishonest as he was, was serving the cause of progress. In spite of himself, he could not help serving it; while Bourbon, a much finer man, could not help opposing it.

De Surcy looked back over the last two hundred years in France: the English domination, the wars with Burgundy and Brittany, the selfish independence of the nobles, the unspeakable misery of the people. And out of this welter of feudal divisions, chronic bloodshed and wretchedness, slowly, often ruthlessly, the Throne had asserted itself, imposing law, creating a nation. If Bourbon succeeded, it meant a return to chaos. De Surcy might lament the persecution of an innocent man and his followers, but he lamented still more the desolation of millions. To avoid this, he had spent his life in the service of three kings. But it was not Charles, Louis, or Francis whom he had served; it was the Throne, as a unifying principle. And for that Throne, he would sacrifice even the gentleness of his heart.

From La Palisse, dominated by the castle of the Marquis's old friend, Jacques de Chabannes, one of the marshals of France and now with the army at Lyons, the road climbed steadily upward toward forest and mountains. At the village of Saint-Martin, de Surcy with his following passed from the Duchy of Bourbonnais into the County of the Forez and could soon expect to see the high-pitched roofs of the Lallière manor house. It had been well over twenty years since he had spent a night there. The place, he imagined, would have changed little (Blaise had once told him that a coat of stucco in modern fashion had been applied to the ancient limestone); it was the people, it was himself, who had changed. And times had changed.

What a different world they had all been young in, twenty-odd years back! How much more understandable! There were no Lutherans then, threatening the unity of Christ's Church. And Charles of Austria, now overshadowing the world, as Emperor of Germany and King of Spain, had not been born. The Italian ferment had not yet possessed the North, with its new costumes, new architecture, new philosophy.

The Marquis could only picture Antoine de Lallière as he had last seen him. A warm heart and inherited loyalties would naturally draw him to Bourbon's side. De Surcy hoped to deter him from that, if

29

possible — perhaps with the help of his wife. As the Marquis remembered her, Constance de Lallière was the direct opposite of her husband, level-headed, disciplined and farsighted. She might listen to reason, even if Antoine was deaf. As for the elder son, Guy, the Marquis knew only that he had been one of Bourbon's lances and had therefore cast in his lot with the Duke. Apparently there was no love lost between him and Blaise.

The thought of Blaise usually brought a smile to de Surcy's mind. He liked the young man, as one likes a prank of one's youth. None of his pages had ever been more heedless or more winning. Blaise had attraction enough; but to take him seriously, except as a good swordsman and cavalier, was impossible. Being childless, de Surcy had originally hoped to train his godson in the career which he had himself followed, and he had been prepared to back him with all his influence. But that idea now seemed only amusing. While Blaise's fellow pages had profited more or less from the system of instruction which the Marquis was at pains to provide for them, Blaise profited from nothing but his fencing and riding lessons. The other pages were prudent enough to avoid escapades, or, at least, to conceal them, but Blaise was forever in a pickle — some row or gallantry — that brought him before his patron for reprimand or caning. Though by no means a blockhead, he was as little fitted for state affairs as a young bull. In the end, de Surcy accepted defeat and won Blaise's eternal gratitude by obtaining a lance for him in the company commanded by Bayard. "Go and seek honor, mon ami," he told him in affectionate farewell. "It is the will of God, who has richly endowed you with muscles. After all, they're less troublesome than brains. Go, then, with my blessing and this purse of fifty crowns. Try not to spend all of it your first night in garrison." That was five years ago. From time to time, the Marquis had heard from him: he had shared in the glorious defense of Mézières and seen service in Italy. But he had gradually slipped to the background of de Surcy's mind until his recent appearance in Paris, gay and irresponsible as ever. It was on an impulse that the Marquis had asked for his attendance on the Swiss journey, principally because the young man was diverting and a good companion.

Rounding a spur of woods, de Surcy now beheld the manor house; and, at the same instant, he gave a *ha!* of surprise. From the opposite direction, some half dozen gentlemen, with their mounted servants, were turning in through the courtyard gates. From beyond the wall, he could hear the hubbub of numerous people. It signified an important event.

Drawing rein, he waited for his retinue to come up and then sent one of his pages ahead for information. He must learn on what foot to present himself. But, after a brief wait, the attendant returned to report that it was only a meeting of the local gentry.

"Hm-m." De Surcy frowned, then nodded. "Well, en avant!" And he guided his mule up the short approach from the road to the gate.

At once, however, he was on guard. In view of the prevailing tension, so large a meeting looked odd. It looked still more odd in the courtyard, as he made his way past various groups toward the main door. His bland expression showed only pleasure and expectancy, but he missed nothing. He noted the covert glances that followed him, the whispering, the cold hush. He could read the faces of these country squires like an open book. He was an enemy, and they had been alerted; but they lacked the art to pretend. By the time he had half crossed the courtyard, he was fully aware of the situation. Casually visiting an old friend, he had stumbled into a wasps' nest. There was danger here.

Antoine de Lallière was striding forward to meet him, and he dismounted. But not only age had altered the face de Surcy remembered. Something else appeared in it: furtiveness and embarrassment, which native honesty could not cover up.

"Denis, mon ami!"

"Antoine! Par la foi de mon corps . . . !"

Embracing, the two old gentlemen kissed each other on both cheeks; and the Marquis felt a ray of affection behind the clouds.

De Lallière clapped him on the shoulder. "Comrade! By God, Denis, you haven't changed too much! Some wrinkles and gray hair. Like mine. I expected to find you hidden behind a beard, but you've kept to the old ways in that. Welcome again! Welcome!"

But when the Marquis feared that his visit at so busy a time might be inconvenient, the other's warmth cooled; or, rather, it became loud. "By no means! By no means! You convey an honor, a privilege, which we all value. I say all of us." He stared at some nearby gentlemen, as if demanding assent, and got back an echo. "You see, Denis. Inconvenient? Fie!"

De Surcy now bowed low to Madame de Lallière and gave her a courtly kiss. De Norville was presented (a practised intriguer,

31

thought the Marquis, who knew a good deal about him and his English visit), then Guy de Lallière, then others. Glancing at Blaise, who stood in the background, de Surcy looked through the young man's transparent face into the trouble behind it. The usual devil-may-care was gone.

"Our meeting," labored Antoine before conducting his guest indoors, "concerns — er — a band of outlaws, who are at large in these mountains. We plan to — er — lay them by the heels if possible . . ." His voice was raised and distinct, as if for the purpose of instructing others than de Surcy or, perhaps, of reminding them.

"Indeed?" said the Marquis lightly, but his words had a barb in certain ears. "That interests me. In the King's service, I've had experience with outlaws — of every sort."

He was aware of the silence behind him, as he entered the house.

Chapter 5

If Pierre de la Barre had not been smitten by the charms of Mademoiselle Renée, he might profitably have listened to the gossip in the courtyard. But, instead of mingling with others, he had sought the seclusion of the garden on the other side of the house. There, propped against the trunk of an apple tree, he languished and gazed into distance. It was a kind of sweet anguish to which he was often subject, but it always seemed to him new and very important. While the attack lasted, his whole nature changed. From bold, he became meek; from confident, shy. Love did not steal gradually upon him; it came with a surge and knocked him into a trance.

Renée, of course, was beyond comparison the loveliest girl he had ever seen. Par Dieu, at last he had found his ideal! She reminded him of spring flowers. He thought of her vaguely in terms of mignonettes, lilies of the valley, forget-me-nots and violets. The rose was not included, as being too usual. What adorable little feet she had, which seemed merely to touch the coarse earth as a zephyr touches it! And, heaven, what eyes! Of the purest hazel? No. Like fern-shaded spring water. And what a delicious voice, whose soft intonation of *Oui, madame ma mère* went rippling up and down Pierre's mind! As to the bow of her lips, the curve of her cheek . . .

Happening to pass one of the windows which overlooked that side of the house, Guy de Lallière frowned suspiciously at the dreamer. Why was the puppy lounging out there by himself? It was close upon the five o'clock supper hour, and as yet no decision had been reached as to how to dispose of him. His rank entitled him to a place at the main table; for, though only an archer, he was no less noble than most of the other guests. But it was bad enough to have the old fox de Vaulx to hoodwink without being forced to worry about this whippersnapper. Besides, the table was crowded. De Lallière had arranged to have the Marquis's physician and secretary served in another room together with the rest of his suite. That would isolate *them* well enough. Now he had to find some excuse which would keep de la Barre out of the way without offending him. Hurt feelings have sharp eyes.

A glimpse of Renée, who was crossing the far end of the room, gave him an idea, and he called her to him. As eldest son and a man of thirty, his authority was almost parental.

He jerked his head toward the window. "Look you there. Do you see that young galliard?"

"But yes, mon frère."

"I'd have you do me a service."

Guy explained the situation in part, though he carefully said nothing of the chief reason for not wanting another king's spy at table. If Renée would take charge of de la Barre, the problem was solved. He would be flattered and got rid of at the same time.

Renée hid her excitement. "But how?"

"Faith, I leave that to you. Dea, mistress, if you haven't the wits to feed a young man and keep him engaged for a couple of hours, you're fit for a nunnery."

"What will Mama say?"

"I'll explain it to her. Hurry on now, while he's alone. Don't primp." Renée's hands were at her headdress. "You look well enough."

She looked more than well to the dazzled eyes of Pierre, when her footstep on the garden path startled him out of his reveries, and he saw the subject of it coming toward him, preceded by Cocorico. This was a miracle. He had barely expected to see her again: to see her now and alone savored of magic. Spellbound, he could only stare.

On the other hand, Renée had never been more fluttered in her life. Brought up in the country, she could count on the fingers of one hand the young men of her own class whom she had seen, not to say met. And even to see one was an adventure. But to meet one, to meet him alone beyond the watchful guard of her mother, to meet this particular one alone, was so giddy an event that she dared not think of it. To her brother, Blaise, she could toss her head about Pierre de la Barre; but he had been steadily in her mind since he had jumped the duckpond almost on top of her. She found him very manly and good-looking. His clothes were superb. She loved his crisp, short hair, the tilt of his nose, the cleft of his chin. More impressive than anything else, and overpowering, was his man-of-the-world assurance, the tone of the court, which made her feel like an ignorant little country mouse. At first, she wanted to run away, but the occasion was too wonderful. Her knees faltered, as she came down the path. Her heart beat strangely. She almost tripped, but steadied herself in time.

The shyness in each of them misread the other's. To Renée, his stare looked haughty; to Pierre's enchanted eyes, she was a princess and he was only a varlet. He forgot to bow; she forgot her mother's lessons, or, rather, the thought of them confused her.

"Monseigneur," she began, but caught herself and changed to *messire*.

"Ha?" breathed Pierre.

"Monsieur," she amended, "I have been sent to ask you in to supper. I mean to say, if you would have the goodness" — it seemed impossible to express herself — "if you would condescend . . ."

"Certainly, madame," said Pierre — "I mean mademoiselle."

She flushed. He was making fun of her.

"Well, sir, if you choose to be pert . . ."

"Pert?" Pierre gasped. "To *you*, mademoiselle?"

It struck Renée that he really looked crestfallen, and the thought gave her courage. "What I meant is that supper's ready. But at the table in the grande salle, there're only old men." (To Renée, anyone over twenty-five belonged to that class.) "Would you like to have supper with me?"

"Cordieu!" His eyes widened. This surely was a dream. "Would I like . . ." he repeated.

"Yes."

"Where?"

"Oh, any place. Here, perhaps." She pointed. "In the arbor. I'll fetch a basket."

She could see from his look how shocked he was that a young girl of good family would throw herself at him in this way.

She wanted to cry. If he came out with some courtly quip, she *would* cry.

"Bon Dieu, mademoiselle," he faltered, "it would be Heaven. I never hoped . . . It would be Heaven, mademoiselle."

A curtain went up for Renée. There was no mistaking that tone of voice. She gave him a sudden smile. "Then I'll bring the basket." And, managing not to hurry, she tripped back up the path, more excited than ever but much less nervous. He was terribly good-looking.

While she was gone, Pierre recovered the use of his reason up to a point. That is, he cursed himself fiercely for a lout. Saint John! To stutter and stare! To let her go alone for the basket! What was the matter with him? Well, he had sense enough to answer *that*. But even if love for the moment had robbed him of his cockiness, it might have left him some manners.

By the time Renée got back, he was able to copy his usual self. He relieved her of the basket, petted Cocorico, made a remark about the pleasure of eating out of doors on a fine evening, and, walking on air, accompanied her to the arbor. Little by little, his dizziness passed; but it left him silent. On the other hand, inspired by his rapt attention, Renée never talked so well. She found him very different from what she expected, not a bit superior. She could even tease him.

"Are you as dangerous to girls as Blaise said?"

"Ah, mademoiselle! Your brother likes to make fun. Do I look dangerous?"

"No," she agreed, then added with a tone of deep experience, "but you can never tell with men."

What a lovely voice she had! The thought struck him that if she dropped the *monsieur* and actually said *Pierre*, his heart would stop beating.

"Aren't you hungry?" she asked. The arbor, which contained a table and benches, was a favorite eating place in summer. She had set out the contents of the basket: half a meat pie, a capon still warm from the spit, two big slices of trencher bread to serve as plates, a jug of wine with a cup, two napkins, two knives, and some

35

pears for dessert. "I had to snatch what I could," she went on. "Everybody's flying round in the kitchen, and Dame Alice, the cook, is so cross. I know it isn't very nice."

"It's marvelous."

"Then eat, I pray you, monsieur."

Jogged by that, he cut two slices of the pie and ladled one of them on his fingers to her trencher bread before serving himself. She admired his elegance. Not a speck of gravy fell on the table.

But, then, having picked up her knife, she dropped it and stared across at him. "Alas, monsieur, what are we about? We've forgot the Blessing."

"By God, yes."

And they both stood up facing each other with heads bowed.

A pause followed. Pierre racked his brains for the benediction which he had heard a thousand times. Finally it came.

"Quicquid appositum est, felix ac sacrum esse jubeat, qui sua benignitate pascit universa. Amen."

They crossed themselves and sat down. The pie was excellent. She filled the cup and touched it with her lips ("Monsieur, to your health!"), before passing it to him. He answered according to rule ("I love it from you, mademoiselle!") and took care to press his lips to the same spot. It pleased her that he now and then slipped a morsel to Cocorico, who showed uncommon approval of the stranger and at last jumped up on the bench beside him.

Afterwards, stiffness faded, though Pierre's enchantment grew. He even contrived to make a full meal, while he listened to the nimblest, most adorable tongue he had ever heard — and the most interesting. For she spoke about important, uncanny things: the spirits who haunted Lallière and raised the hackles on the dogs' necks; the wolf-masters of the Forez, who could lead a pack of wolves through the woods like so many tame hounds (and Monsieur her father had seen this himself); the Good Ladies, the fairies, who were almost everywhere but whose queen, La Fayolle, held her court at the nearby Mare aux Bonnes Dames, a forest pond; the sinister ruins of the Clos des Moines, an abandoned monastery in the woods, the assembly place of wizards.

To Renée, the spirit world was no less real than the highroad from La Palisse. Her hushed voice and the furtive look in her eyes made it real to Pierre, who would have had no doubts anyway. Only scoffers and heretics doubted such things. He nodded gravely or shook his head and crossed himself, putting in now and then some weird bit of his own. The spirits drew them still closer together.

But even this topic could not fix his thought entirely. It mattered more to him than anything else that he was in Paradise, but not for very long. The rays of the setting sun grew more level between the vines of the arbor. It would soon be twilight. Then slowly the garden, with its vegetables and fruit trees, would fade out, and this hour with it. He would be on the road again tomorrow.

The sun went down. Upper windows of the house caught fire. The conical towers stood out sharp against the sky. Swallows were flying low. He could hear the tinkle of cowbells.

At last, what he had been dreading happened. Renée grew silent, glanced uneasily toward the house. "Eh bien, voilà . . . I suppose they'll be wondering . . ."

"Not yet," he begged. "Supper in the grande salle won't be over for hours. I'll wager they haven't finished with the meat yet. Then comes dessert, then talk. It won't be dark for a long while."

She shook her head. "I'm sure Mama will call me."

By this time, he had gained courage. "Then why stay here? It's a lovely evening. We could walk . . ."

The idea was so happy that she agreed at once. A lively girl of fifteen could not help agreeing. Even if she got whipped for it, why not make the most of her one great experience? She, too, was hoarding the minutes. And somewhere in the back of her mind dangled a horseshoe on a pink ribbon.

"Yes! We'll go to the Mare aux Bonnes Dames. It's only a little way through the woods. I'll show you where the fairies dance."

They left the remains of supper on the table, and, keeping the arbor between them and the house, slipped away through the open end of the garden, while Cororico raced off in front. A short path across fields led to the surrounding forest.

Plenty of light still lingered between the pillars of the beeches, and only here and there a black cluster of pine broke the effect of arches stretching on and on. There was no underbrush, since the peasant women collected it for various purposes. Pierre and Renée drifted side by side along the soft path. He gave her his hand on the pretext of helping her over the uneven places, and at her touch his whole body tingled.

But at the moment, physical love was still unconscious. Indeed, in his present mood, Pierre would have considered the least thought of it a villainy. He had had plenty of experience with women on that level. Brought up at a gay court and now cadet in a company of lances, who did not rate chastity as a virtue, he had had the usual affairs of a young man of his class. It was really because of them that Renée seemed different. She was no painted maid of honor nor the young wife of an old bourgeois nor a tavern girl. In his eyes, she was all innocence and grace, something to worship and protect. He had fallen in love, as the phrase went, a dozen times before, but he knew that it had never been like this.

"We'll have storm tonight," she said.

Pierre looked up at the clear evening sky. "But no, mademoiselle."

Their voices broke the hush of the woods, and unconsciously they lowered them.

"I'll wager you. In these mountains, it comes fast. There's a feel of it in the air."

Bets of any kind, on any occasion, had a fatal attraction for Pierre. Indeed, it might almost be said of him that he regarded life itself as a continuous wager. He showed his left wrist. "My bracelet against your earrings." It seemed an easy way to win a token from her.

She hesitated — the earrings were very precious — but she felt sure about the storm. "All right, then," she agreed. "You'll lose your bracelet."

They were suddenly on the edge of a wide pond completely surrounded by trees. Here and there, patches of water lilies darkened the surface, which otherwise looked like a pale mirror in the dusk. An eerie place. No one needed to be told that it was haunted. The strange silence which brooded over it was deepened rather than broken by an occasional lonely sound: the croak of a frog, the quick turn of a fish in the shallows.

Renée whispered: "Over there on the lily pads is where the fairies dance. They dance in front of La Fayolle, who sits under that tree. She has a throne made of silver cobweb. Sire François the Sorcerer has often seen them; but you have to have cat's eyes like his, and it's only on certain nights."

Pierre was utterly unafraid of anything human; but, being now in the presence of spirits, he took comfort in the talisman around his neck. It had been blessed by the Pope himself.

"Blaise used to row me out on the water," she added. "He isn't afraid of anything."

38

The remark put Pierre on his mettle. "Is there a boat?"

"Yes, look." She pointed to a little, triangular skiff moored under the bank. "Sire François fishes here. No one else would dare."

"Then may I be your boatman?"

Renée hung back. The adventure was becoming more fearsome every minute. She had already dared too much by walking alone in the woods with de la Barre, but now to put out with him in the Mare aux Bonnes Dames was rash beyond any excuse. Who knew what terrible enchantment might destroy them both? And, in that case, she would lose not only her life but her soul, for she would die in sin. The pond looked menacing in its dreadful calm.

"Do you think we'd better?"

In spite of the talisman, Pierre did not feel at all sure himself; but he had no intention of falling behind Blaise. "*Allons*, mademoiselle," he said romantically, "let us try our fortune on the water." And they walked down toward the boat.

At this point, Renée spoke out loud for the first time. "Surely the Good Ladies wouldn't harm us. I've always praised them and wished them well. Never have I hurt a beech tree, and I planted hawthorns near the house especially to honor them. We come here as their guests in all courtesy."

Pierre said: "Amen."

The politeness helped. It seemed to Renée that the water looked more kindly, as they crept out from the shore.

She sat in the stern of the skiff, facing Pierre, who handled the oars as quietly as possible. Away from the shadows of the bank, in the pale light beyond, they seemed to float between earth and sky.

Then suddenly both gave a start. Something scratched against the boat. Black goblin hands appeared grasping the side. A hairy head emerged. The thing whimpered at them.

"Mort de ma vie!" Pierre dropped an oar and snatched at his poniard.

"Oh, Mama!" moaned Renée, staring. Then she gave a relieved, "Tiens! It's Cocorico."

They had forgotten him. Chasing a rabbit, he had missed them on the edge of the pond. But water was Cocorico's element.

Renée burst into consolations. "Mon chou! Mon petit mignon!" Feeling silly, Pierre helped her fish the dripping little dog into the boat and was rewarded, together with Renée, by a drenching, as Cocorico shook himself. "Sacristi!" he muttered, wiping off his face on a sleeve. "Oo!" said Renée, looking at her dress. "By God, he's naughty!" Cocorico drenched them again, wagged his tail, and sat down with his tongue out.

After that, they felt more at ease, though talk remained hushed as if in a church. Renée leaned back comfortably and even trailed her hand in the cool water. They skirted the lily pads on the further side, where the air was faintly sweet with the odor of blossoms. Of course, it would have been an outrage to pluck one of them.

In praise of their spirit hostesses, Renée told Pierre about a bride at Varennes in the Bourbonnais, who had a beautiful lace veil. She had spread it out on her bed the night before the wedding, so that it would be the first thing she saw in the morning. It was a night of mist, which, as everyone knows, is most congenial to the Bonnes Dames. When the bride awakened, she found that the Fairy Queen had borrowed her veil to use in an elfin revel and had returned it ruined. A wet wisp of a thing, a rag, monsieur, and no ironing or drying could restore it. The poor girl was in tears, in despair. But wait! The bridal party was gathering. She must wear her veil, limp as it was. The bridesmaids dressed her. You could never guess . . . Renée's eyes were round.

'What?" breathed Pierre.

"Why, sir, it changed in the sunlight to golden lace worth a hundred crowns a foot, so gorgeous you could hardly look at it. The fairies' wedding gift. And, ma foi, it brought her luck as well, for she lived happily ever after."

At last Pierre shipped his oars, and the boat drifted idly. The fairies were forgotten in favor of something still more wondrous. The hour of sentiment began, of long pauses, timid advances.

. . . She would never remember him after tonight. . . . But yes, she would remember. . . . For his part, he would always remember. He would always . . . Yes? . . . Ah, mademoiselle . . .

Doubtless annoyed at being slighted, the Bonnes Dames took revenge by causing Pierre and Renée to forget time. The hour became two hours; twilight became moonlight. But the little boat still drifted on the enchanted pond.

"What do you see in the moon, monsieur?"

"Well, in Poitou, they say it's a man who cut wood on Christmas."

She nodded. "Yes, and now he has to carry a load of thorns forever. I don't believe it. It looks to me like the plume of a cap."

He would have liked to ask whose, but he said, "Or a lock of hair."

40

"Tell me" — she tried to sound casual " — who is your bonne amie? Some court lady?"

"No."

"Does she live at Saint-Maixent?"

"No."

It took a half hour longer to get it settled. By that time, they had made the moon their jewel box. It was safely guarded by the blindness of a world concerned with woodchoppers. Only they could know that it really held his plume and a lock of her hair, as keepsakes of this evening. Would he remember? Would she? To assure themselves of that was the most absorbing part of it.

And while they talked, the moon was being stolen. They looked up just in time to see it disappear into the pouch of a cloud. Suddenly the pond, the shadowy trees, vanished. Shut in by darkness, they could barely see each other. The forest stirred and grew loud beneath the racing of wind.

"Didn't I tell you!" she exclaimed. "We'll have to hurry. Quick! This is no place to be caught by the Wild Hunt."

"The Wild Hunt?" he repeated, fumbling for his oars.

"Yes, la Chasse Gayère. It's the name for a storm like this. Quick!"

But in the darkness, which thickened every moment, it was not easy to make speed. A certain panic rode with the gale which had leaped from the southwest. Cocorico whined and cowered against Renée. Pellets of rain spattered. The mutter of the woods became a roar. Pierre, confused, found himself stopped by a tangle of water lilies, until a flash of lightning gave him his direction. The rain slanted down in earnest before they reached the mooring place on the opposite bank. Scrambling out of the boat, he could see Renée's tense face in another lightning flash.

"We haven't time to get home," she said. "We'd be caught in the fields. There's a hollow tree I know of. It's not far. Hurry . . ."

But at this point, she tripped over Cocorico, who yelped and had to be comforted. "My treasure!" Catching him up under one arm, she gave her hand to Pierre, and led the way between the beeches. A bolt cut the blackness.

"Here," she said.

It was a huge tree, uneven rather than hollow; but what with the deeply indented trunk and thick canopy of branches, it gave some shelter from the rain. He drew his short cloak around her shoulders. She murmured an Ave Maria and a Paternoster.

41

"Don't be afraid," he encouraged. "The storm won't hurt us. You've won the wager."

"I'm not afraid of most storms. This one is different."

"How?"

"Listen . . ."

The center of the gale was drawing closer. It racketed through the forest like a thousand huntsmen whooping on their dogs; it howled like a horde of wolves. Lashes of lightning cracked on the flanks of the rain. Pierre thought he could hear the racing of horses, the padding of hounds. Closer. Closer. "By God," he muttered, "it's a hunt out of hell."

Instinctively they braced themselves against the tree, as if a wave were about to sweep over them.

"It's the Chasse Gayère." Renée's voice barely reached him, near as she was. "It's the ghosts of the old lords riding over their seigniories. They're hunting the souls of men." She pressed harder against the tree. "*Ave Maria, plena gratia . . .*"

He ran his arm around her waist, half covering her with his body against the dazzle of lightning and the pelting rain. But his embrace included Cocorico as well, who, snug in Renée's arms, considered the whole thing a frolic and barked in Pierre's ear.

The crest of the storm passed, raged off into the distance. Almost as suddenly as it had blown up, the rain slackened. Within several minutes, the clouds parted, and the moon crept out.

"Are you very wet?" he asked.

"Not very, thanks to you." She stood silent a moment, watching the pearl-gray light spreading among the beeches. "But I'll never forget it."

"Nor will I, mademoiselle."

Perhaps neither of them was thinking only of the Wild Hunt. For love, too, has its lightning. Their lips still burned with the kiss he had given her, while the old lords rode by.

Chapter 6

A large company, such as was now being entertained at the manor house, required the use of the salle basse or grande salle, the big raftered room to the right of the front door and opposite the kitchen, where de Norville earlier that day had conferred with Antoine and Guy de Lallière. Planks had been laid on wooden horses to form a table accommodating twenty-odd guests; and Madame de Lallière's pride, her embroidered tablecloths, with the silver saltcellars, bowls, trenchers, comfit dishes, vinegar cruets, knives and spoons, that represented a large part of the family capital, gave a rich center to the otherwise grim hall. The napkins had been perfumed with home-made rose-water. The floor was freshly strewn with marjoram and pennyroyal. Pine boughs were stacked in the gaping jaws of the great hearth, which was out of use till winter. Wine coolers, filled with salt and water, were ready. The silver cups on the dresser, whose two shelves indicated the family's noble rank, had been duly shined. Tallow flambeaux, as yet unlighted, stood in their sockets along the wall.

On a last-minute inspection of the room before supper, Constance de Lallière was surprised to find Blaise seated at one side of the cold hearth and with no other companion than Muguet, the falcon, motionless and hooded, on a perch behind him. He was in so deep a study that the bustle of servants, giving final touches to the table, evidently did not disturb it. Such withdrawal on the part of a sociable young man like Blaise was so odd that his mother paused with a stare.

"How now, Guillot the Dreamer? Stop rubbing your head. You look like a molting owl. A penny for your thoughts!"

He looked up, startled; then gave his knee a slap and got to his feet.

"They're worth more than that," he smiled, "a lot more."

"Love, I suppose?"

"Of course." But, from his too hearty voice, she could not be sure that she had guessed right.

"It's supper time," she went on. "You ought to be outside, helping to entertain the company, rather than moping here. I'll have to direct the servants. . . ."

"You're not joining us at table?"

"No, not tonight." On the point of leaving him, she turned back. "This archer of yours, young de la Barre — I hope he's not too great a rogue."

Blaise grinned. "Not too great for God's mercy. Why?"

Madame de Lallière explained that Renée had been permitted to give Pierre his supper in the garden. It was a shocking breach of decorum; but the table here was crowded; de la Barre would not have fitted in. . . .

It seemed to Blaise that she explained too much and too vaguely. He startled her by observing, "Yes, the former page of the Duchesse d'Alençon would hardly fit in."

Her eyelids drooped a moment. "I don't know what you mean. But, in short, I hope that Monsieur de la Barre is a young man of principle, that he'll take no advantage."

"He won't," said Blaise. "From the look of him in the kitchen, I'll bet he fell in love with her at first sight."

"Bon Dieu! But then . . ."

"But then, she's as safe with Pierre de la Barre as with her pet lamb. It's when he's not in love that girls had better take care. Don't worry: I'll vouch for him."

Madame de Lallière shook her head. "Nonsense! I'll have her called in before dark just the same." And she hurried off to marshal the servants.

Blaise smoothed down his ruffled hair and joined the guests, who were assembling in the courtyard close to the main door. But the thoughtfulness which had struck his mother lingered on, though not too apparently, as he exchanged commonplaces with the county gentlemen.

He knew many of them from his youth, and he liked many. There was old Hector d'Angeray, Seigneur de Bruzon, and his son Achille; there was Blaise's kinsman, Hugues Nagu of Varennes, Robert de Grossonne, François de Charency, Louis de la Souche, Charles du Peloux, and others, who were household names in the family. They were rough country squires, independent, stubborn and conservative. Some of them could neither read nor write and were proud of it. They were good fighters, good friends, fierce enemies. They were Blaise's own people, the group he belonged to; and he had a warm fellow feeling toward them. But they were very poor hypocrites. He could not help noticing the reserve, the nascent hostility, which they had never shown him before; and he could not help smarting at it. It was as if he were being disowned and shut out.

He could see de Norville whispering hotly, now with one, now with another, evidently persuading them to something which they had no relish for. Several of the younger men were plainly restive. They scowled and spat and drew away by themselves.

When at last the Marquis de Vaulx appeared, dressed in black, as befitted his age, and wearing the royal Order of Saint Michael, it became at once apparent what de Norville had been whispering about. The more experienced or more docile of the group made a show of politeness to the King's minister. As for the young rebels, the best they could do was to stand aloof and hold their tongues. On his side, the Marquis chatted with his usual grace; but Blaise knew him too well to miss the sardonic glint in his eyes and could see that he understood what was afoot. Indeed, very soon de Norville and everybody else were given to see as much for themselves.

"Ah, monsieur," said the Marquis, interrupting one of de Norville's well-turned compliments, "I thank you. But enough of me. I'm so eager to hear about your recent travels in England. It's an interesting country, which I visited more than once in the days of King Henry, seventh of the name. They tell me there's been much progress there, much building of fine houses and pleasances. Is that true?"

De Norville had a disciplined face; but, for a moment, it turned corpse-white and his mouth sagged. His journey to England had been secret. Until his return two weeks ago, the fact of it was supposed to be known only to the Duke. Since then, the news had got around in the inner circle of the Bourbon party, but that it should have reached Paris in so short a time pointed to a traitor. Unless — and that must be the solution — de Surcy had talked with Blaise since his arrival. Yes, of course that explained it. Well, he couldn't learn much from Blaise.

"What's wrong, sir?" asked the Marquis.

"Nothing, my lord. But to answer your question, I found much wealth in England. The wool trade is flourishing, and I have seen no finer cloth than from the English looms. Great houses are built on commerce."

De Surcy noted that many of the bystanders were now hearing of de Norville's English visit for the first time, while a few others, including the de Lallières, looked stricken. This was interesting as pointing out the leaders of the conspiracy.

"I agree, sir," he nodded to de Norville. "I hope you will give us your views of England in full. What concerns me most perhaps is English policy at the moment or — what comes to the same thing — the policy of Monseigneur Wolsey, Cardinal of York. He's an able minister. I haven't spoken with him since the meeting of the two kings three years ago near Calais, when France was so beautifully

45

tricked. What is he up to now? You had five interviews with him, I believe — no, six."

So deep a hush fell that the clucking of hens near the stables sounded loud. Blaise was no less startled than the others; but he was not so much surprised at the Marquis's accurate knowledge of de Norville in England as at his recklessness in parading it. Standing alone in this crowd of heated partisans, he seemed bent on provoking them, when the most ordinary common sense ought to have kept him quiet. Clearly he had some reason for thus showing his hand; and Blaise, wondering what the game was, felt a tense excitement. That the game might be dangerous rallied his sympathies to the Marquis — that, and Guy de Lallière's black looks. The two brothers were never apt to take the same view of anything.

"Well, sir," de Surcy added, "don't you care to discuss the Cardinal of York? Perhaps my questions are indiscreet."

"My lord . . ." gasped de Norville and then stopped. In the tumult of his mind, anger and hatred had not yet had time to take the lead over astonishment and fear; but they were beginning to stir — fierce anger, black hatred. His seraphic features looked strangely different.

De Surcy smiled. "You're not surprised that I know of your meetings with Wolsey, are you? Surely you don't suppose that the King of France has no friends in England to keep him abreast of such gossip as the doings of my lord of Bourbon's talented agent. You're not that simple." He added on a note of mock regret, "But I see I embarrass you. My apologies."

A servant, waiting to announce supper, had to nudge Antoine de Lallière's arm before he could draw attention.

"Ah, yes," said the old gentleman in a hoarse voice. "To be sure. The table's ready. Do me the honor to enter, sirs. And again welcome to you all."

Headed by de Surcy, whose rank gave him precedence, the company trooped indoors. Madame de Lallière, on duty behind the scenes, wondered at the silence. Not a word, only a shuffle of feet. "Mon Dieu," she thought, "what's happened? It sounds like a funeral."

Silently the guests washed their hands in the basins which the servants presented. The benediction, spoken by Antoine de Lallière, was framed by silence. The loud scraping of benches on the tiled floor did not herald the usual outburst of voices.

46

"Mon Dieu!" she repeated anxiously to herself.

Seated next to young Achille d'Angeray, Blaise made no effort at conversation; nor did his companion. Both had too much to think about. Blaise was aware of an impending crisis, which involved him as well as the others. Here and there people exchanged glances or a muttered word; but, for the most part, each of the guests looked moody and self-absorbed. Only the Marquis, at the center of the table between Antoine de Lallière and de Norville, showed a good appetite.

"Ha!" he exclaimed, his voice distinct above the sullen scraping of spoons. "What an excellent potage à l'oignon! My compliments to the cook, Antoine. He or she must let me have the recipe. Auvergne cheese, eh? There's none better in France. Fill me another half-bowl, mon ami," he directed the servant behind his chair. "I have always maintained that a sound potage is the keystone of good eating. And bring me a cup of hippocras, if you please."

It was not until he had chosen pheasant from among the various kinds of fowl presented and had praised the chestnut stuffing, that he appeared to notice the gloom at table and gave a perplexed glance on either side of him.

"What the devil! It seems that I'm the only one here who hasn't lost his tongue. Monsieur de Norville, I drink your health, sir."

Lifting his cap, he raised a goblet to his lips, then passed it to de Norville, who uncovered, drank and managed to get out something in answer.

The Marquis turned to his host. "Antoine, can you explain why this company looks so distressed? You'd find more talk in a crowd of Cistercians. Let me share the trouble, whatever it is."

De Lallière frowned for help to Guy, who sat across the board; but, when none was forthcoming, he could only think of the earlier, and now inane, excuse.

"Why, Denis, we're all concerned about the business in hand: how best to deal with these rascals in the mountains. They say their leader's one of Montelon's men, who has . . ."

"Come now!" the Marquis interrupted. "Let's be frank, and perhaps these gentlemen will recover their spirits. Why pretend? I'm certain your meeting has nothing to do with outlaws. It concerns politics — no doubt what side to take as between His Majesty and the Constable. Am I right?" De Surcy's gray eyes smiled along the table. "Of course I am; and, of course, you consider me an encumbrance.

47

But let me tell you something. Politics have been my trade, and I know a good deal about the point at issue. Take me into your counsels. I'll give you my advice, if you want it. If not, let's enjoy our food, for God's sake, and I'll bid you good night when we've finished. Then go on with your meeting, as far as I'm concerned. Which will you have?"

Across the table, every eye was on the Marquis; and those who were seated on either side of him along the board craned forward to stare. The room was still silent; but the silence had changed from leaden to breathless. In the dark as to what de Surcy intended, Blaise, nevertheless, admired his courage. It was no small thing to outface the glare around the table.

De Norville put the challenge of it into words. "It would help us to know how much you know."

De Surcy turned on him. "Why, then, I'll tell you. I know the name of every man who escorted the Duke of Bourbon on his supposed pilgrimage to Notre-Dame-du-Puy, which ended at Montbrison two weeks ago. Some of this company were there. I know, moreover, that the Seigneur de Beaurain, envoy of the Emperor, visited said Duke at said place, and that he came away well pleased with his interview. I know, monsieur, of your activities in England. And knowing all this, I know the rest of it. So, before you stir up these gentlemen to lose their lives and their lands in a hopeless venture, they would do well to consult with me."

Then at last dismay and confusion found a tongue. Oaths circled the table. Guy de Lallière brought his fist down on the board with a violence to make the trenchers jump.

"If you and the King know this," he demanded, "why is the Duke of Bourbon still at large in his city of Moulins? Why has he not been dragged to Paris or Loches? I'll tell you why. Because the King knows, too, that a hundred thousand swords are ready to speak for Monseigneur de Bourbon, that his states will rise to a man in defense of his just title. Hopeless venture, you call it? Not so cursed hopeless, but stout and flourishing. And what's *your* aim? To take the heart out of us? Believe me, sir, it will need more than your advice . . ."

He broke off because the Marquis had returned to his pheasant and was apparently giving it his full attention. It is hard to harangue a man who is absorbed in a drumstick.

But now the fog in Blaise's mind was beginning to clear; and, as he guessed de Surcy's purpose, not only the boldness but the brilliancy of it fascinated him. The Marquis had seized upon this occasion to strike a blow for the King, which might have important consequences. What he said and did here would be learned by the entire Bourbon faction in France. A more timid or a duller man would have held his peace and continued his journey next morning, glad to escape from the pickle with a whole skin. As it was, single-handed, de Surcy might accomplish more than an army. The Bourbon venture was very far from being hopeless; but if he could instill that doubt into the veins of the conspiracy, if he could give the impression that he knew more than was actually known, and that the enterprise was stillborn, he might weaken it to the point of collapse. And not only this. Blaise knew him well enough to realize his hatred of bloodshed, particularly of civil bloodshed. It would be hard, at that moment, to say whether loyalty to the King or compassion for humanity was uppermost in the Marquis's mind.

As the perception of this dawned upon Blaise, he felt that for the first time he had learned what statesmanship meant. Thus far he had had a soldier's disdain for any other profession than of arms. Now he could see the splendor and daring of action unconnected with the sword. He waited breathlessly for the next development.

"I ask again why the King has made no move," Guy repeated, "if he knows so much?"

Before answering, de Surcy finished the bone he was gnawing, dipped his fingers in the bowl which a servant presented, and dried them on his napkin. At last he said:

"Because Charles de Bourbon is a prince of the blood and kinsman of His Majesty. The King expects to visit him at Moulins before joining the army at Lyons. He will exhort him to remain a loyal subject and to take up his duties as Constable of France in the coming campaign. Until then, no move will be made; and, by that time, wiser counsels may prevail."

"But if they don't?"

"His Majesty will decide."

De Norville laughed. His glance from guest to guest mustered them behind him. "In other words, rob a man of his property, then hang him if he seeks to recover it. But perhaps you'll admit that it takes a stout rope to hang Leviathan, for that's what Monsieur de Bourbon, with the backing of England and the Empire, has become."

"Tut, tut," shrugged the Marquis, "let us stick to the point." He

49

addressed Guy de Lallière. "You say that my aim is to take the heart out of you, and you're not far wrong, though I'd call it putting water in your wine by pointing out facts. You talk in big terms. Where are your hundred thousand swords? In England, in Germany, in Spain, not here. What will you do when Marshal de la Palisse and the Grand Master of France lead their forces against you from Lyons? Will the hundred thousand swords reach you in time? Nenni, my friend, they will not."

"My lord of Bourbon has a good many strongholds," put in Antoine de Lallière. "It would take time to reduce them."

"No, not much," returned the other. "Even Chantelle could not hold out two days against the King's artillery. And meanwhile your houses would be fair plunder."

"But, by God . . ."

Others joined the debate. The passions of some rose higher. A few of the older guests sat pinching their chins. The Marquis had given them something to think about. The arrival of the meat course brought a pause, but it brought also heavier drinking and hotter blood.

Absorbed by the talk, Blaise was surprised to find that the windows had grown dark and faces less distinct in the uncertain light of the flambeaux. But it was not only the clash between Bourbon and Valois, province and nation, that perplexed him. He was aware now, for the first time in his life, of a cleavage in himself. The slapdash trooper of a few hours ago would not have been so beset. Tradition and family, a sense of fair play, the gallantry of the Duke's cause, all appealed to a young man who lived on the surface of things. They still had the best of it, even now, in spite of this new perception of larger issues that the Marquis's example gave him. They were warm and generous —

"This means nothing to you, of course," young d'Angeray sneered to Blaise. "You'll go on drawing the King's pay. But, by God, I'm not sure that I congratulate you."

They had reached the pears and cheese. The silver nef, loaded with comfits, passed down the table, and the people helped themselves absently. The room now smelled of wine fumes and of the lingering steam of meat. It had become hot, stuffy and feverish.

Blaise remarked that de Norville, with a wink here and a smile there, was egging on the younger element against the Marquis, who remained, however, more than a match for them.

50

A great man, thought Blaise, and then wondered what made de Surcy great. As compared with him, even the older people seemed juvenile and raw. They were wrinkled versions of the younger men present, with the same outlook and prejudices. De Surcy had been like them once, but he had continued to grow; they had not. That was the difference. Greatness meant growing. How did men grow? Blaise did not like to face the answer to that. But a sudden hot restlessness filled him, a discontent with himself.

"So you ask us to knuckle under," stormed Louis de la Souche, "bid honor good-by, abandon Monseigneur in his need, and pay court to the knave who plundered him, because said knave would otherwise plunder us? That may do for shopkeepers, but it happens that we're French noblemen of the Forez."

The Marquis smiled. He had learned long since that noblemen and shopkeepers differed little except in bombast.

"I know who you are," he nodded. "Well, then, *act* French. Ma foi, at the moment, you're a good deal more Spanish and English. Or does France mean less to you than the Forez? For the sake of your Duke and your county, you would tear France to pieces; let in the English again, whom your grandsires helped to drive out; hand over the South to Spain. And you call yourselves *French* noblemen! There's your honor! Fête-Dieu, you're welcome to it!"

By a trick of thought, *Fête-Dieu*, which was Bayard's favorite oath, recalled an incident to Blaise, which he had completely forgotten. It was two years ago at the siege of Mézières, that desperate stand against huge odds, where Bayard had turned back the last Imperial invasion. Even then the Bourbon cause was being discussed. The good Captain and several others, including Blaise, were at dinner – if a little mule meat and water deserved that name – and Bayard listened to the talk with his usual humorous smile. At last he said, "Fête-Dieu, gentlemen, I'm as good a friend as my lord the Constable has. I grieve for his troubles. But when it comes to sidetaking . . . Listen. I know only two things: God and France. That's enough for a plain man." At the time, Blaise had been more concerned with the mule meat than with Bayard's remark. Now, coupled with the Marquis's reply to de la Souche, it returned to his mind with the force of a revelation. France! Not this dukedom or the other! France!

Antoine de Lallière burst out: "We've had enough wrangling. If Monseigneur de Vaulx chooses to uphold a tyrant, he can settle

51

that with his own conscience. He's spoken boldly, at least, and I thank him for it. But, as far as I'm concerned" — de Lallière's rough-hewn features looked more like granite than ever — "I'll not cringe and grovel for fear of the King. I'll not dance with the times. The old ways suit me better — old loyalties, old dignity, by God! A fig for the new age! And, if it comes to dying, I'm well rid of it." He held up his arm. "Gentlemen, fair weather or foul, I'm for the Duke."

Other arms went up. "And I . . . And I . . ." Under the group compulsion, no one dared flinch, though some arms were raised more slowly than others.

Denis de Surcy leaned back. He had done his best. At the moment, his eyes were on Blaise. He could guess how the young man would choose, and he had already forgiven him. At twenty-three, the approval of his own people, the words honor and gallantry, outweigh anything else — as, perhaps, they should.

Everybody stared at Blaise. He sat with his fists clenched, aware of the lifted arms.

Antoine de Lallière tried to keep his voice level. "And you, my son?"

Blaise's mouth was dry. He found it hard to speak, let alone choose his words.

At last, he said, "No, I'll keep my oath to the King."

He heard the scornful mutter around the table and dared not look at his father. He missed, too, the sudden new light in Denis de Surcy's eyes.

Chapter 7

Red meat, red wine, and heroics had now heated tempers to the explosive point. Insolence, on the part of the younger men, began to show in unabashed comments and sneers. To forestall trouble, the Marquis addressed Antoine de Lallière, who, since Blaise's declaration, had not uttered a word.

"Eh bien, mon compère, when thanks have been said, I'll beg your leave to retire. You and your friends will have plans to discuss. I'm riding early tomorrow." He added, "Weather permitting," for the first lunge of the storm struck the house and sent a breath of cool air along the table.

Without answering, de Lallière stood up; and, at that signal, everybody rose, uncovered, and bowed their heads. Habit even required them to look devout for the brief span of the grace. But when that was over, tongues crackled again.

Rounding the table, Blaise joined de Surcy. His father and brother did not appear to see him, and his eyes avoided them.

"And so, good night to the company," said the Marquis.

But he was not to leave without a final skirmish. Raoul de Verney, a hulking young squire, barred the door. He was a bully and trouble-maker somewhat dreaded in the district, but his physical size and assurance gave him a following among the gentry of his own age and rank. He had a heavy face, now more than usually bloated from the recent drinking. Evidently he was bent on showing off before his friends. Standing a head taller than the Marquis, he leered down, though something in de Surcy's bearing and poise made him look like a loutish boy.

"A moment, my lord, *if* you please!"

"Well?"

"I'd like to ask one more question."

"Well?"

De Verney gave a broad wink to several of his admirers who had closed in. "You've been so kind about answering questions. I wouldn't want to impose on you."

"Come to the point, monsieur."

De Verney's tongue got tangled, but it lurched on. "You're sure you don't mind?"

With the indulgence due to a drunken man, the Marquis said that he did not.

"Well, then, monseigneur" — de Verney looked around again at his supporters — "we'd like to know when you last kissed the King's breech."

His guffaw merged with a sound box on the ears delivered by de Surcy. He reeled sideways but then, with a roar, surged back. He confronted, however, not the Marquis but Antoine de Lallière, who stepped between them. The old gentleman's face was grim enough to steady him.

"So! You insult my guest in *my* house, do you? By God, keep your hand from your knife. I'm master here."

De Verney was not easily daunted. "One guest's as good as another. You saw the blow. I'll have satisfaction . . ."

A hand gripping his arm jerked him around. "At your service," said Blaise. It was a relief, after the torment of the evening, to plunge into something straightforward like a fight. "*At your service,*" Blaise repeated, the scar on his nose showing whiter than usual. "Certainly you aren't conceited enough to expect the honor of being chastised by my lord in person. He has better things to do. But he'll not deny *me* that pleasure. I'll satisfy you on horse or afoot with any weapon you please. Or make it now . . ."

"Have done!" The Marquis's voice fell like an axe blow. "Will you fight with a drunken oaf? I even regret that I cuffed him. Satisfaction, indeed! He should be handled by the lackeys."

The storm, which had overtaken Pierre and Renée in the forest, brought this advantage, at least, to the people in the hall that it gave a breathing space to the quarrel. Its fury — the power of the wind, the incessant play of lightning and crash of thunder — dwarfed the human passions and for a short time silenced them.

De Norville, using all the credit which his position with the Duke gave him, fastened on de Verney and succeeded in drawing him and his followers to one side. Almost at once they formed a hushed group intent on what de Norville was saying. The others, startled by the rage of the storm, stood motionless. Superstitious fears rode on the whooping wind. "The Wild Hunt!" several muttered. Their forefathers, the ghost lords racing through the sky, called to them.

"It means evil," said Antoine de Lallière somberly. "It means war and death."

"Do you need a storm to tell you that?" returned the Marquis. "I've been saying as much all evening, and you wouldn't listen. Well, then, believe the wind. At last *think* for yourselves." His glance shifted to de Norville. "There would be fewer wars, if busy rogues didn't hope to profit by them."

De Lallière looked past him. "Your torches are waiting, Denis."

The Marquis bowed. "I thank you. God keep this company."

And, attended by Blaise, he walked out into the entrance hall, pitch-dark except for the flaring lights carried by his two pages and for the now more distant flashes of the storm.

In the bedroom assigned to de Norville, which he was to have shared, Blaise repacked his saddlebags. Further intimacy with the

Bourbon agent had become impossible. Besides, in view of the quarrel with de Verney, prudence suggested a stronger guard for the Marquis than that of his valets, and it had been decided that Blaise would spend the night in his room.

He packed mechanically. He was conscious of a vast ache of mind and heart. Remembering the look in his father's and brother's eyes, Blaise knew that this was probably the last night he would ever spend at Lallière. It meant the amputation of all the past, his boyhood, the sense of belonging here, the roots and tendrils that bound him to his family and the family house. Henceforth, he belonged nowhere. But, at the same time, he had a sense of triumph. He knew that he was a stronger man now than he had been before.

When he had finished stuffing his gear into the bags, he stood for a while, staring at the taper on the bedside table. The storm had now passed. The sound of voices in the grande salle below could still be heard, as the rebels adjusted their plans to de Surcy's warning. No doubt an urgent message would be got off to Bourbon at dawn.

The light of another candle in the doorway caught Blaise's attention, and he looked around to find his mother on the threshold. With her usual calm, she entered and put down her candle beside Blaise's on the table, then stood a moment facing him.

"A sad home-coming, my son."

"You know what happened?"

"Yes, I listened at the side door. It was necessary for me to know." He made a helpless movement with his arms but could find nothing to say.

"You've grown up," she remarked suddenly. "I never thought you would. You acted like a man. I'm proud of you."

"Then you aren't . . . you don't . . ." Blaise could only stammer his amazement.

"No, you did well. You know the proverb: wisdom comes by facing the wind; fools let it carry them. I'm not sure what I should have done in your place, but you did well. You made a hard choice."

He shrugged. "Yes, and now . . ."

"And now you will pay for it." Taking a step forward, she grasped the edges of his short mantle. "Your father and brother will hold by the Duke. My duty is with them. I know it is hard for you to give us up."

He covered her hands with his. "You know why I chose?"

55

"Yes, it is often hard to choose between the past and the future. But the future is bigger than the past; France is bigger than the Forez." She raised her face toward him, and he could see the tears in her eyes. "But listen, son. Do not ever dream that you have no hearth or home. They are here." She clasped her hands against her breast. "They are here. Forever."

She drew him close in her arms. Her warmth passed through him, comforting and healing.

"That's what mothers are for," she added. Then, half ashamed of her emotion, she drew back. "I expect much of you, Blaise. Make me proud of you. If you love me, be great. Promise."

It startled him that she echoed the new ferment in his own mind. But, of course, he could only smile.

"What would you have me? Captain of a hundred lances? Marshal of France?"

"That would be success," she answered. "Greatness doesn't depend on success or luck. It depends on seeing further and deeper than others — that, and losing oneself in a big cause."

He nodded. "I know what you mean."

"Your father and Guy," she went on, "will spend themselves to the utmost for Monseigneur de Bourbon. And, because they are unselfish in this, they should be forgiven. But they are blind. They do not see that fine-sounding phrases cannot replace thought, nor the past, the future. Tonight you have made yourself free. Think of it like that, and not that you are cast out."

"Thank you," he said hoarsely. "At least I know that *you* are great, and I have the honor to be your son."

"Such honor!" Reaching up, she smoothed his hair, her hand lingering a moment. "Touslehead!" she smiled. "Listen, Blaise, you must bear your sister in mind. If the Duke of Bourbon fails and the King takes vengeance, it may be impossible to provide for her." She stopped on a cheerless note. Then, suddenly, her eyes widened. "Mon Dieu, with all this trouble downstairs, I'd forgotten Renée. I don't even know whether she came in or where she is."

Blaise buckled his saddlebags. "Of course she came in. Do you think they would stay out in the garden during the storm? You'll find her in bed asleep."

"God grant it! Wait till I look. Never have I been so careless . . ."

He stood absently while his mother hurried off. But she was soon back.

"You were right. She's sound asleep." It was not Madame de Lallière's fault that the Bonnes Dames had favored Renée by getting her into bed just five minutes before. "You *will* look after her, Blaise, if anything should happen to us?"

He controlled the lump in his throat. "You know I will. But nothing must happen. You'll write me? You'll tell me all the news? I beg you. Try to keep Father from committing himself too deeply."

She shook her head. "I'll try. Of course, I'll write. Any courier into Italy will know of Monsieur de Bayard." She glanced at the saddle-bags. "Where are you sleeping?"

"Monseigneur de Vaulx asked me to share his bed."

"You see," she smiled. "A step forward already. It's no small thing to be the bedfellow of Denis de Surcy. Good night, mon fils, mon amour."

He dropped to one knee and kissed her hand. Then he took her into his arms.

Soon after dawn next morning, all the inhabitants of the manor house gathered for mass in the bleak chapel which opened upon the courtyard. But some of the night's guests — among them de Verney and his friends — had already departed. It was understood that they were off to Moulins with a report for the Duke. Otherwise, masters and servants, alike, knelt on the bare flagstones before the altar, where a village priest intoned his Latin. Many were dressed for the road and would be taking leave when mass was over. Outside in the courtyard, saddle and pack animals were ready.

For Blaise, the service had an unwonted solemnness. Although Antoine de Lallière had not yet spoken out, there was no change in his manner, and he had not answered Blaise's morning greeting. The latter kneeled by the side of Denis de Surcy. Opposite him were the familiar faces, whom he would probably never see together again. He prayed for each one of the family and that the present division might be only a passing cloud.

For Pierre de la Barre, the service was equally solemn, though in a happy sense. From where he kneeled, he had a perfect view of Renée, as she had of him. Neither of them looked at the altar very much, except when calling upon it to witness and remember what their eyes were saying. It was a conversation much more to the point than if it had been carried on in words. It recalled the enchantment of last night but found this morning just as enchanted. It looked forward breathlessly to the future. "Will you be true? Will you remember?" "Ah, mon Dieu, a thousand times — a thousand times!" And both gazed at the altar. She drew up her sleeve a trifle to show him his bracelet on her wrist, then nodded faintly. Something that he had worn would remain close to her always, something of himself. Fortunate bracelet! It startled him when the mass was ended. Never had it seemed so short.

"And now, madame," said de Surcy to his hostess, as the little congregation dispersed outside in the kindling light of the July morning, "and you, Antoine, mon ami, I commend myself to your good grace. It is time for us to mount. Every hour before noon is worth two in the evening, as all travelers know. Thanks for the good cheer, my prayers for your happiness." He lowered his voice. "And would to God that you gave some thought to what I said last night!"

De Lallière overlooked the hint. "I hope it will please you to take a cup and a bite before you ride."

The Marquis accepted the snub in silence. But to Jean de Norville, who now came up, handsome and engaging, he showed a different front. "We can dispense with compliments, sir. I grieve for good men who are mistaken, but I detest the rogues who mislead them. Better return to England or Savoy: you'll find it safer anywhere than in France."

A pale smile showed on the other's lips. "If you're a prophet, monseigneur, it might be wise to consider your own affairs."

"Aha!" the Marquis retorted. *Master Fox, what a long tail you have!*" And he turned away.

After wine and bread had been served to the departing guests, as a stopgap until mid-morning dinner somewhere on the road, Blaise received the sentence he had been expecting. As form required, he kneeled to his mother and father in farewell; but Antoine de Lallière drew back.

"Monsieur," he said in a harsh, distinct voice, "you have chosen a road opposite to mine, so that, if we meet again, it will be as enemies. It pleases you to back a tyrant and to forsake your natural lord when he needs your support. I dare say you expect to profit by it — time-servers often profit — but whether you do or not, you are no longer one of us. If you had remained in your garrison, you might be excused. But you came here. You saw your father and friends preparing to venture everything in an honorable cause which should be yours.

And you dared not play the man. Well, then, you are not to return here while I live. Is that understood?"

It was the measure of Antoine's anger that he said this in public and in the open courtyard. It was the measure of the affection in which Blaise was held that everyone, except de Norville and a few Bourbon partisans, looked crushed. Renée and Pierre, who knew nothing of what had happened at supper, could not have been more astonished if the earth had opened in front of them. The old family servants shook their heads and muttered. Madame de Lallière turned white.

Blaise had no difficulty this time in meeting his father's eyes.

"I am no timeserver or coward," he answered, "and you know it. You do me bitter wrong to call me so. Be assured, monsieur mon père, that I understand your desires."

"Antoine," put in the Marquis, "don't be a blind fool!"

A deeper color rose to the other's cheeks. "I'll be the judge of my son, if you please. We've had enough of your advice. You were received here only on the score of an old friendship. But that debt is paid."

The Marquis smiled. "Nonsense! I pray God to cool your head, Antoine, for He alone can." He turned to Constance de Lallière. "Adieu, madame et très bonne amie. God give you all fair life and long!" Then, with a nod to the page, who was holding his mule, he swung into the saddle.

Blaise kissed Renée, exchanged a stare with his brother, and once more raised his mother's hand to his lips. Her eyes gave him a final benediction. Then, vaulting to his horse, he followed de Surcy through the gate of the courtyard without looking back.

But Pierre de la Barre rode last of the little cavalcade, and he sat half turned in the saddle, with his cap still in hand, until he could no longer see above the dip in the road.

Antoine de Lallière walked back into the house. There his wife found him some minutes later seated on a bench in the grande salle. But his head was bowed, and he did not look up. It seemed to her that he had grown years older since yesterday.

Chapter 8

That morning, François the Sorcerer sat waiting by the roadside at a point not far from the village of Lallière but well out of sight of the last house. Here began the woods, which covered most of the distance to Roanne five leagues off. From his seat between the roots of a great oak, he had an excellent view of the highway, and, while breakfasting on a half-loaf of bread, he kept looking toward the nearby village.

Perhaps of more value to sorcerers than even a pact with Satan and knowledge of spells is the faculty of keeping their ears and eyes open and of piecing together what they learn. By this gift, Sire François had become the best fortuneteller in the Forez and a man of substance. He might carry a medlar staff, with the heavy end down, as the badge of his calling; and he might slaughter black hens at midnight crossroads or forgather with wolves or possess a magic bracelet made of eel-skin: but such things were trappings. His chief asset was a sharp mind.

Having spent last evening in the village tavern, he had learned of events at the manor house almost as soon as they took place; for news of what went on there was highly relished, and the de Lallière servants swelled their importance by spreading it. Thus, Sire François heard of the debate at table and the quarrel with de Verney before lights at the château were out. After that, he needed only to learn that de Verney and his friends with their servants had passed through the village before dawn, riding hard in the direction of Roanne. His quickness of wit and knowledge of people supplied the rest. Here was a chance to make money and pay off an old score at the same time.

He carried the score on his face, which de Verney's whip had once sliced when the sorcerer did not quickly enough make way for him on the highroad. Sire François had hated the rough squire ever since. And, on the other hand, he liked Blaise de Lallière as much as he could like anyone. But neither hatred nor love was uppermost in his thought this morning. He believed that his inference about de Verney was worth a gold crown.

The sun had been up two hours when the Marquis de Vaulx appeared at the head of his suite. Sire François could see the whole column before the first of it reached him: the Marquis on his saddle-mule in front, then Blaise and his archer, then two clerical-looking gentlemen, followed by three young pages riding the grands chevaux, or heavier battle- and parade-horses belonging to de Surcy and the two lances, then six mounted retainers, and, last, a group of lackeys and grooms with the pack mules. For so large a party, it was impressively quiet; and, from the somber faces of the Marquis and Blaise, Sire François could guess that leave-taking at the manor house had not been pleasant. But he was startled when, before coming abreast of him, the Marquis suddenly reined in and gave the order to halt. Then apparently, he conferred about something with Blaise and de la Barre.

Since the talk was out of earshot, Sire François adjusted his position by stealing closer behind the roadside bushes.

"I'm too old a fox," the Marquis was saying, "to be caught off guard by a cub. Besides, I keep remembering that the devil is known by his claws. You heard de Norville's last quip, didn't you? 'If you're a prophet,' said he. Well, I'm not a prophet but I'm not a fool."

Blaise nodded. "I heard him." He glanced along the road. "We'll be riding through hills and woods well nigh to Roanne."

"Just so," said the other, "and here's a good place to arm. I hate wearing steel on a hot day. Perhaps there's no need for it. But who knows that de Verney rode west rather than east?"

This was Sire François's cue. Stepping out from the bushes, he removed his wide-brimmed hat.

"God save your lordship! Monsieur Blaise, your servant!"

"Sainte Barbe!" exclaimed de Surcy. "Who're you?"

He was relieved when Blaise acknowledged the sorcerer's greeting with a "Ha, Sire François!" and then identified him in a couple of words. Pierre de la Barre, remembering that he and Renée had used the magician's boat for their expedition on the fairy pond, regarded him with special interest.

"My lord was saying that he did not know whether Raoul de Verney rode west or east," intoned Sire François in a professional voice, "but I can tell him."

"And how the devil did you happen to be behind that bush?" the Marquis demanded.

The other's voice deepened an octave. "Ah, monseigneur, do not

61

seek to learn by what means those of my guild are present wherever they please."

"Well, what about de Verney?"

"He and his friends made a pretense of heading toward Moulins, then turned back and followed this road. They lead Monseigneur by three hours."

De Surcy exchanged a glance with Blaise. "How many of them?" he asked.

"Six gentlemen with their servants — in all, eighteen horse. They are well armed. They will await Monseigneur at the Col du Torrent two leagues ahead."

"How do you know that?"

Sire François did not explain that anyone planning an ambush would be a fool not to set it at the Col du Torrent, where the winding of the road between forested and almost vertical mountain spurs gave every advantage to the attack. He merely replied, "I have means of knowing. My lord can be assured that I speak the truth."

Blaise put in: "I know the place. It's a fair trap. But we can circle it, if you please, by taking a side path one league short of it. Then, by your lordship's favor, Pierre and I, with some of our people, could take these rascals from behind and give them a good clyster of steel. It would not do to let them think we're afraid."

"Bah!" snapped the Marquis. "What do I care for their opinion! If we can leave them to slap flies in their thicket while we go on to Roanne, we'll have the best of them by a good laugh. However, it's prudent to be ready. Jules! Henri!" he called back. "Send up the pack mules with the armor. Saddle the big horses."

The column sprang into action.

"My lord," intoned Sire François, keeping his nose to the main scent, "was my information of no value to you?"

The Marquis drew out the hoped-for crown. "Here you are, Maître Sorcier, with my thanks. We could use sharp wits like yours in the King's service. Call on me if you should ever want a place."

Sire François bared his teeth in a pleased grin. But, as he bowed himself off, Pierre de la Barre led him to the side of the road.

"You'll be going back to Lallière? You'll be seeing the demoiselle Renée?" he whispered.

The wizard nodded.

"Could you manage to tell her fortune, eh?"

"Likely enough, sir."

Pierre cocked his head. "I depend on you, maître." He slipped a crown into the sorcerer's ready palm. "You'll get plenty more if the fortune comes true."

"Noble and generous prince!" glowed Sire François. "You can rely on me."

In movement again, de Surcy's little troop marched closer together and showed a good sprinkling of steel. The Marquis, Blaise, and Pierre now each wore cuirass, sallet and pauldrons. This somewhat equalized the chances against de Verney's more numerous followers, if, in spite of the detour, they should still be encountered. It also provided for the possibility that one or another of the enemy had a crossbow. The Marquis's six armed lackeys, who now formed the rear guard of the column, had put on their steel caps, and two of them carried arbalests at the ready. Even Dr. Savio, the Italian physician, and Maître Laurence, the Marquis's secretary, had donned corselets, and the grooms were equipped with pikes. On the whole, it was a company which could give some account of itself if it held together and was not taken by surprise.

These preparations had a tonic effect on the spirits of the party. Blaise, for the moment, had something else to think of than the break with his father. The dreaminess which had afflicted Pierre since yesterday afternoon wore off, and he hummed a catch about Madeleine in May. De Surcy, who had exchanged his mule for a spirited horse, rode between the two young men and forgot state affairs in an afterglow of his own distant youth.

"How far to this side path of yours, Blaise?" he asked.

"A quarter of an hour, sir — or close to it."

Blaise went on to explain that the forest trail led steeply uphill for a league, then plunged as steeply down to a little river, l'Arçon, a tributary of the Loire, which would have to be forded. From that point, a short ride uphill again brought one to the northern highroad leading into Roanne.

"Of course it's possible," he added, "that de Verney may have a vedette out to keep us in sight." He glanced up at the thick woods on either hand. "In that case, we should have done better to stay on this road and fight it out at the Col du Torrent. If they learn that we've taken the forest path and ride after us, we'll be tangled in the woods and at a disadvantage, unless we can first reach the ford of the river. We could face them there."

63

"It isn't likely," the Marquis reflected, "that de Verney and his mates have wit enough to reconnoiter us a league this side of them — unless on de Norville's advice. He's the prime mover of this plot. He knows that I know too much about him. Still, everything considered, we'd better risk the side road."

Having reached the turning-off point some minutes later, Blaise advised changing the order of march. "If we take the rear," he suggested, "we'd be the first to know that we're followed, and could then hurry on the others or make a stand or push ahead, as seems best. In front, we'd be apt to hear nothing until they were on us."

The maneuver was carried out. Soon, in a long single file, with a straining of girths and a plying of sticks on the mules' rumps, the column went toiling up the narrow path between the trees. But hardly had he left the road with the Marquis and Pierre, when Blaise drew rein.

From the forested ridge behind them came a prolonged sound like the bellowing of a bull. Only no bull's lungs on earth could have produced such a reverberating groan. One blast followed the other more and more urgently.

"It sounds like a Swiss horn," remarked de Surcy, "the kind those of Uri carry. My faith, didn't we hear enough of them on the night of Marignan!"

"Yes, it's a mountain horn," Blaise agreed. "And it can be heard a league off, certainly as far as the Col du Torrent. It may have nothing to do with us; but, if it's intended to warn de Verney, we have fifteen minutes' start. We'd better make the most of them, whatever it means."

The word to hurry was sent up along the line, and the creaking of leather, the whacks of sticks redoubled. But, to the three horsemen, chafing behind, progress seemed slow to the point of torment. They had not quite reached the summit of the path when a racing of horses' hoofs along the valley road drifted up to them.

"That settles it," frowned Blaise. "The horn was for them right enough. They'll be on us before we reach the ford. Monseigneur, ride ahead, for God's love. You can get away. We'll hold them in check. . . ."

The Marquis cut him off with an abrupt *no*. "Sometimes manhood, friend Blaise, goes even before the King's business. I'll not leave you to pay the reckoning; we'll stay together. But we'll reach the ford if

64

we can. Our people are safe. We're the quarry these rogues are after. So, then, spur!"

Turning out of the path to avoid the line blocking it in front, de Surcy plunged into the woods, topped the crest of the hill, and began the descent on the other side. But there was no need of spurs on that steep slope, where the footing dropped away, and a horse's croup rose higher than its head. Sliding down through leaves and moss, stumbling over roots, avoiding branches here, a fallen trunk there, the riders found the going almost as slow as on the ascent. It was a breakneck business of sheer luck.

Then, suddenly, uproar broke out on the path, where the pursuers had caught up with the single file of the column. Oaths, blows and yells; stampeded mules crashing among the trees; shouts from de Verney's party to make way and be damned. Riders appeared to the left along the path and on either side of it, plunging downhill. One of these caught sight of the Marquis through an opening of branches and, clapping a horn to his lips, sounded the view halloo. Then, wrenching his horse in the Marquis's direction, he headed toward him.

And at that instant, the worst happened. De Surcy's horse stumbled against a half-buried log, missed its footing, and pitched heels-over-head, throwing the Marquis several paces in front of it. De Verney's trooper gave a shout, drew his sword, and swung down toward the prostrate man.

Chapter 9

At the moment of his patron's fall, Blaise de Lallière was some ten paces in front and to the right. A thicket shut out the full view of what had happened, but he caught a glimpse of the somersaulting horse and heard the muffled thud of the Marquis's body. He heard, too, the shout of de Verney's man and the lurching approach downhill. With his heart in his mouth, he turned, breasted the slope, and urged his horse through the thicket just in time to reach de Surcy's outstretched form before the enemy arrived. As it was, their momentum brought the two men together in a head-on collision, and Blaise recognized his opponent as one of last night's ruffling squires.

65

But here the superior weight of de Lallière's mount had the best of it. Practically on his haunches already from the steepness of the descent, the lighter horse toppled to one side and went over, pinning his rider beneath him. In the same breath, Blaise's sword lashed down at the head of the fallen man, who screamed and then lay still. His horse regained its feet and stumbled away with a turned saddle. But Blaise had already dismounted and was bending over de Surcy.

"Monseigneur . . .!"

"Mille diables!" came a dazed voice. "What a tumble! By God, what a tumble!" And, turning over, the Marquis sat up. "Give me a hand, son Blaise. I feel as if I'd dropped from the moon."

Blaise acted instinctively. An instant's thought would have been too long. He could hear the whole chase closing in on them. Fortunately the first pursuer had had a good start of the others, and this gave time — just enough time — to make one more dash for the river five hundred yards below. Blaise's own horse must carry double. He helped de Surcy to his feet, lent him hand and shoulder into the saddle, vaulted up behind him, and, managing the bridle reins with his arms around the Marquis's body, headed downhill.

There was no longer any question of guiding the horse. The gamble had to be taken that somehow, by brute luck, they would reach the bottom without another fall. As it was, a rider, curving in from the side, got in front of them. But again the weight of de Lallière's battle horse, hurtling down, overmatched the lighter hackney and bowled him out of the way, while the rider's sword glanced harmless from Blaise's sallet.

Through another thicket; then, by a miracle, between two boulders without colliding; then slithering down another dip . . . Suddenly the trees thinned. It seemed incredible that they had reached the river.

Not far off, Pierre de la Barre sat his horse and stared anxiously up into the forest.

At sight of them, he gave a shout. "Mordieu! What happened? I couldn't see a thing in that tangle. . . ."

"Spur!" yelled Blaise, turning to the left along the river bank in the direction of the ford. Horsemen were already emerging from the woods at various points, and there was not a moment to lose.

The ford, which lay a hundred yards off, consisted of a rocky ridge about eight feet wide and two feet under water. On either side of it, the river, swollen by last night's rain and accordingly swifter than usual, could only be crossed by swimming. But steep banks on the further side made it almost impossible for a horse, having swum the stream, to gain a footing there. On the other hand, these banks had been graded at the ford end to suit the convenience of travelers. Thus, the ford could be regarded as a submerged bridge, protected on both sides by the depth of the river and narrow enough to be held by a couple of horsemen against superior numbers. If Blaise could only reach it before it was closed by de Verney's people, he could hope for an even fight.

But, at this point, his horse, carrying double, was outclassed. Thirty yards remained to be covered when two riders, galloping down the slope, drew up at the hither end of the ford and closed it. Meanwhile, others were pressing in from behind. Apparently both the efforts and good luck which had got Blaise and de Surcy to the river were in vain. They were trapped, with the Marquis in no condition to fight, and Blaise, cumbered by the latter in front of him, unable to use his sword.

Then Pierre de la Barre passed them, like a thunderbolt, and crashed into the two horsemen. One of them toppled back into the stream; the other, grappling with Pierre, received the full impact of the young man's gauntlet beneath the chin and dropped from his saddle. The ford lay open. A moment later, Blaise had ridden down into the water.

"Good work!" he shouted to Pierre, who had drawn his sword and now faced the oncoming attack. "Get down into the ford and cover me until I bring his lordship across. Then by God, we'll have sport." And he splashed on through the fifty-odd feet of shallow water to the opposite bank.

There, slipping to the ground, he helped de Surcy, still half-dazed from his fall, to dismount.

"It's but a few hundred paces from here to the highroad, monseigneur. If you can reach it, likely enough you'll be safe; for there're King's people these days marching south from Burgundy. Meanwhile, we'll hold the ford."

He was already in the saddle and heading back to join de la Barre, who had turned his horse sideways across the passage and was fighting with three of the enemy who tried to force their way past him. Upon Blaise's arrival, these reined back, and a lull followed, while the two sides faced each other.

67

The Marquis remained standing where he had dismounted. At the moment, he could not have walked ten paces. The best he could do was to lean exhausted against the bank.

"Ha, Raoul!" Blaise called across the strip of water to de Verney. "Here we stand ready to give you the satisfaction you were bawling for last night. Come and take it. Why do you send your lackeys?" He eyed the three men who had backed out of reach of Pierre's blade. "Don't tell me you're disheartened because eighteen of you couldn't cut our throats so easily. Pluck up your spirits. Everybody has to die sometime."

The burly young man, sitting a heavy, half-winded horse on the further shore, replied with a volley of oaths.

"Indeed?" laughed Blaise. "Come and get your mouth washed."

Appraising de Verney's troop, he noticed that the action had so far cost them a third of their number. If they had started with eighteen, they were now twelve. The servants of the young squire whom he had killed or wounded in the forest were probably tending their master. That would mean three or four less. Pierre had accounted for another. A couple, perhaps, had been unhorsed during the ride. But twelve to two were still heavy odds.

"Form column!" ordered de Verney. "Form column and spur all together! We'll blow these two cockerels out of the way."

"Be sure you gentlemen ride in front," Blaise called. "Don't let it be said that noblemen of the Forez charge behind their grooms."

"And what sort of a nobleman are you, you turncoat?" shouted one of the squires, named Jacques Lalisse.

"Why, only of France," Blaise retorted. A hot exaltation leaped up in him. He had fought for France at Mézières and in Italy; but now France suddenly became personal and intimate. This skirmish in the mountains was not merely a random quarrel but the first clash between France and Bourbon. That gave point to it. "Vive le roi!" he added, lifting his sword in salute.

Taunts and jeers answered from the other side. But the horsemen were already forming three abreast. It was sound tactics, since the very pressure of the charge would be apt to carry through, no matter what happened to those in front. As a countermove, Blaise, with Pierre at his side, backed toward their end of the ford, thus enabling them to meet charge with charge and, by the momentum gained, to neutralize the weight against them. Their one advantage, such as it was, lay in the size of their horses and in their armor. But the young squires were well mounted; and several of them, including de Verney himself, wore steel caps and corselets. These gentlemen had not needed Blaise's scoffs to bring them to the front. They formed the first two ranks, with their retainers behind them.

De Verney, glancing back, raised his sword. "Are you ready?" he called. "Charge!"

"Allons!" said Blaise to Pierre. At the same moment, he drove in his spurs.

Hampered somewhat by the depth of the ford and bounding rather than racing forward, the two sides closed in. Denis de Surcy, forgetting his exhaustion and dizziness, stared at the encounter, which was half obscured by the spray of the churned water. "Saint Paul!" he muttered. "Why am I so cursed helpless!" He stood free of the bank, his hands clenched. "Ho, by God, well ridden!"

For the first thrust of de Verney's troop did not break through. Just before the instant of shock, the Marquis saw Blaise swerve slightly to the left, so that he blocked de Verney and another horseman in the front rank, while Pierre contained the third. Swords leaped here and there out of the spray curtain and fell. Horses reared. A mingled din went up of oaths, exclamations, steel grinding on steel, slithering of hoofs on the rocky bottom of the ford, vast splashing as of a number of mad fountains. The morning sunlight wrought an illusive rainbow on the mist of the fight.

"Well ridden!" exclaimed de Surcy again.

But the extreme effort of the two defenders could not last long. The weight against them was too overpowering. Only one chance of success remained. If de Verney, the mainspring of the action, could be eliminated . . .

Catching de Verney's blade on his left arm, Blaise put his entire strength into a slash across the face of the horseman on the outer rim of the ford. The man reeled back in his saddle, lost his stirrups, and pitched over into the stream. Then Blaise turned on de Verney. The latter was no match for him in arms and knew it. His chief weapon was his bulk and strength. Closing in, saddle to saddle and thigh to thigh, de Verney grasped Blaise's sword hand at the wrist and, grappling him around the waist with a bear hug of the other arm, sought to wrench him out of the saddle.

Corselet grated against corselet. Blaise felt the gripping muscles of his legs giving way to the relentless heave that would unhorse him. Desperately his left hand, reaching outside de Verney's straining arm, groped for the hilt of the extra poniard carried at his saddlebow.

He slipped sideways, his whole weight supported now by the right stirrup. He felt the blank hopelessness of defeat. But in that moment his fingers closed upon the hilt of the knife, and he plunged the point of it into the opening between de Verney's corselet and armpit.

The man's head jerked back with a groan; his arm dropped away; and he slid down between the two horses. Blaise reined back to avoid trampling him, as did the rider who had been at his heels.

The latter shouted, "Gare! It's Monsieur de Verney. Back, you others! Hold back!"

In the small space cleared between the horses' legs, de Verney's body could be seen half-submerged in the shallow water, which showed a drifting spume of red.

"Leave him to his servants," roared Jacques Lalisse. "Push on, sirs! We'll have vengeance for him! Will you let these two obscenities carry it against us?"

But the others showed less eagerness. No one cared to ride over de Verney's body. And, as they hesitated, a diversion came from an unexpected quarter.

Shouts rose from the mountain side of the ford. Looking around, the startled survivors of de Verney's band saw a fringe of riders and pikemen behind them, cutting off their retreat. As for Blaise, he at once recognized the Marquis's people headed by Maître Laurence, the secretary. Overridden and scattered by de Verney's pursuit, it had taken them some time to reassemble. But, even so, they had done well, for no more than a half hour had passed since the first clash.

The result was panic among those who remained of the enemy. Lalisse spurred his horse into the river and swam downstream; others followed him. "Our compliments to Monsieur de Norville!" Blaise shouted. Several of the humbler sort gave themselves up. In less than a half minute, the ford was cleared. Only the bodies of three dead men remained, weighted down by their equipment.

Then Blaise and Pierre rode back to the Marquis on the further bank.

"This is no time for me to tell you what's on my heart, gentlemen," said de Surcy. "I shall try to express that later, if I can."

70

Chapter 10

When the pack mules had been rounded up and a general inspection made, it was found that little damage had been done by de Verney's attack. Even the Marquis's horse had suffered nothing more from its fall than a badly strained shoulder. A slight wound on Blaise's left arm, some cuts and bruises among the servants, were the extent of the physical injuries. But, what with the delay, shock and fatigue, it was impossible to continue that day beyond the pleasant little town of Roanne, where the Marquis and his following turned in at *The Red Lion*.

At supper time, de Surcy made his acknowledgments to the two defenders of the ford. Summoned by a page to the Marquis's chamber, Blaise and Pierre knelt, as courtesy required, and hoped that his lordship had sustained no more harm from the adventure than a night's rest would repair. They expressed their regret that so venerable a nobleman had been exposed to such annoyance on his journey.

"Ay, sirs," replied the Marquis, with a wave of the hand that invited them to rise, "*venerable's* the polite word for my trouble. *Old* better hits the mark. If I had been younger — or less venerable — I should have been of some use to you today. But sixty years, alas, is a disease that a night's sleep will not cure. Otherwise, thanks to you, I'm hale enough. And, except for you, I should be a trophy of Monsieur de Norville's huntsmen."

"If your lordship will pardon me," said Blaise, "I don't think I could have taken the fall which you suffered today and now be wearing my shoes. A jolt like that is no trifle at any age."

The Marquis shrugged. "I thank you. However, be that as it may, I did not invite you here to talk about myself. There are other matters." He added with a smile: "Such as Monsieur de la Barre's bracelet. Pierre, my friend, I remarked on our journey that you had one of gold filigree. I perceive now that it is gone. No doubt you lost it at the ford."

Pierre was too schooled a young man to show embarrassment, but he colored slightly. "No, my lord, I lost it at Lallière on a wager."

A twinkle showed in de Surcy's eyes. "And your loss is the gain of someone else. Ah, beau fils, the gambling spirit is a very danger to youth — particularly if your heart's in the bet."

"Pardie, monseigneur, I am well aware of it."

"But it would not do," the Marquis went on, "to leave the wrist of so gallant a cavalier unadorned." He turned to a small box on the table and threw back the cover. "So, I beg you to wear this trinket in token of today and not wager it until you visit Lallière again."

It was a heavy bracelet of gold embossed with figures of Italian workmanship and set with jewels. Pierre dropped again to one knee and poured out his thanks. Then, clasping the bracelet on his wrist, he proclaimed himself forever the servant of Monseigneur de Vaulx.

"Gracefully said," approved the Marquis. "But, for all that, I remain in your debt. And now I should like a word in private with Monsieur de Lallière, who, I hope, will do me the honor of supping with me."

When de la Barre had bowed himself out, de Surcy added to Blaise, "Though, by your leave, we'll sup first and talk later, for I confess I'm sharp-set."

After comfits were served and the pages had retired, the Marquis came to the point he had in mind. Leaning back, toothpick in hand, he remarked: "Well, sir, it's little more than twenty-four hours since we entered the courtyard at Lallière. In that time, a good deal has happened. Among other things, you have been disowned, and you have very much astonished me."

"Astonished?" Blaise repeated.

"Yes. I always considered you a lad of spirit. I admired your hand with a sword or a horse or anything else that takes quickness and muscle. But forgive me if I confess that I believed your head was filled only with butterflies. Last night you showed me that you could think: I was startled. You showed me that you could set your mind against the current and take the consequences: I was impressed. I learned that I had undervalued you. My congratulations!"

The Marquis applied his toothpick, while Blaise, flushed and embarrassed, could think of no adequate answer.

De Surcy relieved him by continuing. "As to my thanks for the service you did me today, I'll not attempt to express them. I can reward young Pierre with a piece of gold. I intend to reward you differently."

Blaise put in: "You'll reward me best by not speaking of it. By God,

72

it would be a sad thing, after all your kindness, if I had to be paid for doing my duty. Why did I come with you on this journey — "

"Taisez-vous!" interrupted the Marquis. "And be good enough to listen. I intend to reward you by asking for another service."

"Ho," said Blaise, "that's different."

"I told you it was." The Marquis took a sip of wine. "You'll set out tomorrow for Paris — no, Fontainebleau. The court has moved down there by now."

"You mean *return?*"

"Yes. Naturally the King must hear of what happened last night and today. He must hear at once. I shall urge him to lose no time in laying hold of the Constable of Bourbon before this fire spreads. Better the death of one man than of thousands, since we have no other choice. You'll carry my letter and satisfy His Grace on any point that needs explaining. You're the only proper messenger."

But de Surcy's matter-of-fact expression did not conceal from Blaise the kindly cunning behind it. Of course the King must be kept informed of the fast approaching rebellion, and he must weigh the Marquis's advice. But almost anyone in de Surcy's following could carry the letter as well as Blaise. It was plainly to bring him to the King's notice under flattering circumstances that he was being sent. He did not need to be told in what terms the Marquis's letter would commend him. If he had looked for a reward, none could have equaled this.

"I quite understand," he said after a pause, "how much I owe to your lordship for such consideration."

"Nonsense! You have your way to make — all the more now that you've broken with your father. It would be absurd if you missed this chance to be thanked by the King. You were with me last night. You heard the wrangle at dinner. You can give His Majesty your own views. In particular of de Norville. I say he's the man to watch." An unwonted grimace of dislike ruffled the Marquis's serene face. "A Judas if there ever was one. Peste! I'll warrant he's the serpent at the Duke's ear. It would be a blessing for France if he could be scotched."

Blaise remembered his conversation yesterday with the Bourbon agent. Absolved from his promise of secrecy by the recent murderous attack, he now reported the talk in detail.

"Thirty lances, eh?" said the Marquis. "Five hundred livres pension. Diable! I'll put that into the letter, too. It may give His

73

Majesty a hint. Certainly it makes your decision last night more notable. So, bribery's in the field as well as treason! And this English girl of de Norville's — I'll wager she's the price of his devotion to England. Do you remember her name?"

"He refused to tell me."

"So? That means probably that it's well known. I'd give a pretty penny — "

"She has reddish hair, monseigneur, and the initials A.R. I looked at the back of the miniature before de Norville came in. He told me that she had spent some time at our court."

"A.R.," de Surcy repeated, "reddish hair . . ." He sat musing. Suddenly his brows went up. "By the Mass! That's interesting. It's possible. If so — " He leaned forward eagerly. "Can you describe her face?"

"It isn't one to forget. Handsome, not pretty — "

"Yes," breathed the Marquis.

"A big mouth — "

"Yes."

"And, by God" — Blaise smiled reminiscently — "the strangest eyes I've ever seen in a woman. I mean the shape and expression of them — "

De Surcy brought his palm down on the table. "Bon Dieu! It can't be anyone else. Blaise, mon ami, if there were no other reason for sending you back to court, this would be enough. I suppose de Norville led you to think that the lady was now in England. No, by Saint John! Unless I'm all wrong, she's this moment at court, and I know who she is. But we have to make certain. You've seen the miniature. You're the only one who can say whether that girl and Anne Russell are the same."

"Anne Russell?" Blaise pondered. "Wasn't there some gossip in Paris about — "

Gaily impatient, the Marquis cut in: "Of course. The King's new favorite, the girl who has given Madame de Chateaubriant more than one turn of the liver. Anne Russell. One of the Queen's ladies. She was slipped into our court three years ago at the time of the Cloth of Gold, when we loved the English so much. To complete her education, ha? And she's still there, under the wing of Madame d'Alençon, who dotes on her, and because the King has taken a fancy to her. Pasque-Dieu! So *she's* betrothed to Jean de Norville!"

74

De Surcy fell into silence, his thought probing the possible bearings of this discovery.

Questions buzzed in Blaise's mind. At last one of them crept out. "Your lordship thinks that this lady is a spy?"

The other glanced up from the table. "Spy?" he repeated. "That's a round word. It has a bad smell that doesn't fit Milady Russell." Absently he selected a grape from the dish in front of him and consumed it before adding: "You don't know her, of course, but I know her a little." He smiled. "Though I may be flattering myself. Who can say that he knows a woman? Still, I've kept an eye on her. She's the half sister and ward of Sir John Russell, one of King Henry's favorites. That she should be at our court, in spite of the war, and popular, too, is an odd enough case to draw attention. But to call her a spy, even if she acts for England? No, the word doesn't fit."

The Marquis fingered his wine cup. Blaise waited expectantly for him to go on.

"Words, my friend, have delicate shades. There are white words and black, but the words in between hit the truth more often. *Spy* is a black word. It suggests villainy. But look at Mademoiselle de Russell. To begin with, she's not more than nineteen. She's not to blame if she has good looks and sharp wits. Is it her fault if her brother and Cardinal Wolsey find a place for her at our court and send her there? Could she refuse to go? Perhaps she loves England; perhaps she would serve her prince. Is it likely that a young girl of that rank would fail to give notice, if possible, of what goes on among us, would not seek in all ways the advantage of England? No, but we are to blame for keeping her at court. I have thought so a long time. The present connection with de Norville proves it. England is bad enough, but Bourbon is still more dangerous."

"If she's like her husband-to-be," said Blaise, "I don't know that the word I used is too black."

De Surcy shook his head. "No, I can tell you that much. She may be an intrigante in her own right, but she's not of his kidney. There's no greater difference between a snake and a falcon."

"She's marrying him."

"And what of it, except that it shows what price England will pay for de Norville's good offices with the Duke? Poor girl! I doubt if she's ever met him. Women don't marry; they are married. But the King must be warned."

This was not too easy, as a courtier like the Marquis realized. The warning might have a recoil, depending on the King's relations with Anne Russell when he received it. An old minister, intervening in a love affair, is not apt to be thanked or believed. On reflection, it seemed best to include no mention of Anne Russell in the main report of last night's meeting and today's fight. The Marquis would dictate this to his secretary. But he would add a separate page with the bald statement in his own hand of de Norville's betrothal to an English girl, who, for such and such reasons, might be Anne Russell, the identification depending on Blaise. It was to be read only by the King, who could then do as he chose.

"And so," ended de Surcy, pushing back his chair, "if you'll fetch me Maître Laurence, I'll get to work on these letters. You should go to bed. Tell Pierre de la Barre that he's to be my chief guard and Janizary from now on to Lucerne. That will sugar the pill for him of your leaving. You'll ride post for greater speed. We'll take your gear and horses with us. I suppose you'll follow the other road north along the Arconce and give Lallière a wide berth."

It was agreed that Blaise should rejoin the Marquis in Switzerland after his errand to Fontainebleau and should bring with him the King's answer.

"Or perhaps by that time," said de Surcy, "I'll have finished at Lucerne, and we could meet in Geneva. I have business there with the Duke of Savoy. Pardie, I'll be on pins and needles to hear your news. We'll ride back together to Lyons. Then you'll return to the army and Monsieur de Bayard, a good deal better off than when you left them, if your business at court turns out as I hope."

But to the Marquis's surprise, Blaise did not respond. He sat rolling a bread crumb between his fingers and gave the impression of a man who wanted to say something without knowing how to begin.

"Well," prodded de Surcy, "you don't seem pleased."

Blaise's cheeks grew darker. "Would your lordship permit me to stay in your service for a time?"

"What? And not return to the army?"

"For a time," Blaise stumbled. "I recall that you once suggested — I mean there was some talk of training me to affairs of state such as your lordship is concerned with. Is that still possible?"

"Pour l'amour de Dieu!" exclaimed the Marquis. He found it hard not to smile at his former plans for Blaise. He looked at the other's muscular, brown hands unfit for a pen; at his open, boyish face; at the ever-mutinous hair in a frolic on his head. The very picture of a guileless, hard-riding, sport-loving lancer. To think of him as a smooth man of business, charged with secret missions and at home on the backstage of politics, seemed peculiarly droll. "Pour l'amour de Dieu!" repeated de Surcy. "What's the meaning of this?"

Blaise kept his eyes on the table. "I don't know that I can put it into words." Suddenly he looked up. "Monseigneur, were you ever young?"

The other laughed. "Parbleu! Wasn't I!"

"But now . . . Monseigneur, I felt last night that the others — I mean old men, like my father — couldn't have changed much in their lives. They talked like the young men. They had never learned anything more."

"Tiens," said the Marquis, interested.

"I pictured myself at their age: just the same as I am now, only with gray hair and stiff joints. It frightened me to think of it. I looked at you, outmatching all of them in wisdom and knowledge of life. Monseigneur, I wanted to be like you. If I go back to the army —" He shrugged and opened his hands in a vague gesture.

Keenly impressed, de Surcy no longer felt tempted to smile. Such words from Blaise were little short of a miracle — like that staff in the legend that put forth green leaves. The boy had, indeed, begun to think, and far be it from de Surcy to discourage him. But the Marquis did not feel sure that the green leaves justified Blaise in quitting the career of arms, for which he was fitted, to become the apprentice of a minister of state.

He said tactfully: "Do you mean that illustrious captains and marshals lack wisdom and knowledge of affairs, or that they have not put away childish things?"

"No, sir!" Blaise flushed to the roots of his hair. "It would be treason to such great men — Monsieur de la Trémouille, Monsieur de la Palisse, Monsieur de Bayard, among others. I spoke only of myself. My lord, it isn't easy for me, when the pack is running, not to run with it. If I go back to the company now, I'll be only what I was before, one of many. Last night, because of you, I got my foot in the stirrup. With your help, I think I could climb into the saddle."

"Of what?" put in de Surcy.

Blaise frowned. After a moment, he answered: "Perhaps I can't say what I mean. All I want is to go forward, not just around in a circle. If a man uses only his muscles, that's what happens. I see that now. He ends where he started. If he uses his brains . . . But it's easier for me to stick in the same place. I need your help to go forward."

If Blaise expected immediate enthusiasm from the Marquis, he did not find it. De Surcy knew the implications of his profession better than the other knew them. He remembered, too, that the fires of youth are often of straw. Only time could show whether Blaise's sudden ambition had stuff in it.

"As far as I'm able," he answered, "you can count on me. Step by step is a good rule. We'll see how your errand to court turns out. The next move may depend on it. And now, fair dreams to you — but send me Maître Laurence."

At the window of the small room, which he shared with the already sleeping Pierre, Blaise stood awhile looking out into the moonlit night. Not far away, he had a glimpse of the Loire, vague and smooth as silver. The stream flowed in the direction of his journey tomorrow. At an angle, along the curving wall of the inn, he could see the lighted casement of de Surcy's room and now and again a dim shadow passing back and forth, as the Marquis dictated to his secretary.

Blaise smiled. "He doesn't expect too much of me. And no wonder!" Suddenly he clenched his fists. He burned with impatience to show de Surcy that he was capable of more than in the past. All his faculties were on the march. He felt confident of the future.

PART TWO

Chapter 11

There were times when the Venetian ambassador, Zuan Badoer, officially called *Orator* to the court of France, a grave, wise, and infinitely practised diplomat, felt tired to the point of despair; and this early August day at Fontainebleau was one of them. His fatigue was of the mind, not the body, and therefore harder to cure. Strolling moodily with his secretary, Niccolò Marin, along a forest path outside the medieval castle, which had not yet been replaced by the later palace, Badoer often sighed and sometimes half raised his hands in agitation. But, finally exploding, he shook his fist at the distant roar and whoop in that part of the forest where the King, with several hundred riders, was coursing the stag.

Marin, a stately old attaché little younger than his chief, sympathized, "I grieve that Your Excellency feels so depressed."

"Depressed?" snapped Badoer. "No, Messere, call it defeated! How many weeks have we dangled since our last interview with this featherheaded King? Two, at least. Two weeks ago I warned the Signory of Venice in haste that His Majesty had gone on pilgrimage to Saint Denis and worshiped the relics at the Sainte Chapelle. Wouldn't you suppose that meant he was leaving Paris to join the army at Lyons? I wrote our senate that he could be expected across the Alps before September. But, instead, he packed down here with the court to Fontainebleau and has done nothing but hunt and make love ever since. In these two weeks, I could have accomplished something for Venice. But you see how he fobs me off. He would rather talk to his horse than me."

"Perhaps," Marin suggested, "our recent alliance with Spain against France has something to do with it."

"No doubt. But a wise prince will attach no great importance to alliances. He knows that they are broken as easily as they are made and looks to the future. Venice might need him tomorrow, and he

79

might need Venice. Of course he would thunder at me, but he would deal; he would burn no bridges."

"The King is young," observed Marin.

Badoer sighed. "There, Messere, you have said everything in four words. There's my cross. That I, Zuan Badoer, a senator of the oldest republic on earth, must spend my time capering around juveniles! By God, I am so glutted with youth that, if this coming war did not put an end to our mission, I should lose my mind. Since the Marquis de Vaulx left court, I have not had a sensible talk with anybody; for the old are as mad as the young. Think of our friends in Venice: the dignity, the polished manners . . ."

His outburst, combined with the heat of the afternoon sun, brought the sweat to his forehead, let alone that the suit he wore of stiff black satin did not make for coolness. With a ringed forefinger, he loosened the laces of his shirt and, turning aside from the path, lowered his large behind upon a bank of moss.

"Let us sit for a while," he puffed. "We shall feel the better for it."

The distant horns quickened to a climax. They were closing in on the stag. Before long they would sound the mort.

"Aye, Your Excellence," agreed Marin, stretching his legs and going on with the topic, "you can't expect manners and grace outside of Italy. They're the fruit of age — like our cypresses."

Badoer nodded. "Yes, and also the sign of it." As he rested in the shade, his irritation passed. He was by nature philosophic and liked to view both sides of a question. Putting his personal grievance out of mind, he reflected, "After all, age is the trouble with Italy."

"I don't follow Your Excellence."

"Why only, friend, that Italy's old and France is young. Spring has moved north in the last twenty-five years. Our great period is closing; now it's the turn of France. Time will cure the imperfections of youth. But what will cure age?"

Marin looked surprised. "And yet, a moment past, Your Signory was saying — "

"I say it again. Personally, I'm sick of young bloods and flaming hussies, pranks and extravagance, passion instead of statesmanship. Take this affair of Bourbon, for example. My God, what a blunder! Or take the King's lightheadedness in my case or a thousand cases. But the truth is I, too, am old; I like an ordered life. And the truth is also that, under the foam here, there's something else."

"What?" sniffed Marin.

"Strength, my friend, creative power, such as we had in Italy seventy-five years ago."

The secretary looked doubtful. He was thinking how much the foam cost in mounting debts and skyrocketing taxes.

Reading the other's expression, Badoer insisted: "After all, the richest grapes give off the hottest ferment. Consider France: the finest soil in Europe, the most varied resources, a vast population of more than fourteen millions. And all of this united under one prince. That's what I mean by strength."

"But there's a limit," Marin countered. "Jewels and women, palaces and wars, cost money. Since he came to the throne eight years ago, this King has spent the savings left him by Louis XII and has so drained every source of revenue that God knows where Treasurer Robertet will turn for the next levy."

The ambassador waved his hand. "I know that, my good Marin. I admit it's shocking to see money wasted. But this limit you speak of — do you know when it will be reached? Does anyone? Centuries away, perhaps, not now. In my experience, every generation feels ruined by its debts. And yet money goes on growing, as long as men can work and the earth can bear. No, it's springtime in France."

He fell silent, as a far-off crowing of horns signaled the end of the chase, then added, "But, you know, women and palaces have their uses."

"I suppose they have," said the practical Marin, "for spendthrifts and moneylenders."

"No, Messere, I mean something else. This King may be a trifler and a wastrel, but no one can deny him a gift for splendor. It's the first time north of the Alps that you find social life worth the name. Graceful living depends on women. We discovered that in Italy years ago. Now they're coming to the front in France. The King has brought them out of their country kennels and given them importance. Palaces are costly, I grant; but they are part of the national treasure and they inspire the arts. The King draws on us for architects and craftsmen, like the great Leonardo or others. He knows how to value them. The beginnings here are crude as yet, but they give the pattern of a court which will set the fashion in Europe. Some day — "

Footsteps along the path interrupted him; and, turning his head, he perceived a young man in high boots, with a dispatch wallet hanging from one shoulder, who was approaching from the direction of Moret. At first glance, he looked like a courier who had lost his horse; and for couriers Badoer had the warmest interest. It was a good part of his charge, as ambassador, to be on the lookout for news, which he relayed to the ever-inquisitive Venetian senate. But, with a shrewd eye for men, he could see almost at once that this was no courier of the usual sort. The tilt of the young man's head, the cock of his cap, and as he came nearer, the gay boldness of his eyes, indicated the gentleman trooper, even if he had not worn a poniard at his belt and a sword carried well behind for greater freedom in walking. To the ambassador, these features made the dispatch wallet all the more appetizing. If a man-at-arms was being used as a courier, he no doubt came from the army and might have news of importance.

On the point of hailing him, Badoer was forestalled by the newcomer himself, who stopped to ask: "Is this the way to the castle, messieurs? I've never been here before. At Moret, they pointed me out a short cut through the woods. But, what with these rocks" — he glanced at the cliffs among the trees — "and a thousand odd paths, I might as well be in Persia."

His speech, like his appearance, had the flavor of the army, a careless, spirited lilt that confirmed the ambassador in his surmise of the young man's profession. Gallants of that kind talked readily and were excellent sources of information.

Badoer stood up. "At your service, monsieur. My friend and I are returning to the castle. It's not far. We can walk together, if you please." He looked down at the other's spurs. "What happened to your horse?"

"No relays, sir, at the last post, and none to be had for several hours. I decided to stretch my legs. One gets stiff after five days in the saddle. The walk from Moret appealed to me."

Figuring rapidly, the Venetian concluded that a good horseman, riding post, would take about five days to cover the distance from Lyons, a fact which again pointed to the army.

"You come from the south, monsieur?"

"Yes, from Roanne-sur-Loire."

This meant nothing to Badoer, since Roanne lay fifteen leagues and better north of Lyons, where the troops for the Lombardy invasion were now concentrating. With the dispatch wallet in mind, he stopped beating about the bush and said in a pleasant tone of query:

82

"I am Zuan Badoer, Doctor and Cavaliere, Orator of the Most Serene Signory of Venice."

The other swept off his cap. "Your servant, sir. My name is Blaise de Lallière, a man-at-arms in Monsieur de Bayard's company but now on detached service with the Marquis de Vaulx."

The ambassador's smiling lips betrayed nothing of his interest in this statement, but he exchanged a glance with Marin and could see that the latter was equally impressed. He knew, of course, of the Marquis's mission to the Cantons. That Denis de Surcy, midway en route, should send back one of his guards with a message posthaste across France meant something urgent. Since he had been traveling through the Bourbonnais, the message very probably concerned affairs in that province and had to do with the Constable of Bourbon. Perhaps the expected revolt was coming to a head. If so, Venice, anxiously watching the course of events, would be eager to know of it.

Badoer expanded with cordiality. "Monseigneur de Vaulx is one of my oldest friends. Monsieur de Marin and I were but now speaking of him and regretting his absence from court. I hope that he's well, that nothing untoward has happened . . ."

It did not escape the Venetian that de Lallière, on the point of speaking, evidently changed his mind as to what he at first intended to say; and the slight hesitation spurred Badoer's curiosity.

"Quite well, sir. When I left him, he had had a prosperous journey in all ways."

"I'm delighted to hear it. I had feared that your mission in such haste meant an accident or some misadventure. I can see" —Badoer glanced hungrily at the wallet — "that you are the bearer of news."

"Yes, a dispatch to His Majesty. I think Monseigneur wished to assure the King of his continued health, and that he desired above all things to remain His Grace's obedient servant."

The ambassador felt aggrieved, but he digested the snub with a smile. He had long since learned that a thin skin had no place in business. The young man disappointed him. From his looks, one would have expected more openness.

"I'm sure," remarked Badoer, "that the King will be pleased to know it. He should reward you for traveling so fast and so far on such a gracious errand."

And he dropped Blaise a wink that brought an answering grin to the young man's mouth.

"But you can, at least, tell me one thing, Master Discretion," Badoer went on, casting his fly from another angle. "Is the report true that the noblemen of the Bourbonnais have thrown off their allegiance to the Constable and have declared themselves loyal subjects of the King? We hear, indeed, that any trouble in those parts is now over, and that Monsieur de Bourbon has made complete submission to His Majesty. He has even joined the army in Lyons. I should be glad to learn from you how matters stand."

The old gentleman put forward this monstrous contradiction of the facts with such a straight face, and he looked so complacent, that this time he hooked his fish.

Blaise exclaimed: "Ma foi, sir, it's the exact opposite. I wonder how such stories are spread. Those counties are all but in arms for the Duke. Submission, nothing! If the King believes that, I think the Marquis's letter —"

The intent, beady eyes of Niccolò Marin, not half so limpid as Badoer's, warned him, and he broke off, crestfallen. Just a moment before he had felt proud of his shrewdness.

"Yes?" probed Badoer gently. "You were saying — ?"

"That no doubt the King is well informed," Blaise floundered; "that Monseigneur de Vaulx's letter may, or may not, refer to these matters."

But the bird was out of the cage, and Blaise knew it, even if he did not know that in due time the Council of Ten in Venice would profit from his slip. Zuan Badoer needed only a hint in order to write a very correct dispatch. The Serenity of the Doge would learn, not many days hence, the purport, if not the details, of de Surcy's letter. And, that being the case, Badoer lost further interest in the wallet.

"Ah, yes," he said blandly, "you're a very discreet young man. I commend you." And, as they walked on toward the castle, he added, "Hot weather, we're having, isn't it?"

Blaise murmured agreement, but it was not the heat of the sun that made him uncomfortable. He had hardly reached the threshold of the court, and the first man he met had drawn him out. A fine beginning! Well, he vowed to take this little episode to heart. No one would catch him again.

He had been aware of the King's hunt in the forest for some time. But now a fanfare of horns sounded close by. Luckily he and the two Italians had reached an open space, where they could draw to one side as a cavalcade poured out of the woods. It was the triumphal procession home.

According to custom, everybody wore red, the color of the chase: a dazzling tide of scarlet, as the sun's rays fell on it. In the front rank rode the King. His horse, a tall bay, with grandly arching neck and mighty shoulders, seemed part of him. Long of leg and body, sinewy, erect, Francis sat a full head higher than those around him. But it was not only the physical man — his stature, the gorgeousness of his clothes — that dominated and glittered. His vitality sparkled still more. The almond-shaped, slanting eyes, black against the pallor of his face, danced with fun. His thin mustache, curving down to meet the edge of his dark beard, accented the smiling mouth. His long nose, projecting above the upper lip, lent a constant whimsical cast to his expression. If any face could be called typically French, as denoting recklessness, gaiety, and high spirits, it was his. Surrounded by a group of ladies, his "little band," as he called them, he resembled a magnificent chanticleer on horseback, attended by scarlet, equestrian hens. And behind him flamed two or three hundred riders: officers of the court, officers of the guard, gentlemen of the chamber, ladies and maids of honor.

Three weeks ago in Paris, Blaise, accompanied by de Surcy, had had only a fleeting interview with the King and no more than a glimpse of the royal palace. But, during his boyhood in the Marquis's household, he had often attended his patron to court, and he could now pick out various faces.

The woman on Francis's right, a tall brunette with a nose very much like the King's, was the latter's sister, Margaret, Duchess of Alençon. Not yet famous as Margaret of Navarre, she was already the most spirituelle woman in France, the most lovable and best beloved. Her brother always called her his darling. The lady on the King's left was Françoise de Chateaubriant, a statuesque beauty with limbs like a goddess and all the pride that belonged to her family, the great House of Foix. Once the ruling favorite but now doomed to make way for another, she still carried her head high. And here and there — most of them six years older than when he had seen them last — Blaise recalled others, great noblemen and ladies, now only vaguely familiar. But all of them blended into one scarlet impression of plumes and jewels, spirited horses and laughing, arrogant eyes.

85

Side by side with the Venetians, he bowed low as the King approached. Badoer made his best leg.

"Ha, Domine Orator," called Francis, catching sight of him. "Taking the air, are you?"

But he was already glancing away when his eyes stopped on Blaise. The dangling dispatch case fixed his attention. Besides, he seemed vaguely to know this man, as one whom he had seen not long since. With a "Halte-là!" that brought the column to a restless stop, he reined in his horse.

"Et vous, mon ami, have you something that concerns us in that wallet?"

Blaise dropped to one knee. "A letter to Your Highness from the Marquis de Vaulx."

"Aha? Well, I can read Monsieur de Vaulx's letters without yawning. Deliver it to one of my secretaries. He'll bring it before me in due time."

"Sire, I was directed to give it only into Your Majesty's hands."

"Indeed?" The slanting eyes sharpened. On the point of a question, the King glanced at Badoer and checked himself. "Good. Then come to me after supper. I have no time for letters now. My lord Chamberlain," Francis called to a nearby official, "instruct an usher to fetch me this" — the King hesitated, took note of Blaise's sword and appearance — "this gentleman before the dance." Then, wrinkling his forehead at Blaise, he added, "Ma foi, I'm usually good at names, but yours — " The frown cleared. "I have it. You're the lance from Monsieur de Bayard, de Vaulx's godson, de Fal — , de Mal — "

"De Lallière, Sire."

"Precisely!" The King's smile flashed warm. "I had it on the tip of my tongue. Well, Monsieur de Lallière, until later. Allons, mesdames!"

He touched his horse with the spur, and the company thronged behind.

Blaise drew back to the side of the neglected ambassador, while the cavalcade passed.

At the heels of the riders followed two huntsmen carrying the slain stag on a pole between them, its antlered head swinging. Then came the whippers-in with the lolling-tongued dogs on leash, hungry for their share of the quarry; then the mounted servants.

"By your leave, lord Orator," said Blaise, "I think I'll watch the curée. It's always a pretty sight when the dogs are fed."

86

"Everyone to his own taste," returned Badoer. "If you want noise, don't let me detain you."

He nodded in reply to de Lallière's bow and gazed after him striding along in the wake of the procession.

"A little raw," he observed to Marin, "a little naïve, as compared with our young Italians. But not without intelligence, let alone vigor. There's promise in him." And with a backward smile at their earlier conversation, he added, "Like France."

Chapter 12

To flesh the dogs was the closing act of the hunt. From a vantage point in the castle courtyard, Blaise keenly enjoyed looking on, not only at the huntsman, circled by hounds, expertly opening the stag and feeding its entrails to the pack, but at the courtyard itself, now vivid in scarlet and gold. Dogs clamored, people shouted and laughed, an occasional horn blared, horse hoofs rattled on the cobbles. He savored not only the show but the smell, the mingled odor of horses, dogs, and fresh blood, of human sweat and heavy perfumes, the familiar smell of a returning hunt.

But the crowd had hardly began to scatter, when a page informed him that *Madame* required his attendance.

"Madame? Madame who?"

"Madame la Régente."

Blaise looked puzzled. "I've been some time in the provinces."

"Doesn't Monsieur know that the King has appointed his mother, the Duchess of Angoulême, Regent of France in view of his march to Italy?"

Formerly, as one of de Surcy's young attendants, Blaise had often seen the redoubtable Louise de Savoie — in fact, she had once had him birched for pinching the behind of a maid of honor — and he remembered that princess with unmixed awe. He wondered how she had heard of his arrival and why on earth she wanted to see him.

"Look you, mon ami," he told the page, "I am still dusty and stinking from the journey. If I could freshen myself — "

"Madame la Régente said *at once,*" returned the other. "This way, sir, if you please."

Making the best of it, Blaise squared his shoulders and followed the youth through the still bustling courtyard, then up and down stairs and along a narrow passage to the more livable part of the old castle. The vast royal retinue crowded everything, so that progress was slow. The modern, brilliant costumes clashed with the medieval building, somber and inconvenient, which recalled a prison rather than a palace. Blaise threading his way, with an occasional *allow me* and *by your leave*, thought it a poor place as compared with his memories of the more recent Amboise and up-to-date Blois.

The page stopped finally at a door, where an archer of the Guard, wearing the royal arms embroidered on his tabard, drew aside.

Beyond, in the long, gothic room, appeared two groups of men and women, each in attendance on a central figure. Of these, Blaise noticed that by far the smallest group surrounded the Queen, Claude of France, who belonged rather to the background than to the front of the stage. At twenty-four the Queen had now fulfilled her function as stud mare of the Throne by bearing the King seven children, and had exhausted herself in the process. Bullied by her mother-in-law, Louise de Savoie, neglected by the King, she was colorless and ailing under the shadow of impending death. People respected and overlooked her as a matter of course. In that room, the King's mother was the focal point. Awaiting her pleasure near the door, Blaise inevitably forgot everyone else.

Louise de Savoie was a thin, dry-looking woman of forty-seven, hard and sharp as steel. The repressions of her youth, the conflict with mighty adversaries — Anne of Beaujeu and Anne of Brittany — whom she had resisted and survived, had tempered her will to an exquisite keenness. The straight, massive nose dominating her meager face — the pinched mouth, small chin and ashen cheeks — expressed her narrowness and her ambition. But she had learned, too, the values of subtlety. Her eyes, gray between puffy lids, tended to sidle rather than assert, and the thin, pointed brows gave another touch of slyness to her expression.

Noticing the arrival of de Lallière and the page, she sent a gentleman to direct Blaise into the next room, a small cabinet, where she would see him presently.

At the heels of his guide and conscious of his travel-stained dress, Blaise covered the length of the apartment, keeping close to the arras-hung wall. He imagined a battery of eyes on him. He could hear the clank of his spurs, the grating of his boots on the tiled floor, the rattle of his sword. Unfortunately he had to skirt that side of the room occupied by the Queen and her ladies, and he could not pass them without stopping to bow. In a hot fluster, he turned, bent one knee, and swept the tiles with his cap. The Queen, in conversation, was not looking at him. But, as Blaise straightened up, his eyes rested a moment on the face of the young woman she was talking with. And at once he forgot his embarrassment.

There could be no doubt about it: this was the girl of the miniature. His casual glance became a stare. She was taller than he had imagined; but he could not mistake the chiseled, regular features and oval, magnetic eyes, which, in that light, were vivid green, the straight eyebrows, slanting upward, that gave a touch of piquancy to her face. The same enigmatic expression which had struck him in the miniature was apparent now, though she seemed to be listening with absorbed attention to the Queen's languid words.

No more than a few seconds passed before Blaise turned away. He was glad that she had not caught him gazing at her.

When he reached the cabinet, he detained his companion long enough to ask, "Who was that lady with the Queen?"

"Milady Anne Russell." The gentleman smiled. "Attendance on the Queen doesn't often prevent her from attending the King at the hunt."

"Ah," nodded Blaise. "A devilish fine girl."

"I agree," said the gentleman, withdrawing, "*devilish* is the right word."

Left alone, de Lallière wondered a moment what the other had meant. But he felt personally unconcerned. The important thing was that he could now positively identify Anne Russell as Jean de Norville's fiancée, if the King questioned him on that point. Then his thought shifted at once to the impending interview with Louise de Savoie.

He decided that she probably wanted to hear what he could tell her about affairs in the Bourbonnais and Forez; and, as Regent of France, she had every right to be informed. But that so unimportant a gentleman as he should be received in private by so great a princess was an overpowering experience. He removed his riding gloves from his belt, where he had tucked them, and flapped off what dust he could come at on his boots and breeches. He was on the point of scraping at a patch of dried mud on the sleeve of his doublet when the door opened.

The Duchess of Angoulême came in, attended by a sleek old personage whom Blaise recognized as the Chancellor, Antoine Duprat. She dismissed her pages and waited until the door had again been closed before she acknowledged de Lallière.

Blaise knelt to kiss the hem of her skirt.

"You're right welcome here, monsieur." She gave him a sign to rise and then came to the point. "I'm told that you bring a letter from Monsieur de Vaulx to the King. Let me have it."

The demand fell like a thunderbolt. It cleared Blaise's mind of self-consciousness by facing him with a deadly peril. He had been ready to answer all questions as best he might; but he could not hand over the letter which he had been instructed to give only to the King in person, and which, by the royal command, he was to deliver that evening. Yet how could he refuse? How was Blaise de Lallière to rebuff the Regent of France in favor of the King? He was like a very small mouse between two enormous cats; and, at the moment, this particular cat held him in her claws.

"Well, monsieur?" she added sharply.

"Madame la Régente, I throw myself upon Your Grace's mercy. Shall I disobey the King, who has ordered me to give him this letter tonight, or shall I affront Your Highness? Either way, I'm guilty."

She gave him a thin smile. "If I caught you disobeying the King, I would have your head. You may recall that I am His Majesty's mother. His will is my will. Of course you'll present the letter to him as he ordered. Meanwhile, I wish to read it." She held out her hand.

"But the seal, madame. What shall I say when — "

"You will say nothing; you will hold your tongue. Seals can be repaired." The extended hand became more imperious.

Blaise stiffened. He might be only a small gentleman but he was a gentleman. "Your Grace does not consider my honor in this matter."

Louise de Savoie's slate-cold eyes met his for a moment, then sidled away; but they were not the less menacing for that reason. "Look you, sir," she said in a flat voice. "I am not used to repeat my commands. Your honor is not concerned in this. If I choose to read Monsieur de Vaulx's letter, it is because I know that a dispatch from him is urgent, and that it merits greater attention than the King, in the press of his affairs, is apt to give it. My concern, now as always, is for his interests. . . . Eh bien, am I to be kept waiting?"

Blaise unbuckled the wallet. To protest further would be absurd, unless he wished to play martyr in a foolish cause. Like everyone else, he knew that the Duchess adored her son and had devoted her life to his advantage. If it was discreditable to open his letters, the discredit attached to her and not to the messenger who carried them. In any case, no wrong would be done the King. If the latter noticed the broken seal and challenged Blaise about it, he would tell the truth, let the Regent command what she pleased.

With a thin knife, which she borrowed from Duprat, and with a skill that showed practice, Louise now gently pried the lower half of the seal from the letter paper. Then, walking over to the window, she began reading, while Duprat studied her face. De Lallière noticed that it was the separate sheet relating to Anne Russell which she read first. Having finished it, with an unchanged expression, she slipped it into the velvet pouch that hung from her girdle and then became engrossed in the main report. But once or twice, she looked up at Blaise with a warmer light in her eyes than he had yet seen; and once she nodded to him with a smile. The Marquis, he reflected, must have been extravagant in his praises to bring so much recognition as that to the Regent's gray face.

Finally she exclaimed, "Excellent!"

Duprat coughed. "May I share Your Highness's pleasure?"

"Yes." She tapped the closely written sheet with a long forefinger. "This Marquis is a man after my own mind. He urges the Duke of Bourbon's arrest as the only proper stroke. *On humane grounds,* he says, *to forestall worse trouble.* I agree with him. Why does the King dally? We have proof enough now to bring that villain to the block. Why do we trifle with parlements and lawsuits in the case of a whoreson traitor? As if we had no power to deal with him! Cré coquin!"

The Chancellor coughed again, with a glance toward Blaise. But a moment passed before the woman's flushed face, framed by the nunlike headdress she was wearing, regained its usual pale calm. Her appearance and tone of voice, even more than her words, confirmed the gossip which everyone at court repeated. Charles of Bourbon's lands and her greed were not the only reason for Louise's persecution of him. Men whispered that the aging, self-possessed woman had once flamed with love for the great nobleman; that, upon the death of his wife two years ago, he had scornfully refused the proffer of her hand, which had been made him by the King.

The dread of the world, he was supposed to have called her. "I would not do such a thing for all the riches on earth."

It is often dangerous to hear too much. Blaise became absorbed in a loose buckle on his wallet.

Louise gave him a sidelong glance and handed the letter to Duprat. "Here, read for yourself. You'll notice that de Vaulx names some of the chief rebels. He should have listed all of them."

Duprat nodded. "The Marquis inclines to softness. He's growing old."

Blaise did not miss the overtones of this. A tiny seed dropped here and there — a shake of the head, a slighting hint — was apt to yield that harvest of disfavor which spelled the end of a rival. Duprat was an expert in such tactics.

But the mutter of names, which now caught Blaise's attention, became suddenly interesting, and he strained his ears to hear better.

"De Norville," the Chancellor was saying. "That troublemaking schemer from Savoy, whose profession is conspiracy and rich marriages. Aha! His property, Chavan-la-Tour, in the Forez, is worth fifteen thousand livres a year if it's worth a sou."

"Excellent!" smiled the Duchess. "See to its confiscation at once. We needn't wait."

"I'll do so, madame." Duprat had his tablets out and was taking notes.

The recent anger in Louise's face had given way to eagerness. "Go on. This is interesting."

Blaise heard a series of names, with an occasional comment: du Peloux, du Puy, Nagu, Grossonne, Bruzon . . . They were, in part, the names of the gentlemen who had met at Lallière. It was obvious that the Regent itched to lay her hands on the rebels' wealth. Some of it would find its way into her own coffers as well as the King's, not to speak of Duprat's. Expecting to hear the only name that concerned him, Blaise drew a sigh of relief when the Chancellor remarked:

"There's the sum of them." He glanced back and forth between the letter and the list he had jotted down. "Yes, I believe that's all."

But Blaise had rejoiced too soon.

"You notice one omission, of course?" observed the Duchess.

"No, madame. Which do you mean? — Ah, I see!" The Chancellor smiled happily. "Trust Your Highness to miss nothing! The Marquis is a friend of Antoine de Lallière. You would hardly expect – " He smiled again.

"No, sir." Louise's voice was ironic. "We must admire Monsieur de Vaulx's delicacy, but we need not imitate it. You can add that name to the others." She glanced at Blaise. "The services of a younger son do not acquit his father. You shall be amply rewarded, sir – but in your own right."

The tragedy of what was happening so coolly in the dim room became vivid pictures in Blaise's mind. His ancestral house gutted and empty. The family condemned to prison or, at best, to want.

"Your Highness," he burst out, "if I have rendered any service – "

She interrupted him with a lift of the hand, but her smile had become gracious, even ingratiating.

"We shall see, Monsieur de Lallière, we shall see. My lord Chancellor, you can put a question after that name. Take no step in regard to said property for the moment. And now, by your leave," she continued, still addressing Duprat. "I should like a word in private with this young man. Be good enough to instruct the usher that we are not to be disturbed for any reason."

When he had pocketed his notebook, Duprat bowed and withdrew.

"What the devil now?" thought Blaise.

Then he remembered the sheet of paper which the Regent had slipped into her purse.

Chapter 13

Seating herself in a straight-backed armchair, Louise de Savoie crooked her finger at Blaise, inviting him to a nearer approach.

"Venez ça, mon ami. You have deserved richly of the King and, therefore, of all who love the King, among whom I am no doubt the first. I have taken a special liking to you. Your courage in defending Monsieur de Vaulx and in saving his life is equaled only by your loyalty to the Crown, for which you incurred the hatred of these rebels and were turned out of your father's house. Bravo, monsieur! You have begun well. I foresee a long and honorable career ahead of you if you remain so happily disposed."

The flat voice could drip milk and honey when it pleased. Blaise would have had to be a much shrewder man than his years permitted not to be enchanted by it. The rewards it implied seemed already in his grasp. He expressed his thanks to the generous princess as best he might.

"But we shall discuss your affairs later and at length," she went on. "Now there's another matter. I rely on you, Monsieur de Lallière; I count on your devotion to me as well as to the King. Am I presuming too much?"

Her smile promoted him to her confidence. He felt that he was being drawn into an inner circle open only to the very great.

"Par Dieu, madame," he said fervently, "Your Highness could never presume too much on my desire to serve you. If there is anything — "

"I thank you, sir. You are a man of sincerity. Believe me, I value it. But now tell me: you are aware, I suppose, of what this letter contains?" She drew out an edge of paper from her purse.

De Lallière bowed. "The Marquis was good enough — "

"And you know that it concerns one of the Queen's ladies?"

"Yes, a Mademoiselle de Russell."

"I gather that you are able to inform us whether this lady is the same as the one shown in a miniature belonging to that traitor de Norville — the girl he is to marry. If so, you must be given the occasion — "

Blaise put in: "By Your Grace's leave, I have already recognized the lady in question. She was speaking with Her Majesty when I passed through the outer room."

"Oho!" Louise brought her hand down in sharp approval on the arm of her chair. "Well, then, that simplifies things. A keen eye, Monsieur de Lallière! By God, you please me!" The thin lips parted in a grimace that showed the teeth. "La putain!" she laughed coarsely. "She took good care to keep her betrothal with this jackal of Bourbon's a close secret. I understand now why she's been asking for a safe-conduct to Savoy."

Leaning back, the Duchess fell silent, her expression matter-of-fact as usual, her eyes absorbed. It was the face of a woman so used to the knavery of the world that she took it for granted. Expecting no moral scruples on the part of others, she entertained few herself. Clearly her opinion of Anne Russell was as bad as possible but no worse than her estimate of women in general. She felt no heat. The girl simply presented a problem to be dealt with.

Now and then, thoughtfully, she clicked her thumbnail between her teeth and at last, with a final click, observed:

"Monsieur, what I am about to tell you is a private matter which I would discuss with no one else on earth. It concerns the King. You see my confidence in you. I must have your word of honor to keep what you hear to yourself."

Still more flattered, Blaise could only vow absolute secrecy.

"Eh bien, monsieur," Louise continued, "I grieve to confess that the King, who is without question the greatest prince in Christendom, has certain weaknesses usually to be found in men of royal and impulsive natures. Where women are concerned, he is frankly blind. Perhaps you will not believe me, but women are an evil race. They are false, lickerish, vain, hypocritical, and most inveterate liars. It takes a woman to see through their deceits and value them as they are. But the King can be taught nothing of this. To him, all geese are swans, and a pretty trollop is an angel. Therefore, his sister and I must protect him if possible." She broke off to ejaculate, "By God, what fools men are!"

If a favorite proverb of Madame de Lallière's to the effect that people reveal their own faults in their judgment of others passed through Blaise's mind, he put it aside as irreverent and said gallantly: "Far be it from me to dissent from Your Grace in regard to the folly of men; but, in this presence, it would be treason to accept Your Highness's opinion of women."

She gave a slight simper. "Nicely put, monsieur. But I can see that you are blind, too. Wait till you have been bitten. However, to the point. This English minx has cast a spell upon His Majesty."

Blaise, taking the words literally, crossed himself.

"No, I don't mean that she deals in the black art. But she's a shrewd hussy who knows that the way with a man or a mule is to keep her carrots dangling in front of him. Now and then, a nibble; but, if he snatches the whole bunch, the game is up. Therefore, she holds His Majesty off but tickles him with her eyes and the shape of her ankle. As a result, he dotes on her, dreams of her, and writes poems to her. He takes the wench for a goddess. If you could persuade him that she is a spy for England and for Bourbon, he would consider her, in his present frame of mind, only the more tempting, the more piquant. The point, then, is this. It would be worse than useless to give him Monsieur de Vaulx's letter about her: worse, because he

95

would not believe it or, if he did, would take no action. And action must be taken. Do you follow me?"

"But, Your Grace, if the King leaves for Italy — "

"He is not yet gone, and he may be delayed. In the meantime, we cannot have de Norville's future wife at court, close to the King's person, alert to our every move. The next two weeks are important. She must be got rid of at once and the King must not prevent it. Of course, if she died — "

A chill crept along Blaise's spine. He began to wish that the Regent had not opened herself to him, that he had never got himself into these waters.

But, after a pause, she added: "No, that would be a mistake. We may not always be at war with England. No, there's a better way. She has been craving permission to leave court, which the King has refused. She alleges the war and her difficult position here. Her brother, she says, directs her to go to Savoy to finish her court polishing. As if she needed it! Someone has found her a place with the Duchess Beatrice. Until today, I put this down to coquetry. Now it may be her marriage with this de Norville or some other trick or both. Perhaps she has a report to make. Perhaps . . ."

Louise broke off again. "Yes," she murmured, "yes, it's more than possible." Then she went on aloud: "The King hunts day after tomorrow, with his gentlemen, in the direction of Paris. He will be gone two days. I shall take it upon myself to pack Milady off. By the time His Majesty returns, she will be out of reach. And the affair will be in your hands."

"*Mine?*" In spite of etiquette, Blaise could only gape.

"Of course. Are you not returning to the Marquis de Vaulx? Does he not state in his letter that, from Lucerne, he will go to Geneva? The court of Savoy is there at present. Some escort must be provided for a young woman and her attendants across France. Who could be more suitable than you? A young man of courage and, I am sure, discretion; a young man who knows my mind and whom I can trust implicitly. Ah, Monsieur de Lallière, what an opportunity for you to win my gratitude! You can trust your future to me. I shall watch over you. For your sake, I am even disposed to abate the rigors of the law against your rebel father."

This was all very fine and dazzling. It fitted in wonderfully with Blaise's new-found ambition and offered the most flattering prospects. But he could not help feeling like a man caught in a quicksand, into which, with every forward step, he sank deeper. First, she had coerced him into giving her the letter which should have been opened only by the King. Next, she had somehow made him her accomplice in abstracting a portion of that letter. Now he was becoming involved in an intrigue, which might be harmless and, indeed, worthy enough, but which had to be carried on behind the King's back. Worse still, he could sense depths beyond this and could not know what he was letting himself in for. But, worst of all, the thought of conducting the mysterious Anne Russell to Geneva filled him with blank dismay. It was a dreadful assignment. Even as he mumbled his thanks to the Regent for her golden promises, he remembered her quip about the mule and the carrots.

Reading his face, the Duchess increased pressure. "Voyons, you don't look happy. I wonder if you know what service I am asking of you. Or were your expressions of devotion to me only so much air? I can't believe it. To be sure, you will guard this minx on the road — though I must confess that I'm not overly concerned about that — but you will do more. You will see to it that she goes to Geneva and not to Moulins or elsewhere. I'm not so much a fool as to let her wander off unwatched through France. You will give the Bourbonnais a wide berth. You will take the road to Dijon, then south to Bourg-en-Bresse, and so to Geneva. But that isn't all of it."

She lowered her voice. Here came the next move, thought Blaise, feeling the tug of the quicksand.

"Monsieur, I don't believe that her marriage alone is taking Milady to Savoy. That may be part of it but not all. She expects to meet someone there — someone from England. Perhaps it's her brother, this Sir John Russell, who stands so close to Wolsey. I wish the arrow that put out his eye last year at Morlaix, when the pirate English raided our coasts, had skewered his brain! And I believe some such meeting is planned because of a secret word from one of our people in England."

For a moment, Louise's expression implied that she regretted having said so much. But, being now committed, she went on.

"It appears that an envoy has been, or soon will be, sent from England to Bourbon with the terms of an alliance between them. This final link is needed in the chain to circle France. But who the said envoy is, we do not know. He will be in disguise. He will slip somewhere across our borders — probably from Savoy, as that is the nearest point — and he will meet the Duke. Now, my friend, do you see what I would have?"

"Your Highness means that, in Geneva, it might be possible to learn who this man is by watching —"

"Exactly, sir. By watching Milady Russell. I count on her to point him out to us. Then let him enter France! He will not leave it soon. And whatever action the King may take against this traitor of a Constable, we shall have the living proof of his treason in our hands. Is this not an important service I am asking of you?"

Important, indeed! Blaise's imagination caught fire. By great good luck, the career which he had newly chosen was already opening to him. He could imagine the Marquis's surprise and approval when they met in Geneva.

"If I can only carry out Your Grace's instructions!" he said.

"I pin my faith on you, Monsieur de Lallière. Of course, if you are clever, you might learn a good deal even before Geneva. Make love to the girl: that's the best play. You'll have time enough in ten days. I wager she's hot enough beneath her English facing — these northern damsels usually are — and you're a handsome galliard. But don't fall in love yourself — at least not too much for our purpose. I say keep your wits about you. She's shrewd enough to cheat the Devil. And, by the way, not a word to her of your service with Monsieur de Vaulx. If she knew that, she would be on guard. No, you are simply a gentleman of Captain Bayard's company, assigned to escort her out of this kingdom and returning afterwards to Lyons . . ."

The Duchess ran on with further directions and advice. Blaise was to report the whole affair to the Marquis de Vaulx upon the latter's arrival in Geneva. For, if matters shaped as the Regent expected, they would require expert handling. Until the Marquis appeared, de Lallière could turn to one Jules Le Tonnelier, a French secret agent in Geneva, for help in detecting any Englishman who might be in touch with Anne Russell. . . .

But though Blaise listened attentively, a part of his mind made its own comments and reservations. He would do what he could to discover the English envoy and, if possible, to lay him by the heels. That was lawful war. But be damned if he would play the role of a Judas and seducer for that purpose! He belonged to France, but his honor belonged to him. And, as the crafty princess spun her web for his benefit, he began to see the pitfalls as well as the rewards of his new career. He must avoid the one, while meriting the other. That was de Surcy's greatness. He would keep the Marquis as his model and try to forget Louise de Savoie's tarnished subtleties.

In the end, she directed him to light her a candle with a tinderbox from the drawer of a nearby table and to bring her a piece of sealing wax from the same drawer. Then, folding the Marquis de Vaulx's letter, she laid the merest touch of hot wax under the original seal and pressed it into place. When she had finished, the keenest inspection could hardly have shown that the letter had been tampered with. Of course, the separate sheet relating to Anne Russell remained in the Duchess's purse.

"There you are," she said. "It was fortunate that Monsieur de Vaulx made no reference here to this further matter." She patted her velvet bag. "If I know the King, he will not look twice at the seal and will not suppose that there was anything else in the letter beyond what he reads. I congratulate you, monsieur. Your behavior, which the Marquis describes, will greatly please him, as it has pleased me. There are few messengers lucky enough to carry their own good fortune in their dispatches and win the thanks of both a king and a regent of France at the same time. But perhaps *my* thanks," she added with a sniff that reminded him of the secret between them, "will be no less valuable to you than his. Go now and refresh yourself from your journey."

Rich as he might be in promises for the future, Blaise felt himself extremely limited in resources for the present. He had only the bedraggled suit and patched boots which he was wearing. The Marquis had provided him with funds for the journey, but he had no time to purchase clothes before his audience with the King. He stood hot and embarrassed.

"What now?" said the Duchess.

"Madame, I have no acquaintances at court. I am hardly in a fit state —"

She made a careless gesture. "To be sure. I shall turn you over to one of my gentlemen, who will look after you. Ask of him anything you please — his best suit, if you wish." She gave him an arch glance. "By the way, la petite Vinette, whom you pinched so delicately some years ago, is now married and has left court. But there are others just as plump and appetizing." And, at the start which he could not conceal, the Duchess observed dryly, "No, monsieur, I never forget anything."

Chapter 14

The gentleman, to whom Louise de Savoie entrusted Blaise, was profuse in civilities. He conducted de Lallière to the small room he occupied under the eaves of the castle and bade him make free of his effects. But, though he would not consent to take a sou for the reasonably adequate clothes selected, his hint that a loan of five gold crowns would vastly accommodate him was not overlooked, so that Blaise did not remain too much in his debt.

"I shall repay you, monsieur, at the first opportunity," said the gentleman. "With my pay two quarters in arrears, you'll understand that I'm a little out of pocket."

Recalling the splendor of the hunt, Blaise was surprised at such need under the glitter. "But if money is owing you —"

"Money is owing to everybody. Not long ago, I explained my embarrassment to Madame d'Angoulême, whom you have just left. Of course, she promised me marvels. But the pawnbrokers won't advance cash on promises; and, like most people at court, I've pledged everything else: my house in Normandy, my three windmills. Promises are the coin here. We're all rich in promises."

"Oh," said Blaise, remembering the Regent's assurances to him.

"That's it, monsieur mon ami. *O* is the symbol of what said coin is worth."

Pondering these remarks, Blaise shifted to the gentleman's clothes, made his toilet and then wandered downstairs to supper in the barrack-like common rooms, which were assigned to the less important followers of the court.

The meal was a thin, pickup affair as compared with the rich procession of courses served to the King and elite in the main hall. The poorer courtiers put up with what they could get. In these circles, nothing except faces had changed from what de Lallière remembered. The girls still laughed and gossiped. Bawdy stories went the round of chimney corners. A stranger, like Blaise, was patronized for having been so long absent from what everyone there considered the center of the world. When at last an usher plucked him away with the command, "Monsieur de Lallière will attend the King," he felt immensely relieved.

* * *

On approaching the royal apartments, Blaise could sense a keener vibration, a growing brilliancy and parade. Here and there, at their posts, were the gentlemen of the Guard, halberd in hand, richly attired. There again was a group of the famous Scottish Archers in their white tabards heavy with gold and the crown embroidered on their chests. And there were the French Archers, the Swiss Guards, the Archers of the Door, gorgeous in the King's colors and the royal device. But the splendor of these was nothing compared with that of the noblemen who thronged the anterooms. Blaise recognized some of them, each the center of a group: Louis de Vendôme, Vidame de Chartres; Robert Stuart, Lord of Aubigny; Philippe Chabot, Sieur de Brion, one of the King's chief favorites; flaxenhaired Robert de la Marck, Lord of Florange, commanding the Swiss Guard, a swarm of other notables. If these men had been gilded court moths fluttering about the royal candle, Blaise could have consoled himself with the pride of a soldier among fops. But they were all distinguished men of war, names to conjure with around the campfires of Europe. Aristocracy still meant valor and leadership. In the neighborhood of these grandees of the sword, Blaise felt duly modest and very humble.

It was the hour of intermission between supper and dancing. The gentlemen stood handling their toothpicks amid a hubbub of talk. Breaths heavy with flesh and wine raised the temperature of corridors and anterooms. In the last of these, Blaise despaired of ever getting through the press of lords and captains; but they fell back before the royal usher, who finally led the way between two resplendent halberdiers. A door opened and closed, shutting out the voices; and Blaise found himself, though at some distance away, in the presence of the King.

As he waited, just over the threshold of the luxuriously furnished room, he had time to steady himself as well as to admire and listen. The King, relaxing after supper, stood with his back to the great stone fireplace in conversation with several gentlemen who had been selected to attend him. One of these was a secretary; another Blaise recognized as Treasurer Robertet; the third was an Italian architect, all attentiveness and dark grace; the last was René de Cossé, called Monsieur le Grand, chief falconer.

Francis had changed from his red hunting costume and now wore evening attire, a dazzlement of richly striped brocade. The large sleeves, half emerging from the folds of his mantle, emphasized the breadth of the King's shoulders. His low, square-cut doublet set off the muscular neck, which was left bare except for a gold chain of the Order of Saint Michael. The darkness of his hair merged with the jeweled black of his cap, which carried a border of white plumes.

"Foi de gentilhomme," he was saying, "I have reached the end of my patience with this old rookery of a castle. How did our grandsires stand it, I ask you? No grace, no spaciousness, nothing to please the eye! They seem to have taken every pains to avoid a level floor in any direction. Since coming here, I have done nothing but walk up and down stairs. Up and down, par Dieu, barking my skins, stepping off into space at the risk of my life. Why, only today Mademoiselle de Limeuil missed her footing on one of these infernal turret stairs and bounced halfway down to the damage of the prettiest behind at court. It's an outrage. Human beings were not made to live like squirrels."

The King underlined his annoyance with a belch. The gentlemen murmured conventional best wishes.

"I thank you, sirs," said Francis. "But to go on with this matter: here's one of the finest hunting grounds in France. It deserves a palace, not a moldy dungeon. That's your affair, Maestro." He smiled at the architect, who stiffened with zeal. "Draw me up plans at once, but remember that each new house of mine must surpass all the others. There's the secret of progress. Always a step forward. People can talk about the good old times as much as they please. Vertu Dieu, I show them Blois and Chambord. By your aid, I'll show them Fontainebleau. This is a new age."

He broke off to press his lips with his fingers. "Too much of that sparkling wine for supper. Yeasty, by Saint Paul. Here, friend," he nodded at a page, "bring me some hippocras in that new Italian cup. Gentlemen, I want you to see the figures on it. The goldsmith has turned out a Leda with thighs grand enough to wake up a corpse. And the neck of the swan — peste!"

The King's smile under his long nose brought an answering smile from his listeners. But the architect had no intention of letting so fruitful a topic as the new Fontainebleau go by the boards. When the cup had been joked over, he put in:

"Sire, these plans? Can Your Majesty give me an idea?"

And the royal attention swung back. "But yes. Grandeur, Maestro. Italian in concept, French in ornament. A blending of the best. I think in terms of a vast court, oval this time, lined with fair buildings. Much space, much light. There shall be fountains, statues . . . Let us have a wonder of the world. And, mark you, plan me stables for a thousand horses, with kennels to match. Build me mews for my hawks and herons greater than those of any other prince. That should please *you*, Monsieur de Cossé."

The falconer grinned. "It would be Paradise, Sire. My pretty birds stifle in their present quarters, which aren't fit for owls. Give me a say when it comes to planning the mews. I have my own ideas."

"Of course," waved the King. "And, Master Architect, I must have your sketches before I leave for Lyons. Then let these old barracks be torn down. . . . What's wrong, Robertet?"

The old Treasurer seemed afflicted by a dry cough. "If Your Majesty would condescend to wait until your return from the war — "

"Wait, monsieur? *Wait?*"

Robertet lifted his shoulders and waved his hands. "Pardon me, Sire. I should have said *delay*." He shrugged and waved again.

"No money, Robertet?"

"Alas!"

"Ah."

A glum pause followed. The King's glance rested on the downcast faces of the architect and the falconer. "There you are, gentlemen. No money. We'll have to go on climbing stairs and fumbling around corners. No amends can be made to the charming de Limeuil's posterior. Our glorious hawks must be packed like hens in a coop, not to speak of our court and the Majesty of France. No money." He shook his head at Robertet.

"But, Sire, you already have Chambord, Blois, Amboise, Les Tourelles — "

"We need Fontainebleau, monsieur. Do not deny us Fontainebleau." Mischief danced in the King's eyes. Suddenly he tilted up his black beard with a laugh. "No money? La belle affaire! Why are you treasurer? Find us money. Clap on another tax."

"But, Sire — "

"Raise me another loan." The diamonds on his strong, beautifully shaped hand sent a rich glitter through the room, as he tapped Robertet's chest with his forefinger. "Ah, mon ami, mon pauvre ami, you will have much ado to keep me from my heart's desires. Have you ever once succeeded with your croak of *no money?* Confess, now."

Robertet wagged his head. "Never, Sire."

103

"And you never will. So, Master Architect, let's have those sketches. It may be that, what with the diversions of war and the Lombard women, I shall be unable . . ." The distant sound of drums and hautboys drifted up from below. "What a fool you are, Robertet, to talk thrift to a man before a dance! By God, we'll have some voltes tonight that will make the ladies' skirts fly above their garters." He waved dismissal. "So — another time, gentlemen."

The secretary, an impersonal, demure man, observed, "Your Grace desired to read a letter from Monseigneur de Vaulx."

Francis chafed, hesitated. "Well, it shouldn't take long." His glance found Blaise. "Come here."

And, conscious of the eyes upon him, the young man crossed to the center of the stage.

It was a tremendous moment. Apart from everything else, that mended seal on the letter. What if the King noticed it and required an explanation —

But without hesitating, Francis broke through the wax, spread open the paper, and began rapidly scanning it by the light of a candelabra, which his page held at one side. The quickened beat of the drums and the wail of the hautboys spurred his reading, though the glint of his dark eyes showed that he missed nothing. He nodded once or twice in approval and gave an occasional *hm-m* of interest. But his slippered foot tapped absently in time with the music, and he had finished reading in two minutes. Then he handed the letter to the secretary.

"Ha, Monsieur de Lallière," he said with the warm kindliness which was one of his most lovable traits, "you have done well. I'd give a thousand crowns to have taken part in that fight at the ford. If there was time, I'd like to hear an account of it stroke by stroke. A dainty bit of action! I commend you. I commend your zeal in our service. Ma foi, you shan't lose by it. Robertet, here's a man who, for love of us, refused a captaincy and thirty lances in the Constable's guard, not to speak of defending the person of Monsieur de Vaulx at the risk of his life. See that he's given a good and sufficient charge somewhere."

This meant one of the thousand nominal offices carrying an annual stipend, with which the King rewarded conspicuous service. Blaise might be an equerry of the stables, a gentleman of the pantry or even of the bedchamber, though no duty was required in that connection. His hopes soared.

104

"I'll consult with the Grand Maître, Your Grace," said Robertet. "Though I'm afraid every place is filled and every vacancy promised."

"Well, *something*," the King insisted, "if it's no more than a token until the proper office turns up. A very deserving young man, Robertet. See to it, I beg." He added to Blaise, "On my honor, you'll not lose by waiting, mon ami. I'll keep you in mind."

But, at the noncommittal look on the Treasurer's face, de Lallière's hopes sagged. At the moment he would have gladly exchanged them for a small sum in cash, had any been offered.

"And now to the main point of the Marquis de Vaulx's letter," Francis went on. A louder cadence of music floated up. The King glanced impatiently toward the door. "I shall outline the answer, Monsieur le Secrétaire. See that you have it ready for my signature by tomorrow morning and that it is then entrusted to this gentleman." He nodded at Blaise. "I would have you listen to the dictation, sir, and stress certain points of it to the Marquis when you rejoin him." He turned to the others. "By your leave, messieurs."

At this sign of dismissal, all except Blaise and the secretary bowed and withdrew. The King stood thoughtful a moment, smoothing down his beard. Then he said: "I note that Monsieur de Vaulx is proceeding from Lucerne to Geneva. A good move. My uncle of Savoy and his young bride from Portugal are there. Clients of the Emperor, both of them. I'll wager their court is a clearinghouse of news. Under cover of assuring the march of our troops through southern Savoy to Lombardy, let the Marquis snap up what he can, in particular any report touching England. (Be sure that's in the letter.) Then let Monsieur de Vaulx rejoin us at Lyons."

Blaise's attention sharpened at the reference to England. The King, no less than his mother, was alert to the next move from that direction. If de Lallière had needed any reminder of the importance of his mission, this remark supplied it. And Francis now proceeded to confirm the Regent's explanation as to why the English contact with Bourbon was especially interesting.

"Tell him that I note his advice with regard to immediate action against the Constable. But tell him this, too — aye, in these words. He who would take the winged stag of Bourbon needs a strong net. Gossamer won't do. The Duke is beloved by most Frenchmen. So far, we have only hearsay of his treason, the reports of spies, our own convictions. We must have more. We must have proof so plain

105

that no Frenchman, however much his admirer, can deny his guilt. Tell Monsieur de Vaulx that an English agent is expected to enter France via Savoy. Let him discover this agent and track him to his meeting with the Duke. This will bell our cat. If Monsieur de Vaulx succeeds, I shall be forever grateful to him. But write also that, meanwhile, I am not asleep." As an afterthought, the King added: "Thank him for the names of these rebels. They shall be punished in due time."

With a sigh of relief, Francis adjusted his mantle and gave his plumed cap a bolder cock.

"Our ladies must not be kept waiting any longer."

The secretary hurried over to the door and threw it open. The guardsmen grounded their halberds. The voices in the anteroom fell silent. An usher appeared, wand in hand.

"You will see," the King instructed him, "that Monsieur de Lallière is permitted to witness the dance. A small token of approval," he smiled, as Blaise kneeled and received the additional favor of kissing the royal hand. "We'll not forget you."

Then, leaving the scent of rose water behind him, Francis strode to the door, while the bowing gentlemen outside opened to left and right.

The King, who was an expert dancer, performed gallantly that evening. He danced a pavane with Madame de Chateaubriant and one with that rising star, Mademoiselle d'Heilly. But he danced most with Milady Anne Russell.

To Blaise, dazzled by the lights of the many flambeaux and plastered against the wall in the rear rank of those favored to watch such grandeur from afar, the scene was magnificent. He caught, to be sure, only glimpses of it at the cost of much craning of the neck: now some figure of the pavane, where masked lords and ladies strutted gravely peacock-fashion around each other; now the branle de la torche, a slow movement of dancers carrying lighted torches; now the pazzamento, another stately parade. But then the drums began racing, the fiddles hurried, the hautboy-players puffed out their cheeks. The running dance of la courante started. Then came the gaillarde, a pirouetting of couples down the length of the hall. And by now only the young, His Majesty leading them, could stand the pace. Then came the voltes. What leaping! What masterly entrechats! What lifting and swinging of ladies, with all that meant of intoxicating glimpses!

For an instant, between the heads of the people in front of him, Blaise saw the King and Anne Russell. They had taken off their masks. He raised her high above his shoulders, swung her around; but she dropped so gracefully, in such perfect time, that there was hardly more than a glimmer of well-gartered legs. The heat of his eyes, the appealing smile, left no doubt of his passion. But when the momentary glimpse had vanished, it was her face that lingered in Blaise's mind. She smiled, too; her eyes answered the King's. But the impression they left was of a poise that not even the royal ardor could flutter, a face schooled in all the courtly serenities and revealing only what the moment demanded.

And this was the girl he had been assigned to escort across France! The coquette of the King, the experienced lady of fashion! Panic swept over him. As compared with her, he was no more than a rough lackey. Picturing in his mind the long road to Geneva, he saw nothing more of the dance.

Chapter 15

A man can be lonelier in a crowd than anywhere else, and this is especially true when the crowd is made up of ruthless self-seekers, each with an eye on the main chance. Blaise had a few acquaintances left over from the time when he attended the Marquis at court. But they had all gone up in the world since then; and, as there was nothing to be got out of him, they were too intent on their own affairs for more than a casual word.

After receiving the letter to Denis de Surcy from the royal secretary, he spent most of a weary day trying to see the Treasurer, Florimond Robertet, in regard to the office promised him by the King. This threatened to be a fruitless quest until, on a chance advice, he tipped the great man's valet, and at last had the satisfaction of an interview.

"A real pleasure," said Robertet, struggling with a yawn, "to see you again, Monsieur de Lallière. Of course, you know that the disposal of places in His Majesty's household is out of my hands. You should see the Grand Maître, who is at present in Lyons, or the Lord Chamberlain. However, as the King directs, I shall put in a word for you. Say, a place at five hundred livres a year, eh?"

"That would be more than ample, monseigneur, and beyond my deserving."

"Not at all. The King is pleased to reward such services as yours. And so, as I am engaged at the moment — " Robertet fingered some papers on the table.

"Would it be possible," Blaise persisted, "to tell me when I might expect the appointment to be made?"

"Ah, ça, monsieur! When? Diable! That's another matter. In a year, two years. How can I say? Places like that don't grow on bushes. You have my best wishes, Monsieur de Lallière. And now, by your leave — "

In the outer corridor, Blaise ruffled up his hair, then put on his cap with a jerk. He felt that he had learned a great deal in the past twenty-four hours. His recent services had been written off with a promise and a royal smile. It was fortunate that his career did not depend on them. If he succeeded in the mission with which the Regent was entrusting him, he would have undeniable claims to the highest preferment. And he meant to succeed.

Meanwhile, the rumor spread that the King's harborers had given notice of five warrantable stags, one of eight tines, to the north of Fontainebleau; and the castle stirred with preparations for tomorrow's hunt. This was lucky for the Regent's plan of using Blaise as an escort to Anne Russell. He could not set out with her until the King had left on his two days' absence; but he also could not delay carrying the royal letter to de Vaulx. The stag of eight tines fitted in perfectly.

Late that afternoon, he received the expected summons from Louise de Savoie and once more faced her alone in yesterday's small cabinet.

"Everything is arranged, monsieur. Mademoiselle de Russell expresses such enchantment at the journey that you would think she was being delivered from prison rather than dismissed from the chief court of Christendom. A chaperon has been found. I have chosen the proper number of domestics. You will leave tomorrow morning by the side gate of the castle, after the King and his gentlemen have set out. Then you will make all possible speed. That is the main point. You must be out of reach by the time His Majesty returns from the hunting. Do you understand?"

De Lallière bowed, but he pointed out tactfully that, even with two or three days' start, women and baggage mules could hardly travel a distance out of range of the King's riders.

"That is your problem," she shrugged. "You may have more than two or three days' start, for I shall do all I can after I have lessoned — I mean reasoned with — the King touching all the advantages which Milady could bring us in Geneva. But the further off you are the better. And that, I say again, is your problem. Why else did I select a young man of courage and resourcefulness like you?"

Blaise groaned inwardly. He could see himself herding the party of women and mules along, like a shepherd with a flock of sheep trailed by wolves. It might be his problem, but, in case of pursuit, it was one that had no solution.

A sudden, furtive glint appeared in the Duchess's eyes. It was almost as if she wished to convey a thought without putting it into words. "Your task is to get this girl to Geneva," she said with hard emphasis. "Nothing else matters — bear that in mind — nothing. And remember this. She does not want to be overtaken on the road. She'll not delay you. By God, she's as bold and shrewd a piece as any I've known. Follow her lead, if your wits fail. But, remember, to Geneva she goes, and nowhere else."

"I hope Your Grace will clear me with the King."

Whatever might be the unexpressed thought in Louise's mind, she replied definitely to this point. "Have no fear of that. You are obeying my orders. You are returning to Geneva, and I have bidden you escort Mademoiselle. I shall be fully accountable to the King. And now, are you prepared for the journey?"

"I must have a horse, madame. I rode the post from Roanne."

"You shall have one of the best." She added casually, "I take it you're provided with funds?"

If Blaise had been a little older and more practical, he would not have missed the chance to fatten his purse. But with great generosity, the Marquis had given him twenty-five crowns when they parted, and he still had enough of these left for his own needs. The flattering assumption implied in the Regent's tone of voice that such a gallant young gentleman as he must, of course, be above the need of money could not be resisted.

He answered grandly, "Mais oui, madame," and felt that he looked

109

like a viscount. But it troubled him that a smile, which might have been one either of relief or of amusement, flickered on the Duchess's thin lips.

"Why, then," she said, "everything's in order, except that I should present you to Milady Russell. It will save awkwardness tomorrow morning. Be good enough to call me a page." And after Louise had instructed the dapper youth, whom Blaise summoned from the next room, to fetch her Mademoiselle de Russell, she added: "I desire the minx to know who you are from me, and that you have my authority."

Then she fell silent, her pallid hands in her lap, her wan face expressionless except for the intent speculation in her eyes.

On his part, while he waited, Blaise's pulses quickened, not so much with curiosity as with a ridiculous sense of fluster. He had been up and down the world enough not to be bashful in the presence of women; but this first meeting with the mysterious girl who, ever since that glimpse of her miniature at Lallière, had been so often in his thoughts and who was to be his charge during the next ten days loomed before him as a critical event. How should he comport himself? What impression would he make on her? His self-consciousness grew as the minutes dragged by. When at last the door opened and the page announced her, he felt unnerved.

She entered the dim little room like a shaft of light. When he thought of her afterwards, it was in those terms. Her tall erectness, the fresh delicacy of her complexion, the olive green of her gown, the vibrancy of youth which she conveyed, were all heightened by contrast with the gray stone background and by the Duchess of Angoulême's colorless age.

She curtsied low before the Regent, "You sent for me, madame?"

Louise's conventional smile gave her face more of a Sphinx-like expression than ever. "But yes, m'amie. I trust that the summons did not inconvenience you. No doubt you are busy with preparations for tomorrow. It is in regard to them that I wished to see you." And, reading the question in the girl's eyes, which she now turned for the first time toward Blaise, the Duchess added: "No fear, ma belle. The gentleman knows of our little project. Indeed, he is concerned in it. I would have you meet Monsieur de Lallière, a cavalier of Captain Bayard's company, whom I have ordered to escort you to Geneva."

It was Blaise's cue to bow. He felt that the girl's eyes, so strangely

110

clear and yet unrevealing under their tip-tilted brows, appraised him an instant. She smiled and inclined her head, then turned again to the Regent.

"Your Highness is more than kind. I am most grateful. But is it necessary to put this gentleman to the trouble of so long a journey? I am sure that Madame de Péronne and the servants whom Your Grace has been good enough to assign me are escort enough."

Was the protest merely courteous, or did her voice imply a hint of disappointment? Blaise could not tell. Perhaps, once free of the court, she had hoped to be her own mistress and choose her own road, likely enough through Moulins and the Bourbonnais. She might have anticipated an interview with the Duke, a meeting with de Norville. Possibly Geneva had been only a pretext, after all. That the Duchess suspected it could be seen by the sardonic glint in her eyes as she waved Anne's objection aside.

"By no means, m'amie. The roads are unsafe. I should never forgive myself if you came to harm within the borders of France. England may be our enemy, but Milady Russell will always be dear to us. So, for our own peace of mind, we must take every precaution regarding you."

If there had been a touch of chagrin before, there was no trace of it now in Anne Russell's expression. Once again, she sank almost to the floor in the deepest of court curtsies.

"How can I thank Your Highness, not only for your care of me, but for such generous words, which I shall always remember and cherish!"

"They are sincerely meant, my child. But, to keep to the point of your journey, I have instructed Monsieur de Lallière that you are to follow the road to Dijon and thence by the shortest route to Geneva. Those are my orders, and I expect him to obey them. You are to avoid the Bourbonnais and other fiefs of the Duke of Bourbon. This is for your protection, since that region of France is at the moment unsettled because of the machinations of said Duke."

"I know," murmured Anne.

"I'm sure you do," nodded the Duchess, with something close to a sniff. "But you can rely on Monsieur de Lallière to keep you out of harm's way."

If she had said *out of mischief*, she would have used the same tone of voice. The two ladies exchanged polite glances of perfect understanding.

"I have explained to Monsieur de Lallière," the Regent continued, "that it is your desire to travel as fast as possible. He will do all in his power to assist you." She turned to Blaise. "As for you, sir, when you have once delivered Mademoiselle into the hands of her friends in Geneva, you will be free to proceed to Lyons and from there rejoin Monsieur de Bayard's company wherever it may be." The Duchess's eyes narrowed slightly, as she eliminated the Marquis of Vaulx from Blaise's recent history. "Thank the good Captain for the good and dutiful letters which you brought us from him, letters which will be answered by a regular courier, and assure him of our continued esteem."

Having, thus, tactfully explained, for Anne Russell's benefit, how Blaise happened to be at court, and having, at the same time, reassured her that a simple man-at-arms returning to his company could not be suspected of knowing anything about political intrigue, Louise closed the interview.

"I would not detain you longer, mademoiselle. It may be that I shall not see you again before you leave. If not, I wish you a safe journey. And may God have you in His holy keeping!"

But when Anne had repeated her thanks in the courtly terms of awe and submission due to so great a princess, and had retired backwards to the door, she glanced again at Blaise. Her eyes warmed a little. She smiled. "Au revoir, monsieur — à demain."

The words renewed themselves and echoed in his mind when the door was closed.

The Duchess gave a ghost of a laugh. "By God, I may be a fool. But if I sent an older man to escort this jade to Savoy, she might turn his head more easily than yours. Well, Monsieur de Lallière, look to yourself. Don't be a lamb to her wolf. Your future, I think, should be worth more to you than a smile and an au revoir."

Chapter 16

"What a pity," observed Anne Russell, with a sideward glance at Blaise through the small mask which formed an essential item of a traveling lady's costume, "that we're living in these dull modern times! No giants, dragons, or even knights-errant to beguile the day.

Otherwise, I should think you would be feeling like a hero of romance."

Blaise took thought before answering and covered up the pause by slapping at a large fly on his horse's neck. Was this, he wondered, the first gun of the engagement? During the last hour from Fontainebleau, except for a civil word or two, Milady Russell had ridden silently, checking her mount to the slower pace of her chaperon's mule. But now this sudden personal remark, spiced with the word *romance*, sounded a warning.

"Got him," she smiled, as the fly dropped from Blaise's glove. "There's one knight-errant who will trouble us no more. But you haven't answered my question."

"As to what, mademoiselle?"

"As to feeling like a hero of romance."

He caught the teasing in her voice and grinned. "Why?"

"Because am I not a forlorn and foreign lady wandering the world, and aren't you sworn to guide, befriend, and guard me — especially guard me? What could be more romantic than that?"

He did not miss the emphasis on guarding her and the double meaning it suggested. The Regent's solicitude about her safety had not hoodwinked her in the least.

"Certainly nothing could be more agreeable," he hedged. And, as a further parry, he spoke to Madame de Péronne on the other side of Anne. "What would you call it, madame?"

The plump gentlewoman, muffled in a hood and voluminous cloak, found it difficult to keep her mask from slipping below a very small, round nose. She pushed it up an inch before answering.

"I should call it nonsense, monsieur. There is nothing romantic about dust and horseflies. There is nothing agreeable in being jostled and belabored by an ill-gaited beast. Monsieur, I have an acute pain in my side. I am drenched with sweat. I am suffering. It is an outrage to continue at this speed. You are most inconsiderate. . . ." The mask slipped again, and some of the lamentations were lost until she had freed her mouth and ended with the word "crucifixion!"

Madame Héloïse de Péronne belonged to that class of women not less frequent in France than elsewhere, whose selfishness takes the form of chronic martyrdom, who would be unhappy if they had nothing to resent, and whose feelings or comfort are being forever outraged. Since the death of Monsieur de Péronne, who had been a gentleman of the late Duke of Angoulême, she had remained a pen-

113

sioner of the now royal family, a prima donna of the background, serving as one of the governesses of the maids of honor. In this office, which gave her temperament full scope, she spent a life of complaint and crisis. That Louise de Savoie, who made few mistakes in her choice of people, should have assigned such a woman to chaperon Anne Russell to Geneva, increasingly puzzled Blaise. He began to suspect a practical joke on the part of the Regent, who perhaps wanted to give the finical lady something real to complain of.

"But, madame," Anne protested, "we have ridden at no more than an easy amble since leaving Fontainebleau. We shall have to make twice this speed to reach Villeneuve tonight. You know that Her Highness — "

"I know that Her Highness did not ask me to kill myself for your whims, mademoiselle. They are not quite so important. It was out of the goodness of my heart that I consented to accompany you on this tedious journey. But I do not intend to be abused. . . ."

The mask slipped. The exasperated lady halted her mule, tightened the fastenings of the strip of velvet, and sat, with one stout leg crooked around the horn of her sidesaddle, in motionless rebellion, while a trickle of perspiration dropped from her chin.

"Eh bien, voilà! I intend to rest. At this moment. I shall not stir a foot until the pain in my side is gone. There is a limit even to my patience, say what you will."

Blaise stared nonplused at the matron, who needed only the long ears of the beast she was riding to look like its sister. Meanwhile, the others of the little party — two mounted lackeys, one of them with Anne's tirewoman on a pillion behind him, and the two muleteers in charge of luggage — drifting up formed a lackadaisical group in the middle of the road.

And this was the haste, thought Blaise, which was to put them beyond the reach of the King! Why, in forty-eight hours, at such a pace, they would still be within an easy canter of Fontainebleau. Chafing at the absurd predicament, he chewed at the thumb of his gauntlet and felt in a stalemate.

But Milady Russell was not so helpless. "Come, Monsieur de Lallière," she proposed, "we'll ride on ahead, and Madame de Péronne can overtake us at her leisure. A plus tard, madame. . . ." She had turned her horse and gathered the reins.

"Never!" cried the lady. "Stop! Stop, do you hear? I forbid it. Never will I permit you to ride off with a strange man. You are in

114

my charge. I am responsible. Ah, misère! Arretez, méchante que vous êtes! Arretez. . . ."

The clatter of hoofs answered her. A cloud of dust volleyed up. Through it, dimly visible, Anne could be seen galloping down the road, then she rounded a turn and was out of sight.

"Monsieur!" cried the distracted chaperon. "Pursue her! Bring her back! Cette diablesse! Ah, Sainte Vierge . . ."

Blaise had not waited to be urged. Behind him the wail of Madame de Péronne grew faint. His horse, which had been supplied from the royal stables, was an excellent courser and needed hardly a touch of the spur. Within two minutes he caught sight of Anne's palfrey halfway up the next hill and drew a breath of relief. It was unlikely that she intended a trick — at least so early in the game. But there were side paths leading from the main road, and one could never tell what a young woman of that feather had in mind.

She drew rein on the crest of the rise and sat waiting for him, a graceful silhouette against the sky. Like all good horsewomen of the period when hunting or on long journeys, she rode astride, her trim legs cased in knee-high, soft leather boots and puffed breeches. She wore a man's doublet, with wide sleeves drawn tight at the wrists, and a loose-fitting sleeveless tunic over it. A linen coif protected her hair from the dust, and this in turn was covered by a felt hat with round, upturned brim.

"We have a proverb in England," she said, as he came up, "that an archer must have two strings to his bow."

Her French, though perfect, blurred at times with a faint drawl that sounded warm and intimate, especially in connection with her smile.

"And that means what, mademoiselle, in this connection?"

"Why, only that if entreaties won't move Madame de Péronne, we must shock her into moving. She's the soul of faithfulness, in spite of her vapors, and would rather die than let me out of her sight. We'll wait for her here. She'll be along presently. But I retract my words."

He looked a question.

"Oh, I mean as to romance. Can you imagine Amadis or Gawain, not to speak of Lancelot du Lac, condemned to herd a party of women, lackeys, and mules across France, especially when one of the women is Madame de Péronne? No, I pity you, Monsieur de Lallière. We ought to be living ages ago."

"Why?" he asked for the sake of argument. "It isn't a question of the time but of how we look at things. It seems that everything past is romantic and everything present is homespun. Pardie, I wonder if Messeigneurs Amadis, Gawain, and the rest, wouldn't be surprised if they knew what the poet fellows have made of them. And I wonder if sometime a scribbler couldn't write a tale about us to match theirs. Speaking of dragons, wait until Madame de Péronne catches up with us!"

Anne laughed. "There's the French of it. Always analyzing. Now we English love sentiment but hate to show it."

Was this an invitation? If so she left it at that, and, suddenly tipping up her mask so that it stood vertically on her forehead, filled her lungs with the summer air. "Hot," she explained. "I don't have to wear a mask with you. It reminds me of court. What happiness to be free — you can't imagine!"

It seemed to him that the day, though bright, was brighter now that her face was uncovered. No mask with him. The phrase perhaps had something more than a literal meaning, and he fancied that she intended something more.

For a while, they sat their horses silently, gazing down from the hill. It was a cloudless August morning and so early that the larks were still up, the twinkling notes of their song filtering through space. Some fields of barley, not yet harvested, stretched from the brow of the hill, where the woods left off, and the golden expanse showed here and there, like vivid jewels, the red of poppies or the blue of cornflowers. But, for the most part, the ancient forest, though occasionally broken by patches of cultivation, rolled eastward to the horizon. A church tower, barely emerging in the middle distance, betokened some invisible hamlet of thatched cottages with the farms around them; two or three clusters of conical turrets in seignorial loneliness marked the location of manor houses, the girdling of fields and peasant huts. One could see, too, a winding of silver flanked by meadows, where the indolent Seine wandered north. The forest, however, dominated as it had for ages and, though declining, still challenged man, the builder, and man, the hunter. Even the great highway to Sens, twelve feet wide, did not wrinkle its surface.

"Par Dieu," exclaimed Anne suddenly, "don't you feel merry to be out of that stinking court! Speak of perfume," — she took a deep breath again — "smell this! Speak of living, what's a life of rules and ceremonies? Monsieur, I was born in the West Country of England. There's no sweeter air and no lovelier land. I like to dream of it.

But I have been long in prison. These courts!" She shrugged. "No use sighing about it. We do what we must. Only, on such a day, out here under the sky — "

She let him complete the thought for himself and fell silent again, her eyes full of light and distance.

Meanwhile, Blaise adjusted himself to the unexpected. He had been prepared for hauteur or ruse or coquetry, the usual airs and manners of a fashionable court belle. He would not have been surprised if she had snubbed or cajoled him. What set him at a loss was her apparent complete naturalness. This did not mean understanding her — far from it — she seemed to him increasingly unpredictable. But the mystery which he felt in her was not fortuitous; it belonged to her as did the strange color of her eyes, or as depth belongs to the sea. He reflected, however, that he had the Regent to thank for presenting him as a simple soldier. Otherwise Anne Russell might have been less open.

"Tell me," she asked abruptly, "do you know why it's necessary for us to make haste, at least until we're past Dijon?"

It was a thorny question to answer. He could not show her that he knew too much without putting her on guard. At the same time, it would seem peculiar if the Regent had sent him on a mission requiring speed without any explanation at all.

He replied cautiously: "I know that you wish to reach Geneva as soon as possible, mademoiselle. And I know that Her Highness of Angoulême is equally eager to speed an English enemy out of France in view of our present war. She hinted, too, that the King does not share either your wish or hers and might seek to detain you. But that's a matter which, for my own sake, as Mademoiselle can understand, I am not supposed to know. Her Grace's instructions to me were simply that we should lose no time."

A wave of color passed over Anne's face. "The King is always gallant, Monsieur de Lallière. Perhaps something of my haste is because of that."

"I understand," he nodded.

Their eyes met, and the frankness in his reassured her. The flush disappeared.

"But Madame d'Angoulême is right," she went on. "In view of the war, I am an enemy of France."

"You are loyal to your prince, Milady, as I am to mine. That is to be expected."

117

"And I have done and I shall do all in my power to aid England while the war lasts."

"You have the right, Milady, as have I — on the opposing side."

"Why, then, we can be friends," she said, with a sudden warmth, "up to the point where we become enemies. I like your honesty. It is hard to live with people on a footing of pretense, and you and I must live together for some days. Thank God you're no courtier! I'm beginning to look forward to the journey."

For some reason a deeper tint showed again in her cheeks. She bit her lip as if she had said too much.

Taken unawares by the glow that swept through him, Blaise answered impulsively, "And I, mademoiselle."

Then their eyes avoided each other, and she began fingering the ribbons of her mask.

The sound of hoofs reached them from the foot of the hill.

"Here comes our dragon," she laughed. "Alas, my poor ears!"

"Aha, friponne!" keened the approaching voice from below. "Is this the respect you owe me! Is this the treatment I deserve! And, bon Dieu, do I find you barefaced in the public road! Wait! Wait!"

Anne slipped down her mask, shrugged her shoulders.

And the storm burst.

Chapter 17

As morning advanced, the highway became increasingly thronged with travelers heading toward Paris, so that, however Blaise and Anne might chafe to get on, speed declined, and Madame de Péronne had now one thing less to complain of. It was all the more maddening, since de Lallière realized that, if he and Anne had been unaccompanied, they could have threaded their way along at a fair clip. Why, in God's name, he kept wondering, had the Regent urged the necessity of haste and, at the same time, imposed conditions that made haste impossible? Of course, a young noblewoman, like Anne, had to be suitably attended; but, this being true, speed — at least on so populous a road as the one to Dijon — was out of the question. It made no more sense than enjoining a man to race and then hamstringing him.

It seemed to Blaise that everything conspired to hold them up. The beggars, with their sores and deformities, who scrambled, like toads, through the dust, planted themselves in front of the horses, and could not, in compassion, be over-ridden. The herds of cattle or swine on their way to the Paris markets; a coffle of half-naked rogues shuffling north in irons to the King's galleys; a gypsy caravan; groups of merchants with their wares; parties of travelers, who were banded together for safety on the road; files of carriers' carts, had each to be negotiated.

At last, but well after the midmorning dinner hour, the wayworn party reached the village of Montereau at the junction of the Seine and the Yonne, where they turned in at the sign of *The Green Cross*.

"And a more distressful five leagues," Blaise confessed to Jean, the lackey, as he washed the dust from his face at the inn well, "I've never made in my life."

"We did wonders to get this far," returned the other. "But I hope that Monsieur doesn't expect to reach Villeneuve tonight. If the old lady lasts beyond Sens, I'll eat my mule."

Blaise nodded glumly. "We must do what we can," he quoted, "when we can't do what we would." And having brushed off his clothes, he rejoined the ladies at dinner in a private room, separate from the noise and confusion of the inn commons.

They had taken off their masks, but the white print of them showed against the sunburn of the morning, which gave the odd effect of being masked and unmasked at the same time. Both ladies looked thoughtful in different ways. Anne seemed lost in a speculation which had nothing to do with the present. She ate and drank mechanically, handling her knife and cup with no attention to the questionable meat or inferior wine. Madame de Péronne, on the other hand, showed the thoughtfulness of a person with saddle blisters. She sat gingerly on her bench and moved as little as possible. The tragic expression of her brown eyes became still more tragic. As she gnawed at the leg of a tough old rooster, which had been cooked in rank oil, the corners of her mouth drooped. It was a thoughtfulness, too, which had to burst; and the meal, when she finally wiped off the grease from her fingers, gave every pretext for plain speech.

"Monsieur," she said icily, "one would think, after the sufferings of this morning, that you might at least have conducted us to a better place than this vile pothouse. It's all of a piece with the rest of your heedlessness and poor management. You are clearly unfitted to escort ladies on a journey. The jakes here is of a filthiness beyond words. The fleas are a menace. The food we have eaten is poison, and if we get off with nothing worse than a flux of the bowels, we can thank God. Monsieur, I protest."

It consoled Blaise at the moment that Anne, withdrawing her eyes from the open window, looked amused and cocked an eyebrow at him.

"I regret, madame," he soothed, "but you could see for yourself that there is no other inn here, and I supposed that you would rather dismount even at so mean a place than ride on without dinner."

"A poor excuse!" snapped the lady. "Are there no private houses where we could have turned in? We have seen a number of them. They would have been delighted to receive people of the court. Or abbeys? I noticed one a half league back. No, sir, this" — she wagged her finger at the stained walls of the room — "is unpardonable."

"But Madame will remember," Blaise urged, "that it is difficult to accept the hospitality of a gentleman or a monastery without lingering in talk for a longer time than our journey permits. If we are to reach Villeneuve-sur-Yonne tonight, we cannot allow ourselves more than an hour — "

"Baste!" interrupted Madame de Péronne. "Monsieur, you are touched on the subject of speed. You think of nothing else. Let us settle the matter once and for all. I, monsieur" — she laid a hand on her stout bosom — "refuse to be dragged along day after day. I am too old for that dance. I stand on my rights, even though you and Mademoiselle de Russell choose to disregard them."

"If Madame will exert herself only as far as Dijon," Blaise pleaded.

"*Only*, nothing! From now on, we travel with dignity. Let that be understood. I have already incurred several wounds this morning, and they must be given leisure to heal."

"Wounds?" Anne repeated. "Bon Dieu! Where?"

"To be blunt, mistress, on my posterior. I am not casehardened like you. I am skinned raw. It is torment even to sit."

"Tilly-vally!" said Anne. "A saddle gall's nothing. I've had scores of them."

"Allow me, mademoiselle, to judge of my own condition. I am well furnished behind and thus liable to blisters. They are apt to become running sores. But, of course, I can look for no compassion from you — " tears welled in Madame de Péronne's eyes — "or from anyone."

An abashed silence followed. Anne conquered a smile.

"Ah, mais non," she deplored, "I know. It's most uncomfortable. I'm more than sorry. But let me assist you. If Monsieur de Lallière will retire, I'll inspect your wounds and tend them."

"Thank you," sniffed the other. "*Monsieur* — "

With the sensation of being swept from the room by the leveled glances of the two ladies, Blaise beat a retreat and closed the door. But he could not help picturing Anne's ministrations. Then, to hurry things up, he found the landlord and paid the reckoning.

It came to a half crown for the party; and, as he waited outside in the courtyard for the horses and mules to be got ready, Blaise reflected that he could not go on acting as paymaster for the whole group. He would have to reach an understanding about that with Milady Russell. It would be embarrassing; but, with only enough money in pocket for his own expenses, he could do nothing else. Remembering his fine gesture to the Regent, he sincerely regretted it. Then, with this uncomfortable problem in one corner of his mind, he saw to the cushioning of Madame de Péronne's saddle for the afternoon ride.

Walking stiffly, and with the air of a martyr on the way to the gridiron, the chaperon, attended by Anne, finally appeared and was installed again on her implacable mule. If *The Green Cross* had afforded even tolerable entertainment, Blaise realized that Madame de Péronne could not have been budged a yard further. That she could be prevailed on to forgo the excellent inn at Sens was so plainly out of the question, that, making a virtue of necessity, he promised to halt there for the night. It was some leagues short of the first stage he had planned; but, what with the morning's delays, eight leagues from Montereau to Sens were a good stint, and what could not be helped must be accepted.

Fortunately the earlier press of traffic had disappeared from the road, and steady, though slow, progress was made up the pleasant valley of the Yonne. By late afternoon, Sens cathedral, bulking above the walls and steep-pitched roofs of the town, came into view; but dusk, with a smell of cooking in the air, had fallen, as the little party dismounted at last in the courtyard of *The Crown Inn.*

Then the ladies, with their tirewoman, repaired at once to their

121

room; supper was ordered for the three of them; and Blaise partook of a solitary meal in his bedchamber, which he was lucky enough to occupy alone.

Reviewing the day, he could see nothing beyond it, except a long train of dull stages to Savoy, beset by constant delays and Madame de Péronne's vapors. As to the Regent's concern about speed, that could be tabled. If the King wished to prevent Milady Russell's flight to Geneva, he would have plenty of time to do so after his return from the two days of hunting.

Then, too, the hitch about money. If food at the humble tavern in Montereau cost a half crown, this night's entertainment at a more expensive inn, would come to, at least, fifteen livres. Blaise had put off broaching the subject to Anne that afternoon, but he could not delay beyond tomorrow morning. It irked him a little that Anne took the matter for granted and did not relieve him of his embarrassment. She could have brought up the topic so much easier than he. But, of course, women —

A sound at the door caught his attention. It was a repeated soft tapping, as of finger tips against the panel. Getting up, he crossed the room and opened, but then drew back in astonishment at the sight of Anne Russell herself on the threshold.

"*You*, mademoiselle?"

"Yes," she whispered, "I know it's scandalous, but I have to speak with you." And, slipping in, she eased the door shut without a click of the latch, then stood a moment listening.

Evidently she had been in bed, for she wore Madame de Péronne's riding cloak over her nightgown and her bare ankles showed above the slippers. Her hair hung loose, and the bronze of it caught the glint of the table candles. She looked taller than in her riding costume and even more charming, perhaps because of the very impromptu of her dress. Blaise would not have been French and young if he had not felt a stir of the blood at being thus suddenly alone with her behind the closed door of his room. That she was aware of it herself showed in her heightened color and the forced casualness of her voice.

"I think no one heard me. They were both snoring when I left. Monsieur, we must come to a decision at once. Tomorrow would be too late. I could not stand a day of twiddling my thumbs in this place because of Madame de Péronne's *wounds*. We have no time to lose, as you know."

Crossing to the table, she sat down, while Blaise took the chair facing her. Still distracted by Anne herself and in something of a flutter, he tried to look as if such an interview were nothing exceptional.

"You think that the King . . ." he began and left the question at that.

"I think that the King may act like a spoiled boy and refuse to put up with his mother's interference. But I have other reasons for haste besides that." Her lids flickered a little over the curiously oval eyes. She paused a moment before adding: "And now Madame de Péronne declares that she will not travel tomorrow. To be fair, I don't believe that she can. She's stiff as a poker and has sores big as thalers on her rear. But, in all conscience, I can't wait for her. I must get on. Why on earth did the Regent saddle us with such a fardel!"

Blaise shrugged his bewilderment. He had chewed on that question all day. Vertu Dieu, what a beauty this English girl was! The lusciousness of her mouth, the full lower lip . . .

"But what do you propose, monsieur? Remember, we're allies."

As far as Blaise could see, there was only one possibility. But he could not suggest anything so outrageous — all the more because of the ferment in his own veins. If he did suggest it, his motives would be suspect, even to himself. An unchaperoned girl of her rank could not dash off with a young trooper. When it came to that, conventions were adamant.

"Saint John, Milady! I wish I knew!"

"Well, *I* know." Then her face fell, as if at some obstacle she had forgotten. After a moment, she hesitated: "Monsieur, will you do me a kindness? Will you lend me some money — a few crowns?" And in reply to his obvious surprise, "You see, the occasion to leave court came so suddenly that I had no chance to draw funds from the agent in Paris who has been instructed to supply me. Madame la Régente, of her generosity" — a smile twitched at Anne's lips — "gave me five crowns for pocket money, as if it were a fortune. And, of these, I had to spend three in pourboires before leaving court. It is embarrassing to be so pinched."

"But, cré Dieu, then, mademoiselle, how did you expect to meet the expenses of yourself and your following to Geneva? Or is Madame de Péronne the treasurer?"

"No, sir, I was led to believe that you are."

123

"*Me?*" Blaise could only stare.

"Yes. Her Highness told me that you were provided with funds."

"But I did not receive a sou from Her Highness. I have only nine crowns and five deniers in my purse. I had meant to ask you — "

They sat staring at each other across the table.

Suddenly Anne's expression cleared. Her eyes blazed into green fire.

"Pardie, the fox! And we have been wondering about Madame de Péronne! This settles it. Don't tell me that you don't see!"

"See what?" Blaise returned. "Except a scurvy trick — "

"No, monsieur, by no means. A shrewd stroke. An excellent play. Listen. Could the Regent have proposed that you and I set out alone to Geneva? Of course *not*. How would she answer it to the King — let alone to common decency? She could not propose it, but she could so manage that we must take the blame on ourselves. Look you, this old woman who can't travel! And, look you, no money for traveling in any case! It's clear as spring water. If we act on our own, what fault is it of the Regent's? She can sigh and shake her head. But act on our own, we must."

"You mean that she *intended* us to quit the others?"

"But evidently. What else could she have intended? And I wager that, if we were so simple as not to take the hint, she would be in a fine rage. Note this: she may be stingy, but not to the point of spoiling her own game. She wants me out of France. You'll remark, too, that, although she provided no money, she mounted us well, while the others have only mules and nags. No, Monsieur de Lallière, I must forfeit my reputation, and you must help me." She gave him one of her baffling smiles and added, "Please!"

Looking back to his interview with the Duchess, Blaise admitted at once that Anne was right. He could now understand the hints and veiled glances which had puzzled him at the time. He recalled the injunction that, at any cost, he was to bring Milady Russell to Geneva with all speed, and that nothing else mattered. The scheme was apparent. Even though he felt his pulses race at the attraction of it, he could not overlook the callousness it implied toward Anne. Provided she was got rid of, and provided the English emissary to Bourbon could be trapped by her means, what happened to her of scandal or worse was indifferent. She served as a pawn in the Regent's game. And what of Blaise himself? He was not so dull that he could not see how easily his flight with Anne might be used to damn her with the King and to damn him. Perhaps Louise de Savoie intended that as a part of her "excellent play." The opportunity to distinguish himself in his new career, which he had hailed so jubilantly a couple of days past, now seemed far less promising than at first.

"You don't look pleased," observed Anne, with another smile. "Some gentlemen I know would leap at the chance. You're not very flattering."

"Is your tirewoman married?" Blaise asked abruptly. "If she is, perhaps we could take her with us."

"Jeannette? No, she's not married, and she's a poor horsewoman besides. There's no escape that way. If I had some money, I'd give you the slip and shift for myself. It's what I had in mind when I asked you for a loan. But now you're forewarned; and I wager you're ordered to bear me company whatever happens. So, we must ride together, and let the Devil make the most of it. A hard lot for you, Monsieur de Lallière!"

The amusement in her voice turned his cheeks brick-red. Did she take him for a bashful ninny or a sanctimonious Joseph? By God, she did not have to tease *him* into compromising her.

"I'm only human, mademoiselle," he retorted, his eyes hot.

He was struck by the sudden change of her expression. She leaned forward, her hands upturned on the table. "You know, I think Her Highness counts on our humanity. She is one of those who use people like musicians their lutes. She knows that we are young, that it is summer. And she hates me because I please the King and am not her slave. Monsieur, I say this to show you that I am on guard, not against you but against myself. I do not choose to become the Regent's puppet. What of you?"

The question was not a challenge or a demand. It expressed uncertainty, as if perhaps she was talking to someone who could not follow what she meant.

"Agreed," Blaise said, although at that moment, under the spell of her charm, he felt no confidence in himself.

A pause followed. He was surprised when she remarked suddenly: "I wish you were different."

"How?"

"Oh, a cavalier of steel and leather, the usual sort. I should find him easier to keep in hand. As it is" — she shook her head — "I'm afraid you are the most dangerous kind."

"I regret, Milady. What do you mean?"

"Why, merely, that — " She caught herself. "I'll not tell you. Perhaps, then, you won't be dangerous."

He wondered if this was coquetry. But she did not smile. With a sudden withdrawal, she stood up, gathering her cloak together.

"When do you think we should ride? Before dawn?"

He nodded. "The earlier the better. I'll see the landlord now — trump up a story and pay the reckoning. That should leave about ten crowns between the two of us. It will be enough if we travel fast and spend no more than we can help on lodgings. What about Madame de Péronne and the others?"

Anne shrugged. "They'll manage. She has enough in her purse to get them back to Fontainebleau. Bon Dieu! The wind of her rage will waft us from here to Savoy!"

"Your saddlebags?"

"I'll pack them now, while Madame and Jeannette are asleep. Alas, the fine dresses to be left behind!" She looked thoughtful. "Perhaps I can bring *one* along. It would ease me to shift now and then from hose. Saints above! How you men can put up with the tight things passes wonder! And so, monsieur, until tomorrow!"

At the door, she gave Blaise her hand, which he stooped to kiss. He held it a moment too long, but she did not draw it back.

On the road beyond Sens, in the first light of morning, while the galloping of their horses sent up a fog of dust between them and the silent town, Anne Russell flourished her riding whip above her head, gained a yard or two on Blaise, and laughed back to him: "Catch me! Catch me, Monsieur de Lallière! I defy you!"

The wind puffed out her cloak; the rhythm of the gallop quickened. She caroled some words in English that Blaise did not understand.

> O saddle me the black, the black,
> Or saddle me the brown,
> O saddle me the swiftest steed . . .

But he understood the lilt of them and would not have changed places at that moment with any lord on earth.

Chapter 18

Villeneuve, Joigny, Tonnerre: twenty-one leagues. Ancy, Nuits-sous-Ravières, Alise-Sainte-Reine: fifteen leagues. Salmaise, Mâlain, Dijon: fifteen leagues.

Saint Paul, how the girl could ride! Blaise himself felt the strain, but she looked as fresh as on that morning out of Sens. The horses needed rest in Dijon, but not she.

"We can afford to catch our breath," Blaise declared at this point. "Unless the King sent out riders at once on his return, and unless they can cover in two days what has taken us four — which, by God, they can't — we're safe enough. Besides, it's no more than a day's ride to the frontier. I don't believe that Pierre de Warthy himself" — he referred to the most famous of the King's messengers — "could overtake us."

They had given themselves the luxury of sleeping late after their arrival in Dijon the night before and were now at mid-morning dinner, following mass. Their inn of *The Three Pheasants* seemed like heaven after the potluck of the road. Traveling as brother and sister, they dined alone in a pretty little room of bull's-eye windows overlooking the street.

"You're probably right," she agreed. "But I shan't feel easy until we're across the border at Saint-Bonnet-en-Bresse. Then we can slow down. If the horses could stand it, I'd like to ride on after dinner." She shot him a smile. "Tired, Monsieur de Lallière?"

"No, but I sometimes wish *you* were, mademoiselle. And if the horses could speak, I'm sure they'd second me."

She shook her head. "Don't put it on them. I admit that the wine here is splendid, the food delicious; the beds are comfortable. But, sir, we are not in this world to pamper our bellies, but to sweat and win honor. So, if your temporary sister can prevail with you, please see to those horses. We might get to Saint-Bonnet by evening."

Blaise gave a mock groan. "Well, let me finish my vittles. Our scandalous life has taken me off ten pounds. I'll be a skeleton by the time we reach Geneva. To wear a man down, reprove his lusts and purge him for heaven, there's no diet like romance. Do you know what I long for most?"

127

"No, monsieur."

"A chaperon."

She burst out laughing. "Poor gentleman! Is it as bad as that?"

"Worse," he grinned.

"Eh bien, in that case, you can have a whole extra half hour, thirty merry minutes, at table. No one shall call me a slave driver. And I'll take another pigeon."

They had fallen naturally into joking a good deal, partly because the rough-and-tumble of the journey, the hours knee-to-knee on the road, the makeshift at inns, made formality silly; but chiefly, no doubt, because it was safer to laugh at each other than to take this equivocal companionship too seriously. Humor was a kind of antidote to self-consciousness.

It occurred often enough to Blaise that he knew actually little more of Anne Russell than when he had first met her in Fontainebleau. She was a wonderful rider, a hardy traveler, a charming companion. But of her personal past and present concerns, he caught only rare glimpses. More than once, too, he reflected that she knew as little about him, while perhaps imagining that she knew everything. Obviously, to her, he was simply the plain soldier-gentleman, ignorant of political intrigue, with whom she did not have to be professionally guarded. She said to him once: "Monsieur, I have had my share of gallants, but you are the only man I have ever really known." It turned him hot to think of the difference to her if she learned of his instructions from the Regent, his commission to watch her in Geneva, his relations with Denis de Surcy, the events at Lallière.

This barrier between them passed through his mind as he looked at her carving the pigeon on her trencher bread. She had shapely, firm hands that were pleasant to watch. He would not have exchanged the lean, tanned lines of her face, the travel-soiled cap and weathered clothes, for all the feminine softness and finery which he had been brought up to admire.

"So, there!" she finished, holding up a wing of the pigeon between thumb and forefinger.

In the street outside, a vendor bawled his wares: fromage de Champagne . . . fromage de Brie. The morning sunlight dappled the table. Life was warm and good.

Then suddenly Anne remarked, "It's not far from here to the

Bourbonnais, is it?" And to Blaise, the casual question — perhaps it was too casual — sounded an alert.

"Fairly," he answered. "A long couple of days to Moulins."

She appeared to turn this over in her mind. "But the Duke of Bourbon has holdings closer than that, around Charolles, in the Beaujolais, along the Saône. Riding south, we shall not be far off."

"True enough," said Blaise, with a greater show of indifference than he felt. "For a stranger, you are marvelously instructed about France, Milady."

She nodded. "Not so ill. Remember, I've lived here three years. . . . Didn't you tell me once that you were from the Bourbonnais?"

"It amounts to that. I was born in the Forez."

"Have you been there recently?"

"Why, yes — en route from Lyons."

He kept his tone as careless as hers, but he would have given a pretty penny to know what she had in mind.

Her next question took his breath.

"I wonder," she hesitated, "if by any chance you have met a gentleman, who is often in those parts, a Monsieur de Norville — Jean de Norville."

He hoped that his amazement did not show, and, to cover it, he drained his cup. Also he thought fast. How should he answer? Some lie was necessary whatever he said. Finally, it seemed best to skirt the truth as closely as possible.

Setting down the cup, he repeated, "Jean de Norville?" as if the name was somehow familiar, and then exclaimed, "Sacristi, yes! And not long ago! Why?"

To cap his surprise, she remarked, "I'm betrothed to him. What is he like?"

That she confessed this was startling enough without the added question. Blaise floundered, "But if you're betrothed, you ought to know."

"Not too much. We've never met. I have his miniature and confess he's good-looking. My brother and the Cardinal of York write wonders of him. But you see, monsieur, like most marriages, mine won't be made in heaven. This is a practical world. What's your notion of him? Where did you meet him?"

Perplexed for an answer, Blaise was not too absorbed to feel a happy relief at her ignorance, though he could not have given a reason for it. That he might be jealous of de Norville had not yet occurred to him.

"Why," he returned with the proper vagueness, "let's see. It was in the house of a gentleman near Roanne. I put up overnight there. Monsieur de Norville was stopping at the same place. As to my notion of him, ma foi, I had little time to form one. He's a handsome gentleman, quite the grand seigneur. He's from Savoy, isn't he?— though I heard he has lands in Forez. They say he stands well with my lord Constable."

She nodded. "Yes, better than well. If Madame la Régente knew of our betrothal, it would have interested her."

"No doubt," said Blaise. The conversation was getting more and more ticklish. He hoped that he could preserve the right tone of innocence.

Anne eyed him through half-lowered lids. "I can see that you don't like Monsieur de Norville."

This was clap in the clout, but how the devil did she guess? "Not like him? Parbleu, a man I've seen no more than a couple of times! Of course, as belonging to the Duke of Bourbon, he's not of my party. But now," Blaise added with more truth than the gallantry implied, "since Monsieur de Norville is betrothed to you, I shall hate him."

She gave an absent smile.

Blaise ventured, "Is your haste to Geneva concerned with him?"

"Partly."

And, as far as talk went, the subject lapsed, though it left questions enough for Blaise to consider. Would de Norville reappear in Geneva? Was she to be married there? Perhaps a wedding, rather than any contact with an English envoy, as the Regent had supposed, was the main point of the journey. It seemed to Blaise the limit of irony that he should be the one to escort Anne Russell to de Norville; that he should spend days alone with her, while her betrothed had never seen her once, he whom de Norville hated. Perhaps it was lucky that the mention of him had shown Blaise the unsuspected degree and quality of his regard for Anne. He must not fall in love with the impossible. That was what the Regent had warned him against — and schemed for. . . .

They finished the meal in silence. Among other things, he wondered what lay behind Milady Russell's sudden interest in the Bourbonnais. From now on, he would have to be doubly on guard. And he loathed the necessity of being on guard with her.

130

Chapter 19

But that afternoon on the road to Saint-Bonnet, suspicion flamed again.

As they followed the highway traversing the broad valley of the Saône, she asked: "I don't imagine I could persuade you to ride further south — through Mâcon? It's not much longer to Bourg that way than through Saint-Amour."

"But it's considerably longer from there to the frontier," he countered, "and I thought you felt pressed to be out of France."

She looked at him sideways. "Really I was thinking of you. The Mâcon wine is famous."

He could not tell whether she was serious or not, but he remembered that only a few leagues separated Mâcon from the Duke of Bourbon's country. She might have planned a meeting here with de Norville or even with the Duke. Geneva might have been only a blind to cover a different objective. Louise de Savoie had apprehended as much. Blaise recalled the dry remark: "To Geneva she goes, and nowhere else."

He said aloud: "Grand merci! But as far as I'm concerned, to help your escape from France outranks even the Mâcon wines."

"Besides," she went on, "it would give me pleasure to see the cathedral there — of Saint Vincent, I think. If I asked it of you, monsieur mon ami, could you refuse?"

She had not called him *monsieur mon ami* before or used that tone of voice.

"Mademoiselle, pour Dieu, why do you make it hard for me? You know my orders. They were to bring you the nearest way into Savoy. Do not ask me to break them."

"But if I did?" she urged.

He swallowed hard. "I should beg of you to excuse me."

Again, as so often, her expression baffled him. Although she tossed her head and remarked, "Why, then, sir, you are what I thought, not only a guide but a bailiff, and I'm your prisoner," some overtone of voice or relenting of the eyes contradicted her. She added, too: "Alas that you won't play Samson to my Delilah! But I don't know that I'm disappointed. I wonder what Delilah thought of Samson."

131

And, at that, she became unusually engaging, as if she was secretly pleased with him. "Ah, monsieur, I wish I could tell you how often I have longed to be a man. We poor women have neither strength nor wit. How I envy and admire you!"

She was plainly making fun, but she kept a straight face.

"Pasque-Dieu! I'd like to know what on earth for, Milady!"

"Why, as an example, take this small matter. Being a woman, I'm a child in your hands. Say it would please me to go to Mâcon; say I should like a meeting with certain gentlemen west of there, who are friends of England and would be glad of news I could bring them. This is only a supposition, monsieur, for perhaps I have no such aim and was merely trying you. . . . Now, if I were a man, it might be possible to defeat you. As a silly woman, I have no choice but to follow where you lead. If I tried to escape, you would no doubt tie me to my horse and drag me along willy-nilly."

"God forbid!" put in Blaise.

"Not at all. You would have to obey your orders. And, being a woman, I should have to submit, as women always must. We are children by nature and never outgrow the rod. Don't protest, Monsieur de Lallière, for it is true."

"Would you call Madame la Régente a child by nature?" he queried.

Anne laughed. "Nenni. But I've heard her say harder things of women than that. Perhaps there're exceptions."

"Perhaps you're one," Blaise complimented. "The nice part of every rule is the exceptions."

"And the trouble with Frenchmen," she retorted, "is that they argue every rule. Now, if you were an Englishman, there could be no argument on so manifest a point. He would take it as much for granted as his oatmeal. Did you ever hear the ballad of the Chevalier Waters?" She hummed the air and then sang:

> All this long day Child Waters rode,
> She ran barefoot by his side;
> Yet was he never so courteous a knight
> To say, "Ellen, will you ride?"
>
> But all this day Child Waters rode,
> She ran barefoot through the broom;
> Yet he was never so courteous a knight
> As to say, "Put on your shoon."

> "Ride softly," she said, "Child Waters;
> Why do you ride so fast?
> The child which is no man's but yours
> My body it will brast."

"That's the right English way."

"A very pretty air," said Blaise, "but what do the words mean?"

"Something like this: 'Le preux Chevalier de Waters chevauchait tout le jour, et à ses côtés la belle Elaine, nu-pieds, courrait toujours. . . .'"

When she had finished translating the last verse, Blaise exploded. "Quel cochon! He had no more manners than a German pikeman. If that's the way in England, it must be a solace to you, Milady, to have lived so long in France, which, everyone knows, is the true home of courtesy. After all, I imagine other nations are only barbarous."

It surprised him that she burst out laughing at this and would not tell him what amused her. But the conversation turned to national differences. She maintained, among other things, that the English were better horsemen than the French, while Blaise, in all honesty, could not help affirming that the French cavaliers had no match on earth.

"Do you call yourself a good rider, monsieur?"

"Average," he answered, and this time modestly, for he was known as an outstanding horseman.

"Like to jump?"

"Sometimes."

"Then look at those heavenly hedges in the field yonder, where the harvest's been cut. Let's take them. I'll decide if you rank with the hunters of England. Or, wait, I'll wager that I can outjump you myself."

This was irresistible. "A vous, Milady!" he took up the challenge. And they turned off from the road.

The first hedges were crossed easily at the lower gaps in them. He admired her grace and assurance and told her so, but she had no praise for him.

"You do well enough, monsieur. But this is no test. Anybody can jump three feet. You've not proved yet that French cavaliers are so wonderful. Now, over there is a more respectable height — see, between the two poplars. Let's try that."

Blaise smiled. The jump was stiff but not exceptional — perhaps a little under four feet. He had done better than that hundreds of times. But he recalled that the horses were stale and were carrying saddlebags.

"If you will," he flourished, "but then, by your leave, we'll have done."

"Shirking?" she teased. "Prudent?"

"Yes, remember I must bring you to Geneva."

"I remember, monsieur. It won't be your fault if I forget it."

They galloped toward the hedge.

"One at a time," he warned. "It's a narrow space. I'll go first. Judge if a French man-at-arms — "

He gathered in his horse, took the jump — and, too late, saw the ditch on the other side.

He fell clear, but the horse came down beside him, with a lashing of hoofs. He tried to avoid them, felt a riveting blow, an explosion of light, then nothing.

Chapter 20

Blaise found himself looking up into a tangle of twigs only a few inches above his nose. Then, at the stabbing pain in his eyes, he closed them again. The earth seesawed up and down; he felt the nausea of drunkenness and dug his fingers into the ground to keep from sliding off somewhere. Like a drunkard, too, he did not at first even wonder where he was or recall what had happened. But gradually the dizziness passed; and, bracing himself to stand the pain of the light, he forced his eyes open, endured the throbbing behind his temples, and tried to raise his head. The first effort failed. He repeated it after a moment and looked vaguely around. Que diable . . .

Fragments of thought began stirring. A highway . . . a broad plain, with mountains in the distance . . . a galloping across some field . . .

Then it flashed back upon him: Milady Russell, the leap, the horse wallowing beside him in the ditch . . .

He struggled to sit up, at length succeeded, and, propped on his two elbows, steadied himself against the giddiness that once more set the earth wheeling back and forth.

He still lay in the ditch not far from where he had fallen. The marks made by the horse's hoofs could be seen on his left. But the horse was gone.

He made shift to call, "Milady! Mademoiselle!" and could hear only the stir of leaves in the hedge above him. How long had he been here? He could form no idea, except that the shadows of the poplars, stretching out in front, hinted of late afternoon.

Raising his gloved hand to his head, he could feel a bandage; then he stared a moment at the red smear on the glove when he lowered it.

Gradually, what had happened became only too clear. He recalled Anne Russell's proposal of riding to Mâcon; her submissiveness, which had been plainly designed to put him off his guard; her challenge to jump their horses. She could not have foreseen the accident with certainty, but she must have schemed for the possibility of one and had been prompt to take advantage of it, when it happened. He remembered, step by step, how cleverly she had worked upon his foolish French pride. . . .

Well, she had proved him a fool and gone her way. All was fair in war. He should not have allowed himself to expect anything else from her, an enemy.

But where was she? Memory slipped. He had a sense of darkness creeping in again and knew that he must exert himself before it was too late. Struggling to his hands and knees, he crawled up the opposite bank, somehow gained his feet, and staggered blindly forward. Stumbling against a rick of barley, he stood, half supported by it, while he caught his breath.

Clarity alternated with haziness in a sort of pulsation, but he derived no comfort from the lucid intervals. Plainly he had a broken head and needed help if he was to survive. But he had no idea how far it might be to the nearest house, nor could he count on hospitality if he got there. Peasants were not always Good Samaritans. The clothes and purse of a helpless man were more tangible than his thanks. Blaise had still six crowns, an attractive sum to an unscrupulous boor. He would do well to transfer them to the inner pocket of his doublet, while he had his wits about him.

Slipping off a glove, he fumbled in his belt pouch and for a moment continued to fumble before the truth dawned on him. It was empty.

Leaning against the rick, he could not help a dry laugh at his predicament. Well, Anne Russell had saved him from thieves. Of course, she needed money for her own purposes and, having carried out the rest of her scheme, would not falter at the last step. But she might have left him one crown. . . .

The throbbing in his head redoubled, and for some minutes, consciousness turned to fog.

When he could think again, he resolved, if possible, to reach the highway. After that, it would be a matter of luck, depending on who happened to pass. But the few hundred yards from the rick to the hedge, which bordered the road, looked endless, and the hedge itself insurmountable, to one who could hardly stand. Still he must try. . . .

The furrows were the worst of it. He tripped on one and fell, got up, stumbled over a second but managed to weave along for several yards until the blind fog shut in again. No, he could not make it. . . . The lord Bayard liked to say that adversity and a stout heart were the recipe of honor. So, take another step . . . another step.

Blaise's mind clogged. He seemed to be advancing to some attack. The breach was not practicable. Too steep. And he had never felt such weight of armor. Besides, where was the company? Surely he could not be expected to carry the place alone. . . .

There was a creaking of wheels, as the artillery came up. A la bonheur! He would wait until they had widened the breach. . . .

He found himself on the ground but in a still more vivid delirium, for his head lay cushioned on something soft and he was gazing into Anne Russell's face upside down above him.

Her voice had a strange tenderness. "Why didn't you stay where I left you?"

Odd as this was, he accepted it. "I thought you had gone," he muttered. "I was trying to get to the road."

"Gone? Gone where?"

"To Mâcon, perhaps."

"But I told you I would bring help. You seemed to understand. Don't you remember? I bandaged your head and took the money for safekeeping."

He stared up blankly. "No, I can't remember. . . ."

The concern in her voice deepened. "Sainte Vierge! I'm sorry I took so long. These good people were in the fields; then they had to hitch up their cart."

Blaise became aware of two men in ragged jerkins, who stood

beside him. They made more sense than Anne's inverted face.

"Why are you upside down?" he asked.

"But I'm not!"

"Then I am. Or perhaps my eyes —" The cushion under his head moved. "Ah," he murmured, "you're very good to me. Your pardon . . ."

She shifted his head gently on her lap. "Tell me how you feel. That was a shrewd knock you had."

It would have been impossible to tell her how he felt. A joke came easier.

He closed his eyes. "Yes. Wages of romance."

Darkness crept over him again, but now he did not fear it.

Chapter 21

It was not until twenty-four hours later that Blaise came finally to himself, with only a vague recollection of intervening time. He knew somehow that he was in a stable and felt no surprise to hear the munching and crunching of animals nearby. He reclined on a heap of hay and could see daylight through the wattled sides and thatch of the barn. Anne's voice, in conversation with some of the farm people, reached him from outside.

The chief surprise consisted in being able to think normally and to feel no more than a wisp of pain in the head. This was such luxury that for a time he basked in the sensation of it.

He remembered certain moments from the confusion of the past hours. The gentleness of Anne's nursing; the coolness of her hand on his forehead; the trickle of water in the pail, as she changed bandage after bandage. He remembered her face, its sympathy and concern, in the dimness of the lantern. He thought he remembered, too, that once, when the pain was hard to bear, she had sat with her arms about him and had spoken English words, which he did not understand, but the sound of which had brought soothing and comfort.

And it was she whom he had suspected not only of robbing and deserting him but of planning the accident which would give her a chance to escape!

137

The voices outside broke off. He heard Anne's light step entering the barn. A moment later, on tiptoe for fear of disturbing him, she appeared from around the haymow, observed that his eyes were open, and caught the new expression in his face.

"Monsieur," she exclaimed. "Dieu merci! You look better."

"Cured," he answered. "Thanks to God and to you!"

Her relief became radiant. "Now, pardie," she smiled, bending over him and holding out both hands, "this is the merriest sight I've ever had. No pain? Are you sure?"

He took her hands. "Certain. But how can I thank you for everything? What shall I say?"

"You mean what shall I say? Perhaps this will cure me of teasing." And sinking down beside him, she felt his forehead. "Perfect! No fever at all."

"Teasing?" he repeated. "I don't understand."

"You wouldn't, monsieur. That's what I like about you. I hate men who understand women. But you don't. You're such a boy!"

She sat smiling at him.

"Won't you explain?"

"Well," she confessed, "I just couldn't resist baiting you a little. I had no interest in Mâcon, but it was fun to make you think I had. You looked so shrewd and manly. Then, too, remember how positive you were that the French cavaliers could outride everybody? Your horse was tired, and I thought that I might have the laugh on you. Of course, I didn't dream — " She shook her head.

"Poor, helpless woman!" Blaise grinned. "You didn't need to prove how clever you are."

"You mean stupid. Look at the mess I made. But I shouldn't let you talk. I'll fetch a bowl of Dame Audette's soup. These people are so kind. They still can't understand why I insisted on putting you in the stable, when they offered their own bed. Bon Dieu, what with no chimney in the house, and the smoke and the dirt, you'd have perished if I hadn't. Their beasts live like lords compared with them."

She stood up, brushing the straw from her jacket. He noticed the circles under her eyes. She had replaced her boots with the slippers which she carried in her saddlebag. Her green-colored hose looked worn and had pouches at the knee.

Catching his glance, she smiled. "Yes, what a scarecrow!"

He said truthfully, "I was just thinking how beautiful you are."

138

She raised a playful finger at him. "You know very well, monsieur, that all Frenchmen are flatterers." Then she hurried away.

Apparently the soup was in the pot, for she came back in a few minutes with a steaming bowl of it, accompanied by Dame Audette herself. The brown-faced, barelegged woman, swathed in a white béguin hood and with her kirtle trussed up over her underskirt, complimented Monsieur on his recovery and apologized for the stable. There were few gentlemen, she maintained, who had *sisters* so devoted and able as Mademoiselle. Happy the man who got her to wife! Evidently Anne had made a deep impression on the family; but the twinkle in Dame Audette's eyes did not indicate her belief in the brother-sister relationship, nor did Anne seem concerned. When the woman had bobbed herself away, with repeated assurances of welcome and service to Monsieur-Dame, Blaise brought up the point.

"Alas, Milady, it looks as if our hostess has a skeptical turn of mind."

"Don't let your soup get cold for that reason," said Anne. "I've told her in private that we're not related. She's enjoying the secret."

"Why did you tell her that?"

"Because we're still in France, and this farm is close to the highway. We may need more than hospitality: we may need devotion. And a pair of escaping lovers charm women like Dame Audette a good deal more than brothers and sisters."

Blaise gave a start. "Parbleu, I'd forgotten! What day is this?"

"Saturday. The fifth day since Fontainebleau."

"But, then, if the King — " He made a swift calculation. The two days of the royal hunting party had given them a good lead, and, until this accident, they had wasted no time since leaving Sens. But the loss of twenty-four hours made a great difference. Assuming that the King, on returning to Fontainebleau, had defied the Regent and sent out messengers at once, the latter would perhaps already have reached Dijon. The thought that Anne might have sacrificed her very escape from France on his account filled Blaise with humiliation. "But, then, mademoiselle, nom de Dieu — "

"Don't worry," she put in, "I'm beginning to believe that the Regent had her way, and that no messengers were sent. I was simply explaining why Dame Audette is so interested in us."

"No," Blaise fretted. "A guess is no certainty. It's little more than five leagues to the frontier. We could reach Saint-Bonnet tonight."

"Folderol! You won't be able to sit a horse until day after to-morrow."

"I'll show you whether I can't!" Putting the bowl aside he began to get up, then clutched at the cover and sat blankly down again. "Where are my hose?"

"Where you won't find them until tomorrow. And you shan't have your boots even then. No, monsieur, you're in the bag. Now, be good and eat your soup."

"Tyranny!" he protested. "But you could go on, Milady. I should never forgive myself if you were overtaken because of me."

The familiar quizzical look showed in her eyes. "What a fine guard you are! What of the Regent's orders? I have a good mind to report you to Her Highness. Weren't you bidden to watch me like a hawk? But you even suggest packing me off by myself — a manifest treason to France and gross disobedience. There I go again! Poor Monsieur de Lallière!" She laid her hand on his. "I can't help teasing you."

Blaise laughed and resumed his bowl of soup.

"Couldn't we make a plot for the sake of appearances? You could wait for me at Saint-Bonnet, and I could guard you from there to Geneva."

"Oh, sir," she bantered, "I wouldn't dare go so far alone. Something might happen to me."

"And all your talk of hasty affairs that call you to Geneva?"

"They can wait a day longer." But, as so often happened when they seemed most at ease with each other, she fell silent and withdrew into herself. In spite of the intimacy which his accident had brought, he was again aware of her essential remoteness from him.

"Is it indiscreet," he said after a pause, "to ask what you are thinking of?"

"Not at all." Yet he was sure that her answer evaded him: "I was wondering where I should sleep tonight. Certainly not in the house. I'm fairly seasoned but not to that point. As to sleeping here, now that you're well — " She tilted an eyebrow.

Blaise gave a sweep of the arm. "This mansion is all yours. I'll retire to the fields — not for the first time in my life. But I *must* have my breeches."

She shook her head. "No, we shouldn't disappoint Dame Audette. We'll use imagination. This side of the hay is yours. The other is mine. And *honi soit qui mal y pense.* I have no reputation anyway,

140

thanks to you, seducer and ribald. Shall I ever live this down, Monsieur de Lallière?"

He had the right answer pat but could not speak it, not now, with his passion for her on so frail a leash. To say what he had on the tip of his tongue would rend the gossamer of their relationship irrevocably. It had become too precious by now to merit the Regent's cynical amusement. Not now. But someday even in spite of de Norville —

He could bridle his tongue but not the flame in his eyes.

Aware of it, she looked confused, then said lightly: "That was an unfair question. I'll answer it myself: never, Monsieur de Lallière." The smile was gone. He wondered what she meant.

Afterwards, alone, he contrived to get up and, on legs that hardly seemed a part of him, searched for his clothes, which he found easily enough in another part of the loft. By the time he had put them on, the truth of Anne's assertion that he could not sit a horse that evening was clear, and he lay down again on his hay couch. But the sound of voices at the supper table outside the neighboring farmhouse, coupled with his determination to reach Saint-Bonnet tomorrow at all costs and with the knowledge that, to do so, he must use his legs as much as possible, roused him to further effort after a while. At some risk, he staggered out of the barn to face Anne's scolding and the astonishment of his peasant hosts.

Sire Audin, Dame Audette, with their three hulking sons and a scattering of other progeny, welcomed him to the table beneath a linden in the little forecourt of the thatched house. The exertion to make himself agreeable, aided by several cups of red wine, the inevitable soup and black bread, worked wonders; and, by the time supper was over, he had even convinced Anne that they could ride tomorrow. Then, after renewed thanks and good nights, with many knowing looks from Dame Audette, the two guests retired again to the barn.

A harvest moon, red and enormous, but still nicked by the horizon, peered through the open door of the loft. The repose of evening, a far-flung softness of light, rested on the brown fields, which would soon turn to silver. Drawn irresistibly to the doorway, Anne and Blaise sat for awhile dangling their legs over the edge and gazing out. That neither of them felt it necessary to talk indicated a great deal more than they were aware of. A few days ago, silence

141

would have been stiff and unnatural; now it fitted their common mood so easily that they were unconscious of it.

In the fields beyond, the shrilling of the crickets rose and fell drowsily; an occasional frog sounded his bass from a nearby pool. The moon rose above the hedges.

Absently, under her breath, Anne hummed a foreign air, which, by association, reminded Blaise of the English words he remembered from last night. He broached the subject indirectly.

"I wish I knew your language, mademoiselle."

"Why?"

"So that you wouldn't have to translate those ballads you sing. It's a rough speech, but not unpleasant. I wonder how you can make the sounds of it."

She smiled. "They're easy. Even children can make them in England."

Blaise showed mock surprise. "Tiens! They must be clever. Do you think I could learn?"

"I do *not*, sir," she returned emphatically. "Frenchmen can never pronounce anything but French. And, if you ask me why, because they scorn to."

"Well, by the Mass, I'll prove that you're wrong. Listen." Blaise got out slowly: "*Ai . . . luf . . . eeou*. Voilà!"

"What does that mean, monsieur?"

He shook his head. "Ma foi, I don't know. But you see that I can make the sounds. What *do* they mean?"

"*Ai luf eeou*," she puzzled. "Alas —" And then, with a sharp glance, "Where did you learn that?"

He lied flatly. "One of your songs. *Ai luf eeou*, then something about *tru luf*."

She continued to eye him suspiciously. "Which song?"

"Fête-Dieu! I can't remember. There's *luf* in all of them. I see you recognize the sound."

"Hardly. But perhaps you mean *love!*"

"The very word. And it signifies — ?"

"Amour, mon ami."

"Ha! What a word for amour! Though on your lips — And the *ai* and the *eeou?*"

She said primly: "You don't need to know that. You know enough as it is."

Silence fell again. Blaise repeated the magical words to himself.

142

Anne was right: he could guess, or rather hoped that he guessed, what she had murmured when her arms were around him — unless it had been a dream.

The darkness outside deepened and then grew more luminous. A gentle breeze, heavy with the scent of harvest, brushed against them. An owl called far off.

"Milady," he said after awhile, "will you tell me what you meant by answering *never* to a question you yourself asked this afternoon? You asked it in fun, I know, but your answer was in earnest, and it troubled me."

She half turned to him. "What question?"

"About this journey of ours. As to whether, in your words, you would ever live it down. It shames me to think that in any way I should cause you shame." The answer which had been on his tongue earlier and which he had left unspoken was there again. The blood pounded in his temples. It was more than flesh and blood could stand to be with her like this in the summer night, to feel the attraction of her spirit and beauty, to breathe the very warmth of her, and yet sit mumchance for the sake of finespun scruples. "Because you —"

"Dear fool!" she said. "Surely you understood what I meant. Shame —" She stopped suddenly, her hand on his arm. "Listen. Do you hear that sound?"

It was far off as yet but distinct. Out of the north, the racketing of horses' hoofs on the road. Not the casual galloping of belated travelers, but purposeful, intent, ominous. With every second, it grew louder, a continuous rattle. Evidently several riders, lifting their horses along in a lather of haste.

"It may be nothing," he whispered, but got to his feet.

They drew back out of the moonlight and stood listening.

Closer, louder in the quiet night. Would the riders pass by? Now they were outside. A voice rose suddenly "Hola!" A scraping halt sounded along the road. "Monsieur de Warthy, this will be the place."

Anne's grasp tightened on Blaise's arm. She repeated, "Monsieur de Warthy! The King's messenger!"

Chapter 22

Blaise had often considered what he would do in the event that the King's riders overtook Anne and himself before they reached the frontier of Savoy, and he had always reached the same conclusion. There was absolutely nothing he could do. As long as he used all haste to get Anne out of France, he was obeying the Regent's orders; and, in the absence of any counterorders from the King, he was beyond blame in the matter. Certainly he could not be supposed to know the royal desires with regard to Anne nor refuse to carry out the Regent's instructions. But once let an accredited messenger of the King overtake him with new commands, and he would have to heed them at once or be guilty of insubordination.

Anne knew this as well as he did. Holding their breaths in the darkness, they were both conscious of the same helplessness.

The wattled construction of the barn permitted them to hear every sound in the yard beneath; and, after a stricken moment or two, having crept to the other side of the loft, they could even peer out through crevices in the wall at the moonlit group of horsemen.

There were four of them; evidently two gentlemen and their lackeys. Blaise and Anne recognized at once the silhouette of the leader, the sharp nose and pointed chin of Pierre de la Bretonnière, Seigneur de Warthy. He was a gentleman of the King's chamber and High Lord of Woods and Forests; a man of iron, indefatigable in the King's business, a magnificent rider to whom distance meant nothing and speed everything; an embodiment of the royal will or caprice. That he had been sent on this errand indicated its importance.

"Well, Monsieur de Fleurac," he said in a dry voice, "we'll dismount, if you please, and present our homages to Milady Russell. There can be no doubt that here's the place. The right distance, the linden before the door. It was a lucky idea of yours to inquire at that last house."

He swung out of the saddle, leaving his horse to one of the servants, and, accompanied by de Fleurac, walked across the yard, his short, slightly bandy-legged shadow black in front of him.

To the two watchers in the stable, his approach to the house was like the final dribble of sand in an hourglass. If it had been a random query on the part of the messengers, as to whether a lady and gentleman had been seen passing on the road, there might have been hope. Sire Audin and his wife could be counted on for a painless lie. But evidently their neighbors had given de Warthy precise information that his quarry was here. To deny this and outface a King's officer could hardly be expected of humble peasants. Anne's fingers tightened again on Blaise's arm, as the knocking sounded from across the yard.

"De par le roi!" came the summons. "Open!" And impatiently, "Are you deaf in there?"

After a pause, bolts were drawn back; the upper panel of the door swung out.

"What's up?" growled the voice of Audin.

"Rascal" — it was de Fleurac speaking — "use a more civil tone, by God, in answer to a gentleman! I told you to open the door, not half of it. Will you keep Monseigneur and me waiting before your pigsty?"

"But, sirs, how do I know who you are?" Agelong servility showed in Audin's stammer. He became putty at once before the noblemen.

"You'll learn who we are in good time. You were bidden to open in the King's name. That's enough for you. Be quick about it."

The other bolts were drawn. "Messeigneurs, I crave pardon, I was asleep. What would you have?"

De Warthy spoke, raising his voice to make sure that it could be heard by anyone in the cottage. "We would have speech with the English milady who is stopping here, the very noble Mademoiselle de Russell."

"But, sirs," quavered Audin, honestly enough, for his wits were slow, "there's no foreign demoiselle here."

"You lie. We were told at a place down the road (what was the animal's name? Flaudrin? Flaudret? Yes, Flaudret it was) that said lady is here with her escort, Monsieur de Lallière, who was hurt by a fall from his horse. Don't trifle with me, you chuff, but present my compliments to Mademoiselle and entreat me the favor of a word."

"Ça y est," breathed Anne in Blaise's ear. "I'd best go down. It's all over."

But he held her back. "Wait . . ."

"Oh," came the now obsequious voice, "of course! Monseigneur

145

means the tall, beautiful demoiselle in hose and boots! I didn't know she was English. But yes, monseigneur — "

Audette's voice — and no doubt her body — thrust itself in front of Audin's. "Ah, but yes, monseigneur. A lady with strange eyes and reddish hair? Much sunburned?"

"No doubt. Where is she?"

"A gentleman with wide cheekbones, a big mouth?"

"Cré Dieu, yes."

"Monseigneur, I am desolated. They are not here. They rode early this morning for Saint-Bonnet-en-Bresse."

"You lie. This Flaudret said that de Lallière's hurt was grievous, that he well could die of it."

"No, monseigneur, do not be deceived by an idiot like Flaudret. What an animal, as Monseigneur justly called him! How should Flaudret know what happened when it was we who picked the poor gentleman up? A bad fall, he had, and a worse headache: but nothing would persuade him to keep his bed this morning. He and the lady were off not long after dawn. N'est-ce pas, Audin?"

Caught between his wife and the terrible messeigneurs, the peasant could only make an equivocal sound in the throat.

De Fleurac burst out: "Bah! Can't you see that the old witch is lying? And, if she is, we'll hang the pack of them from this tree in front here. Look you, cochonne, it's unhealthy to hinder the King's business. Let's have a light. We'll see what's inside." He called suddenly. "Hola! De Lallière!" And, getting no answer, he growled: "For all we know, they may have been murdered. We should look into it, Monsieur de Warthy."

In their loft, Blaise and Anne could feel the vibrations of fear from across the yard. The peasants had nothing to gain, after all, and much to lose, by concealing their guests from the King's pursuit. Audin, evidently on the point of confession, must have muttered something, for de Fleurac barked:

"Ha! What's that? You have something to say, have you?"

His wife cut in, "He can say nothing but the truth, I *hope*." And the promise of future domestic woe conveyed by her tone muzzled him again. She ran on like a hail storm: "That Monseigneur should think us capable of murder! People like us! I would inform Monseigneur that we own our land in fee simple and owe no man a liard." Her voice doubled its pace and heat. "Light a candle at the fire, Jeannot. Let these messieurs enter. Let them search for corpses

146

among us. And may a thousand cartloads of devils take them! Murderers! Us! Sang goy!"

"Jesus, belle dame!" appeased de Warthy. "Hold your tongue, for God's sake! My friend meant nothing, but we are responsible to the King. . . ."

A light showed. The voices faded into the cottage.

Anne drew a long breath. "Stout heart! Lucky that she wears the breeches in the family! Maybe — "

The voices emerged again. "Fi!" someone gasped. "I'm all but strangled. How do they live in that reek, I ask you? Eight of them by my count! Whew! It's no wonder that Milady and de Lallière rode on this morning. They'd have died else. I'd vastly sooner bed in the stable."

De Fleurac appeared from the shadow of the linden.

"You know, that's an idea. We'll have a look in there. In case of foul play, their horses . . ." And he crossed the yard.

"Eh bien, voilà!" muttered Blaise.

One slim chance was left. The horses had been stalled farthest from the door on the other side of the farm animals. De Fleurac carried no light. If he did not search too far —

His footsteps were on the threshold below. De Warthy said carelessly from behind him: "These people seem honest enough. It's likely they're telling the truth. If Mademoiselle rode this morning, she's in Savoy by now — and there's an end on it."

De Fleurac slipped on a piece of muck and all but sat down. He cursed, took several more steps, and slipped again. As his eyes adjusted themselves to the darkness, he made out a couple of oxen, a huddle of sheep, a cow, the thin rump of an undeniable farm horse. A third slip decided him, and he groped his way back.

"Nothing," he said. "Damme, it's worth your neck in there, not to speak of your clothes. What now?"

Anne drooped her head in relief against Blaise's shoulder.

"What now?" repeated de Warthy, in the same careless tone. "Why, we'll ride back to that inn in the last village. It looks passable."

"But we might push on to Saint-Bonnet."

"What for? You must enjoy riding for the fun of it. We have no safe-conduct into Savoy nor any right to stop Mademoiselle there."

"Then you give up the chase?"

"But of course." De Warthy stretched himself and looked up at the moon.

"Parbleu, you take it easily," said the other.

"More than that," yawned de Warthy, "more than that, monsieur. In the first place, do we know that the King would thank us for bringing back his amoret, when he learns how she bolted off with de Lallière? Secondhand goods, my friend — who can doubt it? — decidedly secondhand by now."

De Warthy gave a short laugh, which his companion echoed. Blaise felt Anne stiffen beside him. He turned prickly hot to the roots of his hair.

"Do you think," added the other, "that His Highness would be pleased to continue where his man-at-arms left off, and invite the joke that he had to take by force what de Lallière got for nothing? Nenni, par le diable."

"It's unlikely," agreed de Fleurac. "Lucky man — de Lallière. She's a handsome filly. But he had best keep wide of the King."

"That's his affair," de Warthy shrugged. "To return to us, who can say that we haven't done our best to carry out His Majesty's orders? Since meeting that scandalized old Madame de Péronne at Sens, we've fair ridden our guts out. It's not our fault if the English jade and her gallant had too much the lead of us."

"True enough."

"Besides, monsieur mon ami, there's another point. You didn't have the favor of a word with Madame la Régente before we set out. I did. You know how she looks sideways at a man when she's up to devilment?"

"Don't I!" nodded de Fleurac.

"Well, looking at me in that way, she said: 'Bon voyage, Monsieur de Warthy. I wish you the luck of failing to overtake Milady Russell. Do as the King bids you, of course; but I shall personally regret your success and shall remember it. A word to the wise, Monsieur de Warthy.'"

"Oho!" the other pondered. "If I had known that! Why didn't you tell me?"

"Because of your peace of mind. But now, with a good conscience, we can return more happily to court without Mademoiselle l'Anglaise than with her. Do you agree?"

"A thousand times over." In de Fleurac's voice sounded a note of thanksgiving.

The two men sauntered back to their horses. A minute later, the hoofbeats, at a more leisurely pace than before, receded into the distance.

For a long moment, neither Blaise nor Anne spoke. The silence between them did not need to be interpreted. To hear the world's opinion is more conclusive than to imagine it.

Only when Audette and her husband crept out into the yard, Anne said absently, "We must go down and thank them."

But afterwards, on his side of the haymow, Blaise passed a sleepless night; and he was conscious that, on her side, Anne slept as little as he.

Chapter 23

From Saint-Bonnet to Bourg-en-Bresse to Nantua to Châtillon-de-Michaille. But now, what with the mountains and their spent horses, they traveled no faster than the shrinking funds in Blaise's purse compelled. It was late afternoon on the fifth day from Audin's cottage, when, having crossed the Jura by way of the Crédo and the Pass de l'Écluse, they discovered on their right the far-off dome of Mont Blanc, caught a glimmer of Lake Leman, and saw the clustered spires of Geneva.

At Châtillon, their last stopping-place, Anne had put on a sadly rumpled gold-and-russet dress together with an equally rumpled French hood; and, now that the wrinkles of both had smoothed out, she looked formal enough to be seen by chance members of the Savoy court. She still rode astride, but her skirts reached nearly to the stirrups. Her familiar coif and hat were gone. Her hair, parted in the center and left half exposed by the crescent-shaped headdress, showed a bronze glimmer in the rays of the declining sun. Blaise, too, had smartened himself up with the suit which he had purchased from the gentleman at court and had left off the bandage required by his head wound.

The altered clothes added another touch to the constraint they had felt since overhearing the talk of the King's messengers. But it was a constraint which served rather to deepen than impair the relationship which had developed between them.

"Almost the end," said Blaise thoughtfully, his eyes on distance.

149

She nodded, repeating the words in a half-voice. "Yes, almost the end. Tomorrow I'll be at court. *Your Highness! Your Grace!* The everlasting service! This has been an interlude."

"Which you will never live down." Blaise spoke as lightly as he could. "Remember? I was asking you about that on the night when de Warthy caught up with us. Lord knows, he made it clear what the world thinks. No doubt the Regent wanted to compromise you. I'm sorry we played into her hands."

"Are you?" she said. "Really?"

Their glances met.

"No, by God!"

"And if you believe that I care about what Monsieur de Warthy said, you are very wrong." She fell silent a moment, her lips pressed together. "Care? What I shall always care about are these days — when I was free for once. Ten days out of a lifetime of rules. Our friendship. I'll have this to remember all my life. No, I hope I shall never live it down."

"Is that what you meant?"

"Of course. And besides," she lifted her hand in a gay flourish — "is there a woman at court, high or low, who isn't the butt of gossip? You and I know the truth and can afford to laugh."

"What about your brother?" he queried.

She had spoken in awe more than once of Sir John Russell, the half brother who had taken her father's place and seemed to hold complete authority over her. Blaise somehow gathered that he was a hard man, and that she feared him.

"I think he will understand." But her voice sounded less assured. "He will know why it was necessary for me to reach Geneva in haste. He isn't one to overrate even chastity as compared with reasons of — " she caught herself — "with certain other things."

Had she meant to say *reasons of state?* It was the nearest she had come to touching on the real object of her mission to Geneva. She veered off quickly.

"No, Monsieur de Lallière, as for me, I count this ride of ours well worth the cost of anything that may come of it — except mischance to you. That concerns me most. If the King — " She left the fear unexpressed.

Blaise shrugged. "Her Highness will bear me out, I think."

That aspect of the future did not interest him at the moment. His mind was too full of the recent days, the dust and sunlight of them, glimpses of mountain and woodland and harvest fields, the courtyards and hearth sides of inns, all connected with Anne, forming a background for her. The smell of leather and horses, the wind and rain of August would always remind him of her.

"I wish I had the gift of words," he went on, "to tell you what it has meant to me . . ."

He would have liked to say, if he could have expressed it, that in contrast with the humdrum of his life in garrison and in the field, an almost exclusively masculine life crowded with men and crass sensations, their companionship had brought a sense of enrichment and discovery. Just as Denis de Surcy had opened for him a prospect more varied and enlightening than the career of the army, so through Anne Russell he had caught the glimpse of another level of emotion, higher and more delicate than any he had known. But to have spoken of this, even if he had had the facility, would have seemed inept. More easily, something of it showed in his eyes and the tone of his voice.

"But you speak of it," he added, "as something only to remember. Is that all?"

She put in: "Monsieur, will you do me one more favor? We have only a league or so. Let's be content, for that short time, to look back. Don't you see what I mean? To add nothing."

"As you will," he said. "But don't imagine . . ."

"Please!" she smiled. "Please!"

He bit his lip and smiled in return. "At least promise that I may wait on you in Geneva before I leave. You won't deny me that?"

If she hesitated, it was no more than a moment. "Of course not. I should be so glad to see you — so very glad."

And, for a while, they rode on in silence.

When she spoke again, although it had no apparent connection with what had gone before, he knew that it was in reference to what she had sought to avoid.

"Did I ever show you this?"

She drew up from under her bodice a gold medal which hung from a thin chain about her neck. He had assumed that she was wearing some amulet or keepsake, perhaps one from de Norville, and had scrupled to ask her about it. What he saw was the pentagonal Tudor rose, familiar to him from English escutcheons at the Field of the Cloth of Gold three years before. Detaching it, she handed it to him to look at.

"The English badge," he said, admiring the bossy goldwork and the weight of it. "Here we've been scrimping on the road, while you were so rich!"

She laughed. "Yes, but you don't think I'd part with that short of starvation? It was given me by our sweet prince, King Henry himself, before I came to France. There are not many who have it — only those who are devoted to His Grace and whom he trusts."

"A great honor," Blaise murmured.

"And more than that, monsieur. A seal. A commitment. I don't belong to myself. Isn't it the same with you?"

Blaise recalled the decision he had made at Lallière. "I suppose it is, if you mean the King's service."

She nodded and held out her hand for the medal, which he returned to her. "Service has been the tradition of our family. I was brought up in that faith. I can't tell you how often, at the court of France, this piece of gold has been a consolation to me."

"I understand," he said, but not in reference to the badge. He understood the warning which she sought to convey almost as an apology, the implication of farewell. Side by side, as they were, he could feel the widening chasm between them.

"Perhaps I should tell you," she added lightly, "that I was betrothed to Jean de Norville at the desire of the King."

She said nothing more, nor was anything necessary. Her indirectness had been intended to spare them both.

Evening came on quickly, when the sun dipped behind the Jura. Dusk became darkness. The scattered lights of the approaching city grew more distinct. On the distant lake front, bonfires showed, and then a sputtering of fireworks, as the town, more in a spirit of frolic than of loyalty, still celebrated the temporary presence in Geneva of Their Highnesses, Charles of Savoy and his bride, Beatrice of Portugal.

"The Regent told me," said Blaise, "that the court here is lodged not in the city but outside the walls at the Couvent de Palais. Shall I take you there?"

"No," returned Anne, "I'm informed that lodgings have been found for me at Syndic Richardet's on the Grand Mézel not far from the Cathedral. Monsieur de Norville, to whom I'm indebted for this place at the Duke's court, made the arrangements."

Blaise could not help asking, "Is he in Geneva?"

152

"No, not at this time. He's detained in France on the Duke of Bourbon's business."

They were drawing close now to the suburbs of the city, visible beyond the wooden bridge that crossed the Arve. Gradually the moon, freeing itself from the far-off mountains, transmuted the darkness into silver. It recalled the open door of the loft at Audin's cottage; it recalled other places and moments, which now suddenly appeared distant and long past. Impelled by the same thought, they drew rein at the near end of the bridge and sat looking down at the river.

Finally, slipping off her glove, she gave him her hand and left it awhile in his. No words could have expressed as much. He raised her hand to his lips again and then again, but she did not seek to free it. All that could not, all that did not need to, be said was implied between them. And when she leaned toward him suddenly, he drew her close and kissed her on the mouth. Passionately she returned his kiss. Then, straightening herself in the saddle, she looked away, so that he could not see her eyes.

"We must ride on," she murmured, "if we are to pass the gates."

In the old city, Blaise asked the way to the house of the Syndic, a handsome residence on one of the principal streets. At his knock, a servant with a lantern appeared. Yes, Milady Russell was eagerly awaited. If Monsieur-Dame would enter —

But when Blaise had held her stirrup and Anne stood on the threshold, he drew back.

She curtsied to his bow. "Farewell, Monsieur de Lallière, and, again, my thanks."

Another servant had taken charge of her horse. The door closed.

Absently Blaise found his way downhill through the dark streets to the inn which Denis de Surcy had appointed three weeks ago when they parted in Roanne, *Les Trois Rois* on the square of that name.

Three weeks? It seemed like years.

Chapter 24

It was one of those strokes of luck which strengthen a man's belief in Providence that late the following day, as Blaise sat moodily over a pot of wine in the inn commons, he heard the noise of an arrival in the courtyard outside — a stir of horses and voices — and then the tones of one familiar voice, which brought him to his feet and across the room in a single movement.

Denis de Surcy!

For all Blaise knew, he might have had to dangle a week before the Marquis arrived. He would have had to look up the French secret agent, Le Tonnelier; and, distasteful as it now was, in view of his relations with Anne Russell, he would have had to direct the espionage which, it was hoped, might discover the identity of the British envoy to Bourbon. The Marquis would take that wretched job off his hands, as well as future responsibility for the whole affair. But that was only one of a score of things which he longed to discuss with his patron. What of his own career from now on? He was sick of the intrigue and barren promises at court. As compared with them, life in the army once more appealed to him. With the present ache and emptiness which his ride with Anne had left, the war in Italy offered a tempting distraction. Then, too, he was penniless. . . .

De Surcy's arrival solved everything.

The Marquis was scarcely out of the saddle before Blaise had reached him; and, though the young man tried to kneel, de Surcy folded him in his arms and kissed him roundly on both cheeks. The sight of the shrewd, kindly face, a little more weather-beaten than when they parted, brought the water to Blaise's eyes.

"Eh bien, monsieur mon fils, mon ami!" exclaimed the Marquis. "When did you arrive? How have you prospered? What's the news from court? Vive Dieu! I wish I had a crown for every time I've thought of you since Roanne! Three weeks, isn't it? Yes, three weeks and a day or so. I hope all went well. . . ." Then, reading the question in Blaise's glance, as it passed rapidly over the other members of the party, he threw in: "No, de la Barre's not along; but he'll turn up soon, I expect. By God, friend Blaise, if I've thought of you, it's been often enough with curses for saddling me with that young devil-archer. Saints, what a hellion and scatterbrain! In your best days, you were never his equal. I sent him off to Lyons with a dispatch to Marshal de la Palisse just to get rid of him. He all but wrecked my mission as it was."

"Women?" Blaise groaned.

"No. I wish it had been. He's in love with your sister, and that keeps him chaste while it lasts. No — betting, brawling, chip on shoulder, cock of the walk. And in a town like Lucerne that swarms with the toughest soldiers in Europe, he had plenty of sport. But while I was persuading the Diet to furnish us ten thousand pikemen, it did not help me to have young jackanapes picking fights in the taverns. So I packed him off." De Surcy chuckled. "What'll you wager that he doesn't bring us news from Lallière as well as from Lyons when he gets back?"

"And the pikemen?" asked Blaise.

"No trouble. The first bands are already on the march. His Majesty will be pleased. But you, mon fils? You? I can hardly wait."

"I have a letter to Your Excellence from the King. There's other news."

"Good! We'll sup together and talk."

The inn of *Les Trois Rois* made a specialty of catering to foreigners. When the Marquis, with his suite, had been installed as befitted a minister of France, it was well past the five o'clock supper hour. Then, finally, alone with de Surcy at table, Blaise presented the King's letter and unfolded his story. But supper had been eaten and the table removed before he had finished the report and had answered the Marquis's questions.

He expected de Surcy's interest, but more than interest appeared in the quick, appraising eyes, occasional exclamations and brief comments. Now and then a frown or a sharp breath betrayed the other's excitement.

"So, monseigneur," Blaise concluded, "I think that's the sum of it. You will understand how happy I am to leave the matter in your charge and how badly I need your advice."

The Marquis gave a prolonged puff. "Ma foi, is there anything truer than the saying that man proposes and God disposes? When I sent you to court, how little either of us thought that it would lead to this kettle of fish! I hoped that it would bring you to the King's attention and promote your advancement in whatever career you might follow. Alas, it has certainly brought you to his attention.

155

He won't be apt to forget you, mon pauvre Blaise. I hoped, too, that you would have a glimpse of the service, which you flattered me by admiring that night in Roanne. A glimpse? Pardie, I didn't expect you to be tossed into it neck and crop and be charged with a ticklish mission like this before you were halfway seasoned. You perceive that life is chance, not chess. However, one thing seems clear."

De Surcy sat pinching his chin. The pause grew so long that Blaise asked, "What thing, monseigneur?"

"Why, that being in, you'll have to swim with the current. You can't climb out."

"I don't understand."

Getting up, the Marquis took a turn through the room, then paused at the window to gaze absently down at the square vaguely lighted by the inn lantern and by similar lanterns at house doors opposite. From its far side came the murmur of the Rhône between the piles of the Pont Bâti.

"I'll try to explain," he said, returning at last to his chair. "Let's review the problem — first, from the standpoint of Madame la Régente, whose talents I have always admired and now frankly marvel at. She has served France well in this affair, though at your cost. Having two ends in view, she used you adroitly for both. A double move of great finesse!"

"Two ends?" Blaise repeated.

"Yes. To discover what man Cardinal Wolsey is sending to Bourbon, so that he may be taken, if possible in conference with the Duke. This man is expected shortly. It's probable enough that Milady Russell may have information which would be of value to him. Therefore, the Duchess seconded Milady's desire for speed to Geneva and played you in that connection. But that was not all. Let the King have his favorites, provided his mother controls them. Do you think that Madame de Chateaubriant has lost favor simply because the King is tired of her, or that Mademoiselle d'Heilly is gaining it simply because of her own charms? Certainly not. This English girl might be dangerous if she were caught and returned to court before she could leave France. Therefore, she must be so compromised that the King would have none of her, even if his messengers brought her back. And here again, you fitted the Regent's purpose."

"Yes," said Blaise, "that's clear enough. But what else could I have done?"

"Nothing, being, as I said, unseasoned and inexpert. You will note that Madame la Régente could have employed many others, but she chose you."

"And are promises nothing? She gave me her word to clear me with the King."

De Surcy shook his head. "My poor boy! But now let us consider the King. He will forget Milady Russell, but he will not forget you. Perhaps, if you buried yourself in the army or kept out of sight elsewhere, you might be safe. But promotion? A career? Success? Diable! I should say not. And remember this. If my lord of Bourbon's rebellion fails, the treason of your father and brother will involve you. Ridicule might prevent the King from punishing a nonentity for stealing a prize he coveted; but why should he scruple to punish the son and brother of known traitors? You could be easily accused of the same crime."

"Then I am lost?"

"No, you can do one of two things." The Marquis leaned forward intently. "You can become a traitor, indeed, join with the Duke, take arms against France. You have only to drop a word to Milady Russell of what we have in mind touching the English envoy, and that service alone would establish you with the enemy. Bourbon may win — the issue's very much in doubt — and you would prosper with him. Or, if he fails, you might take comfort in the thought that it is better to hang for a sheep than a lamb. I do not advise this, of course, but I would rather say it than that you should think it, unsaid. You have been badly treated."

Blaise stiffened. "Not by the King. And you say that the Duchess of Angoulême served France well, however ill she has served me. No, monseigneur, I shall not go back from the choice I made at Lallière. France means more to me than the House of Valois, however I am treated."

"And to me," said the Marquis. "So then you have only one other course open: redeem yourself with His Majesty by an action so important that your junket with Milady Russell will seem the trifle it is. Luckily there's the chance of just such an action in the offing. That's why I said you must continue to swim with the current. What do you think would most please the King at this time? Indeed, he mentions it in his letter."

It was clear that what de Surcy meant was the proof of Bourbon's

157

guilt, which would be furnished by his arrest in parley with a British agent. Aware of this, Blaise shrunk in advance from the proposal which he knew that the other was leading up to.

"Suppose," continued de Surcy, "that you are the man who tracks this foreign envoy to his meeting with the Duke. Suppose you are the man whom the King has to thank for a capture so important that it may shape the history of Europe. For I tell you that my lord Constable, at this moment, is more dangerous to France than the Empire and England combined. Suppose, I repeat, that you can accomplish this. If so, you will have made your fortune and saved your country at the same stroke. There is nothing else for you to attempt but that."

To the Marquis's surprise, he encountered a blank silence, and after a pause, he asked, "Did you follow me, Blaise?"

"Grand merci, yes. But, with all this supposing, suppose that said envoy is Milady Russell's brother?"

De Surcy's eyes widened. "Seigneur Dieu! And what of it? Indeed, it's more than likely. But, again, what of it?"

"Why, in that case, I would rather — I would be unable — "

The Marquis sat staring at him. The silence became leaden.

"Hm-m," muttered de Surcy, "so that's it. I thought you told me she was not your mistress!"

"I told the truth, monseigneur."

"Or has the hussy made you a promise, given you hopes, in spite of her contract to de Norville?"

"She has not."

"Then I don't understand." The keen eyes searched Blaise's face. "Ah, I see!" The Marquis could not keep irony out of his voice. "You are in love, pure love! What the devil of a contretemps!"

Umbrage brought a ripple of color to Blaise's face. "Call it that," he said.

Gradually the other's expression changed. He gave a sigh, rather of reminiscence than disapproval and, leaning forward, patted the young man's knee. "Don't be angry. I'd almost forgotten one of the few advantages of being young. In November, it's hard to remember April." Then, in a different tone, he added, "But what I'm suggesting need not trouble your conscience by so much as a breath — unless, that is, your scruples are too finespun for use in a rough-and-ready world."

And when Blaise looked merely skeptical and on guard, the Marquis drew back thoughtfully, as one who chooses his words.

158

"Now, pay attention," he went on, "and then do as you please. I tell you sincerely that I would not ask of you anything remotely dishonorable. I would not ask you to spy on Milady Russell or play the hypocrite with her. Whatever surveillance of her is necessary, I shall take charge of. What I do ask is that, when, or if, I am able to identify this enemy agent here in Geneva, you will follow him into France, whether he is Milady's brother or not, and that you will do everything possible to contrive his arrest in company with Monseigneur de Bourbon. . . . Wait." De Surcy stopped Blaise with a gesture. "I shall ask you one question, and I hope you will answer it honestly. Assume the case were reversed and that someone close to you entered England with the express purpose of disrupting the kingdom, do you think that Milady Russell would abstain from causing his arrest out of fondness for you? If I am any judge of her at all, she would not."

"No, she would not," Blaise agreed. "But the case is not reversed. Let someone else have the mission. Why do you lay it on me?"

"Because there *is* no one else. I am too old; Pierre de la Barre is too young. You are the only Frenchman in Geneva I can use."

In the blank pause that followed, Blaise could only admit the truth. There was no one else, at least no one equally qualified. He felt caught in a vice that offered no escape. As compared with the patriotic service demanded of him, his personal reluctance was inexcusable. And perhaps, after all — perhaps the English envoy was not Sir John Russell.

Weakening, he suggested the possibility to de Surcy.

"Of course," nodded the latter, "he might be one of several — Knight, Pace, Wingfield. But whoever he is, do you accept?"

Blaise shrugged. From any point of view there was no way out of the current of the affair which had involved him since Fontainebleau.

"Good!" approved the Marquis. "I did not suppose you were a shirker. I confess that your future career interests me almost as much as the political side of this; but it's to your credit that it interests you less than your duty as a Frenchman."

"Don't you think," queried Blaise hopefully, "that Mademoiselle de Russell may have had some other object at the Court of Savoy than to meet an agent from England? If she had information for the enemy, it would serve as well to bring it here. The Regent may have been wrong. Perhaps the whole thing's a will-o'-the-wisp."

"It's possible," the other acknowledged. "We'll wait and see. But

Madame la Régente has a keen nose in such matters. I'm inclined to believe she wasn't wrong — Parbleu, what's that?"

The *that* in question was an explosion of noise in the corridor outside, which at once resolved itself into the unmistakable sounds of a cat-and-dog fight — yowls, spittings, barkings, shrieks, snarling, frenzied dashes and leaps — attended now by human voices in high excitement.

"Ha!" cried someone, "I'll give you odds on him, a crown to a livre."

"Done!" shouted another. "If Monsieur Simon can't whip a dog of that size, I'll eat dirt."

"You'll eat it then. On, Cocorico, mon brave! On, my little Saint George! Here's your chance to win honor. . . ."

"On, Monsieur Simon, cat of cats! Comb his ears for him! Eat him alive!"

"Small chance of that! En avant, Cocorico! Remember your ancestors! Ha! Well done, by God! Well done! A shrewd nip . . ."

The Marquis smiled wanly. "I perceive that Monsieur de la Barre is with us again."

Blaise crossed the room in a bound and threw open the door. At the same moment a grizzly object screamed through the air, gained the stairway and vanished, amid shouts of "Poltroon! Chicken-liver! Come back!" from two young gentlemen on the landing.

"Bravo, Cocorico! My little Caesar! My little Roland! One livre, *if you please*, Monsieur le Genevois. . . ."

But, catching sight of Blaise, Pierre forgot his bet and threw himself into the other's arms. Then, aware of de Surcy on the threshold, he detached himself and dropped to one knee.

"Dieu vous garde, monseigneur! I have the honor to report my return. I would report, too, that the King has completed his journey from Fontainebleau and has entered Lyons."

"But this dog?" exclaimed Blaise, eying the ruffled little spaniel, who now returned from pursuing his enemy downstairs. "Surely I've seen him. By the mass, it's Renée's Cocorico!"

"The same," Pierre brushed off his knee and smiled blandly. "A most cherished token from Mademoiselle your sister, whom I saw last week at Lallière."

"What did I tell you?" laughed the Marquis.

"And you carried this dog in your arms all the way from France?" Blaise continued.

160

"By no means. He rides in his own pouch at my saddlebow, like a little marshal. We are companions in arms. . . . Well, sir?" He turned to the young Genevese, with whom he had made the bet and who now waited for a word.

"If you will bear with me, monsieur, I find that I do not have a livre in my purse at the moment, but I shall make shift to pay you presently."

"Forget it," said Pierre with great condescension. "Provided I win a wager, to hell with the stake!"

Chapter 25

Ten days passed and September arrived without the least indication that Anne Russell had any other concern in Geneva than to attend the Duchess Beatrice as one of her ladies of honor. The French agent, Le Tonnelier, whose services de Surcy at once enlisted, employed his spies in vain both at the court itself and at Syndic Richardet's house. It was practically certain that no Englishman, whether disguised or not, had any communication with her during that time.

Meanwhile, de Surcy, whose ostensible errand in Geneva was to obtain the *pro forma* consent of the Duke to the passage of French troops through southern Savoy, and who was daily at court on that business, saw Milady Russell more than once and, as an old acquaintance from France, even had speech with her. Of course, on these occasions, he took care to know nothing of her recent journey, and, in view of the war between France and England, accepted her presence in the neutral state of Savoy as entirely natural. It was she who indirectly referred to the subject one day, when they met in an anteroom of the Couvent de Palais.

"Monseigneur, my escort from France was a young gentleman of the lord Bayard's company, named Blaise de Lallière. Do you happen to know him?"

"Why, yes," said the Marquis. "A personable fellow. He's stopping at my inn. He did me the honor to wait on me the morning after my arrival and, one thing leading to another, offered to sell me his horse. He seemed very much out of pocket. I advanced him a few crowns. One Frenchman should help another, all things being equal."

"Did he tell you why he was so reduced, or anything of our journey?"

The Marquis wrinkled his brow. "Ma foi, wasn't there some mistake at court as to who should pay, so that expenses on the road fell to him? He spoke, too, of a crotchety chaperon. But I confess, Milady, that, what with other matters, I didn't altogether attend. Perhaps," de Surcy added, with the look of a man who is being intentionally polite, "you will tell me."

He produced the exact impression he wanted. She looked relieved.

"No, monseigneur, there's nothing to tell. We had a pleasant journey. Monsieur de Lallière was leaving for Lyons, he said. I hope to see him before he rides."

The Marquis eyed her with the appreciation of an old actor for a talented beginner. She had great promise. But he allowed his attention to wander apparently to a group of courtiers who had just entered.

"No doubt you will, Milady, no doubt." He threw in absently a trite compliment about the moth and the candle, and still more absently, "I dare say he'll rest up a few days before taking the road again. He's hand and glove with one of my people, young de la Barre. Shall I give him your commands?"

"Certainly not!"

The gentlemen approached. De Surcy returned their bows.

"Messeigneurs, your servant."

But it was not Blaise's fault if he did not wait on Anne during the course of the first week. He called twice at the house of Syndic Richardet, only to find that she was detained at court. The round of festivities attending the visit to Geneva of the Duke and Duchess — dances, spectacles, banquets, regattas on the lake — went on incessantly and monopolized the Duchess's ladies. Blaise could have taken part in the more public entertainments if he had wished, but it was not good policy to be seen too much, so he kept aloof. Once or twice, indeed, he caught sight of Anne at a distance in some cavalcade or display; but, in her new, splendid attire, conventionally formal, conventionally debonair, it was not only the distance that made her seem remote. She was the Anne of Fontainebleau, not his comrade of the highway.

The Marquis learned that her betrothal to de Norville was no secret at court, and that she would marry him as soon as his employment with the Duke of Bourbon allowed. People talked openly of the large dowry expected, a dowry further increased by a gift of the English King.

"And that," remarked de Surcy, "implies a good deal: the value England attaches to my lord Constable and the belief in London that said lord is very much ruled by the rogue, de Norville."

"It implies a foul lack of heart," Blaise retorted, "to hand over such a lady to a damned scheming villain, as if she were a bolt of cloth, simply to buy his good offices with a traitor. Has a king no conscience?"

The Marquis coughed. "Statecraft has no conscience. The sooner you learn that, beau fils, the less disheartened and the more effective you'll be."

Then, after Blaise's second call at Syndic Richardet's, a note, often reread and tenderly preserved, was left for him at the inn, expressing Anne's regret that she had not been present to receive him and appointing such and such an evening several days off, when she would expect the honor of his visit.

And believe me, Monsieur de Lallière, that I would much rather speak with you than weary myself in the dull affairs which belong to my office at this court. And I would I were quit of it, remembering certain other days, as I hope you remember them. But it will be true heart's ease to converse with you again if you will so far favor me. Alas, that Dame Richardet must bear us company, but she is not like Madame de P. of the many wounds, Monsieur, je prie Notre Seigneur qu'il vous donne très bonne vie et longue.

If only nothing happened to prevent that rendezvous! Blaise counted the days until then — four of them, no, three, if you didn't count today, which was partly spent. And, as the Marquis de Vaulx took to pinching his chin at the apparent hitch in the calculations touching the English envoy, Blaise's heart grew lighter. It really began to look as if Madame la Régente had shot wide of the mark, after all.

Time in Geneva passed pleasantly. The town, which had not yet become the embattled stronghold of Calvinism, was still Catholic, and as gay as its political factions allowed. It was a semirural city of spacious gardens and orchards, even within the circle of its walls; and the lovely suburbs had not yet been shorn away for purposes of defense. Long imbued, like other medieval towns, with a prickly spirit of independence and already inclining to an alliance with the neighboring Swiss cantons of Bern and Fribourg, it made little secret of hating its feudal overlord, Charles of Savoy, and especially the Duke's arrogant young wife, Beatrice of Portugal. But, nonetheless, it heartily celebrated their recent arrival as a pretext for merry-making and, no doubt, in the interests of trade. A cortege, preceded by trumpeters, flanked by halberdiers, composed of glittering noblemen and ladies, punctuated at every street corner by tableaux and dramatic spectacles, inspired enthusiasm, if not for Their Highnesses, at least for the show. And Geneva, during the late summer of 1523, wore the dress of carnival.

The Marquis de Vaulx enjoyed it especially as a return to French cooking and culture after the Teutonic austerity of Lucerne.

"Mon Dieu," he sighed more than once, "when I think back to that place, I feel the happy release of a soul out of Purgatory. Figurez-vous! Those dreadful Alps! Those terrifying peaks and glaciers! Nothing to look at but distance, nothing to hear but avalanches, cow-bells and German! Quelle supplice! As for the inns, may it please God henceforth to preserve me from another bierstube and the hor-rors of sauerkraut!"

In comparison with the depressing scenery of Lucerne, he liked to view the square beneath his windows, lined with buildings of the French pattern. French voices, that needed no interpreter, rose pleas-antly to his ears. He could look across at the swift-flowing Rhône, which mirrored houses and windmills reminding him of France. He could see at his right the ancient bridge spanning the river, top-heavy with shops and habitations in the manner of the Ponte Vecchio at Florence. And unseen, but present in his consciousness, rose the old city behind him, with its spires and towers. On every hand evi-dences of human age and tradition, the only proper surroundings, he used to repeat, for a civilized man.

Blaise, too, found the time enjoyable. If it was colored by thoughts of Anne Russell and his own future, he was too young to be entirely absorbed by them. There were long talks with de Surcy about the history and politics of Europe, a subject which, under the Marquis's guidance, once more gained the upper hand over recent backward glances toward the army. In particular, and to the Marquis's secret amusement, he would bring the conversation around to England, which the other had visited more than once.

164

No, it was not so barbarous as might be supposed. There were two universities there of age and distinction, and much progress had lately been made in the teaching of Greek. Of course, it should be remembered that whatever culture it had was derived from France and could thus be regarded only as the pale copy of an original. Witness the language, which was formed in great part of corrupted French words so long mispronounced as to be unintelligible.

"*Luve,* for example," said Blaise, "which means amour."

"Ha!" said the Marquis with a twinkle. "You know that one, do you? No, *luve,* I believe, is a Saxon word; for the English have no proper speech of their own but borrow and pillage from other nations. The result is so bad that most people of fashion or learning prefer to speak Latin or French except with the vulgar — as, indeed, who can blame them?"

"And *ai luve eeou,*" Blaise persisted, "means je vous aime."

"Wonderful!" exclaimed the Marquis. "I can see that you have a gift for tongues, and also that you do not waste your time while traveling."

As to the present King of England, de Surcy had sounder views than on the language. His keen eyes had dissected the handsome young prince on several occasions. Henry Tudor, he thought, was promising: he had notable parts and a will of his own. But he was a heavy young man — too heavy — and flesh in youth was a bad sign. It pointed to grossness in age. For flesh, said the Marquis, if there's too much of it, wars with the spirit.

"There, again," he said, "you have the ill effects of imitation. The King of England burns to resemble the King of France. But the only things you can copy from a man are his surface traits. Thus, if Francis of Valois wears a beard, Henry Tudor must have one; if he cocks his hat or cuts his clothes in a certain style, the Englishman follows suit; if he loves display or the chase or women or glory in arms, the other wants them, too. But, in the case of King Francis, all these are only sparks of an inner fire, which the beefy young prince can never copy. And the vices which, in age, may only disfigure the one, may make the other a swine."

On the whole, in de Surcy's opinion, the English were a stanch and enterprising people. They were too much given to piracy on land and sea; but this was because of the smallness of their country, pinned between Scotland and the Channel, which inspired them, like the Swiss, to wander and rob abroad. Their conceit was plainly nothing but the result of dullness and ignorance. Since, neither in wealth nor numbers, could they vie with France or the Empire, their policy must inevitably lead them to shifting alliances, now on one side, now on the other.

And what of Spain? What of Rome or Venice? Above all, what of the rivalry between royal Francis and imperial Charles?

So, as a rule, conversation led back to the impending war and the problem of Bourbon.

"You know," said the Marquis, on one occasion. "I keep remembering that storm at Lallière. I've even dreamed of it more than once. As if it means something. As if there were no escape from what it means. And when I recall it, I think of my lord the Constable. You and I are tangled in his fortunes. The thing haunts me like an omen." He laughed. "Tricks of the mind, of course. Superstitious fancies."

Blaise shook his head. "Perhaps not, my lord. It's strange, but three or four times I've had the same dream myself."

To keep Pierre de la Barre out of trouble required management during these days. Teaching tricks to Cocorico took only a fraction of the young archer's time. By good luck, a sudden urge to express his sentiments for Renée in poetry assailed him for a while. But, after exhausting enough quills to re-equip a goose and enough paper to light several fires, he consigned the Muse to the devil and hired a Genevese rhymster to compose him some verses, which he dispatched to Lallière by a courier headed for Paris. "And the cursed hypocrisy of these poets," he remarked, "was never so plain. The fellow, who had never seen Mademoiselle, grew so impassioned at the thought of a stoup of wine and a veal cutlet that he voiced my admiration of her to a tee. I had only to tell him the color of her hair and eyes. Before leaving this town, I shall buy me a dozen more sonnets to hold in reserve."

But when the poetic fit was over, Pierre fell back again upon betting and ruffling to pass the time. It took all of Blaise's cajolery to keep him out of scrapes. He was like a high-spirited colt kicking his stall down for want of exercise.

"Italy's over there," he said once, as they stood at the edge of the water, gazing down the vista of the lake, which formed a hill-lined corridor to the shadowy ranges of the Valais. "I'll bet you Monsieur de Bayard has crossed the mountains already, he and the company."

Blaise nodded. "Likely enough."

His gaze merged with Pierre's. Both of them pictured some bivouac beyond the passes in a foothill village overlooking the Lombard plain. There were the beloved Captain, the familiar faces and horses and stir of the camp. There was the sense of being poised on the rim of adventure. Both of them felt the same nostalgia.

"When do you think we'll leave for Lyons?" Pierre asked.

"That depends."

"On what? It's a week now since I got back from France, and it seems a year. This mission was well enough when we had nothing to do in garrison, but now — " Pierre tilted his nose. "Monsieur, I intend to ask leave of the Marquis to rejoin our company."

Blaise put a hand on the other's arm. It was imprudent to give more than a hint of what might be pending, but something had to be said. If the pursuit of an English agent ever took place, he would need Pierre with him. "Wait. You're apt to miss good sport if you leave us now. The fighting in Italy hasn't started yet."

"Sport?"

"Yes. Call it a staghunt in the Bourbonnais."

That this might be an allusion to the winged stag on a famous coat of arms did not escape de la Barre.

"That's different. Ma foi, I'll wait for that. Will the chase pass near Lallière?"

"Perhaps."

Pierre swung his arm above his head. The vision of the company was eclipsed by another vision much more radiant.

Finally time resolved itself into hours before the long-awaited call on Anne Russell. But as it happened, another memorable event took place the same afternoon which preceded the six o'clock hour of Blaise's appointment.

The square of the Trois Rois, beneath the Marquis's windows, was thronged, as usual, with people who had gathered this time to witness a half-civic, half-ecclesiastical procession escorting the Prince Bishop of Geneva, Pierre de la Baulme himself, from the suburban church of Saint-Gervais across the Rhône back to the cathedral. The procession would cross the Pont Bâti and then the square, which became a focal point for spectators. And, while waiting, the latter amused themselves. In one part of the square, young men, wearing garlands on their heads, danced a branle with their girls to the accompaniment of song and the piping of a musette. Bystanders

clapped their hands and joined the singing. Further along, an eddy
of onlookers watched a puppet show. Vendors of fruit syrups ped-
dled their wares with cries of "à la fraîche!" Directly below the window, a drawer of the inn bawled that day's menu in a bass voice
and rolled out the long list of available wines. Everybody wore holiday clothes of all colors, with reds, greens and blues predominating.
Ribbons fluttered. The rays of the noonday sun, pleasantly tempered
by the first nip of September, added a buoyancy of light.

"Look at that!" glowed the Marquis. "You'd never find such a
crowd in Lucerne. Charming! How animated! How French!"

Blaise smiled absently and nodded. He was wondering whether,
in spite of Dame Richardet, he could have a word in private with
Anne. And yet, strangely enough, the scene would be one of those
he could never forget: the holiday faces, the dancing colors, even
the words of the song:

> Où est la Marguerite?
> Oh! gai, oh! gai, oh! gai!
> Où est la Marguerite?
> Oh! gai, franc Cavalier!

Perhaps it was made unforgettable by what happened a moment
later.

The Marquis was saying: "It reminds me of last Saint John's Day
at Surcy-le-Château. All my people were there. Parbleu, old as I am,
I danced with — "

Then, at the sudden silence, Blaise looked up to find his patron
gazing intently at someone in the crowd below, with an expression
of mingled wonder and deference. Following de Surcy's glance, he
could see that the object of his scrutiny was an elderly man on a
mule, who was approaching the entrance of the inn, though at a
snail's pace because of the crowd. A baggage mule and its driver
followed him. The elderly man wore a square, biretta-like cap suggesting the scholar or ecclesiastic. He had a long, straight, pointed
nose; a gaunt, though somewhat square, face; and, in spite of the
warm weather, the rich fur collar of his mantle was well gathered
up around his jaws, as if he felt chilly. What there could be about
this middle-class burgher to elicit the admiring attention of a great
nobleman like de Vaulx puzzled Blaise, who glanced further into
the crowd to make sure that they were both looking at the same
person.

168

"Sacristi!" exclaimed the Marquis. "I didn't expect to see *him* here. I thought he was in Basel."

"Does your lordship refer to that old citizen on the mule?"

"What old citizen?"

"The one you appear to be looking at."

The Marquis stared and then laughed. "Heavens! Is that the way you speak of the greatest man in Europe?"

Blaise again scrutinized the elderly burgher. "Greatest . . . ?" he faltered.

"Ma foi, yes. One whose name will live when most of these dull potentates we serve have been long since forgotten. Greater than the Emperor, greater than the Pope, greater — though I speak with reverence — than the King of France. Old citizen, indeed! By God!"

"I regret," Blaise stammered. "I wish your lordship would take me with you. I've never had the honor — "

"Why, mon pauvre ami, it's none other than the great Erasmus himself. The master spirit of our age. Desiderius Erasmus of Rotterdam."

Unlearned as de Lallière was, the famous name startled him. As a boy, he had picked up his smattering of Latin from the *Adagia*. Like most people, he had laughed over *The Defense of Folly* and the *Colloquies*, unaware of the dragon's teeth they concealed. He had heard, too, of those bold annotations of the New Testament, which had raised a storm through Europe and had made the Gospels a revolutionary document.

"Sainte Marie!" he flushed. "I didn't know."

But the Marquis had left the window. "My gown," he said to his page, "the one with the lynx collar. My gold-headed staff. . . . Blaise, you will accompany me downstairs to greet him. What luck that he's stopping at this inn!"

"I didn't know that your lordship was acquainted with the venerable Erasmus."

"Ah, but yes. We were together in Paris years ago. He was even my tutor for a time. We've corresponded since. I wonder what brings him to Geneva — some courtesy to the Duke, I suppose. . . ."

The Marquis's interest in the new arrival and the fact that a minister of France should personally welcome so unpretentious a guest did more to establish the scholar in the landlord's esteem than all the mighty works he had written. As it was, he received every attention. The ostlers busied themselves with his mules and luggage; the landlord bowed low in spite of his paunch; drawers and servant girls frisked about. Then, at the doorway, the two old friends embraced and addressed each other in the sprightliest Latin. Indeed, it appeared that the learned Erasmus spoke no other tongue with ease. Then Blaise was introduced and managed to fish up only a word or so from his forgotten schooling; but with charming grace, the humanist, who was equally a man of the world, helped him out.

There was a great to-do.

Afterwards, when Erasmus had retired to his room, the Marquis ordered supper for them both. It was to be at six o'clock in an arbor of the inn garden. And let the landlord see to the quality of the burgundy to be served, for the illustrious scholar drank nothing else. A page was sent out to invite a certain Canon of the cathedral, whom Erasmus had expressed a desire of seeing. Otherwise, there would be no one else. It would be most intimate, a rare feast of reason. Blaise had never seen the Marquis so elated.

"And for you, mon fils, it will be an evening which you will treasure all your life."

"But Monseigneur recalls that I am to wait on Milady Russell at six o'clock?"

"My dear boy, postpone it. Postpone it, by all means. You will never again have such an opportunity to sit cozily at table with one of the immortals. It's worth a dozen evenings with any woman on earth. Don't you agree?"

A dull pause followed.

"I see you don't. I have a great mind to use my authority and command your attendance. But to what use? You would sit there, like a stockfish, and heed nothing. Well, go your ways. Go and learn some more about *luve*, when you could hear the most elegant Latin since Pliny. I despair of you. It's a sad world."

Blaise could only look abashed and plead guilty. But he hoped to return soon enough to enjoy at least something of the symposium. Then, lest the Marquis should change his mind and detain him after all, he slipped away, put on his best clothes, and ate a hurried supper.

On the stroke of six, he reached the door of the Syndic's house.

170

Chapter 26

Although dusk had fallen, it was still light enough to make out the sacred letters, J. H. S., cut in stone above the pointed arch of Maître Richardet's door, and even to distinguish the elaborate carvings on the door panels. A sign revealed that the Syndic, when not a magistrate, was a notary; and the ground floor of the house, behind its shuttered windows, contained his office. The second-story windows, however, were open and lighted. Here, no doubt, was the formal living room, where guests were received.

Having walked at top speed from the inn, Blaise paused a moment to catch his breath before knocking. It was a warm evening, and the narrow street between its overhanging houses had the pungent, languid smell that clings to cobbles and masonry after sundown. Here and there people loitered home from an after-supper stroll; the last shutters were being put up in front of shops; and the first lanterns were being lighted.

Then, from the windows above him, Blaise heard the rippling chords of a zither and a voice singing, which he would have recognized anywhere. He knew the song, too.

> Child Waters in his stable stood
> And stroked his milk-white steed;
> To him came a fair young lady
> As ere did wear woman's weed.
>
> Says, "Christ you save, good Child Waters!"
> Says, "Christ you save and see! . . ."

How the song brought things back! And how, at a touch, the conventional stiffness which he was beginning to feel, vanished!

He could carry the tune, even if he didn't know the English words; and, from the street, he now joined in gaily. Laughter sounded from the room above.

Almost at once, the door in front of him opened. A manservant with a lighted candelabra in hand, bade him enter, then led the way across the dark inner office and up and around the built-in spiral stairs at one corner, which connected with the second floor. Emerging from the stair well, he found himself at once in a spacious, candlelighted room and, the next moment, saw Anne coming toward him with outstretched hands.

He had pictured the usual formal reception granted to gentlemen by unmarried ladies in the presence of a chaperon; and this unceremonious greeting surprised, as much as it charmed, him. Evidently he was indebted for it to Dame Richardet, to whom he was now presented: a young woman of twenty-five, hearty, robust, and overflowing with good humor, which was unimpaired by a well-advanced pregnancy.

"At last!" she exclaimed. "The famous Monsieur de Lallière! By God, if Milady had not been able to receive you tonight, I should have invited you here for myself. She has so intrigued me with your virtues that I couldn't have waited. Seigneur Dieu, mademoiselle, he doesn't disappoint me. Take this chair, sir, between us, and let me gaze at you."

It was impossible not to feel at ease in Dame Richardet's company.

"I see you haven't forgotten the Chevalier de Waters," said Anne. "I didn't know whether you could hear me from the street. I sang as loud as I could."

Blaise grinned. "Shall I ever forget him?" He turned to Dame Richardet. "Has Mademoiselle told you of the kick my horse gave me just after she sang me that song?"

The Syndic's wife looked interested. "No, I've only heard about your troubles with Madame de Péronne."

Anne put in quickly: "I hope that Madame got back safely from Geneva, Monsieur de Lallière. I've been so occupied that I did not have time to concern myself . . ."

He took the hint at once and assured her that Madame de Péronne and the servants were by now well on their way into France. Evidently the Richardets had heard nothing of the elopement from Sens and assumed that Anne had parted with her attendants at Geneva. The expediency of not having to explain too much was obvious.

"But tell me about yourself, monsieur," Anne went on. "I supposed you would be in Lyons by now. What about the army? Have the ladies of Geneva kept you engaged? And this young companion of yours, de la Barre, of whom the Marquis de Vaulx was telling me? You see, I've been keeping an eye on you."

"Not so much as I have on you, mademoiselle."

172

The gay chitchat continued. He told Anne of the various times he had seen her in the distance. Dame Richardet asked him, of course, how he liked Geneva; and he praised the cleanliness of the city as compared with the filth of Paris or other French towns. The inn of *Les Trois Rois* was excellent. Politics were touched on.

"Have you seen much of Monseigneur de Vaulx?" Anne asked with a casualness which did not escape him.

"Now and then," he replied in the same manner. "The Marquis has honored me with a word or two."

Yes, from day to day, he had put off returning to Lyons, largely because of the hope he had had of this interview. Perhaps now he would wait until the Marquis's departure and ride in his suite. There was no need of haste, as the Italian campaign had not begun.

And yet, pleasant chaperon as Dame Richardet was, conversation between the three of them was not the same as it would have been without her, not the same as it had been on the road.

Blaise grew heavier hearted as the precious minutes went by. No doubt he was seeing Anne Russell for the last time. When there could be no future, what was the use of clinging to a last time? The decent limit of his call had been nearly reached.

"Will you favor me," he asked, "with one song before I leave? Not about that villain de Waters this time. You sang me a ballad once about some gallant named Thomas — I forget his surname — who encountered a foreign lady and became her bondman in a far country. Do you remember?"

Their eyes met. He did not need to stress the analogy.

"Thomas Rymer?"

"The same. Will you sing it, mademoiselle?"

"If you'll hand me the zither."

He would always remember her like this, he thought, and was conscious of mustering every faculty so that he might forget nothing, so that the picture of her might remain forever fresh in his mind. She sat for a moment smiling at him, with the zither on her knees. Then, freeing her wrists of the long, funnel-shaped sleeves of her velvet gown, she struck several chords, letting her fingers apparently drift over the instrument.

The song rose with a depth and tenderness of expression that gave it a new meaning.

> True Thomas lay o'er yon grassy bank.
> And he beheld a lady gay . . .

173

Blaise could see the very stretch of road between Mâlain and Dijon where Anne had sung and then translated the ballad. There was a wood on their right, and rolling vine-covered hills sloped off to the left. The scene hovered vividly an instant before it merged into the candlelit room. He could follow the meaning of the song, but what he followed chiefly at that moment was the personal meaning which she gave to the words and melody.

> True Thomas he took off his hat,
> And bowed him low down till his knee:
> "All hail, thou mighty Queen of Heaven!
> For your peer on earth I never did see."

Blaise re-enacted the scene with a slight bow and a gesture of the hand towards her. Anne shook her head.

> "O no, O no, True Thomas," she says,
> "That name does not belong to me . . ."

The edging of her small crescent hood, set with brilliants, caught the light of the candles. Blaise noticed the gold chain in the square opening of Anne's bodice. He thought of the medal attached to it.

> "But you must go with me now, Thomas,
> True Thomas, you must go with me — "

The song was cut off. A man's voice, sudden and heavy, spoke from the stair well. "Mesdames, votre serviteur." And a tall figure, taller perhaps because of the shadow behind it, entered the room.

Afterwards Blaise remembered that he had heard the street door open and close, with a murmur of voices; but, absorbed in the song, neither he nor the two ladies had heeded it. Subconsciously, perhaps, he had imagined that Maître Richardet, who had been out when he arrived, was returning. And the same vague thought crossed his mind now. But only for an instant.

The zither slid to the floor, with a jangle of wires, as Anne sprang to her feet. She was suddenly pale with excitement. She exclaimed something in English. But the voice of the stranger cut her short with what sounded like a warning.

"Howard Castle of London, mesdames, at your service."

He was a big, broad-shouldered, gaunt man, taller than Blaise. His reddish beard, with a touch of gray in it, did not conceal the arrogant, down-curving mouth or detract prominence from the imperious, cleaver-shaped nose. He wore the cloth cap and sober dress of a merchant; but a sword hilt stuck out from his mantle, and the hand that rested on it was big, sinewy and capable. Altogether, he made a somewhat overpowering impression, and he had not taken three steps into the room before Blaise knew who he was. Even apart from Anne's excitement, even if she had not been present, Blaise would have been struck by the vague resemblance between them. Then he noticed something wrong about the man's eyes and remembered that Sir John Russell had lost the sight of one eye at the attack on Morlaix.

In view of this recognition, what followed had certain elements of farce. No doubt Sir John had been expected, though certainly not on this particular evening. Dame Richardet greeted him with more deference than she might have used toward a merchant; but she repeated the name he had given, without surprise, and expressed regret that her husband, the Syndic, was not at home to welcome him.

Anne had controlled herself at once. "Ah, Master Howard, we have been awaiting you from day to day. We looked for a letter announcing you."

"That's true, mademoiselle," he returned, "but I found no means of dispatching a letter on the journey."

He spoke a French as polished as hers, though with the same slight drawl.

"And the news from London?" she went on. "My brother? Our friends?"

"They were excellent well, Milady, when I set out." His glance wandered to Blaise. "I regret that I should have interrupted the singing. I was not informed that you had a visitor and, hearing a familiar song, I thought to surprise you."

Blaise bowed. He felt caught in a trap and wished himself anywhere else. That it should have been his bad luck to discover that the English envoy was, after all, Anne's brother and to meet him at the moment of his arrival was devastating. It made Blaise seem a hypocrite and double-dealer in spite of himself. It rendered the mission which he had promised de Surcy to undertake more repugnant than ever.

Anne turned to him. "Master Howard Castle is one of my oldest friends, monsieur. He is a wool merchant of London and is traveling

175

in the interests of his trade. I hope he brings me letters." She made a nervous little gesture of introduction — "Monsieur de Lallière."

The newcomer bowed in his turn, then gave an evident start. "De Lallière?" he repeated.

"Yes, monsieur."

"Of the Forez?"

"As it happens," Blaise stared. How the devil did the Englishman know about him?

"Son of Antoine de Lallière?"

"Indeed."

And at that, the other's manner changed completely. He smiled and thrust out his hand. "Ha, Monsieur de Lallière, this is a surprise. I had expected to meet you at Bourg-en-Bresse, but this is much better. Let me present myself: John Russell. Monsieur Château and Captain Loquingham are here with me."

"Brother!" exclaimed Anne in English. But he was so intent that he did not notice. Turning to her, he went on: "Are you ready, mistress? We must set out tomorrow. You will bear us company as far as Bourg — "

"Brother!" She grasped Russell's arm. "Be careful! There's a mistake. . . ."

Struck by Anne's obvious desperation and by the equally plain bewilderment on Blaise's face, Sir John glanced from one to the other.

"Mistake?" he repeated in English. "How could there be any mistake? Why should I preserve my disguise with this gentleman? I was to meet a Guy de Lallière, son of Antoine de Lallière of the Forez at Bourg-en-Bresse. I find him here. I was to present myself to him. You don't know of these plans, mistress — "

"But his name is Blaise de Lallière. He is a man-at-arms of the King of France. He was my escort from Fontainebleau. . . ."

They spoke in a low voice and in English, but Blaise could guess what was said. His brother's name was explanation enough. As a link between Bourbon and the English envoy, none of the Duke's henchmen was more apt to be chosen than Guy de Lallière. None of them better knew the roads of eastern France; none was more coldly daring and resourceful. So, Guy was the appointed guide, and this confusion of names had plunged Blaise willy-nilly into the position of spy and Judas.

He could read consternation and then rage on the Englishman's

176

face. Russell's gloved hand closed suddenly on Anne's shoulder with a grasp that made her wince. Anger at his own blunder vented itself on her. But Blaise could not understand the hushed, hot words, although he caught the menace of them.

Anne, appalled, was evidently pleading her innocence. Then, taking heart, she continued in a low whisper that brought a certain relenting on Russell's side. His hand withdrew from her shoulder; he fingered his beard. Apparently she was assuring him that the slip could be repaired, that Blaise could be managed. In the end, Sir John gave an abrupt nod, and they both turned to Blaise again.

"Monsieur, forgive me," said Russell, "I've been guilty of an error. The gentleman I was to meet is Guy de Lallière. Since he also is the son of Antoine of that name, you must be brothers."

"Yes," said Blaise, "he is my elder brother."

The Englishman made a show of rubbing his hands. "Well, well, that explains everything. My sister tells me that you do not side with your brother in the present unfortunate contention between the King of France and Monseigneur de Bourbon."

"No, I serve the King." It seemed to Blaise that his only course at this point was to tell the truth and cling to his role of unsophisticated soldier.

"Most creditable," approved the other. "Far be it from me to blame anyone for serving his prince." He turned an impatient glance on Dame Richardet. "By your leave, belle dame," he said curtly, "we have certain private matters to discuss between us. If we could be alone, I should be beholden to you."

This was not a request but a command. He dismissed the lady from her own reception room, as if she had been a servant. The arrogant manner of it sent a flush along Blaise's throat. He thought casually of Child Waters. Somewhat startled, Dame Richardet gave a murmur of compliance and withdrew.

"But serving one's king," Russell continued in the tone of schoolmaster to scholar, "does not require a gentleman to take unfair advantage of another. I trust you are a man of honor, Monsieur de Lallière."

"I trust I am," said Blaise stiffly. Somehow Russell infuriated him. He could not help adding, "Have you any doubts about it?"

Anne put in quickly, "One moment, I beg!" She appealed to Blaise. "Of course he hasn't, monsieur mon ami. What a question! My brother meant nothing of the sort. Let me explain. You see, it

177

concerns my marriage. It will be some time before Monsieur de Norville can absent himself long enough from the Duke of Bourbon to make the journey into Savoy. My brother has come from England to conduct me to him. Apparently Monsieur Guy de Lallière was to be our guide from Bourg-en-Bresse. Because of the war and his own rank, my brother travels in disguise, though I have no doubt he has a safe-conduct into France."

She glanced at Russell, who nodded. "Of course, I have. And countersigned by the Regent herself. A pretty penny it cost me through our bankers in Paris. But at last Chancellor Duprat was accommodating."

Blaise murmured something and tried to look as if he accepted the story at its face value. Perhaps the safe-conduct had been forged; or perhaps, indeed, one had been issued to facilitate the entry and capture of the British envoy. At the moment, he did not want to disentangle the true from the false in what they told him. He felt sick of the affair, sick of the service that forced Anne to lie, that forced him to look hypocritically simple. She was not like that, nor was he. They were simply caught in a web of conflicting loyalties and could not help themselves.

"So, you see," she went on lightly, "it would be unfortunate if you spoke to anyone about my brother and did not regard this entire matter as confidential among ourselves. That was all Sir John meant with reference to a man of honor. Monsieur mon ami, I know you so well that I'm sure you will be entirely discreet for my sake."

"I understand," said Blaise, hating himself. He made a movement to leave. "But I have quite outstayed my time, mademoiselle. You and Milord Russell will have matters to discuss — "

"You will give me your word of honor?" she interrupted.

"As to what?"

"That you will inform no one of what has happened here."

He had reached the dead end where no shiftiness would help. He must either refuse what she asked or agree — and lie. No, there was one more move he could make.

"Will you give me your word of honor," he countered, "that what you told me is the truth; that your brother has no other purpose in entering France than to conduct you to Monsieur de Norville; that he is charged with no mission hostile to France or with any that concerns the Duke of Bourbon?"

She drew back a step, her face white, and her eyes avoided him.

178

"Do you doubt me?"

He nodded. "Yes, because you, too, are serving your king. But, if you give me your word of honor, I shall believe it. And I shall give you mine."

Sir John Russell put in harshly, "Of course, she'll give it. I can assure you, sir, that — "

"I was speaking to Mademoiselle."

Russell flared: "Do you hear, mistress? Give him your word and have done."

She remained silent.

"By God," said Russell, "do I have to speak twice? Is this your obedience?"

Then she spoke, but it seemed to Blaise that she was no longer concerned with the immediate issue. "I suppose you will report this to the Marquis de Vaulx?"

"Yes," he said.

"I take it that you were instructed by the Regent to do more than escort me to Geneva?"

He did not answer. He could follow her thought well enough. He had shown his hand. The plain trooper he had pretended to be would not have doubted her, would not so easily have suspected the mission to Bourbon, would not be reporting so promptly to de Vaulx.

"It will do no harm to tell me now, monsieur, now at the end." She seemed to force out the words. "I ask it for certain reasons which you will understand — whether you serve the King only as a soldier or in other ways?"

He might have quibbled but he could not evade the hurt in her eyes. He chose to throw off the last shred of pretense.

"I have been for some time under the command of the Marquis de Vaulx."

"Ah," she said and, after a moment — "so, all those days you were only a spy!"

"Come!" snapped Russell. "We've had enough of this."

She ignored him, her eyes on Blaise. "Now we are enemies, Monsieur de Lallière. Look to yourself."

"I shall never be your enemy."

A sudden movement on the part of Russell warned him in time. His sword was out as soon as the other's.

"No!" cried Anne. She caught at Russell's arm. "Not that way!"

But he flung her off. "The only way. He must not leave the house."

And the swords met. It was merely a trick on Blaise's side, one that he had learned in Italy: a swift enveloping of Russell's blade, a sudden wrench. The Englishman's sword clattered across the room. He stood grimacing at the pain in his wrist.

"Stand back from the stairs," said Blaise.

He had a last glimpse of Russell's baffled face and of Anne, eyeing him steadily, as he crossed the room.

Then he descended the stairs, groped his way through the dark office below, and was soon in the street.

Chapter 27

There was no time to lose. The Marquis de Vaulx must be informed of what had happened as soon as possible. But Blaise was halfway to the inn of the *Trois Rois* before he remembered the Marquis's supper that evening with Erasmus and the ecclesiastic from the cathedral. This meant that he would have to interrupt the conversation; de Surcy must excuse himself to his guests; there would be added delay and, above all, undesirable gossip on the part of the inn people. And, even so, what could the Marquis do except alert the French secret agent, Le Tonnelier, to redouble his vigilance, so that every move of Sir John Russell might be followed? This was the all-important point. Russell was not the man to turn back from a vitally important mission because his identity had been discovered. The hour of his leaving Geneva, by what road, and how accompanied, must be learned if possible.

Blaise, therefore, took matters into his own hands, turned right from the Grand Mézel, threaded his way through the city to the lake front, and knocked at Le Tonnelier's door. He had met the man, an apparently substantial wine merchant, several times in company with the Marquis, so that they were known to each other.

By now, Blaise's earlier distaste for pursuing Anne's brother into France had very much faded. A half hour of Russell's company was enough to prove him an enemy whom it was a pleasure to hate: an arrogant, harsh, unscrupulous man, no doubt bold and devoted to the

180

service of England, but one who inspired no qualms on the part of a Frenchman. To defeat and capture him was a manifest duty to be performed without regrets.

Finding Le Tonnelier at home, Blaise talked with him in a corner of his warehouse, a candle between them. The man, shrewd and energetic, at once caught the urgency of the affair and promised immediate action. Indeed, the arrival of a horseman at Syndic Richardet's house had been already reported to him, although his informant had not learned who the newcomer was. Le Tonnelier would now direct his spies personally. Blaise could be assured that no one would leave the Syndic's house, front or rear, without being followed. But there was a better plan than that. One of Le Tonnelier's people was related to the Richardets' manservant, who had already been bribed to supply any information which might come his way. Le Tonnelier would connect with him at once. He would also attempt to locate the Messieurs Château and Loquingham, whom the English milord had mentioned as being with him. He would report in person to the Marquis later that night. Monsieur de Lallière could rely entirely upon his zeal and dispatch. Monseigneur de Vaulx was an excellent paymaster.

Confident that everything possible had been covered for the moment, Blaise followed the water front around to the Place des Trois Rois. He hoped that the Marquis by now had finished supper and would be free to consider the evening's events with him. But, upon entering the inn, he learned that Monseigneur was still at table with his illustrious guest in an arbor of the garden; and he walked tensely through the house into the darkness behind it. Since the hour was well past eight, he consoled himself that the party could not last much longer.

The inn garden was laid out in paths covered here and there by trellises overgrown with vines, which formed a kind of leafy maze where guests could stroll or talk in private. Occasional arbors, furnished with a table and with sod benches, afforded nooks for conversation or for dining out in good weather. Guided by the sound of voices, Blaise turned toward one of these and stopped at the entrance.

A lamp, hanging from the trellis, cast a subdued light on the group within and glinted on the silver cups and pitchers, which the Marquis carried with him when traveling and which he used in the entertainment of important guests. De Surcy, as host, sat at one end of the table, with Erasmus on his right and a square-set, heavy man, apparently the cathedral Canon, at his left. To Blaise's surprise, a fourth member of the company was Pierre de la Barre, looking chastened and depressed. He sat opposite the Marquis and, therefore, under his direct scrutiny. No doubt de Surcy, with educating zeal, had forced upon Pierre the opportunity which Blaise, in view of his call that evening, had declined. Bread crumbs in geometrical patterns decorated the table in front of the young archer. He sat with his chin rigidly propped on a fist to keep his head up, and his glassy eyes revealed nothing but glum endurance until they brightened a little at the sight of Blaise.

The talk was in Latin, the international language of the day; and so earnest it was that no one else noted Blaise's arrival until he took a step forward. Then de Surcy, glancing up, introduced him briefly to Canon Cartellier, bade him sit down next to Pierre, and resumed the conversation.

"*Dicebas, Erasme eruditissime?*"

"Mon Dieu!" Pierre whispered to Blaise from the corner of his mouth. "Have I suffered! Will it never end?"

"I trust you are speaking Latin, Monsieur de la Barre," observed the Marquis in that tongue. "Nothing but Latin here, if you please."

Pierre turned a moan into a cough.

"You were saying, most learned Erasmus — ?" the Marquis repeated.

Evidently the talk had something to do with Charles V, Emperor of Germany and King of Spain, as compared with Francis of France. Blaise rallied his meager Latin for a moment, but his thoughts raced off to the recent scene at the Richardet house. Absently, he removed his cap and sat ruffling his hair back and forth.

Now that the cat was out of the bag, Sir John Russell would certainly make a bolt from Geneva. Had he already left the Syndic's house? Would Le Tonnelier be able to post the spies in time? If Russell disappeared, it would be difficult to pick up his trail again. Guy de Lallière could slip him into France at one of a number of points along the border.

It was nerve-racking to keep all this bottled up. The Marquis must be warned of the situation. Blaise tried in vain to catch his eye, then coughed once or twice; but de Surcy did not look around. On pins and needles, Blaise suppressed a curse at the eminent Erasmus and wished him at the devil.

"*Et quare Caesarem Francisco regi praeferas, magister illustris-sime?*" the Marquis was saying.

During Blaise's service as a page in de Surcy's household, he had been caned into a knowledge of Latin sufficient to permit his painfully following the trend of a discussion. But the effect on him now was a kind of mental flickering, dim, for the most part, though with patches of light.

"You ask me why I prefer the Emperor to King Francis?" returned Erasmus. "What a question for a poor man of letters!" He opened his thin hands in a wave of disclaimer. "What does a bookworm know of emperors and kings?"

"Nothing," smiled the Marquis. "But who would pretend that Erasmus is a bookworm save Erasmus himself? If there is any point on which your opinion is not worth hearing, be good enough to tell me."

The other sighed. "Those points would take too long to list, *mi domine*. What wisdom I have consists in knowing that I really know little. But — *ecce* — I shall let you answer your question yourself." He took a sip of wine. "By the gods, I have never tasted more delicious Beaune."

It was difficult not to be taken by the man's charm. In spite of his preoccupation, Blaise found himself listening. The sparkle of the gem on Erasmus's sensitive hand, his graceful gestures, the humor of his smile, expressed an inner sparkle and grace that was irresistibly attractive. His eyes and lean, alert face radiated intelligence. The Latin he used had the delicacy of a violin bow — or a poniard.

"Answer my own question?" the Marquis prodded.

"Yes, if you can be frank. But is frankness possible to a courtier? We'll put it to the proof. Imagine, my friend, that I bring before you a prince who is truly aware of the burden on his shoulders; one concerned with the public interest rather than his private affairs; who obeys the laws he has himself enacted; who keeps an eye on his officers and demands a strict accounting; who, above all, remembers his influence for good or evil. What would you say of such a prince?"

"*Crapulos merdas!*" muttered Pierre in a Latin of his own. His jaws stiffened with a yawn. "What an evening!"

"I should say *rara avis in terris*," replied de Surcy. "But I have known one such: my late master, King Louis, twelfth of the name. The description is true of him in his later years."

"I agree," said Eramsus, "and I hear that it is true of the Emperor.

183

But, now, suppose I bring you a prince devoted to pleasure, who leaves care to his ministers, banishing all except those who tickle his ear with pleasant things; one who believes that he has fulfilled the duties of his office if he hunts every day, keeps stables of fine horses, builds himself palaces by the dozen, indulges any whim; one who sells dignities and charges, plunders his nobles in trumped-up lawsuits, and daily invents new ways of draining the citizens' purses into his own? What would Your Excellence say of him? Be frank now."

The Marquis laughed. "And so you take me in your web, most subtle master! First, you portray an ideal prince, craftily implying that he is the Emperor. Then you present me with a caricature, which any honest man would find odious, and trick me into denouncing the King. Shame on you, venerable Erasmus, for using such sleights with a friend! But if I do not accept the caricature, what feint will you employ next?"

"A straight thrust, *vir carissime*," smiled the other: "that, as I foresaw, you are no more frank than a balky mule. But admit that your first question touching Charles and Francis has been partly answered. And I drink your health, as a worthy opponent in the fine art of wordplay. *Prosit!*"

Blaise made the most of the lull at this point. If the talk started on another round, no one could say when it would stop.

"May I have a word with your lordship in private?"

De Surcy, who had taken a sip of wine in response to Erasmus's compliment, lowered his cup with a frown. "Peste! It must be an important word to justify your interrupting us. Can't it wait?"

Tartness was so unusual with his patron that Blaise could only stammer, "I regret it's of the greatest importance."

The Marquis stood up. "Well, then, *domini mei,* I beg you to excuse me a minute. Meanwhile, most ingenious Erasmus, I pray you to consider what you meant by saying that my question had been *partly* answered, for it seems to me that you have something to add. And I shall question you on it when I return. . . . No, Monsieur de la Barre," he continued to Pierre, who had promptly risen and was edging out of the arbor, "you will remain here and entertain our guests."

Together with Blaise, de Surcy walked a short distance along one of the garden paths. Then, stopping, he said impatiently,

"Eh bien?"

But, at the first words, his petulance vanished. He drew a sharp breath and gripped the other's arm.

"Sir John Russell! Par Dieu, you should have told me at once. Well, what then? Go on — "

Blaise explained the confusion of names and what he had learned from Russell's blunder.

"Bourg-en-Bresse," the Marquis repeated. "Yes, it was from there that the Emperor's envoy, de Beaurain, was spirited into France, when he met Bourbon at Montbrison in July. This man, Château, is his secretary; Loquingham is a captain in the Emperor's service. It's clear that they represent the Empire, and Russell, England, at this next conference with the Duke. The three allies together. What a draught of fishes for our net! If it isn't too late! You should not have scrupled to interrupt me. Le Tonnelier must be instructed at once."

"I have already taken the liberty of doing so, monseigneur."

Blaise described his talk with the secret agent and received an enthusiastic clap on the shoulder.

"Bravo! Well done! You're making progress, beau fils. I'm proud of you."

"But what now?" asked Blaise.

The Marquis deliberated. "I can think of nothing until we receive Le Tonnelier's report. No doubt you'll be riding at dawn, but we can discuss those plans later. A good deal depends on what we hear from Le Tonnelier."

He turned back toward the arbor.

"If you'll excuse me," said Blaise, "I think I'll attend to my saddle-bags and drop a word to the ostler about the horses. I find it hard to remember the Latin declensions at this point, not to speak of syntax."

"Of course you do." The Marquis linked his arm with Blaise's. "But, notwithstanding, I want you to go back with me and listen. For two reasons. The first is that calm is a virtue and fussing, a sin. Your bags can wait. But, above all, I want you to hear Desiderius Erasmus. Our little efforts, our concerns and alarms, will be soon forgotten. They're only ripples on the surface of time. The lives and thoughts of great men lie deeper and are really timeless. I hope I can bring him to discuss our age; for, of all men now living, he sees clearer and farther than any. You and I miss the forest for the trees. It will help you to look at the world a moment through his eyes. . . . Mon Dieu, what's happening?"

Merriment sounded from the arbor. As they approached it, Pierre's voice could be heard, now deep, now in falsetto, acting out something, while gusts of laughter interrupted him. Blaise recognized it as the *Farce nouvelle et fort joyeuse du Pet*, in which Pierre took alternate roles of a husband, a wife and a judge. It was not refined and it was not in Latin. It came to a neat conclusion just as the Marquis and Blaise arrived.

The Canon, purple in the face, sat snorting with delight and thumped the table. Erasmus, his long nose in the air, rocked with laughter.

"Ha, monseigneur," he greeted de Surcy in bad French, "you told this young man to entertain us, and so he has — and beyond praise! He's Roscius come to life again!"

The Marquis, smiling, shook his finger at Pierre. "Have you no reverence? Could you not better employ your time with these venerable men, like Christ among the doctors, by asking them questions and improving your mind, rather than affront their ears with lewd and saucy rhymes? I despair of you."

Pierre looked as contrite as he could but managed to flicker an eyelid at Blaise.

Erasmus took up his defense. "And have you never heard, my lord de Vaulx, of that poor acrobat turned monk, who so amused Our Lady with his tumbling before her altar in a certain abbey, that she stepped down in person to wipe his brow when he was spent with entertaining her? A most instructive legend. As for me, I value the humorists higher than the pedants of this world. And I thank Monsieur de la Barre for shaking up my spleen with the gayest story I've heard this year." He fumbled at his belt and drew out a long quill pen, which he handed to Pierre. "Here, master player, wear this feather in your cap, the pen of Erasmus, as his tribute to laughter."

Pierre, with many thanks, at once stuck the quill into his cap at a cocky angle and vowed that he would not part with it for a hundred crowns. He was so flattered by the great man's praise that he even tried to follow the conversation, which was now resumed in Latin, and hung admiringly on Erasmus's words.

For Blaise, a new experience unfolded itself. Except for his brief association with de Surcy and Anne Russell, he had lived in a chiefly physical world of the cruder senses, where muscles and appetites, interwoven with strands of religion and custom, dominated, and

186

where original thought was so completely lacking that no one suspected the possibility of it. Now, as if a low-lying fog had lifted, he caught glimpses of another mode of being, free, bold, and limitless.

"Let us forget our personal and petty concerns," Erasmus was saying: "that your lordship is a servant of France; that you, Canon Cartellier, are dizzy with walking the tightrope between Savoy and the Cantons; and that I, poor wretch, must scratch with my pen for a living. If you please, we'll take a higher ground." His smile, which included Blaise and Pierre, implied a compliment and an invitation. "No, my esteemed de Surcy, you were right, I have still something to say about France and the Empire. For if Charles, the Emperor, were a much worse, and Francis, the Most Christian King, a much better, prince, I should still be a good Imperial. And for this reason. History, in its course, runs mainly from the little to the large in ever-widening circles. An empire crumbles, but a greater empire finally appears. Could Cyrus foresee Alexander or Alexander, Rome? And Rome, you say, has fallen. But can we deny — bear with my fancies — that a mightier state may someday arise, which shall embrace the world?"

"*Quid dicis?*" put in Cartellier, cupping an ear with his hand.

"You dream, Erasmus," exclaimed de Surcy. "But it is a splendid dream."

The other spoke more distinctly for the benefit of the Canon.

"Not wholly a dream, I think. But, in any case, both from conviction and habit of mind, I welcome it. For I would be a citizen of the world and neither a Dutchman, a Frenchman nor a Genevese. O you stanch patriots of one country or another, you will have your turn for a while; you will cut each other's throats to the ruin of Europe and the glory of your flags. But the world tide runs against you, and your day will pass."

The Marquis shrugged. "*Mi amice,* we live in the world as it is, not as it may sometime be."

"True, my lord, but we do not accept what is without striving for something better. My English friend, the delightful Thomas More, serves England no less because he writes the *Utopia*. And note this: being an Imperial, I am, for much the same reason, a good Catholic."

De Surcy arched his brows. "God forbid that you should be anything else! But I do not see the connection. I, too, am a good Catholic, though not an Imperial."

"*Eheu, mi domine,* do you not perceive that a universal faith is the counterpart, on another level, of a universal state? And for that reason I part company with this firebrand, Luther, who, because the house of the Church needs dusting and repairs, would burn it down. Shall the faith of Christendom, which once accommodated all Europe, be parceled out in fragments to become a cause of hatred and of war? I remain a Catholic. I am drawn to universal institutions, within the scope of which men can find peace."

While the conversation turned off to the crisis in Germany, Blaise trembled at the thought of a dismembered Church. A tidal wave seemed to hang over Europe, threatening the chief security of human life. Until now, men had accepted the Catholic faith as they accepted the sunlight, which shone on all indifferently. It was the one bond between peoples, between friend and foe, the ultimate standard. He had long heard talk about the need of reform; but schism was something else, infinitely horrible.

"What, in your opinion," the Marquis was asking, "most erudite Erasmus, is the chief character of our age?"

The other turned his silver cup once or twice between his fingers before answering. Then he said: "That it has so many characters, my friend; that it is so exuberant — chiefly in evil, because of human passions, but also in good. A tangle of weeds, with here and there a rose. The same earth yields both. In the course of time, perhaps, long hence — long hence — men will uproot the one and nourish the other until a garden blossoms more splendid than any the world has known. I would say, too, that our age is so bewildered by novelties that it has forgotten things which will someday have to be painfully remembered."

"What, for example?" put in Cartellier.

"For example, humility. For example, too, that God is not mocked. For example, love, that light from beyond, which Our Lord brought into the world."

"You speak of weeds," said de Surcy, "and, by Jupiter, there's no use pointing them out. But roses? What rose has our age produced?"

"Freedom," said Erasmus. "I mean the freedom of individual man to be distinct from the herd, the ant heap. Or rather, let me say, the new dawn of this freedom, which is the goal of civilization and the hope of humanity. For the tyranny of the herd is the worst of tyrannies, most blind, most debasing. And an age is illustrious in the measure of its distinguished men who are free from this tyranny.

188

That, in our age, such freedom has reawakened is a gain which balances many evils. Does it not foretell an enlightened chapter of history, provided the rose we speak of is guarded and encouraged? But this demands vigilance; for, as a rule, men find it easier to be slaves than free."

The Marquis bowed. "No one in our time can speak with more authority about freedom than you, Erasmus. You have thought your own thoughts, gone your own way. But tell me this. Will not the universal state you dream of, and a universal faith, deny to man an individual freedom?"

"No, *mi domine,* not as I conceive them. For I dream also of universal law, under which war will be curbed or made impossible. And war is the chief enemy of freedom. It is during war that vulgar opinion, which is controlled by instinct, passion, and custom, dominates; and that freedom, such as we are discussing, vanishes. You will find, I think, that those who speak of wars for freedom use the word in a different, or sometimes a hypocritical, sense. But, in any case, war requires conformity; is indifferent to truth; thrives on tyranny, hatred and despair. And consider that wars are growing in extent — these huge armies of several hundred thousand men, these new weapons. You smile at the dream of a universal state. I hope that the nightmare of universal war is incredible. But if it should come to that, do not look for freedom. It is in a world at peace that variety will be most possible. I mean the variety of all the fruits and flowers of the spirit, which include freedom."

Erasmus broke off at the sound of hurried footsteps on the path outside. A dusty, rank-smelling man, evidently a courier, appeared at the entrance of the arbor.

"Monseigneur de Vaulx?"

"Yes," said the Marquis.

The man entered, dropped to one knee, kissed the letter he was holding and handed it to de Surcy.

"From His Majesty in Lyons. My orders were *haste and more haste.*"

"And so," smiled Erasmus, "we descend from the heaven of thought to the dust of action, from the future to the present." He got up, followed by Cartellier. "But for solace to mind and body, we have you to thank, my lord."

"By far the greater debt is mine, *mei domini.*"

There were further compliments. The party re-entered the inn.

Then, after final good nights, the Marquis bade Blaise and the courier attend him upstairs to his room.

Under a lighted candelabra, de Surcy spread out the King's letter. And, as he read, the lines of his face deepened.

Looking up, at last, he beckoned the courier, thanked him for his pains, and gave him a coin.

"You will set out for Lyons in the morning," he directed, "and take my answer to the King. Hold yourself ready without fail."

When the man had bowed himself out, the Marquis added to Blaise: "Well, mon fils, the Constable has shown his hand; the hunt is on. Now, if your brother and Sir John Russell do not fail us, and if all goes well, you may be the man whom the King will delight to honor. Here, read his letter yourself. We must shape our plans to it."

Chapter 28

Monsieur de Vaulx [wrote the King], I have received your letter from Geneva, in which you announce the happy conclusion of your mission to the Swiss Diet. This, you conducted with your usual ability and in all ways according to our desire.

You report also that our letter written from Fontainebleau has been duly delivered to you by Blaise de Lallière, and that the Demoiselle Anne de Russell has safely arrived in Geneva. Whereat I am well pleased, for the headlong conduct of said de Lallière with said lady on the road argued a reckless blade of loose character and gave rise to concern that the letter was not in safe hands. My concern was the greater since de Lallière belongs to a family prominent in the party of the Seigneur de Bourbon, and since, for all I knew, he might have been led to betray the letter or its contents to one of that party. He is certainly not a man to be trusted with secret and important business.

Blaise looked up at this point to meet the eyes of de Surcy. His future, as far as the King was concerned, lay compacted here, like a plant in its seed: the royal resentment, the family treason, which might be used against him.

The letter continued.

Monsieur de Vaulx, that you may be kept informed touching this affair of the Seigneur de Bourbon, know that today, having reached the end of

190

patience, I have sent both the Grand Master and Marshal de la Palisse, with two hundred gentlemen and with the archers of the Guard, in all between four and five hundred horse, together with four thousand foot, into the Bourbonnais. And I have ordered them to seize the person of said lord of Bourbon wherever he may be found. Also I have sent the companies of the Duke of Alençon and the Duke of Vendôme to scour all the country of the Auvergne and Bourbonnais, with a view to stamping out whatever sparks of rebellion there may be in those parts.

Know, monsieur, that, within the week, said Duke of Bourbon, feigning illness but feigning also great desire to please us, had himself carried by litter from Moulins to the town of La Palisse on the road to Lyons. There his supposed sickness turned from bad to worse, the doctors avowing hard pains in the head and kidneys, with his urine surcharged to the point that they gave him but three days of life. Whereupon, said Duke, who was either unable to travel or, if able, might have proceeded to Lyons, turned back toward Moulins. And I, tired of being fobbed off with pretexts, have taken the above means to secure his person, hoping that time may yet serve. And for better measure, I have placed under arrest those of the said Duke's party who were in Lyons; to wit, Monsieur de Saint-Vallier, Monsieur de Prie, the Bishop Antoine de Chabannes, and several others. From them, it may be possible to wring out additional evidence of the said lord of Bourbon's villainy and treasonable practices.

Monsieur de Vaulx, you are aware that, against your advice, I have waited thus long in hope of manifest proof convicting the Constable; for, as I wrote you from Fontainebleau, he is beloved throughout France, and no slight testimony will serve. Be vigilant, therefore, touching the English envoy to the Seigneur de Bourbon, of whom I instructed you. Now more than ever the arrest of such an agent within France, especially if he should be taken in parley with Bourbon, would furnish the proof of treason which I seek.

If, by whatever means, you discover this said agent in Savoy, send us word of him at once by the same courier who brings you this. Should he still attempt to enter France, you will have him straitly followed by at least two competent men equal to the undertaking. In view of this, I have posted horsemen at Belleville, Villefranche and Trévoux, on the Saône River, so that wherever said envoy may cross our borders, one of your people may summon aid, while the other continues the chase. No doubt said Englishman will be conducted to the Duke. And, thus, the two of them would not only be taken together, but we shall learn where said lord of Bourbon now is, a matter at present in doubt. But, I say again, let the man selected by you for this mission be steady and competent, for I consider the affair of the utmost weight.

Monsieur de Vaulx, we are informed that said Duke of Bourbon is resolved ultimately to take refuge in one of his strong places, Chantelle or Carlat, and hold the same against us, pending help from abroad. But this, I believe, he will find hard to do, considering the forces now closing upon him. — And so, à Dieu, qui vous ait en sa garde. FRANÇOIS.

Blaise's eyes lingered on the bold signature and the name of the secretary below it, Babou.

"One thing's plain," he said at last. "In view of this letter, your lordship cannot select me. *Steady and competent!* I marvel that the King did not exclude me by name."

The Marquis nodded. "And yet the fact remains that you and Pierre de la Barre are the only men I *can* select. As I pointed out to you before, I am too old for such a chase. Le Tonnelier and his spies are well enough for Geneva, but they are wholly unsuited to a mission like this. Well, then — Maître Laurence, my secretary? Doctor Savio, the physician? A couple of lackeys or pages? The King forgets how I am accompanied. No, you are the only man to follow Sir John Russell, or he must ride unfollowed. But, let me add that, if I had a company of men-at-arms to choose from, I would still choose you."

"What if I fail?" Blaise countered. "Bon Dieu, monseigneur, there's no certainty that any man alive could track Russell to a meeting with the Duke. The King would hold you guilty for sending me."

"I know that. If you fail, I shall be involved in your disgrace. My enemies at court will see to it. On the other hand, if you succeed, I shall have glory in your honor. It's a case of win-all, lose-all. I'm willing to take the risk."

Blaise drew himself up. "So be it. I'll do my best — all the more because it concerns your lordship."

"No," said the Marquis, "because it concerns France. That's the one thought to bear in mind. . . . And now, as to plans for trailing Russell and, I hope, Château and Loquingham with him. They'll be on their guard. . . ."

The route between Geneva and Bourg-en-Bresse was completely familiar to Blaise from his recent journey with Anne Russell. He reckoned that a party of horsemen riding fast would traverse the defile of the Écluse, cross the Grand Crédo, and reach Nantua in one day. They would reach Bourg-en-Bresse the following day at about noon. Except for a long and, in view of their extreme haste, an utterly impracticable, detour, there was no other route to Bourg from the Écluse onward. However, one had a choice of two roads out of Geneva toward the Écluse Pass: one of them slightly shorter by way of Collonges, and the other through Saint-Julien. If it could be learned which of these Sir John Russell's party would take, Blaise proposed to travel by the other; and, instead of following, he would precede his quarry as far as Nantua. Meanwhile, Pierre de la Barre, who was unknown to Russell, would keep behind at a league's distance, so that, if by any chance the Russell party stopped short of Nantua or took some unexpected route south or north, he could report the fact to Blaise. The same tactics would be repeated from Nantua to Bourg and thence to the River Saône. Beyond that, it was impossible to plan, because everything depended on what direction Russell would take. But Blaise, who, as a boy, had hunted through the Beaujolais, knew the roads well enough to feel confident that he could follow wherever the course led; while Pierre, in the meantime, brought along the nearest detachment of horse from one of the towns mentioned in the King's letter.

These plans were naturally vulnerable to accidents of every sort; but, at long range, they were the best that could be outlined. In this way, Russell and his companions might suspect, but they could not be sure, that they were being followed as long as they were in Savoy. . After crossing the Saône, Blaise would have to improvise his tactics, depending on circumstances; and one could only hope for the best.

It was approaching midnight when a sleepy tavern servant knocked at the door and announced that a citizen of the town, one Maître Le Tonnelier, craved audience with Monseigneur de Vaulx on a matter of urgency, and was told to bring up the visitor at once.

On his appearance, Le Tonnelier showed every sign of satisfaction, which the report that he proceeded to make entirely justified. The Richardets' lackey, an adept of keyholes, had proved especially helpful. In fact, there had been little need of a keyhole at all. He had learned that Sir John Russell proposed to set out for Bourg-en-Bresse at dawn by the south gate on the road to Saint-Julien. Milady Russell would accompany him as far as Bourg and then return to Geneva. Sir John had talked openly with Syndic Richardet, upon the latter's return home, and had described Blaise's visit. But neither of them believed that the Marquis de Vaulx could act quickly enough to launch a pursuit and, much less, to send a warning ahead into France. In short, there was every prospect that Blaise's discovery, though regrettable, would have little effect in hampering the enterprise. The services of the eavesdropping lackey, who was also skilled with the razor, had been enlisted to shave off Sir John's beard, as an added disguise, which had marvelously altered his appearance. The servant, too, had helped with the saddlebags, and everything was ready for an early start.

"Perfect," commented the Marquis. "Almost too perfect. I wonder how much of this was intended for the lackey and other servants to know."

Le Tonnelier's small, round eyes narrowed. "I take your lordship's meaning. I should have wondered myself, except for another point. Milord Russell's attendant, who had made the journey with him, left the house and was followed by one of my men to an inn called the *Écu de Genève*. There, he had speech with Messieurs Château and Loquingham."

"Ha!" exclaimed de Surcy. "Well?"

"What was said, I don't know; but they ordered their horses for dawn."

"And this attendant of Russell's then returned to the Syndic's house?"

"Yes, monseigneur."

"And no one else, except him, has left that house?"

"No. May I ask what concerns your lordship?"

"The Duke of Savoy," returned the Marquis. "It's important that neither he nor the Prince Bishop takes a hand in the game. They would both aid the Emperor and, therefore Bourbon, as far as possible without an open act against France. Of course, you do not know who may have left the *Écu de Genève* after Château and Loquingham were notified?"

Le Tonnelier shrugged. "It would be impossible to follow everyone who leaves an inn, monseigneur."

De Surcy pondered a moment. "It's a faint chance, after all. Yes, I believe it's likely that Russell believes he can outrace us. Besides, he would find it difficult at this hour to communicate with the Duke of Savoy or Monseigneur de la Baulme. You have done wonderfully, my friend, and you shall be richly paid. But do not relax. Keep these people under watch until they leave Geneva by whatever gate they will. Then send me instant word. The rest is our affair."

When the gratified informer had withdrawn, the Marquis turned to Blaise. "There you are, mon fils, mon ami. You'd better warn Pierre de la Barre and see to your horses. Now I can write the King a letter that will rejoice him. Not only Sir John Russell but Château and Loquingham to overbrim the cup! I'll sing your praises and explain why it was necessary to send you on this mission. I'll defend you, too, as regards that affair with Milady Russell, on the strength of the Regent's commands to you. Have no fear; all shall be well, I know it. But I'll hold the letter until after you leave, for fear of some last-minute change. . . ."

Five hours later, dressed for the road, Blaise and Pierre de la Barre took leave of their patron. The faintest gray of dawn showed through the windows, but not as yet bright enough to dim the candles. A stir and champing of horses and the voices of stablemen sounded up from the courtyard.

The two young men kneeled to receive the Marquis's farewell. Word had just come that the Russells, together with Château and Loquingham, were taking the road toward Saint-Julien. Pierre would, accordingly, follow that route, while Blaise rode north across the Arve River. He and Pierre would meet that night at Nantua beyond the pass. After paying homage to the Duke of Savoy and completing his official business at the latter's court, de Surcy would travel to Lyons. Their mission completed, the others would rejoin him there.

"And so, gentlemen, may God have you in His guard! If you speed in this enterprise, you'll win honor not only from the King but among all true Frenchmen."

The Marquis followed them to the door and gave each a parting clap on the shoulder. His heart caught the vibration of their youth and spirit.

"Pierre, mon ami, if you pass by Lallière, don't linger too long, and keep an eye on your bracelet. Blaise, remember I expect to sun myself in your glory at Lyons. Adieu! Adieu . . . !"

Walking over to the window, he watched them mount in the light of the ostlers' lanterns. Pierre gently deposited Cocorico in the pouch on his saddlebow, while Blaise laughed at him. They caught sight of de Surcy behind the windowpane, flourished their caps, and made their horses rear. Then they were gone through the archway of the inn yard.

Chapter 29

An incident at the west gate of the town — the one opening on the fine suburb of Plainpalais — cost Blaise some time and roused misgivings with regard to a possibility which the Marquis de Vaulx had not overlooked.

It was not so strange that the finicky gate warden detained him, while he spelled out the text of Blaise's safe-conduct under a dim lantern and then spelled it out a second time; but, when a horseman, wearing the Duke of Savoy's colors, rode up with a nod, and Blaise was thereupon dismissed, the thing looked queer. It smacked of prearrangement, as if the warden had been marking time until the horseman arrived. And that, in turn, gave Blaise something to consider. Had there been after all, a communication between the Russells and the Duke? Was he, de Lallière, being watched? If Charles of Savoy, who secretly favored the Empire and England, intervened against him, the ride to France might be more than difficult.

But, on second thought, he put aside these fears as making too much of too little. The appearance of the Duke's man at the gate might have had nothing at all to do with him. Besides, the very fact that he had been allowed to proceed on his way, when he could so easily have been held, was more reassuring than not.

Free at last, Blaise now made his way through the suburb and over the wooden bridge across the Arve. It was here on the further side that he and Anne Russell had bidden each other a silent farewell at the end of their journey. He checked his horse at the spot, vividly recalling every instant of that leave-taking: the passion of her kiss, their mutual longing. The rapture, the ache, of it revived. The memory of lost love haunted him, haunted the road. Lost? No, rather, love forbidden. Even now, after the declared war between them, after her disillusionment and her bitter words, he loved her as much as then. He knew that he would always love her. War and the rivalry of kings and unlike destinies could not change that. They made her unattainable, but love remained free. He knew that, however long he lived, no other woman would replace her in his remembrance. He spurred on, making the most of the plain before the ascent toward the mountains began; but, with the recent journey so fresh in his mind, he almost imagined her beside him. Perhaps, sometime before Bourg-en-Bresse, he would catch sight of her in the distance, and yet separated from him by more than distance. . . .

He had forgotten the affair at the gate, when, hearing a clatter of hoofs behind him, he turned his head and gradually recognized the horseman as the same who had nodded him free from the warden an hour ago. A moment later, the man drew abreast.

He was mounted on a superb horse, better by half than de Lallière's; but, except for this, his appearance, in the clear light of morning, would not have inspired confidence, even if the fact that he was there at all had not revived Blaise's suspicions tenfold. To de Lallière's trained eye, the man's burliness, his brutal and low-browed face, the flashiness of his dress, bespoke the ruffler and bravo, the kind usually employed on secret and violent business.

"You're riding fast, sir," he remarked in a heavy voice.

"No faster than you," answered Blaise. "But I suppose we both want to make the best of the level road. You've a good horse there."

"None better in the Duke's stables, when it comes to speed. Wish I owned him."

"You're traveling far, then?"

The man shook his head. "Only to the Fort de l'Écluse with a message from His Highness, which needs haste. And you?"

"To Châtillon or even Nantua perhaps."

"Oho! A long stretch. Do you think you'll get there this evening?"

"Why not?"

The other said nothing but spat sideways and smiled.

The smile did nothing to lessen Blaise's misgivings. "Why not?" he repeated. "It's the regular stage from Geneva."

"Sure it is." The man grinned again and changed the subject. "Well, here's sunrise at last. You can see it on the Old Master yonder." He jerked his head to the left, where the far distant dome of Mont Blanc, behind the Salève mountains, showed pink before the rays of the still invisible sun. "We have another fine day. But I bet you it's the last. A friend of mine from the Duke's castle of Chillon up the lake came in yesterday. Said that the Dent d'Oche, which they can see from there, was smoking. A sure sign of foul weather." He cocked his eye at Blaise. "Still, we must take the bad with the good. It's the way of life, isn't it, monsieur?"

The trite remark seemed to amuse him, and he tossed his head back with a chuckle. Blaise thought of a burly cat who has swallowed a bird. It might be only a mannerism often found in beefy, dull-witted men; but it looked, too, like the mannerism of a bully gloating over a good joke, which Blaise could not help feeling involved him. His suspicions were fast hardening into certainties.

He put two and two together rapidly. Suppose that the Duke of Savoy had resolved to protect the Russells, how could he best help them? The answer was clear: prevent them from being followed by any of de Surcy's people and also prevent the Marquis from sending news of them to France. But, in that case, Blaise asked himself, why had he been released at the town gate? Almost at once, a flash of insight made that plain. Openly to arrest the Marquis de Vaulx's accredited messengers would be a hostile act, and the timeserving Duke had no wish to embroil himself with France. But these messengers could be stopped secretly on the road at some place like the Pass de l'Écluse, where the Duke's men garrisoned a fort that blocked the defile. A word to the captain there, and no suspect Frenchman would get through until the Russells had too long a start to be in danger. De Surcy would know nothing of this for the time being, and afterwards apologies could be found.

As he recalled the episode at the gate, Blaise began to understand it. He could understand, too, his companion's secret amusement; for, while carrying the message from the Duke, to be leading his victim smoothly into the trap could not fail to tickle such a person's sense of humor.

Of course, all this was still only theory. Everything now depended on verifying it.

"Monsieur," said Blaise, when they had slowed down from the gallop to breathe their horses, "you seemed in doubt of my making Châtillon or Nantua tonight. Or was I mistaken?"

The other's hard eyes quizzed him. "But completely, monsieur. I'm in no doubt of your journey. That is, barring mishaps. For, look you, the longer the road, the more accidents can happen. When you consider these mountains in front of us" — his hand outlined the range of the Jura — "and the road you must take across the Grand Crédo, which is close to five thousand feet up, why, damme, who can fail to wonder if you'll get as far as you think tonight? That's all. Don't be discouraged."

Blaise said dryly: "How right you are! We're in God's hands. I thank you for reminding me of it."

"At your service," fleered the horseman.

198

"Now, in my country," Blaise continued, "some people have the gift of second sight — call it presentiments, eh? They can tell fortunes, sniff danger. I have a touch of it myself."

"Indeed?"

"Yes, monsieur. And it seems to me that I may not reach Châtillon tonight, as you suggested. A queer feeling."

For an instant, derision in the other's face gave way to shrewd intentness. Had the victim been put on guard? But, as Blaise looked only guileless and credulous, the bait was too tempting for the coarse-witted soldier. His mockery crept back, and he fetched a deep sigh.

"Ah, sir, that's strange now, curse me if it isn't."

"What's strange?"

"You know, I have a dab of the same gift. It takes me strong at times, like a weight in the belly. And today, thinking of your journey, I'm fair depressed. No, sir, you won't make Châtillon, let alone Nantua, tonight."

"Diable!" muttered Blaise, keenly interested. "And does your foresight extend to the point of knowing what will befall me and where I shall spend the night?"

The man struggled with inward mirth but kept his face straight. "Alas, sir, I can't tell you that. If you want a piece of advice, why not put up with me at the Fort de l'Écluse? I forsake God if the garrison isn't as merry a company as you'll find in Savoy. And take my word for it that the captain will make you welcome, yes, more than welcome." A smile sneaked through at this point but was bit off. "No use kicking against the pricks, since we both have the same presentiments. How about it?"

The plot was now clear as spring water, but Blaise made a final test. If he could only lure the rogue into something more positive than smug sarcasm — a threat, an act — something that would furnish an excuse for killing him! . . . Because he had to be killed. The message he was carrying must not reach the Fort de l'Écluse. If it did, neither Blaise nor Pierre de la Barre nor the courier to the King at Lyons would get through. The entire venture against Bourbon, upon which so much depended, would fail.

The road was now entirely deserted, and the pines of the Jura began closing in on either side of it. The cool scent of the mountains replaced the damper air of the lowland. Now and then, still far beyond and above, the church tower at Collonges came into

199

view. From thence, it was less than two leagues to the fort. Blaise knew that he must take the wolf by the ears as soon as possible. At any moment, travelers might be met on the road, and the chance of action would be lost.

The distant church tower gave him an idea. From Collonges, a road ran north to Gex; and thence, he had heard, it was possible to make one's way across the mountains to Saint-Claude and so to Nantua. For him, of course, such a route was absurd, since it meant covering three sides of a huge square, instead of one, and tripling the distance. But it might serve as a feint to draw the Duke's messenger into the open. Unless Blaise's suspicions were utterly wrong, the man would have to prevent him from taking that route; and this would mean showing his hand. Then he could be killed in honorable fight, not murdered. And, from the look of him, Blaise judged that the fight would be even enough.

"How about it?" the other repeated, staring at Blaise's long silence.

"You tempt me, Monsieur le Savoyard, but unfortunately it can't be. I'm on the King's business and must get forward. However, your presentiments and mine shouldn't be overlooked either. It's clear that I'm in certain danger if I take the road through the pass. On the other hand, the same wouldn't hold for another route. So, I'll part company with you at Collonges and ride to Gex."

"Are you mad?"

"How so?"

"Why, man, it would take you two days to Nantua if not three —"

"Better late than never."

"There's only a goat track over the Col de la Faucille. You'd butcher your horse."

Blaise shook his head. "We'll have to chance it. No, sir, my mind's made up. I never go against intuition, and yours added to mine is proof positive. By the Saints of Rome, I'm grateful to you. A stroke of luck that we met."

The other's suppressed merriment was gone. His face looked heavier, harder and blank. A dark shiftiness crept into his eyes, as he glanced sidewards at Blaise.

"Let me persuade you," he growled.

"Impossible, mon ami. I must take the road to Gex."

"You really mean it?"

"Of course."

The man had been riding on Blaise's right; but now, as if to avoid an unevenness in the road, he dropped back and came up on the left. If Blaise had been as unsuspicious as he appeared, the maneuver would have passed without notice. However, with every faculty alert, it struck him that the change in position exposed his left side and back to the other's poniard hand.

A sixth sense, or perhaps a whisper of sound, warned him. He turned sharply in the saddle and leaned away just as the head of his companion's horse came abreast. At the same instant, the man's dagger, missing its aim, ripped Blaise's cloak at the shoulder. In another moment, a touch of the spur had put several yards between them; de Lallière's sword was out, and he wheeled to face the attacker.

"That," he said grimly, "was a mistake, beau sire. Keep your hand from your sword."

The ruffian's convulsed features looked as if he had swallowed gall. Surprise, rage, and discomfiture stopped his mouth. He sat glaring at Blaise, the luckless poniard in his hand.

Blaise went on in the same voice: "Ça, ça! I wonder how many tall fellows you've served like that. But remember the pitcher and the well, and that every day has its evensong."

The other found his tongue and the right oaths to fit it; a blast of obscenity in bull tones, the louder because of the pine trees that hedged the road. Then gradually sense mingled with profanity. He announced that Blaise was under arrest in the Duke's name; that, if he handed over his arms and went quietly to the Fort de l'Écluse, he, Simon de Montjou, would have mercy on him; but, if not, by God's flesh, he would open his entrails to the flies and leave him to rot in the woods. For such were the Duke's orders. By God's nails, Simon de Montjou had never yet failed in a job, as a good many dead people could testify, if they could talk. What a rotten fig did he give for a namby-pamby French bougre —

"Keep your hand from your sword," Blaise repeated.

"Tes malles bosses!" snarled de Montjou, spurring in.

He dodged Blaise's stroke and took it, glancing, on the upper part of his arm, at the same time thrusting with his poniard. But the movement of their horses carried them past each other. Tossing the knife away, de Montjou plucked out his sword, wheeled and charged again. Blaise parried the blow, whipped his blade down to the other's head, drew blood. The horses carried them apart. They circled, closed. De Montjou made a feint in quarte, delivered his stroke, with a "ha!", in sixte, but met Blaise's steel and, slightly off balance, kept his saddle with an effort. De Lallière's sword flicked, once more drew blood. And the horses carried them apart.

Half blinded by his scalp wounds, the amazed ruffler suddenly realized that he was beaten. A champion in the small army of Savoy, he had never before measured himself against a French man-at-arms. His favorite strokes, the brawn and ferocity which had won him an easy reputation among the Duke's followers, gained him nothing in this fight. When they closed again, he hardly recognized de Lallière's face as the one he had been looking at for the past hour. It was grim as flint — the lips rigid and hooked down, the wide cheekbones prominent as knuckles of a clenched fist, eyes hot but colorless — the face of a fighter happy in his art and, to Simon de Montjou gripped by panic, the face of death.

He would have turned and fled, if he had dared expose his back to Blaise's sword, which now hovered and dazzled, this way and that, above his weakening guard. He tried to rein back, but the other followed pace for pace. A final moulinet swept past his defense. He cried out as the blade sheared down into his brain, then he plunged heavily to the road.

Chapter 30

It was now suddenly very silent in the woods, a silence made more distinct, rather than lessened, by the murmur of the Rhône in its gorge at some distance below the road to the left. Blaise sat for a moment staring down at the motionless body huddled beneath him. His nerveless grip still held the stained sword, hanging limply along his horse's flank.

Then, rousing himself to the need for haste, he wiped off and sheathed his sword, glanced along the road to make sure that it was still vacant, got out of the saddle, and, having caught de Montjou's horse, tethered it with his own. Next, on pins and needles for fear that his luck had run out and that some traveler would appear on the road, he dragged the dead body into the nearby trees and emptied de Montjou's wallet.

Here it was, the oblong paper, bearing the ducal seal and addressed to Captain François de Soliers, Seigneur de Monasterol, at the Fort de l'Écluse. Opening it, he found what he had expected. Beginning with the receipt of the letter, and for the next three days, Captain de Soliers was to detain all Frenchmen proceeding through the pass from Geneva or other eastern points. He was to challenge their papers and make a pretense of referring these to the ducal chancellor. This did not apply to well-known officers of the King, such as Monsieur de Montmorency, Monsieur de Vaulx, and the like, who were to pass unmolested. . . . And Duke Charles of Savoy had every confidence in Captain de Soliers's management and discretion.

Reflecting that the Marquis, and, no doubt, His Majesty, would be interested in the letter, Blaise transferred it to his own wallet. If he had had any doubt as to the righteousness of killing de Montjou, this treachery, on the part of a prince closely related to the French King, would have removed it. The servant had paid the score of his master. Now there would be no message received at the fort; the pass would remain open; and, by the time Duke Charles learned of his failure, it would be beyond mending.

Or so Blaise hoped. A good deal depended on the next few minutes. He must dispose of de Montjou's body before some traveler or travelers passed along the road, caught sight of the tethered horses, the trampled and bloody dust, and investigated. In that case, the fat would be in the fire, and the whole action once more in doubt.

At this point in the woods, the slope ran sharply down to a ravine some fifty paces below. What with the denseness of the pine saplings, it was an ideal spot for concealing a body. Once hidden in that covert, the late bravo of the Duke would probably remain undiscovered for the time being; and, if the hue and cry was raised a couple of days later, pursuit would be impossible.

But it was hard work tugging and shoving the man's bulk down through the undergrowth; and five minutes passed before Blaise, hot and panting, had safely bestowed the body under a covering of thicket. Then he struggled back uphill, thanking the saints for his amazing luck. Within another minute, he would be on the road again. De Montjou's horse must come with him, since he dared not leave such telltale evidence behind. He must also dispose of the empty saddle and appear to be leading a spare mount, a procedure often adopted by travelers on long journeys.

As to the garrison at the Fort de l'Écluse, he now expected no trouble. They had usually nothing to do with travelers through the pass, but remained in their quarters a hundred yards above the road. Since the Duke's message had not arrived, they would have no suspicions of Blaise nor be concerned to stop him. In case some loungers recognized de Montjou's horse, that could be —

"Hola!" The sudden voice sent Blaise's heart into his throat, then down to his boots. His plans faded out.

"Hola! What's afoot here?"

Looking up the slope through the tangle of pine branches, Blaise could see the head of a horseman, who was peering down from the edge of the road. Was he alone or one of a party? Everything hinged on that. Blaise could deal with one man, but several meant checkmate.

"No answer, eh?"

"Why not?" called Blaise, pushing on up as quickly as possible. "Can't a man relieve himself in the bushes without being challenged for it?"

He was closing up, but the other backed away.

"Keep your distance. I'm not so blind that I can't see what's in front of me. There's been a fight here. Where's the body?"

"Nonsense!"

If Blaise could only reach that bridle rein!

"Nonsense, is it? Par le jour Dieu! The devil has dropped me a word about you, my fine bandit. No, you don't!"

The man, now half across the road, jerked his horse around on the point of flight. "The people at the fort will be glad to hear of you. It's their business after all."

"Wait!" shouted Blaise. "If you want ten gold crowns, you can have them."

"And my throat cut, for good measure. No, thank you!"

But the rider hesitated. Blaise took a step or two towards him, calculating a sudden leap. The man drew further away. It was hopeless.

"Wait a moment."

To Blaise's astonishment, the other suddenly wheeled towards him. "Monsieur de Lallière!"

"Que diable!" Blaise looked intently at the man for the first time. His face was vaguely familiar.

"Don't you know me, sir? Denis Le Breton, in His Majesty's courier service? I had the honor of seeing you last night."

204

"Que diable!" Blaise repeated. He felt almost dizzy with relief. Of course he had known that the courier would be early on the road to Lyons with de Surcy's message to the King; but he had had no more than a glimpse of him in the candlelight yesterday evening. "Let me tell you, Sire Denis, that you're the best friend I have in the world at this moment. You're worth more to me than a thousand crowns."

"But what — "

"Mon ami, I'll tell you *what* as we ride. There's no time now. Lend me a hand with that horse. We must get him unsaddled and away from here before someone else happens along. Bon gré Saint George! Quick!"

A minute later, the dust from three galloping horses volleyed up between the pines. Ten minutes later, they traversed Collonges at a sharp trot, then galloped again to Chevrier, the junction point of the road from Saint-Julien. Blaise's delay at the Geneva gate and his fight with de Montjou had cost him valuable time. He did not know how fast the Russells would ride.

In point of fact, it was a near thing. For, looking down the road from Chevrier in the direction of Saint-Julien, Blaise could see horsemen approaching at some distance off, who, he had every reason to believe, were the Russells, accompanied by the Emperor's agents, Château and Loquingham. That he was right in this surmise became even more probable soon afterwards, when, looking back again from a higher point of ground, he noticed a solitary rider about a half-league behind the others and could not doubt that this was Pierre de la Barre.

To lengthen so short a lead, Blaise, with Le Breton, now spurred on up the road to the pass, a ledge between cliffs, on one side, and the gorge of the Rhône, three hundred feet deep, on the other. In spite of confidence that he now had nothing to fear from the garrison of the nearby fort, Blaise's heart beat faster at the sight of soldiers in the defile. But these were only loiterers off duty. A couple of them remembered Le Breton, who had come through yesterday, and waved him a greeting. "Good luck, courier! A kiss to the ladies in Lyons!" Blaise drew a long breath, as he slowed down in the village of Longeret beyond the pass. Unless the Duke of Savoy had another unforeseen trump to play, he was out of the game.

By this time, between bursts of speed, Le Breton had heard

enough about the affair with Montjou and the hide-and-seek with the Russells to content his curiosity, though Blaise told him nothing of the wider plot involving Bourbon. To the simple-minded courier, the doings of great princes were as unaccountable as the weather. The lightning struck as it pleased, and so did a Duke of Savoy or a King of France. A humble man was lucky if the bolt did not strike him, and vague oaths were the only possible comment.

"Monsieur," he remarked, as they toiled up the long, winding ascent that led over the Crédo, "I imagine that you'd find any place on earth healthier than Savoy for a long while to come."

"Yes," nodded Blaise. "So let's get over this cursed mountain as fast as possible. I renounce life if I ever want to see a mountain again."

He reflected that Sir John Russell might possibly stop at the pass long enough to learn that no orders regarding French travelers had been received from the Duke. If the Englishman suspected that Blaise might be on the road and heard that someone resembling him had crossed the Écluse a half hour earlier, he would be put on his guard and would press ahead faster than ever. It was essential, then, that Blaise should keep well in advance of him and out of sight.

Up to the top of the Crédo, at last, and to the great wooden cross which marked the summit. Blaise and the courier stopped long enough to take off their caps to it and mutter a Pater and an Ave. Then, with only a shuddering glance at the dreadful panorama of the mountains, they hurried on and down, not even pausing for a cup at the Capuchin monastery nearby, where the poor brothers were taking their Purgatory on earth by living in such a desolate place. And so, at length, following the loops of the road, they could see Châtillon beneath them. The Jura was past. From here on, the riding would be easier.

It was now midafternoon, and they had been in the saddle since early dawn. Blaise reckoned that their efforts had gained possibly a two-hour advance over the larger and, hence, slower party behind. He had, thus, a safe hour for rest before pushing on to Nantua.

Avoiding the more commodious inn by the side of the road, where he and Anne had recently put up and where the Russells would be sure to stop, he and Le Breton dismounted at a smaller hostelry on a side street of the village.

"And what," asked the courier, as they were eating bread and

206

cheese in the taproom, "if these people behind us decide to stop in Châtillon, while you wait for them in Nantua?"

"Then Monsieur de la Barre will bring me word of it."

"He knows where to find you?"

"Yes, at the *Écu d'Or*. It's the same sort of inn as this. We're sleeping there tonight."

Le Breton shook his head. "No, monsieur, you're not *sleeping* there. It's the worst flea-bitten tavern on the road from Lyons. And fleas, alas, are not all of it. No one sleeps at the *Écu d'Or;* one merely hopes for dawn."

There was a consolation in the thought of these lodgings. If they were as bad as that, Blaise could be certain that the Russells would not turn in there.

The five leagues to Nantua were covered in the next two hours. As Blaise rode through the narrow, arcaded streets of the small town, he thanked God that the first stage of the venture had ended according to plan, when it might so easily have miscarried. It was a good omen for the future. And, being in this grateful mood, he drew up before a shrine of the Virgin, set into the corner of a house at one of the cross streets, doffed his cap, and paid his respects. Le Breton, similarly moved by the thought that he had narrowly missed cooling his heels in the Fort de l'Écluse, showed equal devotion. There remained now only to unsaddle at the inn and await the arrival of Pierre de la Barre.

Spent from the efforts of the day and an almost sleepless night preceding it, Blaise turned from the shrine, at the same moment drawing aside for a couple of approaching horsemen.

"And now, mon ami — "

The words froze on his lips. He stiffened in his saddle.

One of the black-bearded horsemen, who passed them at that instant, was his brother, Guy de Lallière.

Chapter 31

There was no mistaking the proud, saturnine face, the hot, intolerant eyes, nor — when Blaise, after the first moment of shock, turned his head to look after him — the lance-straight erectness of his brother's back. The other horseman had the air of a mounted attendant. And yet, in spite of certainty, Blaise could almost believe that he had been mistaken. However much Guy might condemn him and approve the paternal sentence which had cut him off from the family, it was almost inconceivable that he should have ridden by without, at least, a twitch of recognition. They had been within two yards of each other; Blaise and the courier, with their three horses, stood out like a church front; but not the faintest expression revealed that Guy had seen them. He had gone by like a man in a trance.

Perhaps that was it. Perhaps he had been so absorbed in his own thoughts and so far from expecting Blaise in such an unlikely place, that he had failed to notice him. On the other hand, it was equally possible that Guy, on a secret mission for the Duke of Bourbon, did not want to be recognized and had hoped to slip by unobserved.

Blaise could not tell. In any case, it was certain that his brother was in Nantua to meet the Russells. When they arrived, they would tell him what had happened in Geneva. If he had been aware of Blaise on the street, he would draw the proper conclusions and do what he could to evade pursuit during the ride into France. It would vastly increase Blaise's difficulties. But the chief hope was that he had absent-mindedly failed to notice the dust-covered horseman in front of the shrine. In that event, the casual encounter had changed nothing.

Torn between hope and doubt, Blaise rode on to the *Écu d'Or* with much less satisfaction than he had felt a few minutes earlier. He realized that more than the ambushed insects at the inn would keep him awake that night. Fortunately he would have the company of Pierre de la Barre. It might be necessary to revamp their plans.

The hostelry in the shabbiest part of the town fully confirmed Le Breton's opinion of it. But since, in spite of its name, a gold piece seldom changed hands there, Blaise secured the best lodging to be had, a dirty and drafty but private room, where he ordered supper for Le Breton and himself.

When they had eaten, he bade farewell to the courier, who had other sleeping quarters and was hurrying on to Lyons at dawn. It had been agreed that Le Breton should take Blaise's horse with him, leaving the Duke of Savoy's more powerful mount for tomorrow's effort.

"And here," said Blaise, "are ten livres to pay for the stabling until I arrive."

"That's more than ten times enough, monsieur."

"But not enough to express my thanks."

The man's eyes sparkled. "May God and His saints give Monsieur success! Is there any other way I can be of service?"

"Yes. Commend me to the King when you deliver my lord Marquis's letter. You might tell him what happened on the road today. . . . And a safe journey to you!"

After the courier had gone, there was nothing for Blaise to do but wait for Pierre de la Barre and grind over the same corn in the same mill. Had Guy recognized him or not; and, if so, what then?

Day faded into dusk. A rat scuttled across the floor. Blaise lighted a candle and sat staring at the flame.

Last night, at this time, he had been with Anne and Dame Richardet in the pleasant reception room of the Syndic's house. Turning back the clock, he was perhaps, at that moment, asking Anne to sing him the ballad of Thomas Rymer. The tune of it sprang up again in his mind. None of the events which had crowded the last twenty-four hours had happened. She had not called him a spy or declared him an enemy. They were on the same footing as at Audin's cottage or at the bridge across the Arve. He could still believe that she cared for him. Now —

But what could one do against the stars? He and Anne were born to be on contrary sides: France against England, Valois against Bourbon. He thought wistfully of Erasmus's dream, a world free of petty contentions that made puppets out of men. Vision of the millennium — a long way off.

The stars decreed that Anne should marry Jean de Norville. Blaise's lips curled to an oath. He had known unscrupulous, scheming men but none so cold as Bourbon's handsome agent. Calculation, getting on in the world. The coldness of cold money, cold preferment. How would Anne, warm and generous as she was, endure that cold? But, as the Marquis had said, women were married; they did not marry.

Glancing at the window, he found that it was night outside. Had anything happened to Pierre? Surely by this time, the Russells had arrived in Nantua.

It was well after dark when a rattle of hoofs in the courtyard set him listening, and he sprang to his feet at the sound of Pierre's voice. Throwing open the casement, he leaned out with a *hola*.

"C'est bien vous, monsieur?" came the answer. "Wait till I've stabled this nag, for, my faith, he's had enough. Cocorico, mon vieux, stay where you are till I lift you down. Don't wriggle. Te voilà!"

Blaise waited impatiently until a firm stride and a scurry of paws in the hallway announced Pierre and Cocorico. When they reached the door, he was on the threshold.

"What sort of a ride?"

"So-so." Pierre broke off to make way for a serving-boy with his saddlebags and to order supper. Then, while unbuckling his sword belt and putting off his cloak, he added. "Not bad, but tricky. And, dea, I'll say that that English girl's the match of any trooper in the King's companies. Hour in, hour out, in the saddle. By the mass, what a rider!" Pierre waved his hand in admiration. "I salute her."

Blaise put in, "So, I take it, the Russells got to Nantua?"

"Safe and sound at the *Lion d'Argent,* together with a couple of gentlemen — I suppose they're the Imperials you told me of, Messieurs Château and Loquingham — and three mounted servants. I envy 'em the inn." Pierre turned a quizzical glance around the shabby room. "They'll get a night's rest at least."

"But the ride?" Blaise urged. "You said it was tricky. And that means what?"

"It means, monsieur, that, except for Cocorico, I should have been in a pickle. He brought me through and deserves the credit. According to plan, I kept well behind these foreigners — a league, sometimes two leagues. But they're no fools. They dropped back a rearguard and ambushed me before we had gone an hour from Geneva."

"Ambushed you?"

"At a side road. I came along, thinking nothing, when out rides a hard-looking gallant — it might be this Captain Loquingham, for he carried himself like a captain — and another fellow with him. 'Where away?' they said, barring the road. 'And who are you?' But I noticed that, seeing Cocorico regarding them from his pouch, they were puzzled. Thinking fast, I said: 'Messieurs, to my father's house near Châtillon. And I am Georges de Bonvillars, at your service.' For it was the one Savoy name I could remember on the spur of the moment. 'Verdammt!' said Loquingham, who seems to be German. 'Here's a stout man-at-arms to be scared of! With a lap dog! By God, I bet he has a doll, too, in his saddlebags. Alas for manhood in the world! Why do we waste time?' And they rode, like the devil, to catch up with the others. After that, I had no more trouble. . . . How about you, monsieur?"

210

"I'll tell you," said Blaise.

Breaking off only when the servant brought in Pierre's supper, he described the day's events, ending with Guy de Lallière's appearance.

De la Barre was chiefly impressed by the fight. His eyes smoldered. He forgot to eat. "Talk about luck!" he grumbled. "Talk about luck! I jog along all day, like a carrier, while you have excitement, a duel, something to remember."

"Cheer up!" said Blaise. "You'll have your share of excitement before this is over. What's to do now, with Monsieur Guy in Nantua, when we didn't expect him until Bourg-en-Bresse? If he recognized me, the whole party will know our game. Besides, with him here, they may not go on to Bourg but turn south and ride for Villefranche or Trévoux. If we could only guess where they plan to cross the Saône!" Blaise straightened up in his chair. "They might slip away tonight."

"No," Pierre objected, "horses can stand so much and no more. Theirs are as fagged as ours. They'll not stir tonight."

He sat absently feeding Cocorico with bits from the table. Blaise poured himself a cup of wine but forgot to drink it.

"We can only do our best," he said finally. "The trouble is that, from here, Brother Guy has a choice of roads, while from Bourg there was practically no choice but one. So we have this to do. We must watch the *Lion d'Argent* inn from two hours after midnight on: one of us afoot, not too far from the inn gate, the other with the horses in the nearest lane. These gentlemen will take either the road south toward Trévoux or the one north to Bourg. When we know which, we'll follow as best we can. Once across the Saône, and we can see what way they're heading, I'll keep behind them, while you bring along the King's men-at-arms from the nearest place." Blaise smiled. "I hope you'll find them. There're a good many *hopes* in all this."

His glance fell on Cocorico, who had jumped up on Pierre's knees. "By the way, you can send the dog to Lyons by the courier, Le Breton."

Pierre looked offended. "Send him to Lyons? What for?"

"Why, on the ride we're taking, you can't be bothered with a dog."

"Bothered? Didn't I just tell you how he served us today? Ah, Cocorico, there's gratitude!" The little dog rolled melancholy eyes

211

at his master and seemed to shake his head. "But courage, mon ami! We'll stick together."

"You wouldn't be such a fool," Blaise insisted. "This isn't a pleasure jaunt."

"Where I go, he goes. We're comrades in arms."

"And a brave sight, when you come riding up to His Majesty's lances with that dog's ears flopping! They'll laugh too hard to listen to you."

"Laugh, monsieur?"

"But of course."

Pierre brightened. "Then we shall see what we shall see."

"I don't understand."

"Sacristi, what happens when a gentleman has the honor of wearing his lady's token, and some jackanapes laughs at him? Why, he proposes a different kind of amusement, that's all."

It would be the devil, Blaise reflected, if this hothead fell to quarreling with the men-at-arms he had been sent to call in. But he reflected, too, that Pierre had a manner which did not encourage jokes at his expense.

"You're under my orders in all that affects the King's service," he warned.

Pierre's back was very straight. "I am, sir. But, for a small matter, you would not order me to break a vow or rob me" — his brown hand covered Cocorico's head — "of my chiefest prize. I beg of you."

Blaise knew enough about human nature to yield on trifles. He smiled. "Well, have it your way. So, Cocorico's the equivalent of Renée's garter, is he? It's a pity you can't wear him on your helmet."

Pierre flushed, not because of the teasing, but because Renée's name had come up between them. According to the odd reticences which govern in such matters, an older brother does not discuss his very young sister with a boy who has fallen in love with her, and the boy involved is equally reserved. There had been some chaffing when Pierre returned from France with Cocorico; but, to Blaise, it was only another of his friend's gallantries, harmless this time because so dreamy and high-flown. Cocorico was the living symbol of it. Cock-a-doodle!

"It looks serious," Blaise added.

"Monsieur, how did you guess?"

"By God, I wonder. Perhaps Cocorico told me."

Suddenly the secret came out. Pierre studied his finger tips. "Yes, I intend to seek the hand of Mademoiselle, if she will have me."

"What!" This was serious indeed. "Have you spoken to your father or mine?"

"No, monsieur."

"Alas!" The word expressed all the barriers ahead.

"I know," Pierre nodded. "But however long I may have to wait — " He left the sentence unfinished.

"Mark you," said Blaise, "I'll not have my sister trifled with."

"Trifled with! Holy saints — "

"Yes, haven't you had a dozen girls?"

Pierre looked puzzled. "I've had affairs, bonnes fortunes — what you please. But this" — he gave a deep sigh — "is love. If you had ever been in love, you would know the difference. *Trifled with!* Monsieur, I carry your sister's honor on the point of my sword. If you were not her brother. . . ."

Yes, Pierre had been hard hit. No one could doubt his earnestness. Blaise found himself thinking of Anne Russell again. He envied Pierre. Whatever the difficulties in the latter's case, there was a faint possibility that they could be surmounted.

"I beg pardon," he said.

Pierre leaned toward him. "The point is — do *you* consent, monsieur?"

"What has my consent to do with it? You heard what my father said to me at Lallière."

"No matter. Do you consent? Will you promise to back me?"

"Mon pauvre . . ." Touched and amused by the earnest voice Blaise thrust his hand across the table to grip Pierre's. "Of course, I'll do what I can."

The young man was silent a moment. Then he burst out, "I thank you. I can't tell you how much I thank you!"

Blaise shook his head. He had done nothing to deserve such gratitude.

But Pierre insisted: "It means everything. Don't you see? If we bring off this venture, you'll be in favor with the King. You'll be the one man of your family whose word counts. You'll speak to him about us. He'll arrange matters."

"It's possible."

"Parbleu, it's certain." Pierre's confidence soared.

"I hope so," nodded Blaise. Drugged with fatigue, he struggled vainly against a yawn. "Pierre, my friend, we have four hours for sleep." He glanced at the sinister-looking bed and added: "If possible. Well, there's one good thing. I'm sure we'll wake up in time."

Chapter 32

At two hours after midnight, leaving Pierre to bring the horses along to a side street not far from the *Lion d'Argent,* Blaise groped his way through the practically unlighted town to the Russells' inn. Its courtyard opened on a small square lined with houses and containing a public well together with several linden trees. Behind one of the latter, Blaise took up his watch, a lonesome affair, as time passed, though at first it was pleasant to be in the open again and free from his infested bed at the *Écu d'Or.*

Except for a dim lantern, which marked the courtyard entrance of the hostelry, not a light showed in the inn nor in the surrounding houses. The sky, too, was equally dark. As de Montjou had foretold yesterday, the recent good weather seemed to be breaking up. This, Blaise reflected, would not help the roads, which were apt to turn into quagmires when it rained. Thinking disjointedly of this or that, he leaned against the tree, while time stood still. After an eternity, a drowsy watchman, passing in front of the inn, called the hour of three. Another eternity followed. In all likelihood, Blaise would have to wait until dawn, which, at that season, meant five o'clock. Then, with the light coming on, he would have to move further off from the inn.

Perhaps he was waiting in vain. Perhaps his quarry, in spite of tired horses, had left Nantua, was already on the road. . . .

Suddenly a light flared in one of the tavern windows, then another. He watched tensely as dim figures moved behind the casements of the upper rooms. A stir sounded from the inn, the kind of stir made by a group of people on the point of departure. There were sounds, too, from the kitchen and finally from the courtyard, where horses were being led out.

Blaise drew the hood of his riding cloak over his head and moved behind the trunk of the linden. Muffled up as he was, and in the still

complete darkness, he could not be seen from the inn, but he took
no risks. Time crawled by.

Then, at long last, the courtyard gate opened, and the Russells'
entire party rode through. To Blaise's encouragement, there was no
sign of haste or furtiveness, as might have been expected if his
brother had recognized him yesterday. Indeed, a couple of stablemen carried torches to light the way for the riders. Dimly, in the
flare of these, Blaise could make out Guy's erect figure and bearded
face, Anne's headdress, and Sir John Russell's plain merchant
clothes. He judged that the broad-shouldered horseman behind them
was the German, Loquingham, and that another was de Croy's secretary, Château. There were four mounted lackeys — in all, nine
riders.

But what happened now bewildered him. They were bidding farewell to each other. Sir John Russell leaned outwards in his saddle
to embrace Anne; Guy bowed to her; the men exchanged good
wishes. And before Blaise could adjust himself to this new development, Guy and Sir John, with a final good-by to the others, turned
right from the inn and continued on down the street which led to
the southern road. A moment later, the seven others turned in the
opposite direction of Bourg-en-Bresse.

Blaise stood nonplused. Neither he nor the Marquis de Vaulx had
foreseen this complication. But there was no question as to how
it should be met. Guy de Lallière had been sent to guide Sir John
Russell to Bourbon; he alone knew the Duke's whereabouts. Sir
John, moreover, was the important member of the party, while
Château and Loquingham were clearly subordinate. Doubtless the
conclusion had been reached, that, with time running short and his
mission discovered, Russell should make a dash for it into France.
He, and no one else, was the one to follow.

A few minutes later, Blaise rejoined Pierre de la Barre in the appointed lane.

"Eh bien?" greeted the latter. "We're on our way?"

"Yes," said Blaise, one foot in the stirrup, "and the scent's hot.
But not to Bourg-en-Bresse. We're riding south."

During the last hour of the night, Blaise and Pierre could do
little but follow the road toward Cerdon. This they did slowly and
cautiously. But, when dawn was breaking, they met a carrier, who

had just crossed the mountain ridge separating Cerdon from Nantua and who reported passing two horsemen not long since.

"Yes, one of them had a beard black as the King of Spades. I could see that much, though the light was poor."

By now, the two young men had skirted the mile-long Lake of Nantua and had crossed the level stretch beyond to the foot of the intervening ridge. If the carrier, as he stated, had met the two riders only a half hour since, it reassured Blaise that the slow start had not been too costly. It seemed that Guy and Sir John Russell had made very little better speed. And this was important, because Blaise dared not be too far behind them when they reached Pont d'Ain, the junction of a road which led northwest to Bourg.

At as fast a pace as the steepness of the slope allowed, they now scaled the mountain and could look down at Cerdon stretched out along a stream in the valley below.

Suddenly Pierre exclaimed, "View halloo!" and pointed at two dots beneath them in the far distance. A moment's scrutiny revealed two horsemen.

"Good eye!" Blaise nodded. "We'll have to take care not to press them too close."

At the same moment, the dots began moving more rapidly and vanished around a spur of trees. This was a fortunate glimpse, because a few minutes later the rain, which had been threatening all night, closed in, a steady downpour which reduced visibility to fifty paces.

"Good-by to fair weather!" said Blaise, pulling up the hood of his riding cloak. "We'll have foul roads across the Dombes, if our friends turn that way."

He smiled to notice that Pierre, before covering himself, drew up the leather folds at the back of Cocorico's pouch, which were contrived to form a kind of canopy, so that the little dog's eyes and nose were all that could be seen of him.

"True lover!" he teased.

But, as they rode on downhill, the thought of Pierre and Renée reminded him again, as it had last night, of himself and Anne Russell. What a relief that she was now completely out of this affair! He had not enjoyed the thought of tracking her, even if it was no further than Bourg-en-Bresse. Probably, she would now return at once to Geneva. As to Guy de Lallière and Sir John Russell he had no compunctions. If they were caught dealing with Bourbon, that

216

was their loss. They were men who had taken a chance and must pay the penalty. With Anne, it was a different matter.

On through Cerdon, with the rain sifting down and the little Veyron River loud beside them. Sir John and Guy continued on not very far ahead — so near, indeed, that Blaise once fancied he heard the sound of their horses and drew rein to give them a longer lead.

At Pont d'Ain, it was neck and neck. On the point of leaving the village, Blaise recognized his brother's black gelding, Murat, and Pierre, the big sorrel, which Sir John had ridden yesterday, tethered in front of a wayside tavern. They had all but missed encountering the riders themselves, and they turned back in a quick retreat up the road. There they waited until the sound of hoofs informed them that the two horsemen were under way again.

Soaked through and chilled by the relentless rain, Pierre grumbled: "Cré Dieu, for men who ought to be in a hurry, it strikes me that they're taking their time."

"Yes," said Blaise, "but no doubt they have a reason for it. They may plan to meet Bourbon on a set date at a certain hour — we don't know when. In that case, they might not want to arrive beforehand but simply get within easy distance. And, mark you, if the place was Chantelle or another of the Duke's castles, there would be no point in dawdling; but if it's an open, unfortified place, the luckier for us. The rain's lucky, too," he added. "We can follow them the closer."

This was especially required beyond Pont d'Ain because of the crossroads there. Guy and Russell might, after all, try to slip north to Bourg, which, at that point, was not five leagues off. Accordingly when the telltale hoofbeats started again, Blaise and Pierre kept within earshot of them. But, having crossed the bridge over the Ain and reached the intersection of the two roads, they could hear steady galloping in front, and not to the right along the Bourg highway.

"That settles it," Blaise declared. "They'll turn west at Châtillon-la-Palud and cross the Dombes. They can't do anything else unless they want to ride on to Lyons. It's a help to know we guessed right. Pierrot, I think we have them."

Chapter 33

But the rest of that day and the whole of the next were spent at a jog trot. Russell and Guy de Lallière were indeed killing time. The distance to the Saône, which could have been covered in eight hours of hard riding consumed thirty hours: a slow progress over the rain-swept, undulating plateau of the Dombes, where the road meandered forever between the countless ponds that pitted the surface of the country, and where the slippery earth meant poor footing. Since Sir John and Guy could put up at the only inns of the villages where they stopped — Chalamont and Ars — and since constant vigilance was needed to make sure that they did not slip away during the night, Blaise and Pierre found what quarters they could and kept watch in turn.

On the second night, they stabled their horses at a farmhouse between the village of Ars and the Saône, while they themselves stood guard at the edge of a nearby wood overlooking the river road. Fortunately the two days of rain left off at sunset; but, except for this, they had little comfort, the one sleeping on the ground while the other waked. They were wet, hungry, and thoroughly worn down by the wretched nights since Geneva. Their clothes were caked with mud. They needed a bath and a razor.

"Pardie," said Pierre, "we look more like a couple of brigands than gentlemen men-at-arms. I never stank so in my life. It's a blessing we have papers to show, or we'd be jailed by the first town watch."

Blaise forced a grin. "Darkness before dawn. Tomorrow's our day. I have the feeling that we'll sweep the board tomorrow."

As if to bear this out, everything smiled on the morning of that third day. It broke cloudless, though with an autumn tingle in the air. The two watchers saw their quarry pass down the road, no longer at the dilatory pace of the last two days but riding hard, with every appearance of people bent on business that required dispatch. Some minutes later, Blaise and Pierre were in the saddle galloping after them. Their horses, well fed at the farmhouse and refreshed by a long night in stall, tugged at the bit. Even Cocorico felt the excitement. With his paws on the edge of his pouch and ears flying back before the wind, he lifted his voice in the shrill bark that gave him his name.

"What did I tell you?" said Blaise. "This is our day."

It was lucky that no time had been lost. Before reaching the fork in the road, of which one prong led south to Trévoux and the other straight ahead to the Saône, they caught a far-off glimpse of the horsemen already beyond it and heading directly for the river, which marked the French frontier. Apparently they intended to take the flat-bottomed ferry across to Villefranche. It was one of the places where the King, as he declared in his letter, had posted a detachment of men-at-arms.

But when Blaise and Pierre dismounted behind a bluff overlooking the stream, in order to watch the crossing, they saw the black and the sorrel splash into the water and begin to ford. Pressed for time, as the two riders now seemed to be, they evidently did not choose to wait for the painfully slow barge, which could be seen moored on the other side. The river, shallow and gentle at this season, was dotted with little islands. Now wading, now swimming a few yards from one to the other of these, the horses were soon across. Then, instead of entering Villefranche, they turned north along the further bank toward a road that led inland.

"We're in luck," said Blaise. "I know that road like my hand. It leads to Beaujeu. But I'll wager my neck they cut west along a path through the woods and so over the hills to La Mure. In that case, they're heading for the Forez or Auvergne. It may be Chantelle, after all."

When they had forded the river in their turn, they separated, Pierre to connect with the King's horsemen, while Blaise continued the pursuit.

"Bring them along toward Beaujeu," Blaise directed. "The earth's soft from the rain: you'll notice our tracks. If my brother and Sir John turn off to the left along the path I told you of, I'll leave a tree branch hanging at that point. And the same at any other turn. But keep your eye on the hoofprints." He sat a moment, estimating possible delays and the slower speed of a company of horse. "If the men-at-arms are here, you oughtn't to be more than an hour behind me. Wherever Milord Russell and my brother stop, it's ten to one that Monseigneur de Bourbon will be there. If not, when you arrive,

219

we'll arrest these two and wait for him." He raised his gauntlet. "Bonne chance!"

Then he started in the direction of Beaujeu.

It was a great help that the surface of the highway, though too soft for speed, showed up so distinctly the tracks of the riders ahead of him. He could not tell whether or not they were aware of being followed. Certainly they had given no sign of it during the last two days. But it would be an ordinary precaution, now that they were nearing their goal, to draw off to the side of the road at some point and wait to see who came along. This, Blaise realized, was his chief danger. Being alone, he would stand little chance, if he came to grips with such trained swordsmen as his brother and Sir John Russell. Against that kind of maneuver on their part, the hoofprints of their horses, which he could see for some distance in front, offered a certain protection. But, nevertheless, he rode warily, with all his senses on the alert.

As he had expected, the tracks stopped at the forest trail, leading west toward La Mure; and, having approached it cautiously, he found that they continued along it through the woods. Then, leaving a half-severed branch to dangle at this point, he followed the same path.

From here on, the further he rode west, the more familiar the country became; a succession of forested hills, through which he had hunted as a boy. The morning passed. About midday, he reached the village of La Mure and learned that the black-bearded horseman and his companion were an hour ahead of him towards Belmont. That meant that they were now some distance to the northeast of Roanne and heading definitely towards the Bourbonnais.

He rode on, following little better than a bridle path, intent, as before, on the hoofprints in front of him. But so sure he was of the ultimate destination, that, when the end came, it found him unprepared. He had ridden a couple of hundred yards before he realized that the tracks had vanished.

Returning to pick them up, he found that they entered the woods to the right along a vague trail which had missed his attention. As he followed them again, he drew up just in time to avoid riding out into a clearing, fifty yards square, that contained a long L-shaped stone house.

At once, he recognized it: the hunting lodge of André de Chamand, a gentleman of Beaujolais and a stanch supporter of the Constable. Blaise remembered spending a night there years ago with his father on the occasion of a wolf-hunt, which had been widely attended.

He sat his horse within the covert of the woods, eagerly scanning the house. A strange, almost eerie silence brooded over it, the mid-afternoon quiet of the forest. Except for a wisp of smoke rising from one of the chimneys and the telltale hoofprints that led to the door, one might have considered it uninhabited. In the steady sunlight, crossed now and then by a dragonfly, it was like some enchanted place of legend, upon which a hunter unwittingly stumbles. The leaded windows along the front stared at Blaise like impassive eyes. His imagination helping, he felt an indefinable menace in the very stillness of the house.

So, this was the meeting place of the conspirators, and certainly none could have been more admirably chosen with respect to secrecy and remoteness. Cut off by the hills and woods from the main avenues of travel, few knew of it, and fewer still would suspect it. Perhaps, within there at that moment, the great Duke was betraying France to the envoy of England. Blaise remembered the raftered hall, with its weapons and trophies of the chase, which ran the length of the house, and he could almost picture the scene in front of one of the tall fireplaces: the haughty, commanding figure of the Constable, the rough-hewn features of Russell, papers between them, Guy de Lallière at one side.

It was something to have brought such a quarry as this into the toils. Blaise could not help savoring his triumph. The premonition that today belonged to him, that he could not fail, had been more than justified. What a stroke it was! One to be forever chronicled. And the honor was his. He imagined the King's approval, Denis de Surcy's happiness, the applause of France. Now he had only to wait until the arrival of Pierre and the men-at-arms. Now the only possibility of failure was that they should not arrive in time. But this, he told himself again, was his day.

Then, as he was about to turn back into the deeper cover of the woods, a horse neighed from the stable. And, before he could prevent it by word or spur, his own horse answered. At once the furious barking of a dog rose in the house, and the door opened.

To ride off now would be more dangerous than to remain still, for the sound of the hoofbeats would betray him. As it was, he could not be seen from the house, and he sat holding his breath.

It was only a matter of seconds. A man walked out, followed by another man, who held a dog by the collar. The second man had a full black beard, but it was not Guy de Lallière. The one in front wore the somber dress and cloth cap of a merchant, such as Russell had been wearing, but he was not the Englishman.

In the sunlight, Blaise could see their faces distinctly. A sense of mad unreality crept over him. What he saw could only be a hallucination. But he recognized the black-bearded man as his brother's attendant, who had passed him in the street at Nantua.

The somber-clad merchant was Anne Russell.

Comprehension of what had happened exploded in Blaise's mind: the devastating trick of which he had been the dupe.

He could see her gazing intently at the screen of leaves which concealed him. And at that moment, a branch snapped under his horse's hoof.

"Is it Monsieur de Lallière?" she called. "Welcome, monsieur!" The mockery of her voice made every syllable distinct. "I've been expecting you. Don't be concerned. We're alone here. Come and let me congratulate you."

Chapter 34

It is a merciful provision that the mind cannot grasp the entirety of a disaster at once. A stupefying blow is not immediately so painful as a wasp's sting. After a fashion, Blaise was aware that not only the success of his efforts, the imagined triumph of a few moments ago, but his very life had been blown to pieces, as if a mine had been set off under him. But he was still too dazed to think, much less to analyze what had happened. A witchcraft unreality clung to the silent house, the sun-drenched clearing in front of it, and to the figures on the doorstep. For half a minute, he could only sit his horse in a dull stupor.

Then Anne called again, "Do you hear me, Monsieur de Lallière?"

Mechanically responding, he rode out from the covering of the trees. At the moment, one impulse was as good as another. If he had been able to collect his thoughts, he might perhaps have chosen to escape, ride blindly off in any direction, rather than to face her mockery. As it was, he went through the conventional gestures — bowed, dismounted, tethered his horse — and then followed her into the house.

A fire burned at one end of the great room, not so much for warmth as to take off the musty dampness of the place, which had evidently been closed for some time. Blaise noticed an elderly couple, no doubt caretakers, who replenished the hearth and then went out, with the dog at their heels. Guy de Lallière's bearded servant, after closing the front door, stood grinning at one side.

"Won't you be seated?" said Anne. "You look weary, Monsieur de Lallière, no, desperate. I don't believe that the life of a foxhound agrees with you."

Still mechanically, he took the chair she indicated opposite her.

"And yet I congratulate you," she continued. "When you're once on the scent, you stick to it. I thought we might have thrown you off this morning at the Saône. But no — here you are, faithful to the last!"

She smiled, but the smile was forced. He knew that her words were meant to hurt, but they also exposed a deeper hurt of her own. The pain in her eyes betrayed her.

"You had fair warning," she went on. "I told you to look to yourself. Perhaps now you understand that it's no trifling matter to have me for an enemy. This was my plan from the beginning — yes, from that very night in Geneva. My brother and yours had nothing to do with it. I knew that you would follow us. Who else could the Marquis send? And I foresaw how you might be tricked if the Duke of Savoy failed to close the pass."

Blaise said nothing.

"So, you let yourself be gulled by a change of horses and a black beard. And let me tell you now for your satisfaction that last night, while you were wasting your time in the Dombes, my brother and the Emperor's gentlemen met Monseigneur de Bourbon at Gayete in the Bourbonnais. The alliance with England is signed, and England is on the march. You'll have to ride fast, Monsieur de Lallière, to catch up with yesterday. But take my advice and ride back to the army. Brawn, not brain, is your forte. You don't shine as the Regent's spy and the Marquis's agent."

For the first time, she was struck by his silence and broke off with the challenge, "Well, sir, you don't compliment me."

223

By now, Blaise had recovered from the first shock. He remembered the men-at-arms whom Pierre de la Barre was bringing from Belleville.

"There's no time for compliments, mademoiselle. You deserve well of your King, and I have failed mine. You have my admiration now, as always. But, for God's love, mount and ride from here at once. I think you can still win free. You haven't a minute to lose." In his urgency, he stood up.

"Why?" she asked.

He explained tensely.

She remained seated, though her face showed that this development had not been reckoned with. But the sardonic attendant against the wall lost his grin and stood nervously shifting from foot to foot.

Anne considered Blaise between half-lowered lids. "And what will *you* do, monsieur, when these gentlemen arrive?"

"I shall proceed to Lyons," he said bleakly, "for an interview with the King."

"Escorted perhaps?"

"It may be. I beg you to hurry."

He felt that it cost her an effort to smile. "It's apt to be a stormy interview. If this were England, you would lose your head."

Blaise shrugged. In view of the King's mistrust of him, expressed in the letter to de Surcy, he had no illusions about what would happen. But he did not choose to put on a poor face with her. "Mademoiselle, let me repeat that you have no time to lose. I'll help this man with the horses."

She answered coolly: "Why do you care if I escape or not? I'd suppose you'd want something to show for all your riding. If you hang, you'd have the satisfaction of my company at least."

He found it hard to keep his patience. "Milady, as I reckon it, the King's men are an hour behind me, but they may be closer. More than half of that hour is gone. Excuse me from further talk. You may think of me as you please, but the only satisfaction I ask is to see you clear of this place."

"Why?" she repeated.

"It's an idle question. Answer it yourself. But now, quick! Dépechez-vous!"

She did not stir or speak for so long, that the servant ventured, "Mademoiselle, for God's sake — "

At that she looked up. "Ma foi, Étienne, I'd forgotten you. I'm sorry. Be off at once. I hope you reach Chantelle. Present my homage to Monseigneur de Bourbon and Monsieur de Norville, if he's there. Tell them that I have been taken prisoner and that I'll be brought no doubt before the King at Lyons. Tell them that this is my own choosing because I hope to render service by it. They'll understand. And say to them that I have no fear of the King but expect that he will receive me honorably. And so, adieu and good fortune!"

In a panic of haste as the man was, he still lingered. "But Milady — "

There was no time for polite phrases. Blaise cut in, "Are you mad? Surely you don't suppose, after what has passed, that the King will receive you on the footing that you had before you left Fontainebleau? You remember what de Warthy said, and that concerned merely our ride to Geneva. Since then, you have blocked the King in this most important affair."

"We shall see, monsieur."

"What choice would he have but to deal with you as an enemy spy, even if he wished to show mercy? His captains — "

"We shall see, monsieur."

"Milady, I ask it as a grace: leave with this man. Ride for Chantelle, if you think that you will be safe there. Surely you have brought me low enough without the added distress of seeing you a prisoner."

She said coldly: "What is your distress to me? I marvel that you can still pretend. You are the man who played hypocrite with friendship in order to spy on me, who cheapened my faith in you to please your masters. Your simple-gentleman role is worn out. I shall go to the King in Lyons whether it distresses you or not."

Conscious that, from her standpoint, the bitterness was justified, he could find no answer.

She added to the servant: "What are you waiting for, Étienne? Par Dieu, begone while there's time. You have all my thanks. Your service has been beyond praise. The Duke will reward you. Now obey me and ride at once."

With a fleeting bow and mutter, the man hurried out. Turning away, Blaise walked over to the door, opened it, and stood absently on the threshold. A couple of minutes later, he saw the attendant lead his horse from the stable, throw himself into the saddle, and disappear behind the trees on the other side of the clearing. As far as Anne was concerned, the die was now cast. They had only to wait for the coming of the men-at-arms.

225

After all, why should he care what happened to her? She was an open enemy, whose dash and cleverness had just won a crippling victory against France. She had ruined not only Blaise himself but many another. He turned cold at the thought of the Marquis's disgrace; but that was nothing as compared with the havoc of the English invasion. And now obviously she expected to cajole the King and, at the same time, continue her intrigue for England. If she failed to understand how impossible this was and chose to sacrifice herself in such a forlorn hope, there was nothing he could do about it.

A vague wonder crossed his mind at Sir John Russell's heartlessness in allowing her to take these risks. It was all of a piece with her three isolated years at the court of France. It was of a piece with Russell's harshness towards her at Syndic Richardet's house. Child Waters, again. She could be used to the utmost and then discarded. The King's service, the Tudor Rose on her chain, but no love, no one who cared what happened to her. Perhaps that accounted for certain moments which Blaise recalled on their ride from Fontainebleau: the delight she seemed to take in her freedom, in the naturalness of their friendship. Although defeated, as he was, he could sense her loneliness and pity her.

Expecting at any moment to hear the approaching horsemen, he became increasingly aware of the forest stillness and of the sunlit clearing vacant in front of him. The infinite drone of insects grew louder. It might be that Pierre had not found the troopers at Villefranche, that he had followed the wrong trail, that the men-at-arms would not arrive at all. This offered a possible hope. . . .

"So, you don't care to defend yourself?" said Anne from her chair in the room behind him. They had both been silent so long that her voice startled him.

"From what, mademoiselle?" he asked, turning.

"I called you a hypocrite and spy. Do you accept those titles?"

It seemed futile to discuss words with her, but, after a moment's thought, he answered: "Hypocrite, in a measure, yes; spy, no."

"The first is shabbier than the last." But her tone had lost something of its edge and implied a question.

He said: "If you have grown to hate me, no defense will serve. You, who are so loyal to your King, should be the first to understand my position with you when we met. I did not lie, but I could not tell you the exact truth, either. I wonder if it was not the same with you. And yet so far — and that far only — I was a hypocrite."

226

"That far only?" she repeated.

"On my honor, yes."

He crossed the room and stood near her, looking down. For the first time, their eyes met steadily.

"Mademoiselle, on that last evening of our ride — you remember, before we crossed the Arve — when I wanted to tell you how much — " He paused with a vague gesture. "Well, you asked me to add nothing, to be content to look back, meaning, of course, that there was no future for us — you in the English service and betrothed to Jean de Norville, I in the opposite camp. You remember?"

She nodded slowly.

"And you were right. But now, when there is, indeed, no future for me, it will hurt nothing if I say what I wanted to say then: how much I love you. Certainly you cannot think me a hypocrite in that, for what would hypocrisy gain? A man at the end of life may be allowed to speak the truth. And, loving you, do you imagine me such a Judas that I would betray you to pleasure my masters, as you put it? I did not, nor did the Marquis de Vaulx demand that I should. Or perhaps you condemn me because I would have captured your brother if that had been possible?"

"No, you would have been a traitor otherwise. I am not so unjust." She looked down. Her hands, grasping the arms of the chair, whitened. "But you are still a hypocrite."

"In what way?"

"How can you speak of love to me? No enemy could have served you worse than I. Are you acting the saint? Is that it? Preparing for the next world?"

It was an odd mockery, different from the first and with puzzling undertones. Her lips had softened. He thought casually of that time in the barley field after his fall, when it had been easier to express himself to her in the form of a joke than to attempt the inexpressible. He wondered if she would catch the reference.

"No, mademoiselle, I'm only an incurable romantic."

"Indeed?" But she smiled and he could see that she remembered. "Well, I'm no longer romantic. I've grown harder since those days, more practical. Don't expect me to respond and confess love for you, though I'm glad you're no Judas. Love's a silly thing; it has no place in state affairs. I've been roundly schooled since we met last."

She had turned sharp again, but he could feel that it was not with

227

regard to him. He recalled Sir John Russell's crushing grip on her shoulder that night in Geneva and could guess what school she meant.

"I'm sorry for that," he said, keeping to a light tone, "but having few affairs myself to look forward to from now on, I'll cling to folly. So, let me urge you again, for your own sake, to ride for Chantelle. It may be that the King's lances are delayed. They may not even come. If you'll favor me in this, I'll see you to safety and then go on to Lyons."

She gave a short laugh. "For my own sake! Bon Dieu! No, monsieur, in any case, I'll remain your prisoner. I have business in Lyons. Some of it may even concern you." Her face wore the enigmatic look he so well remembered.

"Me?"

"Yes, how else would the King know the truth about you except from me? His Majesty will grant me some favor. Don't disdain my help."

She got up and, walking over to her saddlebags, drew out a carefully folded long mantle, which she exchanged for the merchant's tunic that she had been wearing. A rearrangement of her coif and cap gave another feminine touch.

"So," she concluded, smoothing out the ribbons of her mask, "you needn't be ashamed for your prisoner."

Returning to the doorway, Blaise caught a distant stir and rattle in the forest. He and Anne stood side by side, listening.

"Monsieur," she said hurriedly — and he was struck by the change in her voice — "why didn't you lie to me that night at the Syndic's house and give me your word of honor and break it like a clever man? If you had, you'd be a success, at this moment, and famous. As it is, you're a failure and traitor. You even worsen your case by consideration for me. Why are you such a fool?"

The raillery sent a glow along his veins.

"And yet," she went on, "you've failed rather gloriously. A fool but a gentleman. Whatever happens to you or me, please remember that I said this."

There were horsemen behind the thicket on the other side of the clearing. A vague movement sounded between the trees. Then came a sudden hail, and several riders emerged followed by others.

But the one in front was not Pierre de la Barre. It was a very notable person, indeed. Any veteran soldier in Western Europe would have recognized the Great Marshal, Jacques de Chabannes, lord of La Palisse.

"What's up?" he demanded, reining in before the door. "Where are Monseigneur de Bourbon and this Englishman you were supposed to be following? Who's this?" He paused, with a glance at Anne, who had not yet put on her mask, and his face lightened with a smile of recognition. "Ha, Milady Russell," he bowed. "I take it your brother's here." And to Blaise again, "Where are these gentlemen?"

"There's been a mistake, monseigneur. I followed the wrong track."

Fixed by the Marshal's stare, Blaise was nonetheless conscious of the disappointment and anger that went the round of the horsemen, who now filled the clearing. They had ridden for hours in confident hope of the great reward which the King had offered for Bourbon's capture.

"Mistake?" rumbled La Palisse. "Well, your explanations had better be adequate to it." He dismounted and walked to the door. "I'll hear them now."

When he had listened to Anne's account, together with the statements of Blaise and Pierre, the Marshal's blue eyes were cold, but he said courteously:

"Dea, Milady, if I were young, I should be your suitor. I can recall no woman more fitted to be a soldier's wife. You have shown great hardihood and management in this business — to our loss but to your credit. However, as you know, by the custom of war, your life is forfeit. You are a spy, taken in the act. The King may show mercy; but you must be brought to Lyons to await his pleasure. All my regrets."

"I had expected as much," she said.

"Yes, and that expectation proves your mettle. My homage."

Then, turning to Blaise, he used a different tone. "As for you, Monsieur de Lallière, consider yourself under arrest. You can keep your sword, if you give me your parole. I hope you may keep your life. For I tell you plain that His Majesty will not easily pardon your bungling. You were charged with an important mission and have failed so wretchedly that your failure amounts to treason."

"But surely, sir, you don't think — "

La Palisse raised his hand. "What I think has nothing to do with it.

I'm pointing out facts. Par Dieu, you didn't even prevent the escape of your brother's servant and this lady's accomplice. It was your luck that I happened to be in Villefranche this morning and so came along in order to give my lord of Bourbon fitting escort. Otherwise, it might have cost you your neck with these gentlemen, whom you have led on such a wild goose chase."

He closed the subject with a glance toward Pierre, who stood stricken next to Blaise. "Monsieur de la Barre, as this gentleman's archer, you had no responsibility except to obey his orders, which you have done. I see no reason for holding you, though doubtless the King will wish to hear your testimony before sentencing Monsieur de Lallière."

Getting up, he strode over to the door and summoned a lieutenant to whom he gave precise instructions.

"Monsieur de Noyret, you and a guard of ten men, including Monsieur de la Barre, will conduct this lady and Blaise de Lallière as prisoners to Lyons. You will carry a letter from me to His Majesty. During the journey, the prisoners are on no account to communicate with each other. They are both to be kept under strict watch. It concerns your neck to bring them safely to the King."

He did not add — but something in his tone and manner brought the words to Blaise's mind — "And God have mercy on their souls!"

PART THREE

Chapter 35

In those days, rumors were thick as horseflies around the city of Lyons. In the encampments of troops destined for the Italian campaign; along the quais of the Saône, which divided the ancient town from its more recent extension; in shops, residences, inns and chapter houses, reports, true and false and of every kind, outmatched each other. But, as might be expected, the greatest buzz of rumor centered in the fortified cloister of Saint-Just on its height above the old town, where the King and his suite had temporary lodgings.

There was a great deal to talk about and to fear. Veteran courtiers declared that they had never seen the King in so black a rage as at the news of the Duke of Bourbon's successful meeting with Sir John Russell and the imperial agents at Gayete, a meeting which might easily have resulted in the arrest of them all and the end of the conspiracy, had it not been for Blaise de Lallière's treasonable failure and the Marquis de Vaulx's obstinacy in appointing him to such an important mission. That the King had not hanged said de Lallière out of hand; that, for more than a week, he had even put off examining him and the English milady personally, was hard to account for. The most apparent explanation of this was the rush of events so urgent that they gave no time for lesser matters.

The Gayete meeting seemed to have touched off a train of dangers, each worse than the last. Almost at once the word passed that Charles of Bourbon had given up the plan of holding his fortresses against the King and was seeking escape from France. This, if it succeeded, would be a master stroke. It would unite him with his allies, give them the benefit of his brilliant leadership, and, at the same time, put him beyond the reach of capture, to remain a spearhead of invasion and a sovereign party in some future dismemberment of the kingdom. Meanwhile, his supporters, if they were not rooted out, lingered on as a secret threat to the national security. Driven into hiding, they were stronger by the Duke's departure than if they had taken the field behind his banner. They could be counted on to assist him with secret intelligence and to rise in his support at the opportune moment.

So there was a great hue and cry for the capture of the Constable before he reached whatever frontier he hoped to cross. And there were arrests and inquisitions among his followers far and wide.

But this was not the worst of it, nor did the Bourbon conspiracy cause most of the hum at Lyons. For the King's anger and misgivings had every day fuel to keep them hot. Reports galloped in of Suffolk's army newly landed in the still English town of Calais and heading through Picardy toward Paris; reports of imperial troops under Fürstenberg menacing Champagne; reports from the South, where Spanish forces had crossed the Pyrenees. Reports, reports — all bad. The best of the French companies were in Italy and unavailable. Great captains, to be sure, covered the points of danger: La Trémouille against Suffolk, de Guise against Fürstenberg, de Lautrec in the South. But their lines were thin. They might not be able to contain the invasions. Since the English wars of a century past, the position of France had never been so critical.

But, whatever happened, as a last personal irritant to the King's exasperation, he would have to give up his long-cherished plan of leading the French army to Milan and stay at home on watch. He was by inclination a soldier. The Italian sports and triumphs, which he so pleasantly remembered from the victories of eight years ago, must be handed over to that lucky dog, his favorite, Bonnivet, now in command south of the Alps. The King himself must continue to stew here in this frontier city, deprived of amusements, curtailed even in his hunting.

Ha, how different if Bourbon and the foreign envoys had been scotched at Gayete, as might so easily have happened! The thought of that checkmate was enough to bring out the veins on the King's temples.

In these circumstances, it came as an unexpected windfall that Jean de Norville, Bourbon's right-hand man, deserted the Duke, betrayed his master's secrets and confederates and, with exquisite courtliness, recommended himself to the King's pardon. When all is black, a ray of light has tenfold value. It was some compensation that in a world of traitors, they were not all on one side.

As a result of de Norville's desertion, the conspiracy lost something of its terrors. De Norville, who knew every detail of it, could point out the key people to arrest and the proper measures to be taken. From him were learned the exact terms of the English treaty with Bourbon, the size of the British army at Calais, the imperial contingents supporting Fürstenberg in Champagne. Through him, it was hoped that the Duke might be captured before leaving France; though, with regard to this, de Norville could only reveal Bourbon's plans at the moment of flight and could not foresee what chances might compel him to alter them.

Surely, in return for such value received, it was not too great a reward that the confiscation of de Norville's estate, Chavan-la-Tour, in the Forez was suspended, and that he could count on its being restored to him in the near future.

Credit for de Norville's amazing change of front belonged to Chancellor Duprat. The Cardinal plumed himself a good deal on landing such a fish, and his already dominant influence with the King prospered accordingly. Even before Gayete, there had been a nibble from de Norville, which Duprat had been prompt to follow up. A tentative meeting in secret led to other meetings. If, as was cynically hinted, the Chancellor not only hooked de Norville but a substantial money bribe along with him, it meant no disloyalty to France but a simple business deal incidental to such a bargain. The King would profit no less from de Norville's revelations because the Chancellor profited from Bourbon's gold, which the traitor disposed of.

That was preliminary. De Norville waited only to attend the Constable at the meeting in Gayete and then slipped off to Lyons, conferred with the King, began circulating at court. He was in Lyons when Blaise de Lallière and Anne Russell arrived, the former to be imprisoned in the Castle of Pierre-Scize, the latter in the Convent of Saint-Pierre. Unobtrusive at first, de Norville became daily more in evidence, was called frequently to the King, was smiled on by the Chancellor, began to shine in the anterooms as a rising star who might be worth cultivating.

No one likes a Judas, but the times were ticklish. Too many at court had once been on good terms with the Duke of Bourbon to affront a man who could so easily denounce them. The tip spread quickly to look out for Monsieur de Norville. This seigneur and that baron would have been well advised not to turn their backs so bluntly or spit so loud when he first appeared in the corridors of Saint-Just. Both of them had since vanished into the Castle to answer charges which they had not yet answered. After that, Monsieur de Norville could not have been more politely accepted.

But fear was not all of it. He had enchanting manners, a handsome person, the gift of leadership. He became at once the center of any group. He rode well, fenced better; no one doubted his personal courage. And, with all this, he was versed in the fashionable arts, newly imported from Italy. People who had seen it spoke of his château in the Forez as a pearl of a place that yielded nothing to the best of the modern houses of Touraine. Indeed, he had lavished such care and expense upon it that not a few could well understand his desire to recover it, even at the cost of his soul. This passion for fine building was a hobby — and not the only one — that he shared with the King.

Monsieur de Bonne, an old hand at court, reflected the growing sentiment in the advice which he gave to his nephew, who reached Lyons about that time. "Mon fils, if you will be guided by me, do not attach yourself to one of the established people about the King. They all have their satellites of long standing, who will not gladly share the pickings with a newcomer. But seek out some rising man for a patron. Be in with him at the start of the race, while he is yet without following. And, for my money, you can do no better than make yourself agreeable to Monsieur de Norville. I have seen many favorites and know their points. As Monsieur de Bonnivet was to begin with, so is Monsieur de Norville now. The same engaging parts, the same absence of scruples. And see to what heights Bonnivet has carried it: Admiral of France, Commander-in-Chief of the Army. But I assure you that said lord did not advance himself with the King in one year so far as Monsieur de Norville has done in the past ten days. Par Dieu, mon ami, fasten yourself upon him. Flatter and copy him. A wonderful model for a young man."

Close to the middle of September, the King at last found time for the treat he had promised himself in dealing with Blaise de Lallière and gave orders that the prisoner, together with Anne Russell and Pierre de la Barre, should be brought before him at the third hour of the afternoon. But, for a few minutes preceding, he refreshed his anger by reviewing the case in consultation with Chancellor Duprat.

An array of documents lay on the table in front of Francis: reports of several examinations which Blaise had undergone in prison; the letter from the Duke of Savoy, which Blaise had found in Simon de Montjou's wallet; the confessions of Guy de Lallière's servant, who had been captured before reaching Chantelle, put to the question, and then hanged; Anne Russell's statement, taken down at the Convent of Saint-Pierre; a very interesting paper contributed by Jean de Norville; a long and detailed report from the same hand.

It was with reference to these last two that the King, having flipped through the rest of the file, observed to Duprat, "Completely damning, Monsieur le Chancelier."

"Completely, Sire."

The tip of Francis's beard curled up. "Not that the case wasn't pretty evident before. That preposterous lie of pursuing Milady Russell for three days — a girl whom he knew as well as his own hand — and mistaking her for Sir John! Saints! And pretending that he confused a servant with his own brother! His stew about Mademoiselle's safety, then letting her man go off — when even such an idiot as had bungled all the rest of it must know that they both ought to be held! No, he would have hanged anyway. But these" — the King's forefinger tapped the two papers in question — "clear up every point and leave no scope for lies. It's another service to the credit of Monsieur de Norville."

The plump Chancellor wagged his head. "It would be no great matter if the rascal de Lallière were the only one involved. He's of no consequence. But I grieve that the charges against him hit a man of stature and rank."

"You mean de Vaulx? Yes, he has more than enough to explain. I'm looking forward to seeing him." The King's smile crooked under his long nose. "Let alone the disobedience of employing de Lallière in the teeth of my warning, I have some questions to ask him about his talk with the rebels that time at the manor house. His account of it and de Norville's are somewhat different, eh?"

Duprat looked sorrowful. "Very different, Sire — alas! Far be it from me to utter a breath against Monsieur de Vaulx's reputation, but the fact will not have escaped Your Majesty that, in the same letter from Roanne, which contained a list of the rebels, he omitted the names of the two most pernicious, the de Lallières themselves."

"Ma foi," stared the King, "I hadn't noticed it, but it's true. And in the light of what's happened since, one can't help drawing conclusions. Peste!"

"Ah," the Chancellor's sigh was like the purr of a cat approaching cream. "Ah, the pity of it! That a man of the Marquis's long service should weaken at the end! I only hope that de Norville's further charges can be disproved — I hope so. That secret interview between de Vaulx and the Duke at Moulins looks odd. Well, well! Of how few can it be said that they finished their course and kept the faith! Let that, at least, be written on my tombstone."

"Amen," said the King absently. He changed the subject. "You know, I had a letter this morning from Madame my mother."

Duprat's eyes quickened. "Indeed?"

"Yes, she doesn't wholly share our confidence in de Norville. She writes, 'Once a traitor, always a traitor.' What is your opinion?"

It was a question that inspired caution. Duprat blinked. "Madame la Régente is a princess of rare insight. I should be the last to deny the truth of such a statement. I do not vouch for de Norville. Your Grace knows as much about him as I do. But, Sire, in this wicked world, we must use what tools we have. Few men are unswervingly loyal and honest. No doubt de Norville would betray Your Highness as he has the Duke, if that were to his interest. So, too, he will remain dependable, if being so is most to his advantage. Self-interest is everything. If he had come over to us with any show of righteousness, I should not rate him a groat. But not at all. He told me that a bird in hand is worth two in the bush. His estate near Feurs is worth more to him than a promised duchy, and he considers Your Highness a more likely gamble than Bourbon. That makes sense. Of course, he needs watching. But who doesn't?"

"Even you?" smiled the King.

Duprat waved his hand. "Present company always excepted. But let me point out something else. So far, his statements have proved right to a tee. Our people in London report the English alliance as he described it. Our scouts in Picardy and Champagne confirm his estimates of the enemy power. He warned us of Monsieur de Bourbon's escape in advance. The rebels whom he has denounced to us have proved guilty. Or take this affair of Milady Russell."

Francis's eyes quickened. "Eh bien? What of it?"

"Sire, Monsieur de Norville has not sought in any way to temper the charges against her. Instead, he took pains to show what service she has rendered to England, even in spite of the personal sentiments which incline her to Your Grace."

"And yet he asks for clemency," put in the King. "Where's the self-interest there? He's lost her dowry by deserting to us."

Duprat coughed. His eyes met the King's, and both glances shifted. Here was delicate ground.

"I should say the desire of pleasing Your Majesty. He believes that a few words from you, Sire — especially after her marriage — will convert her into a better French woman than she has been English. Why else did she make such a point of being arrested and brought to Lyons? Your Highness is irresistible. And to please Your Majesty at this moment is all the self-interest on de Norville's part that we need to seek." Again the glances met and shifted. "Besides, as he points out, she could be used to advantage in any future negotiations with England, and then her dowry need not be lost."

"There's truth in that." The King turned reminiscent. "By God, Monsieur le Chancelier, she has the neatest legs of any woman I know, and report credits her with the other charms to match them. An attractive piece, even if she's an enemy."

The Chancellor murmured, "What woman could be long an enemy of Your Grace?"

"Well, let's have a glimpse of her now. I'd give something to know her real feelings about de Lallière. Perhaps we can learn them." Francis tinkled a bell on the table and instructed the answering usher to have the prisoners brought in. He added to Duprat, "So you think that the Duchess of Angoulême's misgivings — ?"

"I believe, Sire, that Her Highness would be impressed by the facts I have pointed out."

"Yes, I believe she would."

Absently, the King got up and consulted a hand mirror. He ran a comb through his hair and beard, ordered the chain on his neck, plucked up the fullness of his sleeves, ogled the glass.

Duprat smiled.

Chapter 36

The world looked strange to Blaise de Lallière after a week in the twilight of prison. Contours, colors, faces, had become sharp and unfamiliar. His mind, as well as his eyes, groped toward readjustment.

Having cautiously descended the hundred and twenty steps cut into the almost perpendicular rock which supported the Castle of Pierre-Scize, he at once encountered the bustle of the town gate at its foot, the press of people and carriage animals congested in the bottleneck between the rock and the Saône. Looking back a moment and up, it seemed to him that the great medieval fortress, with its battlements and circular keep towering above them, was on the point of toppling over from its hundred-foot base to bury the column of human ants on the road; and a minute passed before he could steady himself. Then, gradually, objects took on their usual proportions, though for a while he felt as if he had descended from the moon.

"This way, monsieur," said one of the two guards, plucking at his sleeve. "You seem lightheaded. The King is at Saint-Just, not at Vaise."

The prisoner smiled. "Of course. But I'm like a man who's been blindfolded and lost the sense of direction." Then, between his guards, he turned to the right down the single narrow street that led into the city.

Since his consignment to the castle prison a week ago, he had been blindfolded in another sense. No news relating to his own case had reached him through the thick walls. Twice he had been interrogated by grim-faced secretaries of the Chancellor, and twice he had fainted after endless, exhausting hours on his feet. They had taken down verbatim his account of the pursuit of Russell from Geneva and of Anne from Nantua. He had been cross-examined about his relations with her; and there had been leading questions, involving de Surcy and even Bayard. But, while eliciting every scrap of information he could give them, his examiners disclosed nothing of the King's intentions nor of what might be going on.

Absorbed in the uncertainties of the impending ordeal at Saint-Just, he paid scant attention to the long, narrow street, flanked by tall houses and churches, which covered every available inch of the hundred yard ledge between the Saône and the steep western slopes. These were still largely rural, an expanse of vineyards, fields and orchards, towering above the dense array of buildings at their foot. With a fraction of his mind, Blaise recognized the arch of the Bourgneuf gate, under which the street passed into the quarter of that name; and, now and then, between the houses on his left, he caught a glimpse of the river, beyond which lay the newer section of Lyons on the peninsula between the Saône and the Rhône. Over there, east of Saint-Nizier, lay the Abbey of Saint-Pierre, in which Anne Russell was confined. He wondered desperately what was happening in her case, and whether they would both be examined and sentenced together that afternoon. Would she be able to appease the King, as she had hoped? And what would be her bearing toward himself? The next hour or two contained the answers to these and a host of questions that thronged incessantly upon him.

Here was the church of Saint-Laurent and the church of Saint-Paul with a cloister between them. The stench of the nearby slaughterhouse filled the air. And here, on the left, was the stone bridge, partially built over, which connected the two banks of the river. And here the street changed its name in honor of the famous inns that lined it, with their stables and coach houses: *The Apple, The Helmet, The Dauphin, The Crowned Hat,* a dozen others. The Marquis de Vaulx, Blaise reflected, would turn in at one of these when he arrived from Geneva. Perhaps he had already arrived.

And now the street circled the mass of the Archbishop's Palace. Beyond it towered the Cathedral of Saint-Jean, surrounded by its walls and buildings, which formed a town within the town.

Blaise shook himself out of his brooding to remark, "Ma foi, you've no lack of churches in Lyons."

"Yes," said one of the guards, "eleven on this bank alone within the space of a half league. Believe me, it hurts your ears when all the bells ring at once. No sleeping on certain nights, I can tell you. And the bells from across the river answer. Yes, Lyons is a godly city. This way, monsieur."

They turned right at the cloister of Saint-Jean, threaded a couple of painfully narrow streets, and emerged on the steep ascent called the Gourgillon, or Gullet, half lane, half ravine, which climbed uphill to Saint-Just.

Almost at once they were in the country. It was only when they took breath and looked back that they were aware of the great city, with its forty thousand inhabitants, spread along both sides of the river beneath them. Then, having passed the line of walls, which had been built a hundred and fifty years before as a defense against the English, they found themselves at the summit of the hill, with the Bourg Saint-Just close at hand.

It was not only a cloister but a fortress that sheltered a thousand people. Surrounded by thirty-six-foot battlements and twenty-two towers, it contained the church of Saint-Just, the great refectory, a tribunal, twelve spacious houses for the canons of the church, twenty-eight other buildings with inner courts, gardens, patches of vineyard — in brief a village of stately edifices. Now, more thronged than usual by the presence of the royal retinue, it glowed with every color of dress and hummed like a vast beehive.

Guided by one of the soldiers on duty at the gate, Blaise and his guards made their way through the come-and-go to the door of the principal residence, where halberdiers wearing the blazon of the King stood watch. Then, passing under the archway, they found themselves in an inner court, with turret staircases at each angle. Up one of these, an usher conducted them into a bare monastic room of leaded windows. And immediately one of the questions which had concerned Blaise was answered. For, seated between a couple of lay sisters, who stood on either side of her chair, he saw Anne Russell, with Pierre de la Barre cooling his heels at some distance from her.

So, the three actors in the tragicomedy of the pursuit from Nantua were to be tried together.

As if in a mirror, he was conscious of his appearance in her eyes, as she gazed toward him. He had managed a shave that morning, and the turnkey had loaned him a clothesbrush; but, otherwise, he reflected the blight of the prison. A man got speedily mildewed in the cells of Pierre-Scize. The stagnant dampness, the wretched fare, above all, the unrelenting dread of torture and death, left their mark in sunken cheeks and hollow eyes. Blaise had seen too many of his fellow prisoners to have any illusions about his own appearance. And he felt this all the more keenly because of the contrast presented by Anne. She was dressed somberly but in the height of fashion. The linen of her coif, the folds of her headdress, the satin of her gown were immaculate. Having lost the tan of the road, her face had regained its dazzling complexion. She breathed freshness, high spirits, and assurance. He had never seen her so enchanting.

Quick to cover up her start of surprise when she first looked at him, though not so quick that he failed to notice it, she answered his bow with a "Ha, Monsieur de Lallière," and a smile which he found hard to interpret. It was distant and yet not too distant. Perhaps it was only a diplomatic smile. He could see that the eyes of the nuns were fixed on her.

And there was no chance to learn more. An officer in charge of a group of archers, who stood in front of a closed door at the end of the room, put in harshly: "The prisoners are forbidden to communicate with each other in any way."

Having exchanged a long glance with Pierre, who shook his head and shrugged his shoulders, Blaise drew back to one side between his two guards.

A long wait followed until the panels of the door swung open and an usher announced: "De par le roi. Let these prisoners now appear before the King."

Francis, with Duprat at his shoulder, sat in an armchair of carved oak and looked resplendent as always. At a table behind him, a secretary tried the nib of his pen before taking notes. Blaise's guards and the nuns who had attended Anne remained outside; it was the King's Scottish archers, bluff, leather-faced men, who now took over and lined the background.

According to custom, Anne, Blaise and Pierre kneeled with bowed heads and remained kneeling until a word from the King would permit them to rise. But, for a long period that word was not given. Stealing a glance at the royal face, Blaise found it inscrutable. Except for a cold glitter of the eyes, which passed over and ignored him, the King's attention centered upon Anne.

At last, he said, "Well, Milady, it's some time since we had the pleasure of seeing you at court."

She looked up and, without smiling, gave the impression of a smile. "Too long, Sire, for one who has been used to the splendor of Your Majesty's hospitality."

"Too long, eh? It's not my fault. Ma foi, you ran off from that hospitality fast enough. Even Pierre de Warthy couldn't catch you."

Anne nodded. "A mistake, which I now seek to repair by recommending myself to Your Grace's forgiveness."

The King tossed back his head with a laugh. "Oh, la belle impertinente! The assurance of you women leaves a man breathless. After conspiring with my enemies, after doing your utmost against me in the service of England, you calmly assume forgiveness."

"No," she murmured, "I presume upon it, remembering that Your Highness surpasses all other princes in gallantry, as he surpasses them in grandeur. Sire, if Your Grace were Charles of Austria and I a French woman taken in this fault, I should be too proud to sue in vain for pardon from that cold man of business. But, kneeling before Your Highness, I am truly humble, being aware that, if my fault is great, your chivalry is infinite."

Music in speech, enchanting modulations of the voice, superb finesse. If there was anything Francis despised, it was business; if there was any renown he craved, it was to be considered the premier gallant gentleman of Europe; if there was anyone he hated, it was Charles, the Emperor. But, above all, he loved beauty, and he found this woman surpassingly beautiful.

To Blaise, it seemed that a spell was being woven about the King. He could see his expression altering from stern to complacent, as if remolded by invisible fingers. His eyes kindled; his smile flashed above the beard; a pleased glow tinted the sallow cheeks. Blaise remembered that Louise de Savoie had accused Anne of casting such a spell upon her son, and he could now understand the reason for the charge. But the adroit suppliant, the charming flatterer, by one of those odd shifts of her personality with which Blaise had grown familiar, had become once more suddenly a stranger to him. This perfect lady of the court had nothing in common with the Anne Russell he knew. Somehow, as he listened to the beguiling voice, he felt more chilled and excluded than when she had scorched him with her anger.

"Par Dieu," said Francis, laughing again, more pleasantly this time, "I fear that you overrate me, mademoiselle. But at least my chivalry extends so far that I beg you will rise and be seated. Ho, someone! A chair for Milady Russell. If all my enemies were as attractive as you, I should be glad to exchange some of my friends for them."

She stood up, then swept him a deep curtsy before taking the chair which one of the attendants provided.

The King added: "But do not mistake me. Your crimes are black and demand severity. No doubt they will cost you your head." His smile suggested a pun. "However, we'll defer sentence for this time and impose it later." If Francis had promised her a duchy, he would have used the same tone of voice. "Meanwhile, I hope that your prison is not too rigorous, that the Ladies of Saint-Pierre incline to mercy."

"Like Your Grace, they are kindness itself. But Saint-Pierre is not Your Majesty's court. It was not to be immured in a convent that I gave myself up to Monsieur de la Palisse. Ah, my lord, how dull I found the court of Savoy after those unforgettable years at Blois and Paris!"

The King beamed. "Homesick, were you?"

"Pardie!"

At least one of Blaise's anxieties had faded out. As a loyal subject, he could now feel more concerned for the King than for Anne. But the next remarks put everything else out of his mind.

"Well, we shall see, we shall see," Francis pondered. "I have been led to believe that you are prepared to become one of us, une bonne française. You have a most active friend at court, Milady."

She hesitated slightly. "Your Grace means Monsieur de Norville?"

"Most certainly. That gentleman has become not the least of our valued servants." The King glanced up at Duprat. "Eh, Monsieur le Chancelier?"

Blaise missed the answer. De Norville? *De Norville* a servant of the King's? Bourbon's chief agent established here at court? The thing made no sense. It was preposterous, like a crazy dream.

Blaise came out of his stupor to hear Anne saying: "When I surrendered myself to Your Grace's lances, I did not know that Monsieur de Norville was in Lyons. I have not at any time had the pleasure of meeting him, betrothed as we are. However, he took the liberty of writing me at the convent, with Your Majesty's permission."

The dream was becoming a nightmare. In the confusion of it, Blaise felt a cold sense of dread, such as attends some victory of evil. And in this Anne was involved.

"I shall see to it," said Francis, "that you meet your betrothed, and that presently. If it were not that your case is so hopeless" — a smile contradicted the words — "I should congratulate him. But that reminds me. You were not summoned here to be judged, but to help me judge this traitor" — the slanting eyes shifted to Blaise; the velvet voice turned to steel — "this shabby villain. Stand up, fellow. I give you leave to defend yourself if you can."

By this time, angry bewilderment had stung Blaise to a point where respect for the King was eclipsed by the raging sense of injustice. It was enough that Anne Russell, a declared enemy of France, should be caressed and forgiven. But that a Judas, like de Norville, should be accepted while honest men were called traitors —

"Sire, I am no traitor nor villain. I have failed in what I was ordered to do — yes; but that is not treason."

The King looked him up and down. "By the Lord, a bold-crowing cock. I think you'll sing lower, when we have finished with you." He turned to Anne, his eyes narrowing. His voice sounded smooth — too smooth. "What's your version of him, Milady? You ought to know him well enough."

If the King expected any trace of emotion, he was disappointed. She glanced at Blaise with the detachment of a great lady toward some groom who has served her once and stands in need of a reference.

"Sire, although it does not concern me, I marvel that you should consider the man a traitor. He was under the orders of Madame la Régente to conduct me out of France. It was I who left Madame de Péronne at Sens, and he could do no less than follow along. As to the recent affair, ma foi, it seems to me that he did his best. Your Majesty knows what trick I played on him. It was very wicked of me."

"Very wicked, mademoiselle."

"Alas, indeed! But he kept on my traces, he and that young gentleman yonder" — she half nodded at Pierre, who stood next to Blaise — "and caught up with me at the last. He's dull-witted, no doubt. If that makes him a traitor, I fear that many another of Your Majesty's lances needs hanging. Yes, a dull-witted, plain man — what else?"

She drew a pomander from the velvet purse at her waist and sniffed it carelessly. Her tone and manner left Blaise chilled. She was play-acting, of course, to establish herself with the King, but Blaise could take no comfort from that. On the other hand, the veiled intentness of the Prince relaxed. He could not catch a single false note in her answer. To imagine that this immaculate, brilliant woman had ever been involved sentimentally with so flat a knave as the prisoner, seemed, of course, laughable. But Francis could not resist a quip.

"At least he had sense enough to admire a certain charming demoiselle and to betray his duty out of regard for her."

Anne looked a question. "Indeed?"

"Yes. You see, we have the confession of that black-bearded rogue who attended you from Nantua. He talked freely enough under torture before he was hanged at Roanne. We know what transpired in Monsieur de Chamand's hunting lodge."

It was a vague solace to Blaise that Anne showed a pulse of feeling. Her eyes filled. "Poor Étienne! He was a faithful servant." Then, absently, "Transpired? I don't follow Your Highness."

244

"Didn't de Lallière permit the rascal's escape and urge you to accompany him? Accepting the rest of his story — which I do *not* — was that the act of a loyal Frenchman?" The King added with a sultry glance, "Though, I confess, the temptation is plain."

Anne stiffened. "I hope that Your Highness does not suggest that this man and *I* — " She broke off with a stare. "Bon Dieu!"

"I suggest nothing, except his treachery."

"Ah? Well, Your Majesty knows best. I should have called it stupidity. Disappointed at not finding my lord of Bourbon at that place, he could see no point in detaining me. He's always been civil. Besides, how could he know" — her voice became music again — "that I chose rather to cast myself on Your Highness's mercy than return to England or Savoy?"

Then the bolt fell. "You seem to be unaware of a certain detail, Milady: he is in Bourbon's pay. Does stupidity cover that?"

"Sire!" Blaise exploded. . . . Up to this point, except for the revelation about de Norville, nothing had greatly surprised him. The rebellion of his family, the King's prejudice, his own wretched blunder at Nantua, would all contribute to a charge of treason. The examinations he had undergone in prison had even prepared him for it. But this monstrous impeachment had no root in anything. . . . "Sire, I protest. Your Majesty knows that it's not true. Monseigneur de Vaulx can vouch — "

"Let him vouch for himself. He has treason of his own to answer for."

"My lord de Vaulx?"

"Aye, like master like man. But we'll leave him out of it for the present. You deny that you are in the Duke's pay?"

"Deny? I call God and the Saints to witness that I deny it."

"Then explain this. Duprat, that receipt, if you please." And when the Chancellor had handed him a paper from the table, Francis beckoned. "Come here. Look at that, and spare your lies."

Dizzily, Blaise could see his own rough signature on the sheet of paper. His name stared up at him, with the familiar flourish under it. It was an instant before he could read the rest, then gradually the words drifted together.

I, Blaise de Lallière, at present man-at-arms in the company of the Seigneur Pierre de Bayard, but henceforth, by appointment, captain of thirty lances in the guard of Monseigneur Charles, Duke of Bourbon, admit receiving from Jean de Norville, councillor and treasurer of said

Duke, the sum in cash of one hundred and fifty livres tournois, as pay in advance for my said captaincy during the current months of August, September and October. And I herewith hold the said Jean de Norville acquitted of said sum. In testimony whereof, I have affixed my signature and seal this twenty-sixth day of July in the year one thousand, five hundred and twenty-three.

Blaise de Lallière

Yes, the signature was his; the seal was his; the amount acknowledged would have been a quarter of the pay which de Norville had offered. But unless he had been completely out of his head at Lallière, he was looking at the paper for the first time. And he recalled vividly every moment of that day.

"Well?" snapped the King.

"Sire, I never signed this paper. A proposal was made to me by de Norville, as Your Majesty knows. I rejected it and was banned from my father's house in consequence."

"You pretend it's a forgery?"

"Most infamous — "

"What of the seal?"

"It has been copied as well as the writing. I implore Your Majesty to tell me how this came here!"

"Why, from the man to whom you gave it, Monsieur de Norville. And let me tell you that forgery is the easiest defense which a rogue, caught as you are, can make."

Blaise found himself speechless, not from confusion but rage. To be condemned for failure was one thing; to be condemned on evidence forged by a scoundrel was another. He stood facing the King, his cheeks flaming and fists clenched.

Pierre de la Barre, equally fuming, burst out: "Sire, may I have a word? I know this de Norville as the cutthroat villain who would have been the death of us all on our ride to Roanne if he had had his way. I've been close to Monsieur de Lallière for the past year. If there's a more loyal gentleman in Your Majesty's companies, I renounce life. And I ask one question — "

"Taisez-vous, monsieur," said the King impatiently. "You're out of your depth here. It's your luck to have been the page of Madame d'Alençon and that the good Bailiff of Paris is your kinsman. Be glad that no one suspects *your* loyalty. And keep quiet till you're spoken to."

Blaise regained his tongue. "I claim the right to face this rogue and

246

cast his lies in his teeth. At least Your Majesty will grant me that."

The King's eyes flamed. "Have a care, speak softly. You forget where you are. As it happens, Monsieur de Norville is just as eager to face you. There's more to your charge than that piece of paper. And I tell you plain that before you're quartered on the Place de la Grenette, you'll sign your name again, and this time to a full confession." He directed one of the attendants, "Fetch us Monsieur de Norville."

Chapter 37

If scorn, hatred and indignation, concentrated in a pair of eyes, could have pierced Jean de Norville's triple-plated assurance, he would have, at least, felt uneasy under Blaise's glare, which followed him through the room and beat upon him, as he made his bow to the King. But there is an integrity of evil as well as of good. Only the second-rate scoundrel feels shame. The thoroughly unscrupulous man is a saint in reverse. He follows the polestar of self-interest without the faintest compunction.

De Norville's glance passed coolly over Blaise, with no touch of shiftiness but too indifferent to return stare for stare. Indeed, he appeared so composed that any third person, comparing his serene face with Blaise's furious expression, would have at once assumed his innocence and the other's guilt.

"Your Majesty sent for me?" Every movement showed grace and reverence. His dress, manners, and handsome features conveyed an impression of strength and dignity. Then, turning toward Anne Russell, he gave a start of admiration and drew back a step. "Is this — ?" The query was left delicately hanging between uncertainty and rapture.

"Yes, mon ami," smiled Francis. "I grieve that you should first meet your betrothed under these circumstances. But I am happy, at least, to be the one to present you to her. Milady Russell, Monsieur de Norville."

Anne rose to curtsy; de Norville half kneeled, as he kissed her hand.

"At last!" he said and contrived to make the two words express

247

passion, delight, and fulfilled longing. He was at the same time tender and magnificent. Whatever her opinion of him, no woman could ignore his charm. Anne smiled and murmured a phrase or two. He bowed again. "It is so rare, Milady, that hope realized should put to shame the utmost flight of anticipation." Then followed solicitude for her welfare, regrets that unhappy events, over which he had no control, had thus far prevented him from casting himself at her feet.

As Blaise listened to de Norville's flow of courtesy, it did not soothe his anger that he was forced to admit the man's brilliancy and envy his address.

"That, since our betrothal," de Norville was saying, "I have renounced old errors and sought the protection of His Majesty, will not, I hope, mademoiselle, prejudice me in your eyes."

She answered diplomatically: "When you have told me the reasons for your conversion, monsieur, I shall no doubt be impressed by them. Certes, I look forward most eagerly to hearing them, and I hope that His Grace will permit me to hear them soon."

"No later than today," put in Francis. "But, for the moment, we have another matter to deal with." He addressed de Norville. "Monsieur, the prisoner here, Blaise de Lallière, affirms that the receipt you gave me is a forgery. This is a most serious charge. What have you to say to it?"

And the focus of the scene shifted at once. But de Norville's eyes lingered a moment on Anne, before they turned absently to Blaise.

"A forgery?"

"You know it is," Blaise flared. "You know, word for word, what was spoken between us: that, when you offered me a captaincy in behalf of the Duke of Bourbon, I did not accept it. You know what followed at dinner, when you and the others were baiting Monseigneur de Vaulx, how I alone with the Marquis stood for the King, and how my father dealt with me in consequence. I cannot yet believe that any man is so foully shameless as to draw up this document and forge my name and seal in direct contradiction to everything that happened."

This time de Norville met Blaise's glare steadily. He looked impassive, though slightly bored. In the end, he smiled.

"Your Majesty, what *can* I say? The paper speaks for itself. Monseigneur Duprat has taken pains, I believe, to compare the signature and seal with others, which are certainly not forgeries. Beyond that, it is this man's word against mine — except that his actions confirm me. I admit that, if he had served Your Highness well, there might be room for doubt. But he has served Your Majesty so ill that, by his connivance, a chief master stroke against the enemy has failed. Certainly his receipt for the one hundred and fifty livres is not the sole count against him. Indeed, trapped as he is, I should have been surprised if he had not claimed forgery. What else could he do?"

"As I told him," nodded the King. "Well answered."

Again Blaise found himself speechless and, for the moment, helpless. What could be urged against brass like this? If he could only take de Norville by the throat —

"No, Sire, by your leave," broke in Pierre, undeterred by the royal frown, "not so well answered. Let him show why, if Monsieur de Lallière had just taken the Duke's pay, he sought to murder him, with the rest of us, on the road to Roanne. That's a devilish odd trick to play on one of your own men, as I see it."

"By God," Francis snapped, "your tongue will land you in the jakes, my lad, and that shortly. But he makes a point there — yes, I confess it — a point, Monsieur de Norville."

The latter arched his brows. "What point, Sire? Surely this young master isn't so lost to truth that he would accuse me of seeking to murder anybody! If a band of hot-tempered squires, over whom I had no control, attacked Monseigneur de Vaulx's party without my knowledge, am I to be held accountable? The said squires have been denounced to Your Highness and are, most of them, now awaiting trial. Let them be questioned as to whether or not I set them on!"

Duprat observed: "They have been already examined. No such charge against Monsieur de Norville was made."

"Eh bien," smiled the King, "that point is disposed of."

Blaise had gained control of himself. This was no time for passion; his plight required cool thinking. It might be the last chance he would ever have to defend himself. Pierre's question gave him a lead.

"But, Sire," he objected, "if I was given a place in the Duke's guard, as this man pretends, is it not strange that I was banished from my father's house because of loyalty to Your Majesty? What else did Monsieur mon père demand but that I should serve the Duke? And, because I refused, he disowned me."

The King shrugged. "That has all been explained. But answer

him, Monsieur de Norville. It is a pleasure to course this fox from one earth to the next."

De Norville bowed. "Gladly, Your Grace. Monsieur de Lallière's memory is as weak as his honesty. I'll try to refresh it. You will remember, sir — though you may not admit it — that your appointment to the Duke's guard was, for the time being, to be kept secret from every living person, except from the Duke himself. Your father, your brother, no one else, was to hear of it. You took a most solemn vow to that effect. And, I notice, you're still keeping it. But don't act surprised that your father, who knew nothing of this agreement behaved as he did. You were not surprised at the time."

"And perhaps you'll remind me," said Blaise, "of the reason for such secrecy."

"Again, gladly, my dear sir. It was considered important that a man of supposed loyalty, though actually in the Duke's service, should be close to the Marquis de Vaulx and work for Monseigneur de Bourbon in the opposite camp. . . . Ah, Your Majesty, how I lament these intrigues now! But, by disclosing, I hope in some sort to atone for them. . . . And let me further remind this gentleman how well the plan turned out — indeed, beyond anything we expected. First, as a good Bourbonian, he had the luck to spirit Milady Russell out of France. Next, he served the Duke by insuring the miscarriage of the arrests which Your Highness had planned. It would have saved Sir John Russell, Milady Anne, and the whole party at Nantua some concern if they had known how little Monsieur Blaise was to be feared. But because no one knew of his relations with the Duke, he would still have been able to excuse himself to Your Majesty, had it not been for the facts which I have had the honor of communicating."

"Hardly, monsieur mon ami," said the King, "hardly. The rat smelled strong enough, even before you uncovered him."

"It is true," bowed de Norville, "that Your Grace is not easily deceived."

But Blaise had withheld his ace of trumps till the last. There was one point, he believed, which no lies could distort. It had only to be stated to prevail. Now was the time to drive it home.

"And has it occurred to you, Sire," he asked, trying to keep his voice level, "that if I were secretly in the Duke's pay, I should hardly have reported Sir John Russell's arrival in Geneva to the Marquis de Vaulx? There would then have been no pursuit at all, and Milord

250

Russell's plans could have been carried out undisturbed. I had only to hold my tongue, as Milady here desired of me. . . . Is it not true, mademoiselle?" he demanded.

Apparently deep in thought, Anne did not answer at once. Then, she looked up. "Yes, quite true. I besought Monsieur de Lallière not to inform the Marquis with regard to my brother, and he refused to content me."

De Norville snapped at this. "In other words, he took pains to put you on your guard. A loyal servant of the King would have avoided doing so. Did it lead you perhaps to suspect that he was in the Duke's service?"

The question required an affirmative, but she shook her head. "No, I had no such suspicion."

The other smiled. "He's an excellent actor."

Blaise stuck to his point. "I have yet to learn why, as a good Bourbonian, I should have betrayed Sir John's presence in Geneva to Monseigneur the Marquis, and why I should set in motion a pursuit which was wholly unnecessary if I intended it to fail. What would be the aim of it?"

Glancing at Anne, he noted a sudden approval in her eyes. She nodded slightly. But, expecting embarrassment on the part of de Norville, he felt a shock of dismay when the latter merely exchanged a smile with the King and Duprat.

"I repeat, Sire, this de Lallière's an excellent actor. Is it the time and place to smoke him out of his last cover?"

The King made a careless movement of the hand. "Why not? The sport's too good to stop."

"Then, by your leave," de Norville said to Blaise, "I'll ask you one more question. Are you not singularly devoted to the Marquis de Vaulx?"

"I am indeed."

"His godson, I think?"

"Yes."

"Brought up in his household?"

"I had that honor."

"So that it may be presumed that he has opened his heart to you, that you know him intimately?"

Blaise lifted his head proudly. "Monseigneur has always treated me like a son."

"Capital!" said de Norville, with a side glance to the King. "We're making progress. For the first time today, Monsieur de Lallière consents to tell the truth." His next remark to Blaise came like a dagger stroke. "Well, then, if you're so intimate with the Marquis, you must be aware of his sympathies for the Constable of Bourbon?"

"I'm aware of nothing of the kind. The thought's ridiculous. Like everyone else in France, he admired the Duke in the old days before these troubles."

"Like your captain, Bayard, perhaps, who not so long ago knighted the Duke's late son."

"As he had the honor of knighting His Majesty." Blaise shook with passion. "By the Cross of God, if you are attempting to cast your dung on my lord Bayard and the Marquis de Vaulx — "

The other interrupted. "Don't declaim, my friend. We're dealing with facts, not with rhetoric. Answer my questions. You accompanied the Marquis on his mission to Switzerland as far as Roanne. You were with him in Moulins on the night of July twenty-fifth."

"Of course. And what of it?"

"Simply this. Being as intimate as you are, you must have known that the Marquis secretly visited Monseigneur de Bourbon that night and stayed with him upwards of an hour."

"He did not. He did not leave the inn."

"Alas!" De Norville shook his head. "The gentleman lapses again. He could not stick to the truth for long. Or perhaps Monseigneur de Bourbon lied, though I can see no reason for it. Certainly the Duke assured me that Monsieur de Vaulx had offered him sympathy and secret support. The Marquis regretted that he must keep up pretenses with His Majesty, such as urging the immediate arrest of the Duke. But he knew full well that the King, in his infinite goodness, would take no such step for the moment. And he advised Monseigneur de Bourbon's escape from France — advice which has since been followed."

"Cré Dieu!" Blaise gasped. "Surely Your Highness will not take this man's unsupported word in such a matter!"

"I shall examine de Vaulx concerning it, when he arrives," said Francis. "Proceed, Monsieur de Norville."

"Well, then, the prisoner here can deny everything else, but he cannot deny that on the night of July twenty-sixth, the Marquis revealed to me and to a group of rebels assembled at Lallière, the whole of the King's knowledge touching the conspiracy, and what plans had been made to deal with it."

Nothing could be shrewder. Point by point, de Norville rehearsed what the Marquis had said; and, on his showing, it looked black enough. De Surcy's bold statesmanship which had sought to cut at the roots of the rebellion was twisted into a betrayal of important secrets. Blaise could not deny these statements. He would merely weaken the Marquis's case by insisting on a different interpretation. And, as he listened, he felt a growing sense of dread. So far, he had been concerned with his own fate, with the injustice to himself. Now he could see the object of the questions which had been put to him in the prison. De Norville's machinations included much more than his personal ruin. That was only incidental to a larger strategy. The Marquis, even Bayard, under attack! Who would come next! What was de Norville's ultimate purpose? The thought was sobering. It excluded mere anger, but it brought a sudden hardening of resolution, a desperate will, somehow to defeat this menace overhanging not only himself but the two men he loved.

So prepared, it no longer surprised him to learn that, aware of the Marquis's secret treason, he would naturally inform him of Russell's arrival in Geneva; that it was de Surcy who directed the sham pursuit in order to keep up appearances with the King; and that the Marquis had given another proof of his treachery by appointing Blaise to the mission in spite of the royal warning against him.

He fell back on irony. "I suppose Monseigneur de Vaulx instructed me to kill Simon de Montjou, although we could easily have kept up these appearances you speak of by allowing the Duke of Savoy to close the pass."

But de Norville was again ready. "I am sure that the Marquis foresaw the likelihood of the Duke's interference and foresaw, too, that such an easy excuse would hardly be allowed by the King."

"No doubt he also foretold that a trick would be played on me at Nantua and bade me follow Milady Russell."

"No, but let me compliment you on your nimbleness in making so obvious a trick the pretext of failure. I agree with His Majesty that it smelled bad, but you might still have faced it out, except for me."

Blaise addressed the King. "Your Grace, would it be possible to summon my father, Antoine de Lallière, to Lyons? He is my declared enemy but he is a man of honor. He would give this fellow the lie on more points than there is time to mention."

Francis yawned. He was growing tired of the case and for several minutes past had been looking admiringly at Anne Russell. "Quite impossible," he said. "When Lallière was confiscated, your father was sent, with other Bourbon rebels, to the prison of Loches — too far for him to be brought back conveniently, even if it served our purpose. He'll be tried there or in Paris. Thanks to this gentleman" — Francis nodded at de Norville — "we know a good deal about him."

Lallière confiscated. A glimpse of the desolate manor house crossed Blaise's mind. And his mother and sister — what had become of them?

"We've had enough of this," the King went on. "Certainly you can't complain that you haven't been given a fair trial and a chance to defend yourself. No one shall ever accuse me of injustice, even to traitors. . . . Monsieur le Chancelier," he glanced at Duprat, "I should prefer that you would review the evidence and favor us with your judgment."

The Chancellor's fat jowls quivered with satisfaction. "In my humble opinion, Sire, the matter looks thus. Suppose that Monsieur de Norville had preferred no charges at all: the prisoner would still be guilty of gross dereliction of duty, of unpardonable failure in executing the orders given him. And since, as a soldier, he is subject not to the civil but to military law, Your Majesty should pronounce the sentence of death. Other and better men have been executed for much less. In the days of King Louis, eleventh of the name . . ." As a lawyer, Duprat could not avoid the recital of precedents. He strung them out.

Using a schoolboy trick, which he had learned years ago, Blaise shot a whisper to Pierre from the corner of his mouth. "My mother — find her and bring her to Lyons. She may be able to testify against this whoreson. Probably she's still near Lallière. Understand?"

"Yes," came back the whisper from Pierre's motionless lips.

"And in the days of King Charles, eighth of the name . . ." Duprat was saying.

Blaise stared at the floor. "Get money — somehow. Try the turnkey. It's a hope. I'm not giving up. Remember it's for the Marquis — others. Understand?"

"Yes."

"Therefore, in any case," Duprat concluded, "he should suffer the penalty for treason."

"So be it," said Francis, drooping his eyelids at Anne.

"One moment, Your Grace," continued Duprat. "Thus far, we have ignored the charges of Monsieur de Norville. But they cannot be ignored. They are most weighty, as touching not only this fellow but the Marquis himself and, it may be, other men. They should be supported by a confession." Duprat raised his voice. "We hope that such a confession may be voluntary and complete. I suggest that the prisoner be given a week to decide whether he will tell the truth painlessly. If, at the end of that time, he remains obstinate, the truth should be racked out of him in such ways as Your Highness's torturers may find most convenient. Then, when a full confession has been signed, the capital sentence should be carried out on the Place de la Grenette. Does this meet with Your Majesty's approval?"

"Understand?" Blaise whispered. He hoped that Pierre would understand the limits of flesh and blood, and that any confession can be got out of anyone, when pain and exhaustion destroy the will.

"Yes. By God, I'll do my best."

Francis stretched himself. "An excellent idea, Monsieur le Chancelier. See that it's carried out." He flung at Blaise: "You have a week of sound limbs, sirrah. Take my advice and keep them sound. You'll make a better showing on the Place de la Grenette." He could not refrain from Anne any longer. "What cheer, Milady? You look white. Toutes mes excuses! One shouldn't speak of certain things in the presence of ladies. But I think you've learned more about this squire of yours than you knew before, eh?"

Anne said faintly, "Indeed yes, Your Grace."

"Well, then, we'll not detain you longer for this time. I promise myself the pleasure of another meeting soon. Meanwhile, Monsieur de Norville, conduct our delightful prisoner to the Abbey of Saint-Pierre. You have my permission to inform her why you have entered our service. She may even be induced to follow your example. I can think of no solicitor more gifted."

"Except yourself, my lord."

The King smiled self-consciously. "You think so? Well, in that case, I may try my hand later."

255

Chapter 38

The Abbey of the Ladies of Saint-Pierre was one of the oldest establishments in France. At this time, it was certainly not less than seven hundred years old and, more likely, not less than a thousand. It occupied an entire quarter of that part of Lyons which lay between the Saône and the Rhône and contained within its walls churches, abbatial buildings, houses, gardens and orchards, a vast, irregular expanse of many acres. But this was only the central core of its domain. Outside, fringing the walls, it possessed houses, shops and taverns, which swelled its revenues. It owned farms at La Guillotière and rights of toll on the two rivers. It disposed of fourteen priories in the environs of the city and of numerous livings and benefices. Great lords were its vassals and owed it homage. Depending directly from the Pope, it maintained for centuries a haughty independence of lesser authorities. Its enrollment of thirty-three regular nuns was not only aristocratic but most aristocratic, and the Abbess was so great a personage that the Pope, the King, and the City of Lyons were all equally concerned in her election.

But grandeur leads to excesses at variance with the strict rule of Saint Benedict, and of late the wings of the abbey had been clipped both by papal and royal interference. The discipline of cloister, refectory and dormitory had been enforced. The nuns, in their stately robes, no longer appeared in public, no longer entertained what friends they pleased in their private residences, were no longer surrounded by their personal servants. They were of somewhat less exalted rank than before, and the lay sisters who served them were more carefully chosen.

However, millennial traditions do not vanish in a decade. The Abbess, Antoinette d'Armagnac, yielded to no one in nobility. The Ladies of Saint-Pierre were still a select community, and the abbey itself remained a power.

That Anne Russell had been nominally imprisoned in such a convent was both a tribute to her rank and a token of the King's regard. Waited on by the lay sisters, she occupied a house, with its own private garden, which had been formerly the residence of one of the dames hôtelières before the rule of the dormitory had been restored.

By order of the Abbess, every courtesy and attention was shown her. No confinement could have been more pleasant or more considerate.

Now, on her mule, attended by the two lay sisters similarly mounted, and by Monsieur de Norville with his lackeys, she descended the steep slopes of Saint-Just, crossed the Saône bridge and the Saint-Nizier quarter beyond it, until, by way of the Place du Chanvre, she reached the main entrance of the Abbey on the Rue Saint-Pierre. The King's orders sufficed for de Norville's admittance, though his grooms remained outside.

Within the walls, they were faced by the two churches of Saint-Pierre and Saint-Saturnin, which served the parish as well as the Abbey. Between and behind these lay the churchyard, a silent place of ancient tombs, disheveled and moss-grown, through which a light wind chased the already falling leaves. It was towards this graveyard that de Norville conducted Anne.

"By your leave," he said in a low voice, "we'd better talk out of doors. There might be listeners inside." And when the lay sisters were on the point of following, he dismissed them with such a show of authority in the King's name, that they vanished at once.

Perhaps an hour of daylight remained until vespers; but the clouds hung low, and the walls of the two churches added a deeper gloom. Threading her way between the graves, Anne felt the chill and drew her long mantle closer. In the extension of the churchyard behind, there was more light, though the irregular space was still overlooked by many windows of the abbatial buildings.

"As long as we're seen," remarked de Norville, "propriety can have no complaint. The chief thing is to be out of earshot. An odd place for our first tête-à-tête, Milady." He smiled at one of the tombstones. "But you and I are beyond superstition."

On the way from Saint-Just, he had made the most of the chance to impress her with his charm and had at last refrained only when he saw that she paid little attention. Now he renewed the heat. He was dressed in black richly brocaded with silver, a white plumed cap on his head, his wide sleeves modishly slashed, a jeweled ring on the forefinger of his glove. The somber background of the graveyard contrasted with his fashionable elegance.

She nodded, and her eyes were level. "I am waiting, monsieur, to hear the reasons for your amazing volte-face. Why?"

He was too shrewd a man to trifle. "Tell me first," he said, "how much you know. Perhaps your brother may have given you a hint."

"Yes, but only that you had some great plan on foot and that you would acquaint me with it when we met. I did not expect this."

"No? And yet what could be more natural, more profitable, than the service of the King? I have already regained my estates in the Forez."

"Monsieur, we are wasting time, for I am still in the service of England."

"And I can't persuade you to turn renegade? I even believe that you don't consider me quite the traitor that I seem. Why not?"

Her face remained as inscrutable as his. "Because a man of your talents, Monsieur de Norville, will expect to gain far more from Monseigneur de Bourbon, backed by King Henry and the Emperor, than from Francis of Valois. And, at this time, the French cause looks sickly enough."

"Well reasoned!" A glow of admiration showed in his eyes. "Well put! You do not babble of loyalty and the like but of profit, the sovereign motive in the world. By the Mass, Milady, I've often dreamed of a woman like you, not a toy, but a companion, an inspiration. Tous mes hommages! Your management of the King today was brilliant. Exactly the proper touch. As to the stroke you brought off against this de Lallière at Nantua, I've never heard of anything more galliard. When we met at Gayete, Milord Russell, who, as you know, is usually tight-lipped, admitted that he owed the success of his mission to you. Messieurs Château and Loquingham were loud in your praises."

"Thank you, monsieur."

"And to think that this prize is mine!" De Norville's voice grew passionate. "When we are married and put our wits together we shall become a power in Europe. We shall be hand in glove."

She did not repel him. In the game of chess they were playing, each had to be very careful. Her tone could be interpreted as he pleased, and it pleased him.

"Meanwhile, my lord, will you give me an earnest of your confidence now?"

He laughed. "The whole of it. Well, then, Milady, you have, of course, guessed right. After years in the Duke's service, after becoming his chief confidant, and now at a time when his fortunes are most promising, I am not such a fool as to betray him for the sake merely of recovering my lands in the Forez. If he triumphs, as I believe he will, I can expect no less than a duchy. The stakes are high, and they deserve a risk." He broke off to bow. "Madame la Duchesse!"

"But you have certainly betrayed him in some measure, from what I could learn today."

"Yes, apparently. One doesn't buy the King's confidence for nothing. But note. As to the Duke's alliance with England, the invading forces, plans of attack, and so forth, I have told the King nothing that his own spies and scouts would not have reported in two weeks. Indeed, much has been already reported — to confirm me."

"You have denounced the Duke's followers."

De Norville smiled. "I congratulate myself on that play. Nothing has so improved my credit with the King. But, mark you, not a single name of importance, except those, like Saint-Vallier, who are already in prison. The rest are little people of small value to the Duke's cause. And they are being exposed to no more than a temporary inconvenience, as most of them know."

"I don't understand."

"You will in a moment, mademoiselle. Ask yourself the reason for these maneuvers. Come, let me see whether you are as shrewd as I think."

She looked absently past him across the tumbled graves. "To judge from your charges against the Marquis de Vaulx, Captain Bayard, and I know not who else — " She stopped, with a question in her eyes.

"Yes," he encouraged, "there will be princes of the blood involved. Well?"

"Then I should suppose that you are stirring up divisions against the King and weakening his power in the face of these invasions."

"Good!" exclaimed de Norville. "Excellent! That is important, but it is still byplay. It will back the main stroke, but another, quicker move is necessary. Can you guess what?"

She gave a start. "You mean against the King's person?"

He raised his arms, as if to embrace her. "By God, Milady, you are sublime. You are adorable. You have put your finger on the very point. And it is exactly here that your services are required to draw this Most Christian King into the trap."

"What trap?"

She was conscious of a slight hesitation on de Norville's part. He seemed to be studying her and balancing one thing against another

259

in his mind. Perhaps now at the moment of showing her his last card, he had some reservation about it. But the delay was only for an instant. He came to a decision.

"The King's capture. You will see the advantage to England, to the Duke, to the Emperor, of having him in their hands. Especially at this time. Par Dieu, what a stroke! It would pluck the heart out of France, blow it asunder like a house of cards. In the confusion, we would sweep the board and do what we please. The game would be over. And, let me add, Milady, the glory of this, the approval of these princes, would be all yours."

He watched her narrowly but could read nothing behind the gray-green of her eyes.

"I suppose you would have me coquette with the King. Well, I've done that before."

"To be sure," he nodded, "and superbly. This would require little in addition. You would entice him to a certain place. Of course it might be necessary to sacrifice your more intimate charms. You would use your judgment as to that." De Norville added some blunt language.

She made the mistake of flushing. "I thought we were betrothed."

"Bon Dieu!" he stared. "Are we not people of the world? Are we concerned with pettifogging prejudices? I marvel that you strain at such a gnat."

She repaired the slip but found it hard to keep an edge of scorn out of her voice. "Then you don't?"

"Of course not."

"In that case, why should I?" Her smile revealed nothing. "As you say, we are people of the world. . . . But are you sure, my lord, that you intend only the capture of the King?"

Although de Norville's eyes remained limpid as ever, it was as if a film crossed them for a moment.

"Most certainly. Why do you ask?"

"Because murder would be final and so much easier. Dead men are beyond rescue."

Again something drifted across his eyes, but it may only have been the regret he expressed. "Alas, Milady, how right you are in this as in everything! I wish the Duke of Bourbon shared your enlightened views. However, he does not. He could not be brought to accept the King's death. To take His Majesty alive is another matter. He would not balk at that, I think."

Anne repeated the words. "*Would* not? Do you mean that the Constable does not know your plan?"

De Norville sighed. "He is troubled with scruples, points of honor and the like. To help him, his friends must act on their own."

"Then by whose authority have you launched this scheme?" Anne's face suddenly looked brighter, younger. "When I came to Lyons, I was prepared to continue the services I rendered at Blois or Paris — provide what information I could. If the King, knowing what he does, could be enticed to accept me, that was his affair. But, Monsieur de Norville, it will require more than your word to engage me in such a plot as this!"

He nodded. "Yes, I haven't yet a husband's control, though I might have hoped — " He let his eyes soften but met nothing in hers. "So I'll produce my authority — I think you will recognize it — the authority of England." And, drawing a letter from a secret pocket of his cloak, he presented it to her. "Be good enough to read this."

Even in the fading light, she could make out her brother's bold hand. The note had been written after the meeting at Gayete. It was hurried and brief, but definite.

Sir John Russell regretted that he had been unable to discuss Monsieur de Norville's plans with her, but he had only now learned them in detail himself. He heartily endorsed them and knew that King Henry and the Cardinal of York would be well pleased. Therefore, he urged her to co-operate with Monsieur de Norville in every way and at any personal sacrifice, for this was to be expected of her allegiance to the Prince and her devotion to England. No womanish qualms or scruples must deter her from rendering the most efficient service. Messieurs Château and Loquingham, representing the Emperor, entirely approved of de Norville's designs, in the name of His Caesarian Majesty.

"And it would be well," Sir John concluded, "that you marry my lord de Norville at once, since I gather, from what he tells me, that you would fit his purposes better as a wife than unwed. He has this day received a portion of the dowry owing him. Therefore, I expect your obedience in this as in the above. And may God have you in His keeping."

She continued to gaze at the letter after she had finished it. Then, at last, she looked up and returned it to de Norville.

"You had best destroy it," she said tonelessly. "If it were mislaid — "

"No fear of that," he put in. "But do you agree that it gives me authority enough?"

"Yes." She paused before adding, "You can count on me up to a certain point."

"What point is that?"

"I will not forfeit my soul on the authority of brother, King or Emperor."

He looked surprised. "Tiens! There's a hitch I hadn't expected. The words are cryptic, Milady. What do they mean in plain terms?"

"In plain terms this. I share the scruples of the Duke of Bourbon. If, for instance, the assassination of the King, rather than his capture, were your object, I would have none of it. To take a man captive is an allowable ruse of war. But I will not stab him in the back."

For some undefined reason, de Norville had the smug look of one who has played his cards exactly right.

"I have already assured you on that point."

"Then, so far, good. How have you planned it?"

He described his scheme in detail. Within a week or ten days, Milady Russell aiding, he hoped to induce the King to visit him at his château in the Forez, a day's ride distant. There would be much to interest the Prince: the house itself, which de Norville considered as charming a piece of architecture as could be found this side of Italy; some excellent hunting; and, above all, the fact that Anne would be hostess. The King would no doubt make such an excursion incognito; he was not apt to be overly well guarded. At the proper moment, a select company of the Duke's faction would close in.

De Norville smiled. "It will be an unusual honeymoon."

"Honeymoon?"

"Yes, you have read your brother's letter. And, I believe, the King of France is no less favorable to our wedding than the King of England. He has even hinted that he would condescend to be present at the ceremony."

"Why should he want our marriage?"

De Norville shrugged. "A young wife is more tempting. One of those whims."

The long sleeves of Anne's cloak hid her clenched hands. Discipline kept her face placid. The chess game had reached a critical point. Jean de Norville was not the only aspiring nobleman content to prostitute his wife to his ambitions. Did not her own brother side with him? But the shabby dishonor seemed to cling to her, like a fetid breath.

"We'll delay for a while," she said.

"Delay? For what reason?"

"Because I find marriage unnecessary to our purpose. You can provide a chaperon at your house. If the King consents to visit you, if he finds me attractive, he will not hold off because I am unmarried."

"But, again, why the delay?"

She lifted her eyebrows. "Ah, Monsieur de Norville, may I be as frank as you?"

"Je vous en prie, mademoiselle."

"Well, then, being, as you remarked, people of the world, we may leave sentiment to the side and treat our marriage from the standpoint of advantage, mine as well as yours. To be blunt, monsieur mon fiancé, I do not trust you beyond the point where your advantage ends."

It was perhaps to de Norville's credit that he did not look offended. On the contrary, his eyes expressed a glint of approval.

"A shrewd lady!"

"And I do not intend," Anne continued, "to commit myself to you until I can see the future a little clearer. Let these plans of yours be carried out. Let England, the Empire, and the Duke hold France between them. You will have your duchy. My brother will be at leisure to give me away at our wedding. Then, if it still seems profitable, we shall marry." She contrived to smile. "You see, I prefer a less unusual honeymoon."

"The King might insist," he hinted, "if I chose to constrain you."

"That might be unwise, monsieur, if you wish me to help in your plans."

"And is this your obedience to Sir John, your service to England?"

"I think I am serving England well in this."

To her surprise, he looked still more approving. "Corbleu, Milady, we were made for each other! I confess that, apart from your beauty, I considered our marriage chiefly as a suitable alliance. But, on my honor, I love you for your prudence and cool wits. There's my advantage, which will not end. But, so be it, let us delay, if you please."

She curtsied. "I thank you, sir. And now, if you love me, I beg a small favor."

"You have only to ask."

"A trifle to one of your influence. . . . Arrange to have Monsieur de Lallière set free."

He was plainly amused. "Oho! Your lover, after all. As I expected. You need have no qualms in admitting it. Why should you not divert yourself on the road to Geneva? Or perhaps it was policy. In any case, I envy him."

Again the clenched hands within her sleeves, again the inscrutable face.

"You need not. I have no qualms, as you say, and I speak frankly. But he was courteous and gallant. He imagines me a friend. If it could have been helped, I would not have led him into this pickle. In short, he's on my conscience. So, oblige me in this."

She could not tell whether de Norville actually considered her plea or not. He went through the motions of deliberating: pursed his lips, stroked his chin, and frowned.

But at last he said: "Milady, it grieves me to deny you. In the first place, even if I would, I could not pry him loose from the King's grip. What excuse have I to offer after the charges you heard me make today?"

She put in casually, "They were false, of course?"

"Naturally. And that leads me to the main point. I am no friend of de Lallière's, but I should not take so much trouble to incriminate him for the sport of it. The policy we have discussed requires his confession to back the case against de Vaulx, Bayard, and several others. That confession will be made."

"You think so?"

"I am sure of it. From all accounts, the torturer at Pierre-Scize is an artist."

She blundered again. "Gold is a possible key to most prisons. Monsieur, if you will favor me in this, I shall agree to — " She caught herself in time. Of all vain oblations, those made to the Devil are the vainest.

"To what?" he asked eagerly, his eyes probing hers. "To what, mademoiselle?"

"To give you this," she amended, drawing out the Tudor badge on its chain from beneath her bodice. "It is worth two hundred livres tournois at the least. It could be sold or used as you please."

He fingered the medal, smiling. "You care for him enough to sacrifice so treasured a token from the King of England?"

"I care for my own peace of mind."

264

"It seemed to me that you might offer more."

"It is all I have."

"Really?" His eyes probed again. "Now, if you had agreed to give me your lovely hand, without delay — "

"I am not such a fool, monsieur."

"No, you are not a fool. How alike we are!"

The vesper bells woke suddenly above them. The wind, quickening, whipped the leaves among the scattered tombs. The light had become dusk.

"No, it is not enough," he said, releasing the badge. "And I must go. But au revoir soon, m'amie. I have no fear for *your* peace of mind."

It almost flattered her that the words were like a taunt. After all, until now, she had held her own in the game between them.

At her desire, he escorted her to the door of Saint-Pierre. But when he was gone, and she could drop her guard, she stood awhile with one hand pressed to her throat. Then, entering the church, she sunk to her knees before a chapel of the Virgin.

"Blessed Mother of God," she whispered, "help me from this fear! Have mercy upon me!"

Chapter 39

As Jean de Norville had observed, the chief torturer at the prison of Pierre-Scize, Maître Thibault-le-Borgne, was an artist in his craft. Among the countless methods, invented from the beginning of time for inflicting physical and mental anguish on human beings, he knew and had tried a remarkable number. Although future science had not yet contributed its techniques to this most ancient and universal profession, Maître Thibault did very well without them; and probably, indeed, he knew several tricks, which have since lapsed from memory and which, if rediscovered, would surprise and delight modern experts. Long experience, joined with natural talent, had given him such a command of the human fiddles he played on, that he could draw out of them any tune he wished. His percentage of failures was negligible. "Only tell me what you want to hear," he would boast, "and leave the rest to me."

As his name indicated, he was a one-eyed man, having once, as an apprentice, been disciplined by the master he studied under. But that single, cold, oyster eye was not the least of his assets. When intent on a screaming patient, its pale glow, so pitiless and so assured, became a hypnotic point of despair. The rest of his physical appearance served him, too. He had the complexion of a prison fungus, due to a life within walls; and the fine, colorless hair which covered his chest and arms recalled the obscene fur of a white spider. His blunt nose and slobbered lips were equally repulsive. It must be said of him that he followed his calling with single-minded devotion, and that he would have sacrificed meat, drink, and pay for the consuming interest he found in it. But since mastery of any useful art brings recognition and reward, he occupied an official position second only to his better known rival, the city executioner. In his own private laboratory he ruled supreme.

Having been informed by the governor of the Castle that Blaise de Lallière had been given a week in which to make voluntary confession of such and such crimes before being put to the torture, and that a voluntary confession would be right pleasing to Chancellor Duprat, Maître Thibault accepted the problem on those terms. He enjoyed any case, like this, which challenged his resourcefulness; and it was a point of pride with him to turn out a deft piece of work according to specifications. Therefore, during the space of a week, he would not touch Blaise with so much as a finger; but this did not mean that a voluntary confession would not be encouraged and the patient softened up.

First, he inspected the material he had to work upon through the grating in the door of Blaise's cell. The view was gratifying. He noted with satisfaction Blaise's wide shoulders and athletic build. Such a patient could stand a lot. Then, too, the prisoner's mental condition promised well. He did not sit moping and woebegone in a corner but strode up and down with the passion of a newly caged lion. It was much more interesting to tame a fellow like that than someone of no spirit.

Pleased with the outlook, Maître Thibault next consulted the jailer about Blaise's diet and, slim as it was, ordered it cut down by two thirds. Experience taught him that nothing more quickly sapped a patient's resistance than starvation. A full-blooded gallant, like de Lallière, could stand a lot of that, too.

These were preparatory steps. Maître Thibault now launched a

266

method of persuasion which he had found excellent in other cases. For this, he needed a clinical specimen, upon whom he could operate in de Lallière's presence, as a foretaste of what would happen if the voluntary confession was not forthcoming. A man's will often snapped under the weight of such an example properly dished up. Of course, the specimen to be chosen must be some unimportant prisoner, about whose fate no one cared. And now, after consultation again with the jailer, Maître Thibault selected a certain André Michelet for the role. In some respects, the choice was a mistake, but neither the jailer nor Thibault could be blamed for that.

The victim in point was one of the many Bourbon rebels denounced by Jean de Norville. He was a man of twenty-eight, a tradesman in a small way, from the Forez; but he had once served as lackey in de Norville's household. When arrested, he had no funds to pay the customary jailer's fees and so existed on such scraps as that officer chose to afford him. Certainly none of the other political prisoners, with whom the Castle was filled, appeared so negligible and forsaken.

Thus far Blaise had been alone in his cell. But, in view of the crowded condition of the prison, it did not surprise him to receive a companion. Naturally, he treated Michelet with reserve, for no trick was more usual than to place a spy next to a man from whom secrets might be learned. Otherwise, he welcomed him as a diversion from the suspense of his own thoughts.

Michelet, on the other hand, felt encouraged and promoted to find himself in relatively better quarters than the underground limbo from which he had been drawn. In this more privileged section of the Castle, tiers of cells, one above the other, lined a great central court, with the towering keep at one end of it. These tiers opened upon wooden platforms connected by short flights of steps. The cells, having no exterior windows, were lighted only from the court and were, hence, dim enough. But, even so, they were preferable to the damp, vermin-infested dungeons, honeycombing the rock below, where Michelet had spent the last ten days.

He was a simple, modest fellow, greatly impressed to be now sharing a cell with a nobleman, and he abounded in deference.

"I suppose, sir, you're one of Monseigneur de Bourbon's gentlemen."

"I'm accused of it," said Blaise cautiously.

"And a friend of Monseigneur de Norville's?"

267

The answer was so long in coming that the other could only consider it the effect of prudence.

"I have met him."

"I know what you're thinking about, sir, but you have nothing to fear from me."

Michelet was so glad to have someone to talk to, that in a short space he had discussed the few bare items of his life and had begun to discuss them again. How such a man could have been denounced as a Bourbon conspirator passed understanding. Blaise wondered, too, at Michelet's calm. He apparently had no dread of the future and seemed to regard his imprisonment as temporary. His village belonged to de Norville's château, and de Norville's name was often mentioned in a tone of abject submission but also of confidence. That he had been denounced by his overlord seemed to be rather in the nature of an understanding than to call for resentment. And the strange part of it was that he evidently considered Blaise a party to some secret which could be taken for granted between them.

What lay behind this? It looked as if at least some of de Norville's accusations were merely for the show and that their victims knew as much. But this, in turn, pointed to a conspiracy between the man who was supposed to be betraying Bourbon and the Bourbon faction itself.

Desperation sharpens the wits. In the dimness of the cell, while Michelet gossiped on, Blaise recalled the fantastic charges against de Surcy, the innuendoes against Bayard. Suppose de Norville was not a traitor to Bourbon at all. The fact, if it was a fact, that he retained the confidence of the very men whom he was accusing to the King, gave food for thought.

"I take it you don't expect to be hanged," Blaise remarked to his cell mate.

"Hardly, monsieur — any more than you do. But we're not supposed to talk about it, are we?"

"No," agreed Blaise, as if he knew what the other meant.

He could get no further that day without putting Michelet on his guard. But, give him another twenty-four hours, and he hoped to learn more.

At this point the turnkey thrust in the evening ration. It consisted of a little bread and water unaccompanied by the usual coarse meat.

"What's this?" Blaise demanded. "You know that I'm paying a livre a day for my fare. Besides, there're two of us now."

The man said nothing and disappeared. Blaise shouted after him, but he did not return.

Next morning there was no food at all; and no amount of banging on the door brought attention. The first touch of faintness began to be felt by both prisoners. Michelet grew increasingly silent as the day wore on.

Toward late afternoon, the door was thrown open, admitting not the usual turnkey but a couple of men in sleeveless jerkins, with bare muscular arms.

"Come along, both of you," ordered one. "You've a little appointment downstairs with Maître Thibault."

Their brutal faces revealed their trade at once. Blaise stiffened. A week's respite had been given him; but, if the prison chose to disregard it, he had no recourse.

However, he kept his voice steady. "Who's Maître Thibault?"

The other snickered. "You'll soon find out. You'll find him interesting — yes, interesting."

Michelet protested: "But you don't want me. I haven't been brought to trial yet."

"You especially, friend," said the man, gripping Michelet's shoulder.

They went out into the brighter light of the courtyard, which, though gray at that hour, was still sharp enough to make them blink; then down a flight of steps, leading from their tier to the pavement below. A group of soldiers, pitching horseshoes at a peg, stopped the game to stare at them. One laughed and pointed, but a couple shook their heads.

A door at the base of the keep opened on steps, leading downward a long way. Then followed a rock-hewn corridor, with side lanes branching off from it. The place was utterly silent, though probably life went on somehow behind the squat dungeon entrances. The corridor ended finally at a heavy door, which one of the guards opened and then closed with a deep boom, when they had crossed the threshold. A couple of steps led down into a vaulted place full of odd implements.

This was Maître Thibault's workshop. Blaise, at a glance, recognized some of the tools — the rack, the estrapade — but he had no leisure to speculate on the uses of all the overhead ropes and pulleys, the neat array of iron, leather and copper instruments — forceps, tongs, ewers, and the like. His attention was focused on Thibault himself, who stood warming his hands over a brazier. Like his assist-ants, the master wore a sleeveless leather jerkin, wide open on the chest and much spattered from long usage. He was bareheaded, and his grizzled, close-cropped hair stood up stiff but sparse, like the bristles of a currycomb. His shapeless, putty-hued features centered about his one moon eye, which, in spite of its color, looked singularly alert. When the door opened, he was not the only living creature in the room. Near him stood brooding a large goat, Maître Thibault's sole pet and one of his favorite tools for certain operations. As yet, Blaise did not know of the animal's utility; but, as the symbol of Satan, it seemed to him appropriate.

"Bring them over here," Thibault directed in his flat voice, which was nevertheless amplified by the vaulting of the room. But when Blaise and Michelet stood before him, he confined himself to the white-faced tradesman. "Look you, fellow," he drawled, "when you were brought here, we thought we had only a little rebel to deal with. It seems that the net took a bigger fish. We have now learned that you were one of three men appointed by Monseigneur de Bourbon to contrive the death of the King on his recent journey from Moulins to Lyons." Thibault glanced at a sheet of paper. "This has been surely attested. It remains for you to confess it."

If poor André Michelet had been accused of plotting against the Pope, he could not have been more astounded.

"But, sir," he gaped, "it's impossible. It is a mistake. I've never even seen Monseigneur de Bourbon."

"A sturdy liar," cut in Thibault. "Will you confess the crime?"

"How can I confess what is impossible?"

"You have a tongue. You can sign your name or make your mark."

"But —"

"Strip and shave him," the other commanded. "I want him naked as a newborn babe." Maître Thibault knew the daunting effect on a patient — the mingled shame and helplessness — of the preparatory treatment he had ordered. For the first time, his pale eye now slid around to Blaise. "And, Jacques, see to it that this other traitor pays good heed to what we do. It may give him something to think about before his own time comes."

The point of the atrocity was now crystal-clear to Blaise. The whole proceeding was aimed at him. No one would bother about the ruined body of an obscure peasant like Michelet. Hence the bare-faced illegality of his torture. The very preposterousness of the charge against him should convince Blaise that a confession of any sort could be got out of a man who was properly sifted by Maître Thibault. A voluntary confession offered the only escape. In a sense, Blaise was responsible for this poor wretch's torments.

Raging indignation swept personal fears out of mind.

"Have you no shame?" he burst out. "Par Dieu, quel cochon! Where are the judges? Where is the clerk? What reading of the testimony? Since when has a butcher, like you, been given the right to accuse, judge and examine? If I were out of this place — "

"But you are not out," drawled Thibault.

"Even so, I'll inform the governor of the Castle."

Thibault laughed. "Will you?"

By now, they had stripped off Michelet's clothes.

"Better confess, mon ami," Blaise called to him. "You have a clear conscience. Don't give these dogs the satisfaction — "

"If you confess," Thibault interrupted, "you'll burn."

What followed need not be described. It lasted several hours, for Michelet was a strong man and he was fighting for his life. He could not tell whether his confession, in absence of a trial, would be conclusive or not. He dared not risk it. With true virtuosity, Maître Thibault showed much of his art; and, now and then, his eye, shifting from the patient, took stock of Blaise. With regard to him, Maître Thibault could congratulate himself that the performance had a salutary effect.

In the end, sane, delirious or mad — it hardly mattered which — Michelet confessed. He made his mark on the paper with his right hand, which had been spared for the purpose. Then, clothed again — an added torment — the husk of him was carried back to the cell.

During that night, Blaise tended him as best he could. Michelet would not die (an expert like Thibault rarely killed his patients); he was apt to recover in a crippled fashion, and he would never hear again of the confession he had made. But something in his mind was broken forever. Blaise had ample occasion that night to ponder the effects of torture. As this man now was, so would he soon be.

What Michelet could not understand — between the convulsions of pain — was that de Norville, the all-powerful, should have brought him into this plight. He babbled disjointedly of the word which had been passed and the reward held out to him before his arrest. Two weeks of prison at most, he had been told, and then a whole arpent of land, fifty livres. . . . Only he must not speak of this to a soul. Now he did not care.

"But why arrest you at all?" Blaise questioned.

"Some scheme of Monseigneur's. Monsieur should know."

"I swear on my honor that I don't."

"Then how could *I* know?"

"Some plot against the King?"

"By God's cross, I was never told."

But he knew other things. De Norville's name threaded the hours of the night. Only a fool would trust him . . . after what happened at the château . . . to his own wife. She was a pretty lady, monsieur, and rich. . . . She served his turn, allez! Then she died. People said . . .

"What did people say?"

"We servants knew how she died."

Blaise never learned exactly what the servants knew. Michelet's fear of de Norville silenced him even now. Perhaps, after all, he was only delirious. Blaise hoped as much. In hell, as he was, his thought turned to Anne. Like him, she was tangled in de Norville's web.

But when the next day passed and the next, without submission from Blaise, Maître Thibault-le-Borgne tried a further expedient. He had often observed that nothing, short of his laboratory, so crushed a prisoner's resistance as hope built up to a point of certainty and then completely dashed. Indeed, he had developed this technique to a point where it brought him in a sizable revenue. For why should a man forgo legitimate profit when it could be made without betraying his office, and would serve not only his own advantage but that of others as well? It was a scheme which required the aid of several guards, who enjoyed a percentage of the intake; and it had a neat ironic turn that appealed to Thibault's sense of humor. If the governor of the Castle knew anything about it, he may well have closed his eyes to such a useful fraud.

So, once more Thibault's assistants escorted Blaise, now considerably weakened by hunger, to a second meeting with the master. But this time, when the prisoner had been brought to his workshop, Thibault directed his helpers to withdraw, as he wished, he said, to reason with de Lallière alone.

Then, to Blaise's astonishment, the door being closed, Thibault lowered his voice to a whisper and asked a singular question.

"You're a rich man, I take it?"

The possible point of the query was not lost on Blaise. He clutched at the straw. "No, but I have friends."

"It's all one," said Thibault. "I am a poor man and could well use a thousand livres tournois."

"It's a vast sum."

Thibault grinned. "Is it too vast for Monsieur's escape? There are three days left until Monsieur will be shaved — that is, barring a free confession. But, even so, there's the Place de la Grenette."

"Say what you mean."

The other appeared to hesitate: pursed his thick lips, spat thoughtfully. Then, in a still lower voice, he proposed: "See that I get a thousand livres tournois, and I'll put you across the walls."

"How?"

"Cré Dieu, with a rope. That's how."

There was nothing incredible in this offer. A thousand livres meant great riches to one of Thibault's class. Blaise had no reason for supposing him less corruptible than others — quite the reverse. Besides, the biggest hope all along had been bribery, as he had suggested to Pierre.

"You know that I can't communicate with my friends."

"Leave that to me. I'll communicate with them."

Here was the hitch. What friends? Pierre de la Barre would move heaven and earth to raise the money, but the sum stipulated was beyond him. To approach the Marquis, even if he had now reached Lyons, was out of the question. Under heavy suspicion himself, it would be like asking de Surcy to put his head in the noose, providing Thibault was a double-dealer. At all costs, the Marquis must know nothing about it. No, Pierre was the only possibility. He had been the favorite page of the King's beloved sister; he was the cousin of the royal favorite, Jean de la Barre. He was reasonably safe from any treachery of Thibault's. But the Lord only knew how he could procure a thousand livres.

"You ask too much."

"Perhaps Monsieur's friends will decide that I don't."

"And what assurance have they or I that you will not play us false?"

"None," said Thibault with perfect truth. "But they and I can discuss the terms of payment."

A drowning man has no choice. He must grasp even a rotten branch for lack of better.

"Look up Monsieur Pierre de la Barre," said Blaise. "You'll find him, I think, at *The Dauphin* on the Rue de l'Albergerie."

"Pierre de la Barre," nodded the other.

"And how shall I know if the bargain is struck?"

"If the bargain is struck," Thibault repeated, "you'll have a full dish of meat on the night of your escape. It isn't too much in return for a thousand livres."

But when Blaise had been led out, Maître Thibault indulged himself in a moment of soundless laughter. The fool could now build up his hopes; and the higher he built, the deeper his fall.

Chapter 40

On the very afternoon of Blaise's appearance before the King at Saint-Just, Pierre de la Barre left Lyons at top speed, having delayed only long enough to entrust Cocorico to the special care of the landlord at *The Dauphin*. Late that night, he had reached Tarare. An early start next day brought him to Lallière by midmorning.

He had quite understood the importance of fetching Madame de Lallière to Lyons as soon as possible. The King was notably gracious to women. Her testimony in Blaise's case might offset de Norville's. If it did not, Pierre must still have time to establish contact with one of the minor functionaries at the Castle and see what bribery could do. At the moment, however, everything depended on what had become of Madame de Lallière. If she had left the neighborhood of the confiscated manor house, no time could be lost in following her. But Pierre hoped that she and Renée might have been charitably permitted to remain at the château for the present until final disposition was made of it by the Crown. Oppressed, as he was, by Blaise's terrible plight, anxiety for Renée lent him added wings on the ride from Lyons.

Arriving at the hamlet of Lallière, he swept through it and topped the rise to the manor house. Locked gates, painted yellow in token of confiscation, confronted him. The sight of them was as chilling as a dead man's face. Riding closer, he hammered on the panels with his sword hilt, waking desolate echoes from within. No other sound reached him. Still, it was possible that the house might be occupied, and some other entrance used.

Tethering his horse out of sight, he found a foothold in the masonry of the wall and, having scaled it, dropped down into the courtyard beyond. But a glance about him, the very feel of the place, showed utter abandonment. Weeds already pushed up between the cobbles; kitchen gardens were overgrown; a green scum clothed the surface of the duckpond; grass stood high on the summit of the belvedere, where Clairon had once kept watch. The lifeless windows of the house stared at vacancy. Not only men and animals, but the very pigeons of the dovecote had disappeared.

Haunted by the stillness that magnified his own loud footsteps, Pierre crossed over to the main door and knocked. But here, too, only an empty sound came back to him, and he did not repeat the futile gesture. Though not of a reflective turn, he stood for a while distraught by the contrast between now and six weeks ago. He had often pictured his return to Lallière, strong in the King's favor and Blaise's success, as the accredited suitor of Renée. He had varied the scene according to fancy, tricking it out in the gayest colors. And, instead of it, this was the reality.

Well, he must return to the village and make inquiries. He had no time to lose.

So absorbed he was that a dry cough at his shoulder startled him like a cannon shot, and he flung around with one hand on his poniard.

But at once he relaxed. It was Sire François the Sorcerer, who, at the time of Pierre's recent short visit, had helped him to a couple of meetings with Renée in the nearby forest. Indeed, Pierre had never spent a gold crown to better advantage than the one he gave Sire François at their first encounter that morning before the fight at the ford. Since then, the old charlatan, refreshed by another donation, had used all his magical arts to further his young patron's cause.

"Mordieu, beau sire!" Pierre exclaimed. "What do you mean by stealing up on a man like a ghost! You fair jolted me. But I'm glad to see something alive in this place. How did you get here?"

François removed his wide-brimmed hat and bowed so low that his elflocks hung down along his jaws.

"God shield you, monseigneur. I grieve that you were taken aback.

275

Seeing you pass through the village, I followed and entered through the stable wicket. I hope that all is well with Your Grace?"

Pierre flung out both arms. "*Well?*" he echoed. "By Our Lady of the Sorrows, what a question! Where is Mademoiselle Renée? Where is Madame?"

The Sorcerer shook his head. "Yes, there have been great changes since your lordship was here last."

"Jehan!" Pierre snapped. "I can see the changes well enough. But where are the ladies?"

To his immense relief, François answered, "Patience, monseigneur. They're not far off. I took it upon myself to find them a residence when they were cast out from here, and when no one else had the courage to harbor them. I have also provided for their needs out of my own purse to the amount of nine livres and eight deniers. Believe me, they have lacked for nothing."

"Well done!" said Pierre. "Grand merci! You shall be repaid double. . . . A residence?"

"To speak honestly," François admitted, "it's only a hut in the woods; but a roof's a roof. There's such fear of the King and Monsieur de Norville in these parts that the families tainted with treason can expect no help even from kinsfolk. Besides, these ladies do well to stay hidden."

"But they're alone, I take it. The country's full of roving bands."

"They have Clairon," returned the other. He added proudly, "And they're under my protection. I have set up my marks: the black hens and a wolf's head. It's a bold man who wants my curse."

"I must go to them at once. But first tell me what happened when the château was seized."

François described the arrival of the King's people; the arrest of Antoine de Lallière, who had been taken first to Tarare and now, it was said, to Loches; the gutting of the house down to the last clout, the last hen. The ladies had been stripped of every trinket they owned and had been turned out with only the clothes on their backs.

"You spoke of de Norville?" Pierre asked.

The other replied that de Norville's indictments had struck a number of people in the district. Everybody, even the poorest, lived in terror of arrest.

"But, my lord," François went on, "I wonder that Monsieur Blaise and the good Marquis de Vaulx, who stand high with the King, have done nothing to protect Madame and Mademoiselle. And I know that these ladies wonder as much. Perhaps, Monsieur Blaise being in Savoy, the news did not reach him. Now he will take steps — "

"Alas!" Pierre groaned. There was no reason to conceal what had happened, and he outlined the facts. "So you see, my friend, that Madame may be of more help to Monsieur Blaise than he to her. But I doubt if anything she can do will answer. And that leaves only one last shot."

Sire François's colorless wolf-eyes blinked. He made the money sign with his thumb and forefinger.

Pierre nodded. "Yes, if I can get in touch with somebody at the Castle. But it's not so easy."

The sorcerer blinked again and said amazingly, "Leave that to me."

"*You?*"

"If your lordship will take me with him to Lyons, perhaps I can be of service."

"How? I don't understand."

"These are secrets, monseigneur, but I'll tell you. The Sorcerers' Guild is a well-knit fellowship. We stand by each other and find it profitable. I know Maître Thomas-le-Rodeur in Lyons, a most notable member of our brotherhood. The prisons furnish certain ingredients we need for charms, which means that if Maître Thomas isn't pot-fellow with every turnkey in the Castle, I'll eat my staff."

Here was an unexpected ray of light. Pierre gave a deep "ha" of satisfaction. "Corbleu, mon ami, if you can help me pull this off, I'll fill your purse."

The other waved a modest hand. "We can speak of that, my lord, when the bear is skinned."

"Entendu!" said Pierre. "And now conduct me to the ladies. I hope they can set out this afternoon. Will you arrange for the post horses?"

"Without fail," bowed François. "But if Your Grace will be advised by me, you will not descend on these ladies unannounced. They would not wish to be taken by surprise. It might embarrass them."

Pierre understood. "What do you propose?"

"Why not meet the Demoiselle Renée at the Clos des Moines, as your lordship did last time. The cottage is hard by, and I'll bring her word at once. Would that not please Your Grace?"

The sorcerer's knowledge of human nature was more potent than his charms. It had not occurred to Pierre that a meeting between him and Renée alone at this time was possible. But now, thanks to the wizard, it seemed natural.

He glowed. "The very thing. You're my friend, Sire François. I'll meet her at the Clos des Moines. Then we'll wait on Madame together."

No one knew when the ruined monastery, called the Clos des Moines, had been built nor when it had been abandoned. Its heyday belonged to the far off past, hundreds of years ago. Perhaps war had ravaged it, or pestilence; perhaps the monks had simply removed to another abbey. Since then, the forest had crept over it. Ancient oaks and beeches grew here and there in what had once been cloisters and assembly rooms. Fallen columns and arches lay covered with moss or bedded deep under the decay of countless autumns. But fragments of walls remained, or a dim inscription or carving, an occasional broken vault, a doorway leading nowhere. The high altar, now a bank of moss, still overlooked the round which had been a chapel.

And, like the forest, legend had drifted over the Clos des Moines. It was now, of course, haunted and full of dread, given up to midnight sorceries. Sensible people avoided it. Therefore, as guests of Sire François, who erased all evil influences for their benefit, Pierre and Renée could not have found a more private meeting place in the county.

Here, too, as he waited, Pierre was conscious of the change brought by the last weeks; but the change, being natural, soothed rather than distressed him. He had kept a vivid memory of the Clos des Moines at the green crest of summer. Now the golden light of autumn, traversed by falling leaves, brooded over everything. In its crimson and amber, he found the place even more enchanting.

For the moment, recent disaster and impending tragedy faded in his mind. To be on the point of seeing Renée again eclipsed everything else. Seated on the moss-covered base of a vanished column, he kept his eyes fixed on the path which entered the enclosure and listened intently for the first sound of footsteps. She walked so lightly that he would not be apt to hear them far off. The stir of leaves, the shifting of his horse tethered under a nearby oak, deceived him more than once. He had not been waiting long, but it seemed to him hours.

Then, without warning, she was there, under the broken arch at the entrance of the chapel; and, springing up, he crossed the space between them in an instant, dropped to one knee, and pressed her hand to his lips.

In her plain gown, with only a linen scarf on her head, she seemed to him lovelier even than he remembered her. But at once he felt a difference in her and was aware, too, of the difference in himself. Under the shadow of events, they had both grown older and, at the same time, had been drawn much closer. The airs and byplay of a little time ago no longer occurred to either of them.

He slipped his arm around her, as they followed the nave of the ruined chapel.

After a moment, she said: "I knew you would come. I knew you wouldn't be afraid — even of the King. Madame ma mère didn't believe me when I told her you would come."

"Then she knows about our meetings?"

"Yes. I had to talk of you; I couldn't keep it to myself."

"What did she say?"

"She wasn't angry. But she said I mustn't expect to see you again: you belonged to the King and had your way to make; you couldn't marry a girl who has nothing and is the daughter of a rebel. Unless Blaise and Monseigneur de Vaulx — where is Blaise? Why didn't he come?"

He put off the answer. *"Then Madame votre mère approves!"*

Renée looked surprised. "There's no question of approving. When Sire François brought word of you, she hardly believed him. Do you think she would have let me come to you if she didn't approve?"

"Bon Dieu! Bon Dieu! Bon Dieu!" By this time, they were seated on the moss-covered steps of the ancient chancel. In his rapture, Pierre caught her to him and kissed her until the scarf slipped down from her hair. "Bon Dieu!" What he had scarcely been able to hope from success had come to him from ruin. He could not credit such luck as to obtain Renée's hand without bargains and barriers. He kissed her more recklessly than before. "M'amie! M'amour! Then we'll go to her at once and ask her blessing."

Renée hesitated. "Of course, my father hasn't been told."

"It doesn't matter. That will be as it may."

"Or your father."

"Sacristi! Why should he care? I'm only a younger son. In these times, we can't wait to ask everybody. Madame's blessing is enough. No one could call us runaways then."

"And, of course, there's Blaise," said Renée. "Why didn't he come with you?"

Pierre could not spoil the moment by telling her the grim truth. He muttered something about Blaise's being detained and drew her protectively closer to him. She pressed her head against his shoulder. The living silence of the forest closed around them.

They spoke of the recent disaster at Lallière, but not for long. Love was more important. They talked of their first meeting: the Wild Hunt, their adventure on the nearby lily pond, Cocorico, her story about the fairies' wedding veil of golden lace. "Your veil will look finer than that on our wedding day, m'amour," he said. She half lay in his arms, gazing up at him, her dark ringlets matching the color of her eyes. After all, what they spoke of did not matter.

A sudden idea struck him. "Wasn't this a church?"

"Yes, long ago."

"Once a church, always a church."

"But it hasn't a cross," she objected.

"You're right."

He thought a moment. Then, getting up, he walked over to the horse and fetched back his sword, which he had left hanging at the saddlebow.

"Here we are."

Drawing the blade, he plunged it deep into the mound which had once been an altar, so that the gilded hilt stood erect, like a cross.

"Will you give me your promise now," he asked, "and receive mine?"

"But we've already promised."

"Not like this — before God and Heaven."

"Our betrothal! Oh, Pierre . . ." The intonation of her voice lingered like music. Her absolute surrender to him gave her an added radiance.

Then, kneeling in front of the crossed hilt, they said a Paternoster and three Aves. It was irregular, because they forgot how betrothals went; but, if Heaven regards intention, nothing could have been more valid.

"I, Pierre Louis, plight my troth to you, Renée Antoinette, before God, the Blessed Virgin, Saint Michael, and All Saints. . ."

"I, Renée Antoinette, plight my troth. . ."

They were hand in hand. They solemnly kissed when the vows had been made. He gave her his signet ring, the gift of Madame d'Alençon. Except marriage itself, nothing could be so final. He lifted her in the air to kiss her again.

"Now, let us go to Madame votre mère and ask her blessing."

It would take more than her husband's arrest, more than destitution and the utmost of the King's anger, to bend Constance de Lallière's head one jot from its proud erectness. She reserved such bending for God, not men. She might suffer, but she would never strike the flag of her own inmost citadel. As she, together with Clairon, awaited Renée's return in front of the poor hovel which was the best that Sire François could provide, she gave distinction to the place by a sort of reflected nobility.

She had been waiting for some time. Renée was to have brought back young de la Barre after a brief delay, which should permit Madame de Lallière to set things in order. Now one hour had passed. With such a featherhead as Renée, thought her mother, you could count on nothing.

But finally Clairon barked. She caught the sound of hoofs and then saw Pierre leading his horse and walking hand in hand with Renée. Such informality was shocking to one of her school. And yet, inspecting Pierre with keen eyes, she had to admit that he appeared, to the last degree, comme il faut. His carriage, the tilt of his head, the whip-leather grace of him, all showed good form and breeding. His family was, of course, excellent. But what Madame de Lallière could not help doubting was that such a young nobleman could now be serious in his attentions to Renée. She knew the world too well to credit such unworldliness. If Pierre supposed that he could take liberties with Renée, because she was penniless and unprotected, he was apt to have met his match.

"Ha, Monsieur de la Barre," she greeted him, "it is some time since we met. But I grieve to learn that since then, you have been meeting Mademoiselle without my knowledge or consent. You are both much to blame."

If she had been standing in the grande salle of her manor house, she could not have looked more imperious. But Renée did not give Pierre the time to find his words. She flung her arms around her mother's neck.

"Mama, we're betrothed! We've just taken our vows on the cross. See my beautiful ring." She held out Pierre's signet, that hung loosely on her small finger. "Isn't it magnificent?"

281

"Betrothed? Without witnesses?"

"Are the saints no witnesses?"

"But without your father's permission or mine?"

"Ah, Mama, we couldn't wait. It would have been wrong to wait. Pierre — " Renée gave him a glance and her hand. They both knelt.

He said, "We beg your forgiveness, madame, and your blessing."

It was all unusual beyond words. Constance de Lallière's orderly mind turned a little dizzy; but her eyes filled, as she looked down at Renée and Pierre.

"One moment, monsieur," she said. "I wonder if you understand that my daughter has no portion and, worse than that, is the child of a man now guilty of treason against the King. You are a fool, monsieur."

He looked up. "If mademoiselle, in her own right, were Countess of the Forez and ward of His Majesty, she would not be one half so dear to me."

"Is it so, par Dieu! Then I think there are still great hearts in the world." She laid her hands on their heads. "My children, you have my blessing and all my prayers. May God keep and prosper you."

Then she drew them close to her and kissed them.

"But I marvel," she said a moment later, "that Blaise is not here. Did he not know of your coming, sir? Or does he lack your courage? I can't believe it."

Pierre could no longer withhold the bad news. He related the failure of Blaise's mission, de Norville's charges against him and the Marquis, the King's wrath, Blaise's sentence. He expressed the faint hope that Madame de Lallière's testimony might help in some way.

She listened intently, her face white but her eyes undaunted.

When she spoke at last, it was about de Norville. "I always considered the man a serpent and I warned Monsieur de Lallière of him. But I have never heard such villainy as this. Of course, I shall tell the King what I know if he will receive me. But how shall we travel? I have no money. I'm even owing to Sire François who has befriended us."

"No trouble for that," said Pierre. "The post horses have been ordered."

She took thought a moment. "At least, we shall not be at your charge in Lyons. The Abbess of Saint-Pierre is my friend and kinswoman. She will welcome us. It is more fitting anyway than a public inn."

It struck Pierre as ironic that Blaise's mother and Anne Russell should be together in the same convent.

"You will find the English Milady there, of whom I have just been telling you," he warned.

The other's eyes flashed. "I shall not wish to meet the wanton. But, in so vast a place, there is no need of meeting her."

An hour later, they were on the road, with Clairon beside them and with Sire François as a most uncouth but formidable attendant. Any vagabond outlaws would think twice before challenging the wizard's right of way.

Renée sat on a pillion behind Pierre. Now and then, she would lean her cheek against his back; and, feeling her arms about him, he would cover one of her hands with his. Again it occurred to him that misfortune had brought a happiness which he would not exchange for the brightest trophy of success.

Chapter 41

Rumors of Blaise's failure, arrest and sentence reached Denis de Surcy on the way from Geneva. Realizing the gravity of the case, he quickened his speed; but, though prepared for bad news upon reaching Lyons, he did not learn the worst until Pierre de la Barre had given him a complete account on the night of his arrival.

By this time, the young archer had been back two days from the ride to Lallière and could report, in addition to everything else, that the King had refused audience to Blaise's mother. This hope being gone, he concealed from the Marquis his own efforts to secure Blaise's escape from Pierre-Scize before the end of the week. A man in de Surcy's critical position had to be kept clear from any such attempt. Otherwise, he related, step by step, all that had happened since their parting in Geneva.

It was very still in the upper room at *The Dauphin* when he had finished. For awhile the Marquis said nothing but sat clasping one knee, his eyes vacant, his face impassive.

He was considering de Norville's amazing about-face. What accounted, too, for the preposterous charges against Blaise and himself? Vengeance for the rebuff at Lallière? Some connivance between him and Duprat? Perhaps. But the Marquis, with a long experience of intrigue and intriguers, did not feel convinced by such obvious motives.

At last he said half to himself, "Bayard, eh?"

"Yes," returned Pierre, "he also cast doubts on Monsieur de Bayard."

"Ah? Was there anyone else?"

"Not at that time. But there's gossip, which I'd swear rises from him, about the Marshals de Lautrec and de la Palisse. Even the Duke of Alençon is mentioned."

"Ah?"

Then, vengeance could be eliminated. Connivance with Duprat did not cover the case. De Surcy asked himself why Admiral Bonnivet was not involved, and the answer suggested itself that the inefficient Bonnivet could be disregarded. Suspicions were being directed precisely against the King's most devoted and able officers. The Marquis would have given a good deal to know what other names beside his own and Bayard's were to be pressed out of Blaise in the torture room of the Castle.

But one point above all struck the Marquis. Assuming de Norville to be a traitor, no one could call him a fool. On the contrary, he was obviously a genius of intrigue, a very conjurer so to cast his spell not only upon the King but upon Chancellor Duprat, who, though venal, was devoted to the Crown. Why, then, should de Norville forfeit his position with Bourbon and Bourbon's great allies, England and the Empire? Why should he do so, especially at this time when France had her back to the wall?

"Hm-m," murmured de Surcy.

Well, at least he was forewarned as to what he had to expect in tomorrow's interview with the King and could steel himself accordingly. Meekness and appeasing would not do, even if he could have brought himself to truckle. He must meet charge with charge, lies with outspoken frankness. De Norville must be exposed and defeated if the Marquis was to save not only Blaise and himself but perhaps others, perhaps even France. De Surcy did not underestimate the task. He had little time; his enemies were entrenched.

"Alas!" he regretted aloud. "If Madame la Régente were only here, it would be a great help."

"But she *is* here," said Pierre. "The Duchess of Angoulême arrived today unexpectedly and is lodging at Saint-Just."

"Par Dieu!" the Marquis exclaimed, sitting bolt upright. "Why didn't you tell me of it?"

"I did not know that your lordship was especially concerned."

"She's a very bow of promise," returned de Surcy. "There's a cool-headed woman who doesn't snap at the first bait. I don't think Monsieur de Norville will dazzle her. Is there any report as to why she came?"

Pierre shrugged. "State affairs. Some conference with the King."

But it did not seem to the Marquis unlikely that the ever-watchful Louise de Savoie, hearing of de Norville and perhaps of Anne Russell, wished to look over matters for herself. At any rate, here was a possible ally. If he failed with the King, he must turn to the Regent. What troubled him most was the shortness of time.

Next morning, in an anteroom at Saint-Just, de Surcy had leisure to reflect on the brittleness of worldly honors. He was like a man stricken with the plague, whose very neighborhood is dangerous. Six weeks ago, these courtiers, chatting with each other here and there, would have flocked about him, eager for a word from the great Marquis. Now he might almost as well have been invisible. A few saluted him furtively and distantly, but all kept away from the window alcove where he was seated. Chancellor Duprat emerging from the royal apartment passed by but did not appear to see him. De Norville, surrounded by a group of admirers, strolled down the room, handsome as an Apollo, and had the effrontery to glance at him with a smile. Long familiar with the ways of princes, de Surcy had often seen a career of devoted service go out in snuff. That this now threatened him was not surprising. The sun must set for everyone.

But it took all his philosophy to endure the long wait, until at last a black-clad usher summoned him to attendance on the King. Then, head up and serene, he disregarded the heavy silence which followed him to the door.

In the room beyond, Francis sat at the end of a long table, which had served for a council meeting earlier in the day. The chairs around it were still disarranged, and a litter of papers had not yet been removed. That de Surcy, for many years a member of the council, had not been invited to attend it was a fitting preface to the interview.

For a space, the King said nothing but went on reading a letter, while the Marquis waited. The gorgeousness of the royal dress struck a discordant note in the thin light from the gothic windows. It recalled the King's chronic disease, his incurable youthfulness, which would never adapt itself to the graver colors of life, which would keep him twenty-one as long as he lived. He was not a cruel man or even less honest than most people: he was only young, in spite of his thirty years, and had the flaws as well as the charms of youth. But the storm that was now breaking upon him could not be daffed aside by inexperience.

An ironic smile twitched the Marquis's thin lips. Looking up suddenly, the King noticed it and flushed above the line of his beard. He was somewhat in the position of a grown-up schoolboy sitting in judgment on his old master, and he could not quite shake off the earlier sense of inferiority. How often, as a mere stripling, in the days of the late King, when he was only Duke of Angoulême and by no means sure of the Throne, had he listened with deference to the instructions of the Marquis and courted his approval! Now something of this lingered on and daunted him, in spite of himself.

"Ha, Monsieur de Vaulx!" he snapped. "You seem merry."

"No, Sire, only philosophical."

"Then I wish you'd lend me some of your philosophy. Things are in a sorry pickle. Do you agree with me?"

"I can think of none sorrier since the days of the English a hundred years ago."

With a scowl, Francis hinted at the issue between them. "Perhaps Bourbon may still be taken — no thanks to you. In that case, we'll have one enemy the less."

Inflexibly, the other discouraged the hope. "I should not count on it, Sire. Except for an accident, I believe he will escape."

"And then?"

"Then he will be more dangerous than if he had headed a rebellion here in France. His flight was a shrewd stroke. We shall have much to suffer from him for a long time."

"By God, you're cool!" The King wrenched his chair around from the table. His eyes burned; his long nose quivered. "And who's to blame for it? Who's to blame that Bourbon isn't in my hands at this moment?"

"You are, Sire."

"Bon Dieu!" choked Francis. "I like your insolence!"

"Is it insolence to recall to Your Grace that you had Monseigneur the Constable in your hands a month ago, when you visited him at Moulins, and that I urged his arrest at that time?"

"I gave you my reasons," fumed the King.

"You did, Sire. It is for you to judge whether they were good reasons."

"And does that clear you?" Francis's rage boiled into sarcasm. "When, by God's favor, you had Monsieur de Bourbon and his fellow plotters of England and the Empire in a sack, perhaps I'm to blame that you so managed as to let them out of it. What do you say?"

"What Your Majesty thinks. I am guilty of failure and have no excuse."

"No excuse, indeed! But you are guilty of more than failure, Monsieur le Marquis. You are guilty of treason."

The King had the triumphant look of one who is about to spring a trap. Evidently he expected the other to show confusion and dismay. He was visibly taken aback when de Surcy smiled.

"Nonsense — if Your Highness will forgive the word. Sire, by your leave, we shall not beat about the bush. I know what infamous charges a notorious traitor has invented against Blaise de Lallière and me. There is no use soiling Your Majesty's lips by repeating them nor my ears by hearing them. They are as flimsy as they are vicious, and that is saying a great deal."

It was clear that Francis had looked forward to playing cat-and-mouse with his victim, gradually hemming him in with the unexpected knowledge of his treachery. De Surcy's boldness took the wind from the King's sails. For a moment, he sat crestfallen.

"How did you know?"

"From Pierre de la Barre, who was present when the scoundrel told these lies to Your Grace. But I could have learned of them just as well from anybody else. They seem to be common property of the court. It appears that Your Majesty does not care enough for the reputation of an old servant to protect it from slander until said lies have been disproved."

The King actually gulped. From his standpoint, the conversation was taking a very unfortunate turn. He felt the teacher-pupil constraint more strongly than ever. Instead of accusing, he was being accused. The only remedy for this was bluster.

"By God, sir," he rapped, "if you were anyone else, you would now be in chains."

"I thank Your Majesty. As the reward for a lifetime of service, not to be in chains is, I suppose, the utmost that I could expect."

"But, if you know these charges, man, disprove them, disprove them. It is all I ask."

"Then I summon the Duke of Bourbon to deny that I met or had any communication whatever with him at Moulins."

"You're safe enough there," retorted the King. "He will hardly answer the summons."

"Precisely. So that that point rests on the word of a self-confessed liar as opposed to mine."

"Self-confessed? What do you mean?"

"If he betrays the Duke, has he not lied to him? But I go on to the charge that I disclosed valuable information to the rebels at Lallière. And against this, I summon two witnesses. First, the King of France. Your Majesty was informed in detail of what I said on that occasion and why I said it. Next, I summon Constance de Lallière, now in Lyons. She overheard everything at the dinner. She will testify what small comfort those gentlemen derived from my disclosures — so small, indeed, that I all but lost my life because of it next day."

The King was impressed. He looked down; he fiddled with a piece of paper on the table. "There may be something in this. But I notice that you do not defend the notable rascal, Blaise de Lallière, whom you employed against my warning."

De Surcy did not yield an inch. "Why should I defend him? Do you not perceive, Sire, that if de Norville lies about me, he lies about de Lallière? Clear water and foul does not proceed from the same source. As to my employing him, I ask what would have been Your Grace's judgment of me if I had sent no one at all upon the traces of Sir John Russell. For there was no one else to send. I had always found Blaise de Lallière able and devoted. But, for my sending him and for his failure, I take the entire blame, and I take it all the more because I forced the mission upon him."

"Oho!" said the King, feeling that here was an important admission. "That confirms de Norville."

"It confirms him no whit." The Marquis swept his hand as if clearing away cobwebs. "My defense, though I scorn to use the word, is a countercharge. I accuse this knave of conspiring against Your Grace; of betraying my lord of Bourbon in order to set him up; of sowing dissension among Your Majesty's true followers; of malicious lies to that end; of a secret understanding with Milady Russell, a known agent of England."

This last may have been a shrewd guess; but, at that moment, it was poor tactics. The King's face darkened. He had had a pleasant visit yesterday at the Abbey of Saint-Pierre.

"Let him be brought to trial," de Surcy went on. "Let him confess these crimes or else be put to the torture. I wager my head that he'll confess them in due time. Is it not topsy-turvy justice that this fate is reserved for a man like Blaise de Lallière, who has fought and bled for Your Majesty, and that he should be condemned to death on the word of a turncoat, who has thus far served the enemies of France? Is it justice that he should suffer imprisonment and death, because of a trick played on him by a woman, and that she should go free?"

The King's eyes smoldered, but he said nothing.

De Surcy should not have been guilty of the next blunder.

"I should like to know what Madame la Régente will say to that, for I believe it was she who considered it wise to dispatch Milady Russell from France."

A great blunder. If the Marquis had not been carried away by his indignation, he would not have fallen into it. It is not well to remind a king of his mother's authority.

Francis rose from his chair, trembling with anger. Passion freed him from any boyhood deference. He stood towering above the older man.

"We have had enough of this. You have taken it upon yourself to lesson me, monsieur, and I do not choose to be lessoned. I think you need to cool your head at Pierre-Scize, as well as your accomplice."

De Surcy's eyes met the King's, and something of their gray coolness tempered the other's heat.

"I am in Your Majesty's power. But, for the sake of the Throne, which I have long served, I ask you, Sire, to take thought of the effect which my arrest will have in France at a time when unity and loyalty are most needed."

"You threaten?"

"Yes, if facts be threats and to point them out be to threaten. I tell Your Highness plain that self-willed tyranny cannot long replace justice. I demand, for Blaise de Lallière and myself, a fair trial before judges appointed by the Parlement of Paris, with benefit of counsel and proper hearing of witnesses."

"*Demand* is a round word. . . ."

"I have the right to use it, I think, if not as a nobleman of France, then on the even better ground of forty years' service."

In the contest of eye to eye, the King did not get the best of it. It was an unusual experience for him to meet flint instead of putty, so unusual that it checked his anger in mid-course.

"Begone!" he said abruptly. "But do not venture to leave Lyons. If I bear with you for the moment, it is because of those years when you were not a traitor nor the protector of traitors. Not a word more! Do not goad me too far, Monsieur le Marquis. As for Blaise de Lallière, he has had his trial and will undergo his punishment. As for you, do not be concerned: you will have your trial, too. And I think that de Lallière's confession will add something to it."

De Surcy bowed as low as etiquette required but not an inch lower. Nor did the King silence him.

Bold as ever, he answered: "May Your Majesty discover the truth in time — not for my sake but your own!"

The courtiers outside could draw no conclusions from the Marquis's bearing. Some even feared that they had been mistaken in assuming his disgrace. But, as he rode down the steep path from Saint-Just, dread rode behind him. He must lose no time in seeking an audience with Louise de Savoie. That was the last hope.

In the courtyard of *The Dauphin,* a man passed him of so odd and sinister an appearance that it drew his attention. Glancing over his shoulder, the Marquis noticed that people made way for this person as if to avoid contact with him.

"Who is he?" de Surcy asked one of the ostlers.

The fellow spat before answering. "That, monseigneur, is Thibault-le-Borgne, torturer at Pierre-Scize."

With this omen in mind, the Marquis repaired to his room and finished a letter to the Regent, which he dispatched at once.

Chapter 42

Sire François the Sorcerer's eminent colleague at Lyons, Thomas-le-Rodeur, showed no lack of good will toward his fellow wizard from the Forez and treated him to an excellent dinner at the sign of *The Goat,* an ill-famed tavern in the suburbs. But, with regard to corrupting one of the turnkeys at Pierre-Scize, he confessed himself helpless. If it had been any of the other prisons in Lyons, he might have been useful; but Pierre-Scize was a royal castle reserved for political prisoners and independent of the city. From the governor down to the youngest turnkey, it was staffed by appointees of the Crown, between whom and the Sorcerers' Guild no business relations existed. On the other hand, through underground leakage, Maître Thomas knew a good deal about the methods of Thibault-le-Borgne and urged Sire François, for God's love, to stay clear of him.

So, when a private communication from Thibault reached Pierre, summoning him to a meeting that night at the slaughterhouse near Saint-Paul's, Sire François warned him urgently against the rendezvous.

"It's an old game of Thibault's, your lordship."

"How so?" asked Pierre, his hopes dashed by the other's bleak expression.

"Why, just that. This Thibault, it seems, is a very honest man. He'd as soon forgo the chance of tormenting a poor fellow into jelly as to cut off his own right hand. But he sees no harm in a little side-profit. You pay him your money, and he keeps the prisoner. They say, too, he finds it useful in his work to let said prisoner believe that he has escaped and then seize him at the last moment. Cat-and-mouse business, your honor. Breaks a man's nerve."

"What do you mean, *believe he has escaped?*"

"Well, sir, it's like this. As I said, Maître Thibault's an honest man. He promises to set the prisoner across the walls. There's the bargain, and he keeps it. What happens then can't be blamed on him. He lets the prisoner down by a rope from the battlement — into a squad of soldiers at the bottom. They each get their cut, and everybody's happy except the prisoner. It's as neat as that."

"Cré fils de putain!" Pierre cursed. "But if the trick's so well known, how is anyone fooled by it?"

291

"Ah, monsieur, the people he deals with are not so privileged as your honor. They haven't the advantage of a private tip. They only hear afterwards that the stroke has failed, no fault of Maître Thibault's. What can they do about it? Besides, the trick isn't played too often. The last time was a year ago. My friend, Thomas, heard about it from one of the soldiers."

Pierre fell into thought. Sire François did some mind reading.

"If you're thinking of a rescue, when Monsieur Blaise has once been taken by the guards, it's impossible, my lord. The rope is let down to the steep path on the north front of the Castle, where supplies are brought up by muleback. The soldiers line up against the wall and can't be seen from above. There's no point from which they can be attacked. They simply march the prisoner in through the door at the top of the path."

"So that's it," said Pierre. He sat scratching his head.

François added: "Believe me, there's nothing to be done through Maître Thibault, monsieur."

"Perhaps not," Pierre agreed. "But I'll see the fellow anyway. I'll hear what he says." A grimace twisted the young man's lips. "At least I might have the satisfaction of slipping a knife into him."

Sire François sympathized. "I can well understand the pleasure. But where's the profit? You would only ruin yourself without helping Monsieur Blaise. Believe me, this meeting with you is known to others at the Castle. I see no good in it. But if your honor must go, act simple, my lord. Don't let him guess that you're onto him."

"Trust me for that," said Pierre. "We'll talk things over when I get back."

The slaughterhouse and meat market close to the church of Saint-Paul could be reached within a few minutes' walk from *The Dauphin*. To find it in the tangle of narrow streets behind the church, one had only to follow one's nose. The stench deepened on nearer approach until, even in absolute darkness, there could be no doubt that this was the place. But the darkness was not absolute. An occasional house lantern or a lamp before some shrine served as guides along the nine-foot-wide alleyways and revealed the scurrying rats, which became more numerous in proximity to the butcher shops. There, too, the sounds of penned animals, awaiting slaughter in the morning, grew louder.

Half groping his way along, Pierre now and then held his nose;

but every minute he remained alert against possible attack of foot-pad or night prowler, and, upon meeting some rare passer-by, he handled his poniard, as no doubt the other man was handling his. At last, when the stench had reached its worst, a shrine lamp indicated rather then revealed the row of shuttered stalls, which gave a kind of façade to the abattoir. Along this, he walked slowly and still more watchfully, for here was the assigned place.

Then, without warning, the door of one of the shops swung open, a bull's-eye lantern flashed on him, and a flat voice enquired, "Monsieur de la Barre?"

"The same."

"In here, if you please."

Upon entering, Pierre found himself in a confined space little larger than a vestibule and connected with the shed behind it, from which came the sound of pent-up animals. The light from the lantern roused a hum of flies, which clung to a couple of raw carcasses swinging on hooks from the rafters of the shop. The fetor here was indescribable, as if one had stepped into the belly of a decayed whale.

To Pierre, the man confronting him seemed appropriate to the place. In spite of good nerves, it was hard to repress a shudder at the corpse-white face, with its one clammy and speculative eye; the thick, moist lips; the dense fuzz on the hand closest to the lantern.

On his side, Maître Thibault saw in Pierre an inexperienced youth ripe for picking.

"By your leave," he drawled, "we'll get down to business at once."

The proposal he made followed the pattern which Sire François had outlined. He would furnish a rope by which Blaise could descend from the walls, providing his terms were met. Three days remained of the week of grace. "After that," said Thibault dryly, "he'll be in no condition to move."

"And your price?"

"A thousand livres tournois."

"Sang Dieu, where do you think I can find a thousand livres?"

"That's your affair. I'll not take a penny less. It's worth the while to risk my neck for that sum but for nothing under it."

"Five hundred livres," Pierre countered.

"We're wasting time, young man. I said a thousand to the penny."

"After Monsieur de Lallière is free?"

Maître Thibault gave a silent laugh. "No, before — and counted down."

"How do I know you will keep your bargain?"

"My word on it."

Pierre reached a conclusion. He must play the fellow's game and outplay him, if possible. It was a long chance but the only one.

"See here," he said, "your word means nothing to me. But I'll do this. Slip me into the Castle, and I'll pay you the thousand livres before Monsieur de Lallière and I go down the rope. I'll escape with him."

On the point of a flat refusal, Thibault checked himself. He was struck by an excellent idea. Why not let this cocky blade become involved in the same coil as his friend? Let him be taken by the waiting guards as well as the other. It would be easy to show that he had entered the Castle in disguise, that he had provided the rope. As an abettor of de Lallière's attempted escape, he would be guilty of a capital crime. And then what a laboratory specimen he would make to secure Blaise's confession! What had been done to Michelet would be nothing in comparison to Pierre's treatment. The very thought of it brought a trickle to the corner of Thibault's ugly mouth.

But he pretended to hesitate. "We'll have no time on the walls to count up money. By God, I intend to assay every piece of it. No tricks or counterfeits for me!"

"You can reckon and assay beforehand. But I'll keep the purse until we're ready to cross the walls."

"You'll enter the Castle unarmed, mind that."

"Why not? Do you expect me to carry the place singlehanded?"

Again Thibault hid his eagerness. "Well, have it your way. It's a peck of trouble for nothing, but I don't object. Young gentlemen like you oughtn't to be so mistrustful. Anybody could tell you that my word's my bond. If I undertake to see your friend across the walls, I'll do it. For a thousand livres, remember! Don't come short by a groat."

Pierre showed confidence on that score which he was far from feeling. "You'll have your money. But how do I get into the Castle?"

Maître Thibault thought it over. "Dress yourself up as a muleboy, and speak to Sire André, who's in charge of the supply mules. I'll drop him a word about you. When you're once inside, he'll bring me word that you're there." Thibault added significantly, "You have just three days."

They parted without farewells. The torturer congratulated himself on as good a stroke of business as he had ever pulled off. The amount of the bribe was exactly right: big enough to make Pierre believe that the recipient was in earnest, but not too big to be raised. Thibault felt certain that a showy young fellow like de la Barre could find that much cash — from the moneylenders, if necessary.

But Pierre's thoughts on the way back to *The Dauphin* were dark enough. How to raise the sum demanded was the first big obstacle. Pierre reckoned that he could sell the bracelet which de Surcy had given him for perhaps five hundred livres. He might borrow a hundred more. But where the balance would come from, he had no idea. Doubtless prayers and vows to Our Lady furnished the best hope; for, to raise that balance, without involving the Marquis, required a miracle.

Chapter 43

Meanwhile, penned up with the crippled Michelet in the cell at Pierre-Scize, Blaise de Lallière continued to suffer the pangs of starvation and the anguish of suspense. Had Thibault communicated with Pierre de la Barre? Would Pierre be able to get together the money needed? Could the torturer be depended on to carry out his agreement? As the days and nights passed, each of them incredibly long, there was not even a hint of an answer to any of these questions. The signal that the bargain had been struck was to be a full meal on the night of escape. With his heart pounding, Blaise would listen to the approach of the turnkey bringing the evening ration. The door would open; the wretched fragment of moldy bread would be thrust in; the sickening disappointment would be repeated; then the torment of waiting and hoping until the next night would begin over again.

With Michelet before him, it was harrowing to look forward to his own torture. Imagination kept rehearsing every detail of the process. These hands and limbs and muscles, now so strong, would presently cease to belong to him except as a burden of pain to be carted off at last to excruciating death on the Place de la Grenette. Hanging or decapitation would have been mild as compared with his sentence of quartering, which meant being torn apart by four horses. But that was not the worst of it. The supreme fear was of dishonor, that in the delirium of suffering, he might be forced to incriminate falsely the men he most admired and to whom he was most indebted, de Surcy and Bayard.

Meanwhile, too, by constant attendance on Michelet, he had learned enough to convince him that Jean de Norville, however unscrupulous, was at least not a traitor to Bourbon; that he was heading a conspiracy against the King, which, unless blocked in time, was even more dangerous than the armed invasions. And yet what could Blaise, shut up here and convicted of treason, do about it? No ear that he could reach would believe him.

Often his mind turned to Anne Russell, wondering at the conjunction of the stars which had brought them so fatefully together. He owed his destruction to her, and yet, strange as it was, he never thought of her bitterly. Instead, it comforted him to review their days together on the road to Geneva. Under the shadow of approaching death, romance offered a brief anodyne. The memory that she had acclaimed him a gentleman challenged his courage. His one remaining hope was that he might continue worthy of that title.

Four days dwindled to three, then to two, then to one. Only two more nights remained of the week's respite. Why fool himself any longer? Either Pierre had not been reached or he could do nothing. Obviously any appeal that Madame de Lallière might have made to the King had been rejected.

On this last night but one, Blaise resolved to expect nothing. As on other nights, the door opened, the turnkey entered and went out. Blaise, seated next to Michelet's pallet, did not turn his head. But then he became aware of a strange odor. The next moment, springing up, he stood gazing at two heaping bowls of meat.

The first effect was one of faintness so acute that he leaned against the wall, fighting down the pumping of his heart. Now that the despaired-of signal had come, he could hardly rally himself to accept it.

Michelet was staring. "Meat?" he said feebly. "Monsieur, is it meat?"

"Yes."

The crippled man cried, "Thank God! Oh, thank God!"

Mechanically Blaise fetched him the vittles, then threw himself upon his own ration. At first, he could think of nothing but eating.

It took an effort at last to hold back. In view of the night's work, he must not gorge himself. He would need all his alertness. So he ate slowly and put off finishing. Probably he would not be summoned by Thibault for some hours.

All his faculties now focused on escape. Evidently Thibault had received the bribe and intended to keep the bargain, or he would not have given the proposed signal. The possibility of a cat-and-mouse trick did not cross Blaise's mind. Escape, he felt, was certain. As to what would happen beyond the walls of Pierre-Scize, he hardly gave it a thought. He was sure of only one thing, that he would never again be taken alive.

Pretending to sleep, he lay on his straw, tense as a drawn bowstring. Without benefit of a clock, he could only guess at the passing of the hours. He heard the remote sound of the guard changing in the courtyard below. That meant close to midnight. But a long time seemed to pass after that before the lock of the door rattled, and the turnkey, accompanied by one of Thibault's valets, summoned him forth. Doubtless the turnkey assumed that the prisoner was to be subjected to another inquisition. Michelet, drugged by the unaccustomed food, did not stir.

Once again, with Thibault's bare-armed apprentice, Blaise descended the steps to the courtyard. It was a moonless night with only a faint show of stars. Entering the door at the base of the keep, he followed the underground corridor to Thibault's sanctum.

But this time, when his guard left him at the threshold and the door was closed, he found that Thibault was not alone. A tall, ragged fellow, with a muleteer's whip in one hand, stood facing him. It took more than one glance before he recognized Pierre de la Barre.

"Bon Dieu!" he exclaimed. "It isn't possible! C'est bien toi?"

They threw their arms about each other, though Blaise, who had not seen a mirror for a week, wondered at the shocked expression on Pierre's face.

"Mon ami, how can I thank you?"

To Maître Thibault, almost bursting with ironic glee, which his one fishy eye managed to conceal, this scene, except for one to be enjoyed later on, was the dessert and payoff of his calculations. He could not resist prolonging it. His lips parted in a moist grin.

"Surprises you, doesn't it, monsieur?" he said to Blaise. "I like to surprise people."

Blaise continued to feast his eyes on Pierre. After the week of hell he had passed, the sight of his friend's face was heaven. But he noticed an odd intenseness in the other's gaze, that puzzled him. It seemed as if Pierre wanted to communicate something but was deterred by Thibault's presence.

"Yes, I'm surprised indeed," Blaise answered absently. What was Pierre trying to tell him?

"You see," Thibault went on, "this young gentleman thinks the worst of people. He wouldn't take my word that I meant to deal squarely by you, but insisted on overseeing the job himself."

"You've counted the money, haven't you?" said Pierre. "It's the full sum." He slapped his belt-purse. "But I'll keep it until we're on the walls. How about starting?"

Thibault grinned again. "You're a bold one, Monsieur Cock. Suppose I wanted to lay you by the heels and take your money, what could you do about it?"

"I'd show you when the time came," said Pierre.

The other shook with mirth. It issued in a snicker. "Yes, you're a bold one. I'd like to have the handling of you. Perhaps some day I shall. But, for now, we'll finish off this business. You'll see how Thibault-le-Borgne keeps an agreement." He reached behind him on the table and laid hold of a coiled rope. "Here you are — as good hemp as ever hanged a rogue." Then, pointing to a low door across the room, he added: "We'll get to the walls that way. . . . Oh, no, gentlemen, you in front. I'll keep behind you."

Along a shoulder-high tunnel ascending through the rock, each followed the other. Blaise longed to exchange a word with Pierre but found no opportunity. Thibault was at his shoulder, and the foul breath of the man reached past him. They emerged in the pitch-dark courtyard behind the bulge of the keep and were thus screened from the sentinel patrolling beneath the tiers of cells. Immediately at hand, steps led up to the battlement.

"Dépechez-vous!" hissed Thibault.

A few seconds later, they were on the walls, and were still concealed by the huge mass of the keep from any eyes in the courtyard.

"Now, mark you," Thibault whispered, "when I loop the rope around that merlon, the end of it will just reach the mule path up from the Porte de Pierre-Scize. Bonne chance, messieurs! But first hand over my money."

In the darkness, Blaise could hear Pierre unbuckling the purse. "There you are."

But, in handling the purse, it must have slipped from his hand or Thibault's and it dropped between them. With an oath, Thibault stooped to retrieve it. And, in the same instant began a furious struggle, one man on the back of the other, the pair reeling to and fro, but no sound except the scuffle of feet.

"Hold the bastard," gasped Pierre, "hold him, for God's sake. If I lose my grip on this thong — "

Blaise's arms found Thibault and closed about him. Completely bewildered as to what was on foot, Blaise could only follow Pierre's lead. There was a sound as if a bone snapped. Thibault's head sagged abruptly to one side. But, for a moment, Pierre continued to twist the loop he had made of the muleteer's whip, which had unexpectedly become a strangling thong. When he left off, Thibault lay huddled on his face against the battlement.

"What's the game?" Blaise whispered.

Pierre snatched up the rope and the purse. "No time to talk. Come on. Keep behind me." And he began running along the wall toward the west, bending forward to merge with the breast-high rampart of the battlement, so that his silhouette could not be seen from the courtyard. Still at a loss, Blaise followed him close, up and down the steps which connected one level with another, around the occasional turrets which broke the continuity of the ramparts — and so to a point on the walls almost opposite the one which Thibault had selected. Since, at that time, no enemy menaced Lyons, guards were not posted on the battlements; and the hour of the night precluded casual encounters.

"Here," said Pierre, knotting the rope to form a noose, which he dropped over one of the merlons in the rampart. Then he drew it taut, with one foot braced against the masonry. The rest of the rope he tossed down over the wall.

But something had caught the attention of guards in the courtyard. A hail sounded, "Qui va là?" At the same moment, another distant hail rose from outside the walls beneath the point where Thibault had been strangled.

"Hurry!" breathed Pierre. Straddling the rampart, he grasped the rope and swung clear. "Come on."

Blaise waited an instant, then followed. The rope burned his hands as he went down. At the foot of the rope, he found Pierre waiting but not alone; another shape loomed beside him.

"Who's this?" Blaise challenged.

"A friend," came the answer, "François from Lallière. This way. Quick!"

The shadowy form set off running up the steep slope of Fourvière which faced this side of the Castle with its fields and vineyards. Breathing hard, Blaise and Pierre kept behind him.

But now a roar of oaths came from the walls. "Halte-là!"

Something sang next to Blaise's ear and buried itself in the ground in front of him. A trumpet sounded within the castle.

"They'll lay on the dogs," he thought. "I hope we have horses waiting."

Exhausted from prison, he found it hard to keep up the pace which their guide set. Then suddenly the latter stopped at what seemed to be a rubble of stones, among which a brook flowed downhill.

"Follow close," said François.

For some thirty yards, he waded up stream, then disappeared through a clump of low bushes to the right. A moment later Blaise found himself underground in the complete darkness of what seemed a vault.

"No dogs will find us here," said François, striking a light from his tinderbox, "unless they can follow scent through water. This is the meeting place of our guild in Lyons."

Chapter 44

For centuries, the walls of the Roman city of Lugdunum, which formerly stood on the heights of Fourvière, a name derived, indeed, from the original Forum, had supplied the stone and lime for the building of the newer town of Lyons. At length the earth absorbed what remained of them; fields and vineyards covered the site of temples, villas and amphitheaters. Even the memory of the ancient city faded to only a few pale references in ancient manuscripts. But, beneath the surface of the vine-clad hill, fragments of old foundations remained, arches that still defied the weight of earth and time, secret chambers paved with broken mosaic.

It was in one of these that Blaise now found himself. Candles were lighted, and he caught his breath sufficiently to glance around. Here stood something that looked like an altar; a serpent-entwined head lay pictured on the floor. Between two columns, blocked by rubble, peered out a marble face with ghostly, startling features. The pediments of other columns had been arranged to serve as seats. Perhaps it had once formed part of a temple to Hecate, goddess of magic. If so, it was highly appropriate as a meeting place of the latter-day sorcerers, themselves a most ancient fraternity, who claimed descent from the Druids. In any event, it had long been used for this purpose, no one knew how long. The place smelled of damp age, the more pungent because of a lingering odor of incense used by the magicians in certain rites. To Blaise, it smacked uncannily of the Devil, and he crossed himself when Sire François was not looking.

"You will give me your solemn oaths," said the latter, "to keep this place secret from every living soul. I doubt if any layman has ever before entered it. And, with all modesty, I can tell you that no one but François of the Forez could have obtained the privilege of bringing you here. As it was, my good friend, Le Rodeur, made such objections —" He broke off with a stare at Blaise, "Cré matin de matin! What a change! I hardly recognize you, monsieur. A very skeleton! That gray in your hair!"

"Gray?"

"A white lock, like a plume," Pierre put in. "And your beard!"

Blaise sat down on one of the pediments. He felt very tired and a little faint. "Three weeks of the Castle, mes amis. But this last week —" The horror of it in retrospect, the incredible relief of escape, swept over him suddenly. He covered his face with his hands.

Pierre filled the pause with a profanity which might have been envied by any trooper in the King's forces. He concluded with the bitter regret that he could not have taken his time to kill the obscenity torturer, who deserved impalement among other things.

Blaise forgot the past sufferings in curiosity. "I still don't know why you strangled him. It was well done, of course; but he had kept his bargain."

"The cursed double-dealer!" Pierre growled. "Didn't you hear those shouts on the other side of the Castle, where we were supposed to go down? Wait till I tell you. . . ."

He gave an account of Thibault's game, as he had heard it from Sire François. The idea of taking the rascal in his own trap had come to him during their meeting at the slaughterhouse. Then he and

301

François had worked it out together. Since he could take no arms into the Castle, some means of killing had to be devised, which would be both silent and effective. The muleteer's whip suited his disguise and could not be challenged. It had been especially prepared for the use to be made of it. Pierre and François had rehearsed the dropping of the money-pouch, the sudden placing of the thong. They had reconnoitered the walls of the Castle from the outside to determine where the final descent should be made. Thomas-le-Rodeur had been talked into permitting the use of this vault as a hiding place. But, though carefully worked out, the scheme needed luck, and luck had served them.

"Saint John!" said Blaise, his voice a little husky with gratitude, "I don't see how I can ever thank you both." He paused a moment to clear his throat. "You haven't told me, though, how you ever raised a thousand livres in two days. That strikes me as the most wonderful part of it. I suppose Monseigneur the Marquis —"

"No," Pierre interrupted. He looked unusually solemn. "That, monsieur, was a downright miracle. You owe your escape to Our Blessed Lady herself, and I owe her a pilgrimage to Loreto as soon as possible. It was like this. The best I could do was to raise five hundred livres — not a sou more. If it couldn't be helped, I meant to turn to the Marquis, as a last resort, but only then, because he's in the black of the King's disfavor as it is. Our friend, Sire François, offered to turn me out some magical coins, which would fool almost anybody; but that took time, and we shouldn't have dared to try them on a fox like Thibault anyway. So, nothing remained but heaven. I put the case before Our Lady at her chapel in Saint-John's. And, presto, I had hardly finished praying, when the thought came to me of the good Abbess of Saint-Pierre, Madame Antoinette d'Armagnac. Until then, she hadn't even crossed my mind. Here, said this thought, is a friend of Madame de Lallière's, and she certainly has the cash if she can be brought to lend it. So, at once I crossed the city to that convent, talked with Madame your mother and Renée, and left them to do what they could in the next couple of hours. At the end of which time, back I came, still praying most fervently to Our Lady. Well, monsieur, the prayers were not in vain." Pierre broke off for effect. His eyes grew rounder. "If anyone ever scoffs to me after this about the value of prayer, I'll have the bastard's blood. There was Mademoiselle Renée, who gave me three rings of value, item a piece of gold worth two hundred and fifty livres. But — wait — this said piece of gold was in the shape of a rose, a manifest token of the Rose of Heaven."

"A rose?" Blaise exclaimed. "Can you describe it?"

"As if I couldn't! It was eight-sided and hung on a thin chain. Such a medallion as the Blessed Virgin herself might have worn."

"And this came from the Abbess?"

"From who else? Though naturally, in such a case, no names were mentioned. For her own sake and the convent's, Madame d'Armagnac could not risk the charge of treason against the King. Well, what do you think of *that* miracle? With the rings and the gold piece, I had a hundred and fifty livres too much."

Blaise sat silent in elated wonder. Far from questioning the miracle, he alone knew how great it was. That Anne Russell should have parted with her chief treasure for his sake filled him with new life and new purpose. No other restorative in the gift of Heaven could have brought so quick a cure. He could feel returning strength tingle through him.

"Marvelous!" he muttered. "Look you, Pierre, did you leave this rose in pledge, or did you sell it?"

"In pledge, with the Italian bankers on the Place du Change. Since we lost no money to the dog, Thibault, it can now be redeemed, together with the rings, and returned to Madame l'Abbesse."

"Not the rose!" said Blaise. "Pierre, mon ami, if you will do me the grace to return the money for it and let me have this rose, I shall make it good to you for twice the value, if I live. And, if not, I still ask it of your friendship. What! Give back such a talisman, the very proof of God's favor? I should say not! I'll wear it from henceforth, and it shall bring me luck. Say that you'll pleasure me in this."

Pierre could well understand the value of such an amulet: the direct answer to prayer, if not a gift of the Blessed Virgin herself. It would be no theft to keep it under the circumstances; and, if anybody needed luck, it was Blaise.

"Of course I will," he said heartily. "And may it profit you! All I want is to redeem my bracelet when we're once out of this coil. I value it for memory's sake." He stopped with a sudden frown. "But how the deuce can I show up at the Medici bank after this? The hue and cry will be on my traces just as much as on yours. It would cost me my neck to be found in Lyons."

Sire François put in, "Your lordship has the receipt for these jewels?"

303

Pierre slapped his chest. "Next my skin."

"Why, then, Your Grace, I could arrange matters, if you sign the paper and are willing to trust me with the money."

It was a big risk, but Pierre agreed at once. "We're trusting you with our lives as it is. You could make a handsome thing of it, beau sire, if you wanted to sell us out."

Perhaps François wondered a little at his own virtue. Strange as it may seem, he loved Renée de Lallière in the sentimental fashion of an old rogue who allows himself one benevolence. He had seen her grow up and had favored her with his most powerful charms. He valued her confidence in him. It was flattering to be a sort of goblin protector to her and this open-handed young nobleman. Of course, in the end, he expected to profit by his honesty; but he would have been the last person on earth to betray them.

Now his yellow teeth showed in a grin. "Well said, my lord. I am a sorcerer, not a Judas. Your honor shows sense. I'll take charge of this affair in the morning, return the money and rings to Mademoiselle Renée, and bring the gold piece here. Your worships can rest assured that you won't lose by it; and," he added significantly, "knowing your bounty, neither shall I."

Pierre took oath that he certainly would not. "And now," he directed, "set forth the vittles and wine we laid by. We'll feed and talk over plans."

While eating, Pierre, with some complacency in his role of leader, sketched out what ought to be done. They would lie low tomorrow until the hunt had died down, then start across country to the first point where horses could be hired and ride the post into central France. It would be unsafe to head for the de la Barre homestead in Poitou, as the King's officers would no doubt search in that direction. But Pierre had kinsmen near Turenne in the Limousin, who would put them up for the time being. Meanwhile, it could be hoped that the storm would blow over. The Marquis was counting on the good offices of Madame la Régente.

"So Her Highness is in Lyons?" Blaise interrupted.

"Yes, Monseigneur de Vaulx has an audience with her tomorrow. When he hears that you're out of the Castle, he'll draw calm breath for the first time. Tomorrow your week would have been up, and he feared that his audience with the Duchess came too late."

"What time does he wait upon her, do you know?"

"Close before supper. Why?" Blaise said nothing. After a moment,

Pierre added. "Well, monsieur, those are the plans for us and they're good ones. I hope you approve."

He was astonished when Blaise shook his head. "They're good enough, but not for me. I intend to wait on the Regent tomorrow myself — with my lord de Vaulx, if possible."

Pierre shook his head. "Mon pauvre ami! No wonder you're unsettled. But a little rest — "

"Nonsense!" smiled Blaise. "I'm not mad. You ought to see that it's the only thing I can do."

"You mean, enter the King's headquarters at Saint-Just, appear before Her Highness at the very moment when a price has been put on your head? And you say you're not mad! Why not walk straight back to the Castle? It would save trouble."

"I'll have to take the risk that Madame la Régente will not give me up. Listen, Pierre." Blaise leaned forward to tap his friend on the knee. "There are two reasons for seeing her: first, because the Marquis will be charged with my escape, though he had nothing to do with it. He has enough on his shoulders without that. Second, I have something to tell Her Grace regarding Jean de Norville that she doesn't know. It concerns the King and the safety of France. Yes, and there's a third reason. I have a score to settle with de Norville himself; the score of his lies about me, the score of this last week at Pierre-Scize. I don't intend to scurry off and leave him riding high — not if I can pluck him down. Do you understand?"

François the Sorcerer's eyes looked intent. "Cré coquin!" he rumbled. "I think I can guess what Monsieur will point out to Her Highness. This Seigneur de Norville's game has a queer smell even to a poor bonhomme like me."

"But how?" Pierre demanded. "How will you even pass the gates of Saint-Just? You'll be collared by the first guard."

"Not if I've changed as much as you and Sire François have been telling me. A bag of bones; a dusty, round-shouldered courier, with gray in his beard and hair. And that change can be improved. A courier who has ridden day and night from Paris with an urgent message to Her Highness. Who would recognize me? For, mark you, the last place on earth where anyone expects to find Blaise de Lallière is at Saint-Just. In any case, I'll chance it."

Apparently far off but actually near at hand sounded the belling of dogs and hallooing of riders along the slope of the hill. The sounds died away. Sire François grinned.

For a moment, Pierre sat listening, then he snapped his fingers.

"Well, *Out of the frying-pan into the fire* is our motto. We'll chance it together. And God send us another miracle!"

Chapter 45

"Do you suspect Duprat?"

Louise de Savoie's toneless voice betrayed no more emotion than if she had asked today's quotation on barley per bushel, and her face looked as blank as a chess player's who had just made a move. But the Marquis, an old hand at the verbal game, gave the question a moment's thought before answering. Duprat was his enemy. This was an invitation to denounce him. It must be declined.

"If Your Grace means do I suspect him of being false to the King, most certainly not."

"But of being mistaken in his estimate of Monsieur de Norville?"

"Most certainly yes."

"And perhaps of receiving — shall we say — a valuable gift in return for his support of that gentleman?"

Again, the invitation. De Surcy shrugged. "Your Highness knows Monsieur le Chancelier more intimately than I."

Louise gave one of her sidelong smiles, which expressed so much experience and so much disillusionment. Then she remarked: "If I had asked him these questions about you, I hardly believe that he would have been so charitable."

But, as the Marquis said nothing, she let the subject drop and sat for a while in silence, tapping the arm of her chair with long, blunt fingers.

De Surcy's guess that her unexpected visit to Lyons might be concerned with Jean de Norville's activities and with the King's revived passion for Anne Russell had proved completely accurate. The disturbing news of both had alerted the maternal devotion which was the one unvarying principle of her life. She suspected the Savoy adventurer and the English milady to such an extent that not even the crisis in northern France could prevent her from making a brief excursion south to appraise the situation for herself. But, with customary indirectness, she disguised her motives to the King and others, alleging only the need of a conference with His Grace — on measures to be taken for the defense of the frontiers.

Caution was necessary. The King had outgrown her leading strings, if not the need for them, and resented interference on her part. Until Francis had crossed the Alps, her office as Regent did not become fully operative; the power remained his, and he was apt to assert it. So, casually and obliquely, she had probed the de Norville-Russell affair; questioning, now, Duprat, now, some other courtier in a pleasant, offhand fashion; treating de Norville himself with distinguished favor; and drawing inferences, the one more disquieting than the last. If the Marquis had been kept waiting several days for his audience with her, it was because of her caution in receiving a man so out of favor with the King and from no lack of eagerness on her side. Their present meeting was furtive, almost secret. De Surcy, disguised in the mask so often worn by noblemen of the time, had been accompanied to Saint-Just by Giovanni Passano, her Italian maître d'hôtel, who vouched for him at the gates. She received him in private.

Now, having heard his account, she thought it over in silence. As far as her expression went, he could not tell whether she sided with him or his enemies. But they had known each other a long time and shared one talent in common, the talent of shrewdness. He could not believe that she would be taken in by de Norville's sleight of hand.

When she spoke again, it was apparently once more in reference to Duprat, but the remark had a further bearing.

"You may not have heard that the Chancellor urged your arrest today following last night's escape of your protégé, de Lallière, from prison, and the murder of that fellow, Thibault. He vows you contrived it through young de la Barre, for fear of what the said de Lallière might confess. I had some trouble to prevent His Majesty from issuing the order. It is the first time that I have taken action in this affair." She added, as if to disclaim any partiality toward the Marquis, "I did not wish to be deprived of learning your opinion of it."

He bowed his acknowledgment.

"I suppose the Chancellor is right?" she added, with a lift of her thin brows. "You need have no fear of admitting it to me. It was only natural that you should wish to procure the young man's escape — for every reason."

"On my honor," said the Marquis, "I had nothing to do with it

307

nor was I a party to the plan in any way. But let me confess that I rejoice at his freedom and am sorry that I had no hand in helping him."

Louise nodded. "Well, if you say you did not, I believe you." She paused a moment. "And I shall go further. I believe all your statements to me touching this man de Norville. I believe them the sooner because he has slandered me to His Majesty as well as you."

De Surcy gave a start of amazement. "You, madame? It's incredible."

"Not so incredible. Of course, he does not as yet accuse me of betraying the King. That would be a mistake. His approach is gradual. He must prepare the ground, instill the poison drop by drop. A hint, a smile, the air of knowing more than he says. But, ah, with so much reverence for me!"

She broke off, impassive as before. But de Surcy became conscious of a strange tension in the atmosphere of the room.

To break the silence, he said: "What poison? What does he hint at?"

And at that, he perceived that Louise's cool objectivity was, on this occasion, neither cool nor objective at all, but the effect of an anger so intense that it found no adequate outlet. As in the case of any extreme emotion, grief or hatred, it seemed frozen because it could not express itself. For an instant, the Marquis looked into the eyes of incarnate fury; Louise's nunlike face was distorted. Then, almost at once, she controlled herself; but her words came like the hiss of vapor from a cauldron.

"What does the triple obscenity hint at? God uphold me! Why, that the regard I once had for Charles de Bourbon, the favor I deigned to show him — " She was unable to complete the sentence. "That I am still an apple ripe for his teeth. Sang Dieu! That he, the Duke, I say, has confided his passion for me to this whoreson — his hope of possessing me when he has seized the Kingdom. That my hatred of him is only the other face of an old love which could be renewed. That, hence, the King should bear this in mind with regard to all business concerning the Duke."

Words failed her again. The Marquis, remembering her bitter persecution of Bourbon, could only exclaim:

"De Norville must be mad!"

"Yes, if Satan be mad." The flame of the Duchess's anger subsided again. "For, like the Devil, his aim is to separate heart from heart, friend from friend, loyalty from allegiance. That much is clear. For whose benefit? I think that is clear, too. And, like the Devil, he has the power of enchantment."

De Surcy nodded. In his long experience, he had never encountered so matchless an intriguer. "But, in attacking Your Highness, he overreaches himself. How did you learn of it, madame?"

"I have means of knowing," she said evasively, "and I can put two and two together. . . . Now, look you, Monsieur de Vaulx, we shall get nowhere if we do not believe this man capable of anything. He will not overreach himself; for, mark my word, he can read the King like a book, and has planned his game to the last trick. I repeat, an enchanter. He makes people believe what he pleases. The Chancellor is his puppet. The court flocks around him. He has the King on several hooks: love of art, love of sport, love of a woman. Who could imagine that the King has even consented to visit him next week at his place in the Forez!"

"No!" exclaimed the Marquis.

"Yes — with Milady Russell to greet him there. You can judge from that how much a prisoner she is!"

"It must be prevented, madame."

"How?"

"By force, if necessary. Monsieur de la Palisse or Monsieur le Grand Maître might agree to — "

"To what? Armed disobedience? And give de Norville at once the stake he seems to be playing for — disunity, strife at such a time as this? Nenni."

"At least they could accompany the King."

"If he would accept their company. I doubt it. Par Dieu, the trouble is that we have no proof against de Norville except our own convictions."

The Marquis was a realist. "There is always a last expedient."

"Yes, I had thought of it — for him and his English trollop. It may be the best plan. The objection is — "

A knock sounded.

"Your mask," she whispered. And, rising so that she stood between the Marquis and the door, she called sharply, "Yes?"

A voice answered from the threshold. "Your Highness, a courier — "

"Did I not make it plain that I wished to be private at this time? Are my orders to be overlooked because some courier arrives? Cré Dieu! Begone!"

"Madame, I cry you mercy. The fellow is from the North in all haste with a dispatch from Monseigneur de la Trémouille. He says that he must give it into Your Grace's own hands, that it is of the utmost consequence."

A pause followed. The English were advancing from Calais. This might be the news of some disaster. The Regent could not delay receiving it.

"Well," she directed, "send him in then — alone." And, while the Marquis stood half concealed in the shadow of a window alcove, she waited near the door.

A bearded man, gray with dust, in clothes that looked too big for him, entered and knelt. She was struck by the lock of white hair across his head. Otherwise she might have considered him young.

"Eh bien, cette lettre," she demanded. "I hope you bring no ill tidings."

He looked up. "I beg forgiveness. There is no letter. Does Your Highness recognize me?"

"*No letter?*" She drew a step back, at once on the alert. "What has my recognizing you to do with your impertinence — "

"I am Blaise de Lallière."

She eyed him, speechless; while, at the same moment, de Surcy turned from the window with a sharp exclamation and crossed the room. "Blaise! You! What does this mean?"

They had not met since that last night in Geneva. Since then a lifetime seemed to have intervened. For the length of an embrace, the Regent was forgotten. Then, remembering her, the Marquis drew back.

"I crave your pardon, madame. The surprise . . ."

"Yes," said the Regent, "and I have still to know what it means." Her face showed curiosity mingled with speculation. "Are you mad, sir, to show yourself here? Do you forget that it is my duty to hand you over at once to the King's justice? An escaped traitor, who has added one more crime to the list by killing a servant of His Majesty at the Castle? And you force yourself in upon me under false pretenses. I marvel at your effrontery. What have you to say?"

Perhaps it surprised the Regent that Blaise kept his head up and his voice firm. "As to handing me over to justice, Your Grace will do as seems best, when I have explained what brings me here. You will judge, too, madame, whether the ruse which I contrived to gain admittance was warranted or not. I could think of no other way to

310

speak with Your Highness and Monseigneur de Vaulx at the same time, as it was important that I should."

"Who told you of our meeting?" Louise interrupted. "Pierre de la Barre, I suppose?"

"Yes, he knew that Monseigneur was summoned by Your Grace for this hour. Since I could have no doubt of the topic to be discussed, and since I have information which bears on it, Your Grace will perhaps agree that I consulted my duty rather than my safety in venturing here, even if I am no more than an escaped traitor."

"Well enough put," she said dryly. "And what topic were we discussing?"

"Jean de Norville, madame. There could be no other."

"Ah? Well, say on. What information have you?"

"Of a definite conspiracy, which de Norville, under cover of betraying the Seigneur de Bourbon, has hatched against the King."

The Duchess, who had seated herself, leaned forward intently. "Eh bien?"

Blaise described the past week at Pierre-Scize. He reported in detail what he had learned from Michelet as to the compensation promised him for his imprisonment and the assurances that said imprisonment would be brief. There could be no doubt of a similar understanding on the part of others whom de Norville had denounced.

"These promises," de Surcy asked, "were they made by de Norville in person?"

"No, by the steward of his manor house."

"Hm-m. And did Michelet give the names of others to whom like promises were made?"

"He did not, my lord, but he gathered that he was not the only one so favored."

"Of course, he would," the Marquis agreed. "If one, then many. But alas, this brings us little further than we were. Though it points suspicion, it proves nothing. The promises of a steward, the babblings of a man unhinged by torture, are not in themselves of weight enough to convict de Norville. We must have facts so absolute that they cannot be smiled away. Is it not so, Your Highness?"

Louise nodded. "Yes, Monsieur Satan would make short work of this."

"By your leave," said Blaise, "it seems to me that your lordships miss one point. Michelet was given to understand that he would

311

soon be freed. Why *soon?* How could he soon be freed unless by some event now pending, which in itself would set at liberty those of the Bourbon faction? Perhaps the victory in arms of England and the Empire. But another event is possible here in Lyons, of no less danger to France and of help to the Duke of Bourbon. If de Norville is no traitor to the Duke but is conspiring against the person of the King, your lordships will gather what event I mean and will seek to prevent it. That, to my thinking, is the chief value of what I learned from Michelet: not charges against de Norville, but a warning to act at once in defense of His Majesty."

"By God," exclaimed the Regent approvingly, "spoken like a Daniel! Prison has sharpened your wits, Monsieur de Lallière. The reasons you give are sound. De Norville cannot hope to continue his present course for long. He must know that the charges he makes are too absurd for credit and will recoil against him. But they fog the air for another thrust which he must soon press home. Sow dissension among us, then strike at the King — and farewell France! Aha! The scent is hot. Do you smell it, Monsieur le Marquis?"

De Surcy nodded. "Yes, but what then, madame, as long as the King takes this devil for an angel of light?"

With her head tipped back against the cushion of her chair, Louise gazed upward at the ceiling. After a pause, she said to Blaise: "I take it that vengeance as well as duty brought you here, monsieur? You have every reason to hate de Norville."

Blaise clenched his fists but said nothing.

"Hatred is a thirsty passion," she went on. "We must help you to quench that thirst." She glanced at the Marquis. "Here, Monsieur de Vaulx, is one man we can count on, one who will stop at nothing. There are not many such at the moment."

"Your Grace has only to command me," Blaise put in.

For a brief space, she looked tempted, then shook her head. "It may come to killing him, but not now. That would settle nothing. The King would consider him a victim. It would only make his lies seem true and inflame the canker of them. No . . ."

She fell to pondering.

"Sirs," she said at last, "there is nothing for it but this. The King must himself discover de Norville's treachery. Anything short of that will not serve the purpose. And that, I grant you, entails a risk; but the risk must be taken. Now, as I told you, Monsieur le Marquis, the King rides next Thursday week to de Norville's estate, Chavan-la-Tour, in the Forez. He will ride incognito and, except for his lackeys, poorly attended. If de Norville is plotting anything against His Majesty's person, the stroke will be made there. As the custom is, when the King travels, a number of servants will be sent before him with baggage and oddments to ready his chambers to receive him. Now, mark you, I shall so arrange it through the maître d'hôtel, Monsieur de Luppé, who is my friend, that you, Monsieur de Lallière, shall be one of those domestics. And I shall see to your disguise myself. I'm rather good at masquerade. Of course, the said de Luppé will know only that you are one of my people. Do you follow me?"

"Yes, madame," Blaise said eagerly. "And then?"

"You will keep your eyes and ears open: study the manor house, arrangement of rooms and the like; give heed to gossip and rumors, especially of any armed men in the neighborhood. The King will arrive with de Norville and a few of his gentlemen. But I shall see to it that Monsieur de la Palisse, with some men-at-arms, arrives also from Feurs that same evening, as if by accident. You will report whatever you have learned to him and take his orders. He will be informed of you."

De Surcy objected. "But, Your Highness, will not the show of force compel de Norville to postpone any attempt he might have planned?"

"There will be no show of force. A few men only but well chosen. They will be instructed not to seem on the alert. However, Monsieur de Lallière will so arrange that he and La Palisse shall at all times shadow the King."

"It is hard to foresee every move," demurred the Marquis.

"Yes, there's the risk. But I think the English girl will be used. She and her room are especially to be watched. Your chance, perhaps" — Louise smiled at Blaise — "to even the score with her, mon ami."

Blaise concealed a start under a bow. So, Anne Russell was to be at Chavan, too — in what role he could easily guess. The relentless stars remained implacable, and suddenly the adventure which he had been welcoming lost its savor. It was likely enough to prove again a dilemma between love and hate. But there was no possible retreat from it. He must meet and solve it as best he could.

"If I may make so bold," he said, "I should like to have Pierre de la Barre with me in this. Two are better than one, as I see it, for the purpose."

She nodded. "A good idea. Where is he now?"

313

"He arrived with me. He is dressed as a muleteer and, ma foi, he looks the part."

"Good. I shall put you and him in the hands of my maître d'hôtel, Messer Giovanni, who has all the craft of Italy. He will enlist you among my people and keep you hidden until you set out for the Forez. . . . Ah, Monsieur de Lallière, if you serve me well in this, your fortune is made. Think what honor will be yours with the King, all the greater because of his misjudgment of you."

Once, Blaise had rejoiced in the Regent's promises. By now, he had learned their value and took them as routine. If he could retrieve himself, restore the Marquis to favor, and at the same time scotch a serpent in this venture at Chavan, he asked nothing more. He contrived to smile, but his heart did not flutter.

The Marquis's glance met his with a twinkle. "Are there no promises for me, madame?" asked de Surcy.

She understood the irony but overlooked it. "Yes, my good lord. I shall follow the King to the Forez. If things go as we hope, I shall join him next day at Chavan and celebrate a little triumph of my own. You shall be with me. I can think of no finer promise than that."

"Nor I," said the Marquis, "providing Your Grace will but add one more, that this time there shall be no slip between the cup and the lip."

PART FOUR

Chapter 46

Seen from a distance, the white façades of Chavan-la-Tour, de Norville's splendid mansion in the Forez, resembled a stately swan riding the water of the small lake surrounding it. And, like the reflection of a swan, the mirrored picture of its walls, now clear, now vague with ripples, added depth and softness and ever-varying beauty. In many ways it was similar to Azay-le-Rideau, that pearl of handsome residences, which had just been completed in distant Touraine. It had the same L shape, half inclosing the courtyard or court d'honneur, the same principal wing four stories high, connected at right angles with a shorter wing, the same round-bellied turrets with conical roofs at every outer corner of the building. And, like Azay, it retained no features of a medieval castle except those which served to adorn it: the corner turrets, the battlement connecting them along the whole outer side of the château. But the turrets were only for symmetry, and the battlement had become a third-floor inclosed gallery of many windows affording an excellent view of the surrounding country. Indeed, as compared with the dark castles of the past, this had a wealth of mullioned windows on every side, now single, now in pairs extending up to the handsome dormers of the lofty and steep-pitched roofs. And everywhere could be felt the Italian passion for artistry and grace: in the rich decoration of the courtyard façades; the fluted columns that flanked the windows; the niches, friezes, and fan-shaped transoms; the sculptured cupids, garlands, and medallions.

Hardly less than the château itself, the landscape around it was the effect of art. Originally the old castle of Chavan, of which one turret still remained at the southeast corner of the building, had stood in an open field, its moat supplied by a stream flowing down from the Tarare hills to the nearby Loire. Now a shallow lake replaced the field; an artificial island, formed of piles, supported the new

315

château; a fine stone bridge of several arches led from the courtyard to the mainland. And around the lake, screening from sight the stables, kennels and other dependencies, together with the village beyond them, stretched a league or more of parkland, the preserve of deer and wild boar. Thus, in concentric rings, like the setting of some rich jewel, forest and water relieved the dazzle of white stone, softened its outlines, and gave the impression of enchanted peace.

Altogether, Chavan-la-Tour, brand-new and still smelling of mortar, proclaimed the new age, the age born in Italy and now permeating the North. It symbolized many things: the revived cult of beauty, the worship of human intelligence, the passionate concern in all that ministers to the senses. And, by implication, it bore witness to the passing of the former age, dark and gothic, perhaps, but more convinced of spiritual values.

To Blaise de Lallière, arriving with the King's baggage train, the first view of it was breath-taking. He stood bemused on the shore of the lake, as if the gracious house beyond the bridge were glamoury and a vision. Even the muleteers and lackeys of the convoy stopped their chatter for a moment to gape at it. But then an odd idea struck Blaise and gradually tempered his enthusiasm. He found a resemblance between the magnificent château and its owner. According to this notion, which went on developing in his mind, Chavan-la-Tour became an architectural portrait of de Norville. The same external grace, the same fair-seeming. It was the kind of house that de Norville would inevitably build. It showed his versatility, finesse, and intelligence; but, while displaying art, it also implied artfulness and artificiality. No shadow of the past, no accent of the soil, such as clung to the weathered walls of Lallière, were apparent here. Disdainfully modern, its self-assurance rejected tradition and traditional standards. The result was disquieting, even menacing, in spite of the superficial beauty. It seemed to Blaise that he learned more about de Norville from each new facet of the château, and that the man's personality, subtle and dangerous, attended him from the very moment of his setting foot on the bridge.

Monsieur de Luppé, who had been selected from the King's maîtres d'hôtel to oversee the luggage and servants on this occasion, had been well coached by Louise de Savoie. Concerning Blaise and Pierre, under the names of Goujon and Berthelet, he was told that they were men appointed by the Regent to watch over His Majesty's safety during the excursion to Chavan. He was, therefore, to treat them as secret agents and to give them every facility in his power to learn the arrangement of the château and to pick up whatever information they could from de Norville's household. Accordingly, with this end in view, he attached them to his person, as valet and groom; so that, while others of the convoy were lodged in the dependencies on the mainland, Blaise and Pierre had quarters in the château itself adjoining de Luppé's room. And accordingly, too, Blaise, carrying the sword and cloak of his supposed master, accompanied the latter on a tour of the mansion, which de Luppé's office as the royal harbinger required him to make.

They were shown around by de Norville's steward, one Charles Bertran, whose name Blaise recalled from Michelet's talk in the cell at Pierre-Scize. Bertran was the man who had promised Michelet compensation for his imprisonment. No doubt, then, more than anyone else at Chavan, he enjoyed de Norville's confidence; and Blaise studied him narrowly, but he could read nothing on the steward's bland features save the desire to please so great a gentleman as the King's maître d'hôtel and pride in the house which he was exhibiting.

There was every reason for pride. The stately rooms of the first floor with their panels and tapestry, their richly decorated beams and superb, canopied fireplaces, made a fine showing. Monsieur de Luppé gratified the steward by remarking that none of His Majesty's palaces could show more splendid furniture. He exclaimed, too, at the magnificent stairway, adapted from Italy, no longer spiral but ascending straight from landing to landing, of which there were then but two other examples in France. Equally new was the generous lighting of these stairs by the row of mullioned windows on each landing. As for the bedrooms on the second floor, they yielded nothing in splendor to the formal apartments below them. Here was Monsieur de Norville's room, which had been prepared for the King's use. The stonecutters, said Bertran, had finished but yesterday the King's crowned salamander carved in stone above the canopy of the fireplace with the royal device *nutrisco et extinquo*. As a further compliment, a frieze of F's, the King's initial, had been painted in gold around the edge of the canopy, while a wrought-iron fireback in the form of a shield with the three fleurs-de-lis had been newly installed. The vast bed occupied an alcove, which accounted for half of one wall. It was shut off from the rest of the room by heavy damask curtains and could be reached only by velvet-covered steps leading up three feet from the floor.

This room and bed Monsieur de Luppé dutifully examined but found nothing to criticize. The bedcords had been properly strung and the sheets lavendered. Perfume pastilles were ready for lighting. The King's chests had been unpacked, and his extensive wardrobe, toilet articles and the like, had been duly arranged in the right places.

"Perfect," said Monsieur de Luppé, who then inspected the accommodations for the King's gentlemen in adjoining rooms and found them excellent. "You know your business, Maître Bertran. I congratulate you. And what rooms are those down the corridor on the other side of the landing?"

"They are occupied by the ladies, monseigneur, the very noble Milady Russell, Monsieur de Norville's fiancée, and her chaperon, the noble Madame de Saint-Martin of Lyons, together with their women."

"At no inconvenient distance," winked de Luppé. "The more I see of Chavan, the more certain I am that the King my master will be well pleased. This chaperon — I take it she's no dragon?"

Bertran gave a sleek smile. "Most carefully selected by the Abbess of Saint-Pierre — at His Majesty's command."

"Ah, alors," chuckled de Luppé, "tout est en train."

In the background, Blaise stiffened. Hints of this kind were commonplace; but now, as applied to Anne, they nettled him. He glanced down the vacant corridor, both hoping and dreading to catch a glimpse of her.

"You will wish," said Bertran, "to view the gallery above," and led the way up the magnificent stairs to the third floor.

Here the crenelations of the mock battlement, which crowned the exterior façades of the house, were so many windows lining an inclosed promenade that extended two thirds around the château. It was a broad gallery with tapestried walls, hung here and there with paintings acquired in Italy or diversified by sculptures and objets d'art. The fine parquet floor, beautifully polished, was not the least of its features. But today, more than anything else, de Luppé and Blaise were attracted by the magnificent view to be had from its windows, westward across the Loire toward the mountains dividing Forez from Auvergne; southward, a distant glimpse of the town of Feurs; eastward, the hills of Tarare and the Lyonnais: a charming landscape of woodland and meadows, water and mountains, infinitely pleasing to the eye.

Blaise reckoned the distance to Feurs as no more than a league.

This was the place from which Marshal de la Palisse would lead his men-at-arms day after tomorrow night, and where the Regent, together with Denis de Surcy, would await the news of what happened at Chavan. It was reassuringly near. Today was Tuesday; the King and de Norville would arrive Thursday evening. By that time, Blaise hoped to have smelled out something of de Norville's plans.

In the great, vaulted kitchen, where he and Pierre supped with their comrades of the baggage train and with the numerous servants of the château, there was gossip enough but none which remotely indicated any conspiracy at Chavan. If a plot existed, the servants probably had no part in it. On the other hand, casual remarks showed more than once how clearly the assembled lackeys sized up the reason for the King's visit to the château. Coarse language was a custom of the day. In the democracy of the kitchen, as bellies filled with meat and wine, it spared neither lord nor lady. Indeed, de Norville came in for the greater share of the jokes; and a lively discussion started as to whether a man could be fitted with horns by his fiancée before marriage. The serving wenches took sides as well as the men. The air grew thick with round words, round oaths, and unbuttoned laughter. As someone put it, it might have been the eve of a wedding, and, cré Dieu, what was the difference? But behind it all could be felt the pride of those of Chavan that their future mistress had taken the fancy of the King. A royal amour brought honor to the château; and, if horns came with it, those horns were gilded.

Anne Russell, who had arrived two days ago with her chaperon and other attendants, had already caught the admiration of the household.

"God grant her better luck than our last mistress," said an elderly groom at Blaise's elbow.

"What luck was that? She died, of course."

"Yes, she died." The groom exchanged glances with another servant across the narrow table.

"How?" asked Blaise, remembering Michelet's babble after the torture at Pierre-Scize.

"Ah, monsieur, how indeed?" said the groom, drawing back like an old turtle in its shell. "That's the question."

But his vis-à-vis had either drunk too much or was less discreet. Emptying a tankard, he swept the back of his hand across his mouth. "You see, monsieur — "

"Chut!" hissed the groom.

"Diable!" said the other. "Everybody knows it. What's the harm of telling our friend here? I'm not accusing anyone — Well, monsieur, you see, not' maîtresse — who was a true saint in this world, if ever one lived — had been ill of the migraine, to which — poor lady! — she was much subject. On the night of her death, she slept alone in the room where our mistress-to-be, the English lady, is now lodged."

"Slept alone?" Blaise repeated.

"Yes, because of said migraine, she could not stomach even her maid to sleep with her. Note, too, that she bolted the door on the inside and that the room has no other door. In the morning, she could not be roused by knocking. Monseigneur de Norville ordered the door broken in. And a main hard job it was, too, because of the stoutness of the wood. But when my lord and the servants had at last got in, they found her dead."

Blaise shrugged. "La pauvre! And yet I see no great wonder in it. Other sick people have died alone in their beds."

The man lowered his voice. "Beau sire, there were marks on her throat."

Blaise managed to look less stirred than he felt. "You mean she was murdered?"

"Sapristi! Who knows? Monseigneur de Norville refused to believe it. And, indeed, how could she have been killed? The windows, too, were bolted on the inside. They say that Richard le Diable, who was one of the old lords of Chavan and deserved his nickname, still haunts the castle, though it has been newly rebuilt. . . ."

The man drifted into legend. Blaise shook his head at the thought that Richard de Chavan must have been a devil indeed to equal the present lord. Then his scalp prickled at what the other was saying.

"And, by God's cross, I've heard the footsteps myself."

"What footsteps?"

"Those that pass at night — but no one's there; doors that open when all the doors stay closed."

"Nonsense!"

"And I wasn't drunk, either," said the man.

"How did Monsieur de Norville take his wife's death?"

"Brokenhearted. No one has ever seen a more profound grief. It touched us all."

"Ha!" said Blaise. He found de Norville's sorrow harder to credit than Richard the Devil's ghost, but he could well imagine how beautifully de Norville would act the grief-stricken part. "By the way," he asked, "does Mademoiselle de Russell know that she is sleeping in that room?"

"God, no!" exclaimed the man. "Who would be such a blockhead as to tell her? But, speaking of Mademoiselle, she's not like our old mistress, who was meek as a lamb. She can take her own part, allez! I pity the phantom who steals in on her. He'll have his face scratched."

And the salty gossip closed in again.

Supper had been early. It was still daylight when Blaise sauntered out into the courtyard to clear his lungs of the kitchen fumes. Pierre, also sauntering, joined him.

"Well?" Blaise queried.

The other shook his head. "Not a whiff of a plot came my way. All I smelled was garlic. Those scullions know nothing. And, mark you, scullions they are, not men of the sword in disguise, which might have been possible. The whole mob of them would be no match for however few gentlemen the King has with him."

Blaise nodded. "Yes, the swordsmen will come from outside. But I heard no talk about the Constable, no reference to armed gatherings in the neighborhood. Did you?"

"Not a word," said Pierre. "The people around me stuck to women. It seems that Milady Russell brought a good-looking dame de compagnie with her from Lyons." He sighed; his thoughts were evidently far from Chavan-la-Tour.

After a pause, the friends separated: Pierre to keep up appearances by attending Monsieur de Luppé; Blaise to determine the depth of the lake around the château. For many reasons, it was important to learn how much the island depended on the bridge linking it to the mainland. If flight became necessary and if the bridge was blocked, what then?

Circling the house on the margin of land between it and the lake, Blaise, apparently idling, studied the water. After a while, he could look through the glimmering reflection of the walls and was relieved to see bottom. To judge by an occasional reed further off, the depth was no more than three feet and could thus be waded in case of need. Like the turrets and battlement, the lake was only an architectural ornament.

So also was the peacock, which he now caught sight of on the stone railing of a terrace, as he rounded the western end of the château. In the last rays of sunset, the bird proudly spread its tail for Blaise's benefit, a mingling of emerald and sapphire. On its white pedestal against the background of the terrace, which nestled between the two corner turrets, it looked so gorgeous that Blaise stopped in admiration. A moment passed before he was suddenly startled to notice that the peacock was not in sole possession of the stage and that a girl in a blue cloak stood half on the threshold of the turret doorway.

The full light of sunset showed her distinctly, but for an instant he could not credit his eyes. It was his sister, Renée.

At the same moment, becoming aware of him, she came forward across the terrace, though, since he had his back to the sun and the wide servant's hat shaded his face, she gave no sign of recognizing him.

"Bon soir, beau sire," she remarked. "It's a fine evening."

He thought quickly. Should he reveal himself or not? But curiosity as to why she was at Chavan, coupled with the assurance that he could fully depend on her, had the best of it.

"Renée!" he said in a low voice, removing his hat.

She stared at him, bewildered. If he had any doubt regarding the effectiveness of his disguise, her completely blank expression would remove it. His face had not yet regained its fullness since Pierre-Scize, and a three weeks' beard further altered his features. The gray lock of hair, which he had acquired in prison, had been artfully spread to give him a grizzled appearance.

"I don't understand," she froze. "You are impudent — "

"Look at me closely."

Her eyes widened. He could read incredulous recognition in them.

"Blaise! Grand Dieu! Is it you, Blaise?"

He laid a finger on his lips. "Careful! No one must know that I'm here. Understand? No one. I count on you. And, if you see Pierre de la Barre, don't give a sign that you know him."

"But how? . . . Why?" Her surprise could not find words.

"I'll tell you later. It's a long story. But what of *you* in God's name? How do *you* happen to be here?"

"I came with Milady. She — "

"Renée!" called a voice in the house. "Renée, m'amie?"

"Je vous attends, mademoiselle," the girl answered.

Footsteps were descending the turret stairs.

"Where could we meet?" Blaise whispered.

322

Renée hesitated. "Wait . . . Yes . . . In the upper gallery tomorrow morning after dinner. I can get away then."

Blaise stepped back, with a deep servant's bow.

He was already some yards off when Anne Russell appeared on the terrace.

"Who's that man you were talking with?" he heard her ask. "I could see you from the window."

"A gardener, I think," Renée said carelessly.

On this side, an oval tongue of lawn edged by dwarf willows completed the island. Taking his cue from Renée's answer, Blaise made a show of plucking up a weed here and there from the grass, but he kept his eyes on the terrace. He could see Anne clearly: the familiar tilt of her head with the crescent hood at the back of it, her graceful slenderness. Now and then, the slightly foreign intonations of her voice reached him. She wore a gold-brocaded gown, which caught the fires of sunset. Standing with one arm around Renée against the pearl-white background of the walls and flanked by the preening peacock, she recalled some Venetian painting, such as Blaise had wondered at in Italy.

And yet — though doubtless it was only his knowledge of impending events, the uncertainty of what the next days would bring forth — he felt a tightening of the heart as he gazed at her. Their odd relationship, in which the bitter so mingled with the sweet, had now reached its ultimate stage and still found them on opposite sides: she the fellow conspirator and promised wife of his bitterest enemy; he, risking his life to defeat and perhaps to destroy her. If he failed, France was undone; if he succeeded, he would find only desolation in victory. And the board was ready; the final moves were about to be made. Nothing that he or she might do could prevent it. He wondered what thoughts were passing through her mind these days, as she awaited the King's coming. What was her real attitude toward de Norville? To what lengths was she prepared to go in her loyalty to England? At least once, for his sake, he mused, fingering the Tudor Rose beneath his doublet, she had been disloyal.

Glancing again at the terrace, he saw that the vivid sunset light had faded: the colors were gone.

"Rentrons, m'amie," he heard her saying. "It grows chill."

That night, after rejoicing Pierre with the great news about Renée and speculating with him on the reasons which had brought her to

Chavan, Blaise lay awake on his pallet in Monsieur de Luppé's ante-room. The fatigue of the journey from Lyons did not bring sleep. A jumble of disturbing thoughts swept back and forth through his mind, the more unmanageable as time passed. It was as if something brooded over Chavan, rendering the air leaden and hard to breathe. Owls hooted from the woods on the mainland. He could hear the monotonous lapping of ripples beneath the windows.

Then, at the dead hour of night, his ears caught a sound which froze him to attention. It was distant at first but came nearer, the sound of footsteps. He could not be mistaken. It was no draft of air, no rat behind the paneling, but a furtive, muffled advance. Now the footsteps were in this very room. He sat bolt upright, every nerve taut, one hand on the pommel of the dagger beneath his pillow. Through the casement, oblique rays of a declining moon afforded some light, so that the place was only in semidarkness. But he could see no one, no passing shadow, even when the footsteps were close beside him. They continued on, grew faint; a door closed somewhere.

A trickle of sweat crossed his face. He sat listening a long time, but the sound was not repeated. Pierre, sleeping near by, had not awakened. At last, crossing himself, Blaise stretched out again. He knew, as well as everyone else, that damned spirits haunted the places of their former crimes. No doubt this was one of them — Richard de Chavan, perhaps. The groom's story had been substantiated.

So, behind the lovely façades of Chavan-la-Tour, behind the beauties of art and intelligence assembled here, lurked hidden shapes of lust and violence, like devils in ambush. Perhaps, indeed, they alone were real, and the rest of it was a delusive vision.

But, as sleep at last crept over him, it was not the glimmering château that lingered in Blaise's dreams; it was the smiling face of Jean de Norville, handsome as an angel's.

Chapter 47

As was the general custom at that time, the household at Chavan rose early, attended mass, and dined in the midmorning. It was close to noon when Blaise reached the gallery on the third floor and, sauntering about, as if admiring the view from the many windows, awaited Renée. He reflected that this was the hour when people were apt to withdraw for a siesta, which probably accounted for Renée's choice of it as the most convenient time to meet him. The gallery itself was equally well chosen. It was not a private room, and the casual meeting there of Monsieur de Luppé's valet and Milady Russell's companion should rouse no suspicions, if anyone else entered.

By now, Blaise's surprise at finding his sister in Chavan had considerably faded. The fact that Anne had given her rings and the Tudor badge to Renée to be used as a bribe in his escape from Pierre-Scize explained a great deal. No doubt Anne had become acquainted with Madame de Lallière and Renée at the convent and had somehow won their friendship. Her help at the time of his escape would have also assured their gratitude. That a warm affection existed between her and Renée was obvious enough. In view of this, she might naturally desire the young girl's company on the journey to Chavan.

Walking up and down, he considered how much Renée could be told of his and Pierre's mission at the château. Finally he decided that he could be entirely open with her. It was a great stroke of luck to have Renée as an ally and a source of information.

He had been strolling about in a part of the gallery at some distance from the stairway and had repeatedly crossed a portion of the floor between two of the windows when he became gradually conscious of something which, in the end, fixed his attention. Why, at a certain spot, did the floor yield slightly under him as he crossed it? The amount of give was hardly perceptible, but, once noticed, there could be no doubt of it. The rest of the parqueted floor was solid as rock. Only at this point he could feel a springiness which indicated no support underneath. At first absently and then alert, as a sudden notion formed in his mind, he tried his weight now here, now there, until he was fairly certain that the soft spot, to call it so, consisted of a square, two and a half feet in each direction.

In other words, the size of a small trap door. And one edge of it was along the outer wall.

During yesterday's tour of the château, Blaise had been constantly impressed by the extreme thickness of the walls, shown not only in the doorways but by the depth of the window recesses. That this square of parquetry might cover the mouth of a passage within the wall was entirely possible. And the wall in question formed the exterior side of the principal bedrooms on the second floor: de Norville's (the one to be occupied by the King), Anne's room, de Luppé's, and several others.

With one eye on the entrance to the gallery, Blaise drew his poniard and, stooping down, examined the flooring. Although beautifully joined, the parquet at this point seemed to fit a trifle looser than elsewhere. Between it and the wall extended a crack, into which, with some difficulty, he inserted his knife to the hilt; but the blade encountered nothing underneath. He could see no means of lifting this square of flooring and concluded that it could only be raised from below, if, indeed, a passageway existed. It was, therefore, an exit, not an entrance.

As he considered the theory of a secret passage within the wall, he was struck by its implications. The trap door here in the gallery might cover the mouth of a narrow stairway leading up from the second floor. That in turn indicated a lateral passage along this side of the house, with entrances to bedrooms, no doubt artfully concealed behind tapestry or paneling. Could this explain the mysterious death of de Norville's late wife without recourse to the ghost of Richard de Chavan? Could it explain the eerie footsteps? As to those of last night, he suspected Charles Bertran, the maître d'hôtel, who, he had every reason to believe, was in de Norville's confidence. It was improbable that anyone else now at Chavan would know the secret of a passageway.

But of chief importance was the bearing which all of this had on any conspiracy against the King. It vastly increased the difficulty of protecting him. For it was useless to post guards here and there when his room and the rooms of his gentlemen could be secretly entered at de Norville's pleasure. Besides, it seemed more than possible that such a hidden passage would extend down to the first floor and to a concealed entrance there, which could be used by de Norville to introduce reinforcements into the château or for other purposes.

However, forewarned is forearmed. Blaise had now, at least, something tangible to discuss with La Palisse, when the latter "casually" arrived on the King's heels tomorrow night. The most ticklish part of the whole affair was that some attempt on the King (though parried at the last moment) was to be encouraged in order to convince Francis of de Norville's treachery. And Louise de Savoie had not foreseen this complication. . . .

A light step mounting the stairs to the gallery caught Blaise's attention, and a moment later Renée appeared, hurrying toward him.

When the first rush of questions was over, it turned out that the motives which had brought his sister to Chavan were very much as Blaise had imagined.

"It began with Clairon and Cocorico," she explained. "Milady Russell had a whole house to herself and a little garden at Saint-Pierre. The dogs wandered over to it. When I came looking for them, we met; and she asked my name. 'Are you kin, by chance, to a certain gentleman, Blaise de Lallière?' she said. Of course, we had heard from Pierre how she had tricked you and caused your disgrace with the King. I was more than cold to her. But when she learned that I was your sister, you should have seen the kind look she gave me. 'Then you are very dear to me,' she said, 'very dear, m'amie.' I couldn't help telling her what I knew. 'Yes,' she said, 'but if I could save your brother, I would do anything.' And save you, she did, though she made me promise not to tell Pierre that it was her rings and gold badge I gave him. So, now you know, and you mustn't hate her, Blaise."

He shook his head and preferred to let that pale negative express him.

"It's not her fault," Renée continued, "that she's on the side of England and the Duke."

"No," he agreed.

"It's not her fault that the King makes love to her — so great a lord — and that she's betrothed to a man like de Norville."

"No," he said again, much more doubtfully. He could not help adding, "Does she ever speak of me?"

"Sometimes — about your ride to Geneva. I know she cares for you. She doesn't often show her thoughts."

How he recognized Anne in that! As to her caring for him beyond a certain point, he could not be sure and probably he would never learn.

In any case, there could be no doubt of the affection which had sprung up between her and Renée and Madame de Lallière. On the eve of her journey to Chavan, she had begged so earnestly for Renée's companionship that the plea could not be denied.

"She's afraid of Monsieur de Norville," said the girl. "I know it, though she's not one to show fear. She's often at her prayers. We share the same bed, and I know that she lies awake hour after hour. Perhaps, too, she's afraid of the King. He visited almost every day at Saint-Pierre."

"Does de Norville know that you're here?" Blaise put in.

"No, Milady asked permission to bring a companion with her from the convent. He agreed."

"You'll do well to keep out of his way when he comes," Blaise said. "He'd be quick to suspect something if he recognized you. And, believe me, Milady Russell has every reason for fear."

Renée grasped his arm. "I don't yet understand about you and Pierre at Chavan . . . in disguise . . . I thought you would be hiding somewhere. . . . You've hardly told me anything."

"Listen." As briefly as possible, he informed her of the situation: de Norville's mock betrayal of Bourbon, the probable conspiracy against the King, the Regent's counterstrategy.

"Why should you care about the King?" she interrupted. "What have you had from him but injustice?"

"I care about France," he retorted, "and so do you if you love Pierre de la Barre. Remember, he's with me, heart and soul, in this."

It was a master word for Renée. Politics to her depended on personalities; her heart determined her creed; and now one person mattered above all others.

"That's true," she nodded. "We saw each other in the courtyard before dinner — "

"You didn't speak, I hope?"

"No — only our eyes."

"Be careful, m'amie. We need your help. You will help us?"

"Yes, but not against Milady, not even for Pierre's sake. She's been good to me; I love her. From what you say, I can understand why she's afraid. She's in Monsieur de Norville's trap. She doesn't like what she's forced to do."

"By God," said Blaise, "I want to believe that. I do believe it. Help us to free her from de Norville."

Renée's eyes narrowed. "And what will happen when the King learns of this plot — if there is a plot? What will happen to her?"

What, indeed? Blaise wished that he could answer the question. He could only say: "One thing at a time. Don't you see that I love her? Do you think that I would ask you to harm her? But neither she nor I can help ourselves. We must face what comes."

His expression, the torment in his eyes, revealed more than his words. Renée understood. "Tell me what you want me to do."

"First, this. If you hear or see anything which you think I should know in view of what I've told you, try to bring me word of it. And if you can't find me, tell Pierre."

"Yes," she nodded.

"Now, another thing. What kind of a room has Milady? Can you describe it?"

"Very large and stately, with a canopied bed in the center against the wall. A beautiful hearth. Two fine windows. There's a little ante-room adjoining."

"How many doors?"

"Only one — except the door to the anteroom."

"Can you enter this anteroom from the corridor?"

"No. It's really a large alcove, with two small windows high up. Milady uses it as a wardrobe and to dress in."

"But it has a door, you say?"

"Yes, it can be locked."

"And the small windows" — Blaise's thought was still on Madame de Norville's death — "could anyone get in through them?"

"No, they're much too narrow and high. They let in air and a little light."

"Have you heard anything — this is important, Renée — of a secret passage to the room?"

The girl looked startled. "But, no — and I'm sure Milady hasn't either. Why do you ask?"

"Just an idea." He came to the next point. "When is Milady apt to be out of her room? I should like to look over it."

He could not forget Louise de Savoie's remark that this was the room which should be especially watched. And the Regent's intuition was oddly borne out by Blaise's present theory of a secret passage.

Renée gave a puzzled frown. "I hardly know. Mademoiselle spends most of the time in her room. We have our meals there together. But when the King and Monsieur de Norville arrive, I suppose she will be at supper with him in the grande salle. Or there will be other occasions."

"If you could let me know when the room is empty, I should be grateful. . . . Some signal . . . Wait a moment . . . What of this? I'll know, of course, when Milady is downstairs with the King, but

329

there might be a maid or some other servant in the room. I'll be loitering close to Monsieur de Luppé's door. As his valet, no one would look at me twice. If I see you come out of Milady's room and drop your scarf, I'll know it's empty."

"Very well," she agreed.

"And one last point. Is there any place in the room where I could hide if someone came in?"

Renée pondered. "The anteroom — but you'd be seen at once, if whoever it was looked in there. The bed has heavy curtains, with folds wide enough to stand behind. I can't think of anything else — "

From the tail of his eye, Blaise caught a glimpse of someone mounting the stairs at the entrance to the gallery.

"Bonjour, Monsieur le Maître," he said, bowing to the steward, Charles Bertran, who approached them. "Mademoiselle here has been good enough to point me out some of the beauties of Chavan."

"Is it so?" the other answered coolly. And to Renée, "Milady Russell has been asking for you, mistress." But when the girl had tripped off with a civil smile and nod to Blaise, Bertran snapped: "Look you, fellow, your duty is to your master, Monsieur de Luppé. We don't care to have idle lackeys sauntering about the house. Be off to your work and take care that I do not find you away from your quarters again, or you'll taste my cane."

The man's eyes were slits of suspicion. Blaise could feel them between his shoulders, as he walked toward the stairs.

Chapter 48

That afternoon, Blaise and Pierre, attending de Luppé, rode on a wide circle of the Chavan estate under the guidance of de Norville's chief forester. Not less important than the cheer within doors was the entertainment which the King would expect from the chase, and it behooved de Luppé to look over both the terrain and its possibilities. As for Blaise, having accomplished what he could at the château, the ride furnished a pretext to avoid Bertran's speculative scrutiny and at the same time to learn the lay of the land. So, for several hours, they jogged through the autumn woods, sighted a couple of herds of deer and as many of boar, then, coming out on the plain, admired the quantity of game birds, which would provide good sport if the King took a notion to hawking.

De Luppé, who had previously inspected the stables, kennels and mews, was emphatically pleased. His Majesty would find all that his heart desired at Chavan-la-Tour. And he quoted the King as saying that no prince on earth needed more for his entertainment than a fine woman, an excellent greyhound, and a noble horse, all of which were present at this pearl of a château, with every facility for making the most of them.

At one point Erasmus's estimate of King Francis, on that now distant evening in Geneva, crossed Blaise's mind, and he could not help admitting its verity. France was invaded, affairs were at sixes and sevens; but that did not prevent the King from junketing over here on a pleasure excursion. And yet there was something about him — an exuberance, a gusto and charm — that covered the multitude of his faults and almost redeemed them. In spite of personal grievances, Blaise was too French not to relish the quintessence of the French élan in Francis. One might disapprove, but one liked and forgave at the same time.

Once, silhouetted against the sky on the crest of a hill, Blaise caught sight of several horsemen, who disappeared into the valley beyond. De Luppé, aware of them at the same time, asked the forester if he knew them.

"Ma foi, no, monseigneur, they were too far off. I should think they are neighbors — perhaps Monsieur de Vivray and guests. He has the estate next to ours on the north."

But Blaise could have sworn that the riders wore steel caps. He would have liked to know how many guests were assembled at Monsieur de Vivray's. Here was another item which should be reported to La Palisse tomorrow night. However, it seemed unlikely that de Norville could reckon on any sizable force. The district was pretty well patrolled by the King's troops, and no large gathering of the Bourbon faction was possible. On the whole, the measures taken for the King's protection should prove adequate. Francis would arrive with, at least, some gentlemen and archers; La Palisse could be depended on to bring fifteen of his ablest men-at-arms. If an attempt on the King was actually intended, de Norville's one advantage would be surprise; and, with that failing him, the match was more than even.

Having finished their ride, and leaving their horses to be stabled on the mainland, the little party walked back across the bridge to the château.

Then, at a stroke, the unexpected made a hash of calculations.

The courtyard was a-flutter. Servants hurrying about, Bertran, the steward, speeding them. From the house came a sound of bustle. Smoke poured from the kitchen chimneys.

De Luppé hailed Bertran. "Nom de Dieu! What's up?"

"The King," fidgeted the steward, turning a moment from the lackeys. "He arrives within the hour. A courier rode in just after you left. His Majesty decided to come a day earlier."

"A day earlier," Blaise's thought echoed. He exchanged blank glances with Pierre. What now? What of the Regent's instructions to La Palisse? They concerned tomorrow night. What if, taken unawares, she had been unable to notify the Marshal? Then there would be no reinforcement of men-at-arms from Feurs; then the King would indeed be without sufficient guard, if the necessity arose. And, in view of this, how ought Blaise to act? He had been specifically ordered not to confide in de Luppé beyond allowing that officer to understand that he was in the Regent's service. De Luppé was too much a courtier, too much impressed by de Norville, to be trusted. The whole point of the maneuver at Chavan would be lost if somehow or other de Norville got wind of the trap which the Regent designed for him. He would then avoid it with the same adroitness which he had shown throughout and could even use it to strengthen his position with the King. No, the one thing left was for Pierre to slip off to Feurs in the hope that La Palisse had by now taken up his quarters there. Nothing would be lost if the Marshal already knew of the change in the King's plans; and, if he did not, everything could still be set right.

But, for the moment, ill luck made this move impossible. Blaise had hardly whispered his instructions to Pierre when a flourish of horns sounded on the mainland; and the royal cavalcade, emerging from the woods, rattled in across the bridge.

True to his incognito, the King wore a mask, as did de Norville and several of the party. But the disguise was only a gesture. Almost anyone could have identified the tall figure in the white-plumed cap, the distinctive smile, the panache of ostrich feathers affixed to the crownpiece of the horse's bridle. Blaise noted that the King had no more than a dozen or so attendants, including de Norville and doubtless several of de Norville's men. He recognized Captain

Fédéric of the Archers; de Montpezat and de la Guiche, both gentlemen of the bedchamber; a few others of the King's intimates; Louis de Bruges, Antoine de Hallwin, Tristan Gouffier; the royal trumpeter, Francisque de Branques; some pages and grooms — a poor guard, indeed, if La Palisse failed to arrive.

The King brought his horse to a rear in front of the twin doors which formed the main entrance to the château, then swung gracefully from the saddle. But de Norville had already dismounted to kneel before his guest, kiss the royal hand, and express appreciation of the honor conferred upon him and Chavan-la-Tour by the King's visit. If his courtliness was conventionally elegant, he gave it a warmth which would have convinced anyone of its sincerity. Francis, visibly touched, made a hearty rejoinder, and called de Norville his good friend.

"But where, mon ami — "

The question was already answered. The doors swung open. Anne Russell and her chaperon, Madame de Saint-Martin, hastily informed of the King's sudden arrival, now appeared on the threshold to curtsy their welcome. In compliment to the guest, Anne wore a gown of his colors, tawny and silver; and the front of her hood formed a silver crescent. Beneath the delicate arch of the doorway, she seemed to Blaise, from where he stood on the outskirts of the courtyard, a glimmer of loveliness.

The King whipped off his mask. "Behold Diana," he bowed in allusion to the crescent, "the goddess of this Arcadia! And I rejoice to see by your colors, divine mademoiselle, that England at last has declined in your favor, and that you are now" — he linked nationality with his name — "a good *Françoise*."

"All the more, Sire," she answered, "because I find Your Majesty's colors becoming — a potent temptation to a woman. I hope Your Highness agrees with me."

"Like your mirror, Milady," he glowed. "And I shall write you a poem to express how much."

"Then, Sire, I shall need no other claim to immortality."

"Meanwhile, let's seal your conversion, ma belle Françoise."

He kissed her but was tactful enough to bestow the same honor on Madame de Saint-Martin, adding a word or two of esteem for her late husband, one of the magistrates of Lyons. Then, between the two ladies and attentive to both, he entered the house, while de Norville and some of the gentlemen followed him.

333

Blaise grew conscious again of the courtyard, the stomping horses and babble of voices. Nearby, he overheard Monsieur de Luppé talking with one of the newcomers, Louis de Bruges.

"You say this was Monsieur de Norville's suggestion?"

"Yes, somehow he heard that Madame la Régente looked askance at our outing and sought ways to supervise it. You may know that she and de Norville lose no love between them. Rumor had it that Monsieur de la Palisse, her good friend, might join our party. De Norville had only to drop a hint to the King, who wants no gray-beard chaperons on this occasion." De Bruges paused to wink. "His Majesty flared up and resolved to make an issue of it. 'But no,' says de Norville, 'how much simpler to leave Wednesday rather than Thursday! If Her Highness has plans, it would catch her napping.' So up we rose before dawn this morning and rode hard. Meanwhile, it was given out that His Majesty had gone to inspect the works on the Rhône below Ainay. Cré Dieu, I've never seen the King in higher glee — like a runaway schoolboy. It's two to one that the Regent hasn't yet heard of the trick. As for La Palisse, if he turns up here, His Majesty vows to give him a sermon he will long remember."

Another gentleman sauntered up. The conversation broke off. Glancing at Pierre, Blaise could see, from the bleak look on his face, that he had overheard the talk and got the point of it. First, La Palisse could not yet have learned that the King was already at Chavan-la-Tour. Unless he had word of this at once, there would be no sufficient guard that night at the château. But, second and worse, if any attempt was actually planned against the King, de Norville's maneuver indicated that it would be made tonight. Aware of the Regent's suspicions, he must feel desperately short for time. The change of schedule had gained him a free hand during twenty-four hours, after which anything might happen.

"What about de Luppé?" queried Pierre, when he and Blaise had drifted out of earshot. "He knows we were sent here by the Regent. If he wants to curry favor with the King, he has only to drop him a word about us, and our goose is cooked."

Blaise shook his head. "No fear. He's in too deep already. The King would ask him why he had not spoken up in Lyons. Besides, the Regent is a nasty enemy."

"Then, tant mieux," said Pierre. "I'll slip across the bridge now, when these horses are taken to the stables. The devil's in it if I can't strike into the woods from there — and make it on foot to Feurs in an hour. I noticed a short cut during our ride."

"Good luck," Blaise nodded. "You know as well as I how much depends on you tonight."

He watched Pierre cross the bridge and then, waiting until Monsieur de Luppé went upstairs to dress, he attended him. This would provide an occasion later on to wait in the corridor for Renée's signal.

"By the way, Goujon," remarked de Luppé, when they were alone, "you will do well to keep very quiet about your service to a princess we know of. The King would be angry to hear of it."

"Rest assured, monseigneur," he answered, "that I am quite aware when to remain only your lordship's valet."

But, meanwhile, Pierre de la Barre got no further than the stables. "Where away, fellow?" called one of de Norville's grooms, as he started toward the woods.

"A stroll," said Pierre.

The other came over to him. "No strolling tonight for any of us. King's orders."

"Parbleu, why?"

The man shrugged. "How should I know? Someone told me that His Grace doesn't want the news spread that he's here."

"You're sure it's his orders?"

"Yes, through Monseigneur de Norville. If you're free, give me a hand with that horse, will you?"

Pierre obliged. At that moment, he could not afford to rouse the faintest suspicion. But, having rubbed down the horse, he eluded this particular groom and tried again in another direction. This time he was stopped by a forester at the edge of the woods.

"Halte-là, mon ami."

Once again Pierre listened to the King's orders and returned raging to the stables, accompanied by the forester.

By now it was close upon supper, and all hands were trooping over to the kitchen in the château. Pierre could find no excuse to remain behind, all the more as he saw the forester in talk with the groom who had first detained him, and they both glanced his way. In the end, he joined them, set them laughing at some tale, and proposed supper together. He must wait now until dark and watch his chance then. But it was infuriating to sit there in the reek and babble, knowing that Blaise imagined him already at Feurs. And precious time was slipping past.

As he watched the parade of viands being marshaled for the various courses at the King's table in the grande salle, he wondered about these orders. He did not believe that the King had issued them. It looked rather as if de Norville was making sure of his game.

Chapter 49

In a gorgeous brocade of white and gold, heavily perfumed, the jeweled clasp on his cap matching the blaze of rings on his hands, Francis strolled through the château before supper, in company with Anne Russell, Jean de Norville, and two other gentlemen. His trained eye admired every architectural beauty. He praised the hanging keystones of the lovely arches in the entrance hall; the spacious stairway, which heralded, as he put it, a new age in building; the lordly spacing of the windows and the rich ornateness of their frames.

"Foi de gentilhomme, my friend," he told de Norville, "when we have peace again, I shall put you in charge of all our new buildings. You know how to blend the French and Italian into something new and glorious. I must have a Chavan-la-Tour of my own — on a larger scale, of course — and there's an island in the Loire a few leagues from Tours which will exactly fit it."

With a passion for every form of art, he seemed to miss nothing, not the design of a tapestry or the ornamentation of the ceiling beams, not a Cupid or nymph or medallion, not one feature of the chimney canopies. He had noticed and did not fail to appreciate the salamander of his coat of arms newly carved in his room.

"It is I who should thank Your Grace," said de Norville. "You have brought history, Sire, to Chavan-la-Tour. Henceforth, that room will be known as la Chambre du Roi."

But de Norville's art collections interested the King no less than the château itself. He paused to fondle some handsome bindings in his host's library, several of them enriched with precious stones, the work of Lyonnaise craftsmen. And he took such delight in the miniatures of a Book of Hours that he graciously accepted the volume as a gift from de Norville, who humbly thanked him for the condescension.

Lacemaking in Western Europe had not yet attained the perfection of a later period and could not rival the products of Greece or Asia. The King marveled at some Venetian importations acquired by de Norville, especially at one piece wrought in gold threads.

"The needlework even of Italy, not to speak of France," he declared, "is only a clout by the side of such elfin cobweb."

But the King was especially struck by various capital paintings and bronzes — a Bellini "Madonna and Child" in the grande salle, a rich Giorgione in the adjoining room, a "Rape of Lucrece" by Mantegna, a fine copy of Donatello's "Saint George" in the third-floor gallery — and complimented de Norville on his enlightened taste.

"Ma foi, I pity our poor old ancestors," he remarked, "who did not live to see this modern age. They missed so much." But, since Anne had now excused herself, he could not help observing, "Bon Dieu, monsieur, your late wife must have been rich. For I take it your Savoy estates could not meet the charge of all this."

De Norville sighed. "Rich and most generous. I shall never cease to mourn her. No doubt I spent more than I should, but Your Majesty knows the temptations of art."

"Do I not, pardie! Do I not!" The King agreed. "It's a pity, though, that you're losing Milady Russell's dowry by your adherence to us. It would have recouped you. Well, I shall take care that you're none the poorer."

"As Your Highness will grant," de Norville murmured, "the lady's self is a supreme temptation."

Their eyes met in a veiled understanding. The King glanced impatiently at his two gentlemen, de la Guiche and de Monpezat. "By your leave, sirs, I would have a word in private with Monsieur de Norville."

They were now in the wide corridor on the second floor. When the gentlemen had withdrawn, Francis repeated in a low voice: "None the poorer, monsieur. On the contrary, richer by much. I have an eye for men and can read your devotion, your most rare devotion. Sir, we have touched on this matter before. We are both men of the world. Do you think that Milady can be brought to — " He paused and smiled. "Eh?"

De Norville bowed. "I am sure that her warmest desire is to please Your Majesty."

"Her room?" asked the King.

"At the end of the corridor on the left."

There was a moment of silence. De Norville could easily read the Prince's thought. Anne's room was at some distance from the King's. Guards would be stationed in the corridor at night. Of course, they could be withdrawn, but gossip was undesirable. . . .

"Sire, might I have speech with you in Your Highness's apartment?"

Somewhat puzzled, the King walked with his host to the room assigned him and dismissed the pages on duty there.

"Well?" he asked.

"I have not yet shown Your Majesty all the conveniences of Chavan."

Entering one of the window recesses, de Norville reached up to an apparent molding on the panel above him. A click sounded. He then pushed slightly against the side, which swung back, leaving a narrow doorway. Out of it drew a cold breath of stone and mortar.

"Diable!" wondered Francis. "What's this?"

"One moment, Sire." De Norville stepped back into the room and lighted a candle with his tinderbox. "Now — if Your Highness will permit me to lead the way."

The King found himself in a narrow space within the wall, but not so narrow that it cramped the shoulders. It lay between two flights of steps, one leading from above and the other communicating with a passage higher than the line of windows. De Norville then closed the concealed door to the room. He pointed out a lever two feet above his head.

"Pull down on that, and the door opens. Will Your Majesty try it?"

Francis did so, with the stated result. De Norville again closed the door and standing sideways with his candle, so that the King could see past him, he explained: "One has only to mount those steps to reach a passage running the length of the house. At the far end other steps lead down to a door which, like this, is concealed in a window bay. Your Grace can easily guess into which room it opens. The device for entering is the same as here. Need I say more?"

"Saint John!" exclaimed Francis. "You are a nonpareil, mon cher ami, you are beyond praise. But I would not frighten the lady by appearing, like a phantom, out of the wall."

"Leave that to me, Sire. She will not be frightened — and she will be alone."

"Monsieur de Norville, you can expect a dukedom from this."

"I hope only for Your Majesty's continued favor."

But perhaps the shadow of a misgiving crossed the King's mind. Secret passageways can serve other purposes than those of gallantry. "And those steps — " he pointed to the longer flight — "where do they lead?"

"To the gallery, Sire. And at the opposite end of the passage, other steps lead down to the first floor. I shall be open with Your Grace. To my thinking, a house should afford privacy of movement as well as other comforts. Am I to have no freedom to enter or leave my house, visit my wife or bonne amie, save under the eyes of my lackeys? No, this way I keep my eye on *them*. Let me recommend so convenient a feature to Your Majesty."

Francis was charmed. "Ma foi, I shall bear it in mind. An excellent arrangement which I could make good use of. Are there others who know the secret?"

"None but the masons, whom I imported from Touraine, and who have returned there. Of course, with my King, I would have no secrets of any kind. Apart from the service which this passage may render Your Grace, I should have been derelict in my duty, Sire, if I had not apprised you of it."

Honest fidelity in every accent. Completely reassured, Francis now re-entered his room; and, to assure him still further, de Norville explained how, by a simple-looking device concealed on the molding of the panel, the door could not be opened from the passage.

"Monsieur de Norville, mon ami," said the King. "I foresee that this visit to Chavan will be one of my pleasantest memories. You anticipate my every thought and wish."

"Would that I might, good my lord!" returned the other. "But, in view of today's journey, I hope I'm not wrong in anticipating Your Grace's willingness to partake of supper."

"There you are!" smiled Francis. "I'd forgotten I was hungry until you reminded me. Allons! No, arm-in-arm. On such an outing as this, we can drop ceremony."

On their way down to the grande salle, where tables had been set up, the King's gentlemen took good note of this distinguished honor to de Norville.

"Mark my word," de la Guiche whispered to Montpezat, "he's on his way to becoming a peer of France."

And during the elaborate meal, which the cooks of the château had managed to prepare in spite of short notice, the informal, friendly note was maintained. Relaxing from court etiquette in a picnic spirit, the King insisted on placing Anne at his right and the much overwhelmed Madame de Saint-Martin at his left. He ate from the same trencher as Anne and shared his cup with her — an arrangement which gave occasion for intimate glances on the King's part, while drinking her health, and for none too subtle jokes, especially when it came to carving up a fowl. Behind the chair of his royal guest stood de Norville, quick to serve him, quick to put in the right word at the right moment.

The watchful gentlemen, who supped at a neighboring table, decided that Anne Russell was perfection. If her eyes drooped before the King's stare, if she listened more often than she spoke, if she smiled rather than laughed, it expressed modesty, an excellent thing in a woman — and much more piquant than boldness to a man of good taste. Besides, she was ravishing to look at. Bon Dieu, what skin and teeth! What grace of body! No wonder His Highness had a soft spot for English women. Some of the gentlemen recalled that he had risked his succession in the late King's days out of too warm a fondness for Louis's English Queen, the young Mary Tudor. If he had given the King an heir, he would have remained Duke of Angoulême; and his mother was properly anxious.

Wines and food were excellent. The peacock, with gilded beak, was a work of art. The flaming boar's head lighted up the room and set shadows dancing. As for pastry and comfits of every shape, the King declared that Paris could not rival them.

But when the dessert wines had been served, Francis rose from table. The day had been a long one; there would be hunting tomorrow. He proposed an hour of cards in his room and then bed.

His gentlemen were careful to look innocent. "Whose bed?" murmured Louis de Bruges from the corner of his mouth.

On watch outside of Monsieur de Luppé's room on the second floor, Blaise could see the length of the corridor beyond the stair landing to the extreme end of the house. That is, he could see it as well as the dim light of a cloth-covered lantern hanging above the staircase permitted, and this was dim enough after nightfall. At first, other attendants loitered about, but these gradually disappeared to snatch a bite of supper in the kitchen, while their masters were at table. At length a couple of vague figures, whom he took to be chambermaids, issued from Anne's room on the extreme left and entered another door. He waited on pins and needles. Then a third figure emerged, but he could not have told that it was Renée if she had not walked toward him as far as the landing and stood a minute listening to the voices in the grande salle below. She wore a brocaded dress of white and silver, probably a gift from Anne. When she turned away, her scarf fluttered down; but, without appearing to notice it, she continued on and disappeared through a door at the right.

Blaise took note of this door, at which he would stop and knock, if anyone appeared in the corridor before he reached Anne's room. Returning her scarf to Renée would provide the only excuse he could think of for being found on that side of the landing. He snatched it up, as he passed, and hurried along, holding his sword to keep it from rattling; but the corridor remained empty. A moment later, careful to make no sound with the latch, he slipped into Anne's room and eased the door shut behind him.

It was lighted by only a pair of tapers, though a candelabra stood ready against her return. In the dusk, he could make out the bed, flanked by its heavy curtains; the deep, canopied fireplace, from which the pine boughs of summer had not yet been removed. This might furnish a better hiding place than the curtains of the bed. Such a hearth had been used more than once for that purpose. The door of the alcove stood open, and Blaise glanced within; but, as Renée had said, it offered no means of concealment.

He now set about his first object in coming to the room. If his theory of a secret passage was right, the exterior wall (to judge by the position of the trap in the gallery) could alone contain it. And, as the most likely place, he turned first to the window recesses.

If he could prove the existence of a concealed passage and, better still, how the room could be entered from it, he would be much better prepared for the night's task. Failing La Palisse, the whole responsibility for the mission imposed by the Regent devolved upon him. And the odds were desperate. He could not be everywhere. He could only be present at that point which the Regent herself considered the most vulnerable and which his own suspicions centered on.

By now, supper below had been in progress over an hour. Reckoning from experience, Blaise felt that he could count on at least a half hour longer before it would be necessary for him to conceal himself. To his satisfaction, he soon found a hollow-sounding panel in the second of the window recesses. But it was one thing to have confirmed his theory regarding the passage, and quite another to learn how the panel might be opened.

In vain, his fingers ran here and there from top to bottom of that side of the recess. He investigated even the window frame, the flooring, for some token of a hidden mechanism. It was maddening to know that the device was probably simple, but he could not hit on it. And the minutes slipped by. He now fingered the paneling above his head —

Sudden voices just outside the door spun him around. He had only time to reach the far side of the bed, but he was still fumbling with the heavy, tapestried curtain, when the door opened.

He heard Anne bidding good night to Madame de Saint-Martin. The light of flambeaux carried by the escorting pages struck for an instant into the room, then was shut off by the closing door. But at once Blaise was aware of suspense. Anne evidently stood close to the door listening. A long minute passed. Then he heard the faint click of the latch, and someone entered.

"You're quite alone?" said a voice so toneless that he could not recognize it.

"Yes."

"I'll make sure."

Footsteps passed here and there through the room, paused in front of the hearth, entered the small adjoining room, skirted the bedside within a foot of Blaise, stopped, while the searcher parted the curtains and peered between them. Blaise held his breath, hopeless of remaining undetected. But luck favored him. The footsteps crossed back to Anne, who was now lighting the candelabra from one of the tapers. The dusk of the room grew brighter.

"And now, at last, for tonight's plans, Milady," said de Norville.

Chapter 50

"It will be tonight then?" Anne's voice sounded coldly impersonal.

"Yes," said de Norville. "The old witch of a Regent suspects too much. Even tomorrow would have been too late: we should have had the house garrisoned by La Palisse, and the venture would have been twice as hard. It was wonderful luck that I could talk the King into coming a day earlier."

He paused, as if for a word of agreement, but she said only, "What are the plans?"

"I have assembled twenty men at Monsieur de Vivray's, a league and a half from here. They are close at hand. They will take care of the King's gentlemen. Meanwhile, their leader, Achille d'Angeray, and I will be dealing separately with the King."

"How *separately?*"

"His Majesty will be paying a visit to you. It was that I especially wanted to prepare you for."

A moment of strained silence followed. When Anne spoke again, it was evident that she found it hard to keep her voice level.

"A shabby role for both of us. But, having lent myself to it — " She broke off. "Couldn't you have spared me this?"

De Norville explained how much more desirable it was to take the King by surprise, unarmed and alone, than if he could call upon his gentlemen. "We want no useless bloodshed."

"We want none at all, Monsieur de Norville. In other words, you intend to ambush the King, when he enters this room, and take him prisoner?"

"Something like that."

An evasive note in the other's voice struck her attention, and she repeated: "*Something like that?* Look you, sir, I want plain speech. You have not yet told me — when you have captured the King — how you will get him across the frontier or, indeed, which frontier. Is he to be placed in the hands of the Emperor, of Monsieur de Bourbon, or of the English?"

There was no answer to this; or, rather, de Norville seemed at a loss how to answer.

"Well?" she insisted.

"Milady, I shall be frank with you. That plan has been discarded. It would be impossible to convey the King out of France, especially now that the Regent's dogs are on our traces. I have often remembered the prudent suggestion you made at our first meeting at Saint-Pierre and have resolved to adopt it."

"What suggestion do you mean?"

"Why, dea, to the effect that death is simple and final."

Again, silence, at first heavy with the word *death,* but then vibrant with mounting passion.

Anne burst out: "By God, do you shift your villainy to me? Do you fail to recall how I wondered that a man without scruples, like you, did not take the easier way of assassination, and how you answered me? I accepted that answer in good faith and agreed to assist you, provided that only the capture of the King was involved. You seem to forget my plain statement that under no conditions would I have anything to do with murder!"

De Norville threw in a compliment. "I forget nothing, Milady. Your gentleness of heart is equaled only by your beauty."

It was oil upon fire. "And, so, having tricked me with false pretenses and used me for your purpose, you now speak truth at last when you think that truth can do no harm. The trap is set; I am the bait, whether I please or not. Is that it?"

De Norville's suave voice changed. He gave a sharp laugh. "How quickly your ladyship always seizes the gist of a matter! But, listen. I should not have caused you this annoyance, except for the reasons I mentioned. The King can be more easily dealt with here than in his own quarters. There is a further reason. If he dies in this room, I shall be the better able to justify his death to the world at large and especially to my lord of Bourbon. I shall have vindicated your honor and mine. It pays to be a hero. I'm sure you agree, ma belle!"

She disregarded both his candor and his irony.

"Thank God I knew of this in time!"

"Time for what, Milady?"

"To warn the King, of course. Do you think that I will have any part in this? From henceforth, happen what may, I shall at least be quit of you and your infamy." Her voice rose. "Unhand me! What do you mean — "

"Nothing — certainly not to startle you, ma très chère." His voice went on, like the purring of a great cat. "But I beg you to consider. What will you gain by betraying not only me but the interests of

344

England, by proving false to your nation and your prince for the sake of this lecher King, who does not rate you a snap of his fingers?"

"Gain?" she repeated. "Perhaps a trifle of self-respect."

"I fail to understand."

It was truthfully spoken. For all his intelligence, he actually could not understand. That was the horror of him.

"I shall not trouble to explain, monsieur."

He went on. "Did you help me to lure the King here, or did you not? Of course you did. And magnificently. And he is on the hook — your hook. Warn him? To what purpose? For, by God, he shall not leave this house alive. Infamy? Call it so, if you wish — yours as well as mine — but don't imagine that a feeble gesture at the last minute would gain you pardon for your share of it."

Like a snake with a bird, the man cast a spell. Behind his curtain, Blaise could picture the handsome, intent face and Anne unable to remove her eyes from it.

"Come, Milady, you are not a fool. A moment's thought will convince you that what I have planned is the only possible solution both in the interest of our several princes and — frankly — to save our own lives. To balk at the last hurdle is a poor way of losing a race."

"I've made my decision."

"That would be unfortunate," said de Norville, "if it were not impossible."

"Why?"

"Because I should prevent it." He did not raise his voice; he simply, as it were, drew it out of its sheath.

"You could kill me. Do you think I'm afraid of that?"

"Kill you?" he exclaimed. "Bon Dieu! I would as soon deface my Giorgione painting. You are much too beautiful."

"Very well . . ." she began.

What occurred then was too sudden to realize before it was over. Hurried footsteps across the room; a smothered cry; a door closing; a key turned in the lock; then Anne's muffled voice on the other side of the alcove door and the thudding of her hands against the panels. It was this that fortunately kept Blaise where he was. She had taken no harm except to be locked in the small adjoining room.

"Doucement!" said de Norville, loud enough to be heard by Anne. "Ne vous tourmentez pas, m'amie. The decision has merely been taken out of your hands. Call for help, if you please, but no one will

345

hear you. When the King arrives, perhaps he will let you out — if he has time."

Then, crossing over to the main door, he removed the key from the inside, let himself out into the corridor, locked the door and put the key in his pocket.

So absorbed he was that he failed to notice the slight figure of Renée standing against the opposite wall until, turning away, he confronted her.

"Who are you?" he challenged in a low, threatening voice. It was too dim in the corridor to make out her face.

"Milady's maid in waiting."

"Your mistress will not need your services tonight." He would have liked to throttle her; but, at the far end of the passage, Captain Fédéric had taken up his post in front of the King's door. "Be off!" But, then, raging as he was, de Norville mastered himself and detained her. "A word, pretty mistress. With strange gentlemen in the house, one takes precautions. You understand?"

"Yes, monseigneur."

"Good!" He fished in his purse for a coin. "And one holds one's tongue, eh? It would be embarrassing else."

"Indeed, monseigneur." She felt weak with fear.

A flame of the passion in him licked out. "By God, you'd better!" He fingered his knife hilt. "Now, be off."

He watched her until she was gone. Then, serenely inscrutable, he walked downstairs to a vaulted basement room, where armed men, ferried by twos and threes across the few score yards of water from the western shore, had been gathering since nightfall. Admitted by the steward, Charles Bertran, through a secret entrance, nearly all had arrived.

Blaise waited a long minute. Then leaving his hiding place, he rounded the bed and unlocked the alcove door.

Out of the darkness, Anne came toward him. With his back to the light, she could see only a broad-shouldered man, a bearded face and a jutting sword hilt.

"You're sent by Monsieur de Norville, are you?" she asked. "I expected it." She crossed herself. "Do your office."

His mind in a turmoil, Blaise could not find words for a moment. Then he said: "You are always brave and true to yourself, Milady, but I am not here on de Norville's errand."

At the sound of his voice, she stood rigid as if facing an apparition.

"Monsieur de Lallière! It's impossible. Am I mad, or is this an answer from Heaven?"

Blaise thought of Pierre's miracle and his prayer for a second miracle on the night of their escape. He answered gravely: "Notre Seigneur does as it pleases Him in spite of kings and Monsieur de Norville."

"Then Dieu merci!"

In an outburst of relief, she threw her arms around his neck and pressed her face against his shoulder.

Chapter 51

But there was no time for sentiment in the crisis now confronting Anne and Blaise.

"The King," said the latter, after accounting for his presence at the château and in the room, "has but this one sure trump left" — he patted his sword hilt — "and that has to be saved for the last trick. We could hammer at the door there, stir up the household, demand to speak with His Majesty — and what then? I am an escaped traitor and accused murderer with a price on my head. I am found here in your room. On the other hand, de Norville has never stood so high in the King's favor. He would twist our charges to fit his purpose. And, indeed, Milady, you, as well as I, would be hard put to clear yourself."

"Yes," she nodded, "I've been a hypocrite in what I considered a good cause — as if false means are ever justified! I've learned that they're not and am willing to pay for the lesson."

"But destroying ourselves," he countered, "will not help. I'll warrant de Norville's people are now here or are closing in."

"So, perhaps, is Marshal de la Palisse, if, as you say, Monseiur de la Barre carried word to him!"

Blaise rubbed his hand across his head. "That's the devil of it. La Palisse should be here now. It's a scant league to Feurs. Pierre could make it on foot in an hour. He set out just after the King arrived. Something's wrong. Perhaps the Marshal has not yet reached Feurs."

"What do you propose, then?"

He shrugged. "Fête-Dieu, we must make the best of a poor hand and our one trump. We know that the King will visit this room. No doubt de Norville has given him the key which was in that door. We know that he will be attacked here at once by de Norville and d'Angeray — probably from the secret passage which I can swear exists. Most likely, too, at that same moment, the King's gentlemen will be surrounded and cut off. But what de Norville does not know is that I am here and that tables may be turned. There's our only advantage."

"They will be two to one."

"Not for long if I'm lucky. The King is a tall man-at-arms, remember that!"

"And then?"

"Perhaps we can win free; perhaps, after all, La Palisse will have come. If he does not — " Blaise shrugged again.

She shook her head. "Too many perhaps."

"Yes, but have we any other choice?"

For a long moment, she studied the candle flames. "No, you're right. We can only wait. But isn't it likely that de Norville and the other man will hide themselves in this room before the King comes? If so, they mustn't find you and must be sure that I'm still in the alcove. They're apt to use the curtains of the bed as you did. Where will *you* hide?"

He pointed to the great hearth. "Behind those branches. But I still believe in the panel yonder. They'll strike from there."

"How much time have we, do you think?" she asked. "The King is at cards."

Figuring roughly on the probable length of the game and allowing an equal length afterwards, in which the King would go through the form of retiring, Blaise guessed at two hours.

"Well then, we have time to talk — at least for a while . . ."

"It's strange, Milady, that we're on the same side at last."

She gave him her hand. "At last."

Meanwhile, in the kitchen, Pierre's exasperation became homicidal. Time was passing and he found himself virtually a prisoner. He was soon aware that some word had passed among de Norville's servants to keep those of the King's following under watch. It was tactfully managed. The personal lackeys were not detained from attending

348

their masters, when the King rose from supper. But Pierre noticed that the royal grooms, who had their quarters in the dependencies beyond the bridge, were well plied with wine and that none of them left the kitchen. If anyone withdrew to satisfy a natural necessity, one of the Chavan people, similarly moved at the same time, accompanied him out and returned with him. Pierre heard a man, who had somehow escaped notice, complain that he had been turned back by a guard at the bridge. In short, it was plain that the King's servants were being kept on the island, and the reason for that was not far to seek, if de Norville planned some coup during the night and did not wish a breath of it to leak out.

At first, because of his two abortive attempts to slip away from the stables, Pierre could feel the suspicion of the groom and the forester, who flanked him at table, and he dared not revive it by any new attempt to escape. To counter this, he lent himself heartily to the drinking and chatter, told a couple of salty stories, and established himself as a good fellow. But he succeeded too well. The company would not part with him, when, a little later, he stretched, yawned, and remarked that it was time for him to seek his quarters in Monsieur de Luppé's anteroom. They demanded another merry tale and filled his cup again. It was maddening to be so baffled. If he did not start for Feurs at once, it would be useless to start at all.

Then, at the blackest moment, he got his chance. A chambermaid, tripping up, announced that the demoiselle of Milady Russell desired a word with Pierre Berthelet, and that she awaited him in the passage outside.

Pierre managed skillfully. Lovers, in France, have special privileges. He gave the impression that here was a possible bonne fortune. There were some jokes when he got up, but no one stopped him. A moment later, he found Renée in the passage which connected the kitchen with the main wing of the house.

At once she was in his arms. If anyone happened to spy, the report of Pierre's good luck would go the rounds and excite no suspicion. But at the moment he thought only of her.

"M'amie! M'amie!" he kept saying. "My dear!" Then, as she clung to him, "You're trembling. You're frightened. What is it?"

In the dimly lit passage, her eyes looked darker and larger than ever against the dead whiteness of her face.

Faltering, she told him of her encounter with de Norville. "I

349

don't know where Blaise is. He was in that room. . . . I heard voices, then the banging of a door in there. . . . Do you think de Norville has killed Milady? . . . The look on his face when he came out . . . Why did he lock the door and take away the key? . . . What can we do?"

Pierre thought quickly. "Only one thing: to reach Monseiur de la Palisse somehow, if there's still time. I'd have been in Feurs an hour ago if that pack of kitchen loons hadn't held me up. Wonderful luck you sent for me. I'll wade the lake. No use trying the bridge. Do you know any way out of the house except through the courtyard? I mustn't be seen."

"Yes," she said, "from the terrace door at the far end. I'll go ahead and see if the way's clear."

While he waited, she crossed the entrance hall and peered into the grande salle beyond it. Then, at a sign, he joined her; and they hurried through the long room, where the supper tables had not yet been removed. The petite salle was equally empty. A door at the far side opened on to the terrace balcony.

She showed him the tongue of lawn pale in the moonlight, with its fringe of dwarf willows. "It points toward Feurs. You can't be seen here from the courtyard. I'll walk down with you."

They scaled the low balcony and were soon among the trees. In front of them stretched the pallid water of the little lake, two hundred yards or so of it from that point to the woods on the mainland.

"Pierre, I wish I could go with you."

"I wish you could, m'amour. I'd like to carry you across in my arms. But I'll be running to Feurs, once I get to shore. What'll you bet I don't cover that league in a half hour?"

She tried to smile. "Your bracelet. Remember our wager at Lallière?"

"This time I'll win. If the Marshal's there, I'll have him back here in an hour." He added half to himself, "God grant he's there!"

"I'm so afraid."

He drew her to him. "Of what, chérie?"

"I don't know."

"You have nothing to fear. Whatever happens, no one will harm you. Go to some room, shut yourself in and stay there till morning."

"But I'm afraid for you."

"Bah! I'm a cat that always lands on its feet. And, mark you, if I serve the King well tonight, do you know what it means? We'll be married at once. I'll ask that reward of him. So, good cheer, darling!"

They kissed passionately. "God speed!" she said. "God speed! I love you — forever . . ."

He stepped down into the shallow water, which did not reach above his waist, and moved as quickly off as the depth permitted, stooping a little when he had passed the shadows of the trees. Once, in a deeper part, she saw him swim a stroke or two. Then he reached the farther bank, a dim figure in the moonlight. It seemed to her that he gave a flourish of his arm, and she waved mechanically, though he could not have seen her. There was no sound from the woods where he had disappeared, no hail from any guard who might have been posted there. She drew a long breath of relief.

She did not hear the footsteps in the grass behind her. A grip of steel closed on her shoulder, spun her around. She looked up into the white face of de Norville.

"What are you doing here?"

Terror-stricken, she could not speak for a moment, then managed to breathe, "Nothing, my lord."

"You lie. I was told but now that you were with a certain Pierre Berthelet, Monsieur de Luppé's groom. Where is he?"

"Monseigneur . . . I don't know. . . ."

"You had better speak. Did he leave the island?"

She thought now only of Pierre. She must gain him time.

"No, monseigneur. He went to his quarters in Monsieur de Luppé's room."

"Indeed? And you stand here alone? Why?"

Fear silenced her again.

"I found you outside Milady's door a half hour since. I warned you to hold your tongue. What did you have to say to a groom of one of the King's gentlemen?"

She struggled to speak but could not.

"By God, your face is familiar." He drew her out into the clearer moonlight. "What's your name?"

She answered helplessly, "Renée de Lallière."

Something in his very quietness horrified her. She whispered, "Have mercy, seigneur."

He stood looking down into her face, his eyelids drooping. "Renée de Lallière! That's interesting. Well, a girl of your rank does not consort with grooms. Who is the man?"

Her mind went blank. "Have mercy," she repeated.

351

He spoke softly. "Who is he? I have little patience tonight. Tell me the truth. Tell me what you know."

Betray Pierre? She answered, "I know nothing."

"I'll make sure of that."

She tried to scream, but his hands closed suddenly about her throat.

Chapter 52

When he had finished, de Norville drew the body back into the shadow of the trees and stooped down an instant to assure himself that she was dead. His pulses kept their usual steady beat. Glancing toward the house, he felt convinced that no one had seen him. The bedrooms faced in the other direction. There had been no sound.

Coolly his thought balanced possibilities. Yes, from where she had been standing, Renée might easily have seen the last of d'Angeray's men cross over to the château. They had but now arrived. It was this fear, rather than her communication with de Luppé's groom, which had brought him after her in hot haste, when the report reached him that she and the groom were out on the point of land. A word among the King's men of this arrival, and the whole enterprise became much more difficult. He could take no chances of that. The little spy had got her wages. Obviously the groom, whoever he was, had escaped from the island. That was unfortunate — but much good it would do him! The nearest royal garrison was in Montbrison. On foot through the woods, it would take the man hours to fetch help from there, and by that time the King would be far beyond help and de Norville himself well on the road to Auvergne. Then would come the Bourbon rising. He looked ahead a couple of weeks. Chaos. France in a turmoil, while the English and Imperials swept everything before them. But one thought troubled him: La Palisse. Still, it was impossible that the Marshal could have covered the road from Lyons that day in the short time since the King's secret departure had been learned. No, reckoned de Norville, he was safe enough.

Re-entering the château, he now joined the party at cards in the King's room and excused himself for his absence on the score of household matters.

Francis had been winning and was in high good humor.

"Everything prospers me on this jaunt of ours, Monsieur de Norville," he declared: "good weather, good cheer, even luck at play. And I have no doubt that these are but tokens of the remainder of our visit. In life or in cards, the tide runs one way or another. You know when you're in a winning vein and you should make the most of it. Now, if we'd come tomorrow, everything might have been different. Take time by the forelock, eh?"

"Your Grace could not be more right," said de Norville, making his bet for a large amount and gathering up the hand which had been dealt him. "Timing's the chief point in the art of living. Would that I had Your Majesty's knack for it!" He noticed a dark strand of hair on his cuff and removed it absently. "But I share Your Grace's opinion that Chavan-la-Tour has only begun to afford the entertainment which may be found here." His eyes met the King's. "For instance, Sire, you have not yet sampled the chase. I warrant that the goddess Diana will prove favorable."

Overlooking the game, Louis de Bruges, who was not playing at the moment, whispered to Tristan Gouffier, "Damned pimp!" though his steady lips smiled approvingly.

"Then I drink to her with all my heart," said Francis, emptying his cup. He tossed out a card. "Your play, Monsieur de Norville."

The latter lost heavily in the game, though it was noted by the subtle courtiers that he might have won except for two obvious blunders; and his gold went to the heap of the King's winnings.

"You see," Francis exulted, "I'm unbeatable tonight. I refuse to pillage my friends any longer." He affected a yawn. "It's time to retire, gentlemen. Here, you pages, divide the coin between you. . . . Monsieur de Norville, Monsieur de la Guiche, mes amis, will you see me to bed tonight?"

The two selected acknowledged the honor with deep bows. The others withdrew; a couple to the anteroom, where they would sleep within call, the rest to adjoining quarters. Captain Fédéric stood guard at the door; he would be relieved later by de Bruges.

Assisted by the pages, de Norville and de la Guiche performed the ritual of the royal coucher, much abbreviated on such an informal occasion: stood aside reverently as the King kneeled at his prie-dieu, solemnly handled the royal garments, presented the nightshirt. Unclothed, the King was a fine figure of a man, broad of chest and shoulder, lean of hip, with the hard, flat legs of a horseman. Even without his shoes, he stood a half head taller than the two gentle-men. Finally in bed, he gave them good night, and they bowed themselves out.

Then, on the pretext of seeing personally to the doors and windows of the château, de Norville went downstairs again. Almost as if he were present, he knew what was happening in the King's room. At first a pause to let the household settle down; then a sharp whisper to the two pages who slept at the threshold; a hurried dressing but not so hurried that due attention was not paid to the right set of the hair, a few jewels, renewed perfuming. The lads would be sworn to secrecy; the King would vanish behind the panel of the window recess.

In the vaulted basement, a rattle of steel greeted de Norville's en-trance. He nodded to d'Angeray and others of the tense group.

"Nearly time," he said.

Tossing aside his short mantle, he slipped on a back-and-front corselet, which d'Angeray helped him buckle, then belted on sword and poniard, drew down a close-fitting coif on his head, covered it with a steel cap.

"These are your instructions, gentlemen. Monsieur d'Angeray and I will post ourselves at the top of the stairs in the secret passage, leading from this place to the second floor. When the King enters Milady Russell's room, we shall follow and attack him at once. Our good Master Bertran here will stand at the foot of the passage stairs and know when this occurs. He will pass the word to you. Then pro-ceed at once to the second floor by way of the grand staircase. You know the number and the names of the King's gentlemen with their lackeys. Overpower but do not harm them unless need requires it. They may be good Bourbonians yet. And so, God prosper you! Bear yourselves well in this, and your fortunes are made. Monsieur d'Angeray, we had best get to our post now, though it's likely we'll have some time to wait."

At his touch, an unsuspected door opened in the masonry of the cellar. Before entering, he turned with a smile to face the company again. "Vive Bourbon!" he said, lifting his arm in salute. "Vive la victoire!" Then, followed by d'Angeray, he disappeared into the hol-low of the wall. Many a better man might have envied his gift of leadership.

* * *

354

Hidden behind the screen of pine branches which filled the great canopied fireplace, Blaise had an excellent view of the window recesses and especially of the one with the suspected side panel. On the other hand, he could not see the main door, and it was through this, he of course assumed, the King would enter. That de Norville would disclose the secret of the passageway to his guest did not even occur to him. Accordingly, with ears attentive to any sound at the door, and with his eyes on the panel, he awaited the next development.

It seemed a long time since Anne had shut herself up again in the small adjoining room. But that she was there, close to him, acted like a cordial. Even the suspense of waiting for the fierce game which was about to take place here, the extreme doubt that he would be able to protect the King, the probability of his own death before the candles had burned much lower, did not lessen the glow which her nearby presence brought him. Together at last, if only at the end. No longer division, cross purposes, distrust. Together, masks off. The sense of this colored everything, gave zest even to the desperate affair at hand.

Surely it was more than an hour, to judge by the shrinking candles. Silence everywhere in the house, but, to Blaise's taut nerves, not the usual silence of night: the oppressive quiet of ambush, of coiled alertness.

Then, suddenly, a footstep. Perhaps overhead. He could not place it. A footstep, then another, as of someone walking softly. But even with this warning, the click, gentle as it was, in the window recess startled him. He had only time enough to admit that Anne's guess had been right and that the assassins would await their victim in the room itself, when the panel swung inward, and an unexpected face appeared in the opening.

The King! What was the meaning of this? How would he know of the secret passage? Blaise could not credit his eyesight.

Francis did not enter at once but, with an arch smile, glanced here and there about the room. Then, slipping in and drawing the panel noiselessly to behind him, he began tiptoeing toward the bed.

He wore a long brocaded robe with a lynx collar over his shirt and trunk hose. A filigree bracelet, set with jewels, appeared at one cuff. His perfume filled the room. The light of the candelabra set the gold threads of his robe glimmering as he moved.

Gently parting the curtains of the bed, he peered in but, finding it empty, drew back with a stare and called in a low voice, "Milady!"

No doubt she had been listening as intently as Blaise; for the alcove door opened at once, and she appeared on the threshold.

"Your Majesty is in grave danger," she hurried. "I beg — "

Enchanted at the sight of her, he broke in: "Danger, indeed! A mild word to describe my condition, mademoiselle! Not in danger, but lost — "

"Sire, for the love of God, look behind you!"

It all happened at once. De Norville and d'Angeray were across the room before Blaise could free himself from the pine boughs in the hearth. The King, turning, faced two raised swords. He cried out, "What's this?" At the same moment, Anne stepped in front of him.

De Norville's blow, aimed at the King, whipped down. He could not stop it. But in the last fraction of a second, a turn of his wrist saved her from the edge and brought the flat of the heavy blade upon her head. She sank blindly to her knees, then to her hands, and lay outstretched on the floor. At the same moment, Blaise's sword from behind rang on de Norville's steel cap, glanced from it to his shoulder and severed the hinge connecting the front and back of his corselet. In amazement, de Norville wheeled to meet this attack out of nowhere; while d'Angeray, lashing down at the King, missed his aim, and found himself grappled, wrist and waist.

"A moi!" roared the King, bearing his opponent in front of him across the room until they crashed against the wall. "A moi! Fédéric, La Guiche, Gouffier! Mes amis! A moi!"

He was no weakling to be tamely slaughtered. At once the fop and philanderer reverted to his basic self, the fighter and man-at-arms, the tough soldier of Marignan.

"Ha! By God, whoreson," he raged, heaving d'Angeray from his feet, "look to yourself!"

"Hold him close, Sire," Blaise shouted, parrying a blow of de Norville's and returning it, "until I can deal with him."

"Until you can deal with him, eh?" jeered de Norville, parrying in his turn and changing edge to point in a thrust that ripped the skin at Blaise's side. "We'll see to that! Who the devil are you?"

Blaise saved his breath. But as they circled out closer to the lighted candelabra, he could see that de Norville recognized him.

"De Lallière, by God! This is a pleasure." The two swords grated against each other until the hilts clashed. Body strained against

356

body. Both poniards were out at the same moment. De Norville's gashed Blaise's right shoulder. Blaise aimed at the opening between the other's throat and corselet but missed, and the knife, plunging down, severed the connecting strap on that side. As they broke away, de Norville's corselet hung only by the hinge on the left shoulder, an impediment rather than a protection. He shook it off, and it fell with a clatter.

"On more even terms," hissed Blaise.

"I accept them," de Norville panted. "The de Lallières are my specialty tonight. The brat, your sister — " He parried a blow and returned it. "I say — "

Tumult burst against the locked door. Sword hilts pounded on the panels.

"A moi!" thundered the King, still locked with d'Angeray. "A moi, messieurs!"

But the hope vanished at once. "Bourbon!" yelled de Norville. And "Bourbon!" came the answering roar from outside. The King's few gentlemen had been cut off.

"Break down the door!" shouted de Norville, parrying and thrusting.

The door, stout oak as it was, shook and cracked under the shoulders against it.

Francis, an expert wrestler, brought his opponent down at last, but could not keep uppermost; and they rolled together, now one on top, now the other, though the King did not lose his grip of d'Angeray's wrist.

"God's blood!" cried de Norville, his face running with sweat, a growing horror on it. "Will you not break in that door, you obscenities! — Ah, Christ!" He reeled back, plucking at Blaise's sword that spitted his chest. "Christ!" His blade dropped from his hand, stood an instant upright, then slithered across the room. He collapsed against a table, sank to the floor, the weight of his body freeing Blaise's steel.

A panel of the door burst in.

Blaise sprang to the King's help. At the moment, d'Angeray had the best of it. Tearing his wrist loose, he raised his sword hilt to bring it down on the other's head. The blow did not fall. Blaise's dagger plunged into the nape of d'Angeray's neck.

At once the King was on foot and had snatched up his opponent's sword.

"This way," Blaise gasped, "this way." He pointed to the still open door of the secret passage. "Quick, Sire!"

Anne Russell had struggled to her knees, her hands to her head. Following the King, Blaise stooped to lift her up, one arm around her waist and, half carrying, half supporting her, reached the aperture, helped her through in front of him; then, entering the passage, clicked the panel shut.

In the room behind them, the door crashed open. A torrent of voices swept through.

Blaise stood fighting for breath. It was pitch black in the passage.

"We'd be trapped if we go down," panted the King. "We could make a stand in the gallery — perhaps give them the slip."

"Does Your Grace know the way?"

"Yes, up these steps."

A choked voice reached them from beyond the partition. "The secret passage . . . you'll find them there . . . draw down that molding. . . ."

Chapter 53

Blind in the complete darkness, they reached the upper level of the passage and hurried along it, guided by the walls on either hand; but so black it was that they seemed almost to force their way through a wall in front of them. More than once, Blaise, his arm stretched forward to support Anne, felt her stumble; and the dread of her collapsing in the narrow place crossed his mind. The distance seemed much longer than it actually was until they stood suddenly close together at the foot of the steps leading to the gallery.

"Nous y sommes," boomed the King's voice, magnified by the tunnel. "But curse me if I know how to open whatever door is up there. No time to look for hidden catches. Ha! Par Dieu, they're on our heels."

A glimmer showed at the far end of the passage. No time indeed. The pursuers, directed by the mortally wounded de Norville, had entered through the secret panel and were closing in.

"I believe it's a trap door that can be lifted," said Blaise. "We can try."

358

The King was already climbing the steps.

"Up, Milady!" urged Blaise. But his heart was in his mouth. If the trap could not be lifted, they were pinned there, like rats in a hole.

An oath of satisfaction came from the King. A pale square showed above them from the diffused moonlight in the gallery. An instant later, they were through. But, in that same instant, footsteps were pressing up behind them. Blaise slammed down the trap and could feel the heave under his feet. The King, looking about for some weight, caught sight of the bronze statue of Saint George across the gallery and, half lifting, half dragging, set it up at last with Blaise's help over the square of flooring.

"Stand guard there, Monseigneur le Saint," he breathed. "And a hundred candles if you bear us aid tonight — for, faith, we need it!"

If a couple of men from below could have lifted at one time, the statue might not have held them back. As it was, the narrowness of the passage gave room for only one, and Saint George did not budge.

Blaise said, "The roof perhaps . . ."

But a glimpse through the nearest window put an end to any hope of escape that way. There were no gutters. The wall dropped sheer.

Francis tested the sword which he had acquired from d'Angeray, its balance and temper. "Not bad," he commended. His robe had been thrown off after the struggle, and he now looked a tall, lean figure in his full, white shirt and trunk hose, an excellent costume for swordplay. "Monsieur," he went on, "if you agree, we shall make our stand at the top of the main stairs rather than await the rascals here. It will give us, at least, the advantage of position and elbow-room. I perceive that we shall have a lively passage at arms, with the event in doubt. But no one shall say that the King of France did not give these wolves something to remember. Monsieur, it is odd that I do not know your name or by what good fortune you were in that room to save my life. Let me tell you that I could not wish a braver companion to fight or die with — if it comes to that. Your name?"

Oblivious to everything else except his hand-to-hand fight with d'Angeray, Francis had not heard de Norville's remarks to Blaise; and the semi- or complete darkness in which the entire action had taken place made recognition impossible, apart from Blaise's altered appearance.

"Your Grace," said the latter, "I am a servant of Madame la

Régente, whom she sent here to be of use to Your Highness in case of need. She and the Marquis de Vaulx had strong suspicion of some such stroke as de Norville has just made. My name will not be pleasing to Your Highness. I am Blaise de Lallière."

The King stood motionless an instant, with d'Angeray's blade half bent in his hands. Then he repeated in a low voice "De Lallière! Bon Dieu!" And, after a moment: "No time to speak now of my injustice to you, sir, and to my other friends. But, if I live, I shall speak of it later and at length." Voices hurrying along the corridor of the second floor reached them. "We had better take up our position." Turning to Anne, he said coldly — and Blaise realized that it was the first time he had seemed aware of her since the attack on him — "Milady, you will do well to join your friends below. I thank you for risking your life but now to save mine. When it came to the point, I suppose, you had no stomach for murder. Judas had the same qualms. Precede us, if you please."

When they reached the top of the stairs, a couple of armed men were already on the landing a few yards below them. At the sight of the King and Blaise, they stopped short, waiting for their comrades to come up. The great cloth-covered lantern, hanging down in the stair well from the ceiling, showed their troubled faces and their uncertainty. Without leaders, the Bourbon gentlemen hardly knew what course to take. It was no small matter for simple squires to confront the King.

"A truce," called Francis, "to let this lady pass. She belongs to your party rather than mine."

Anne's headdress had been lost, and her hair, a cascade of bronze, fell to her shoulders. She stood leaning against the doorway of the gallery.

"No," she said. "I'll stay here." Her eyes were on Blaise. "It makes no difference where I am."

A stir in the corridor below interrupted. "Set me down," came a voice, now distinct, now laboring, but unmistakably de Norville's. "God's name! . . . What are you waiting for? . . . You, Le Pont . . . You, Berauld, take the lead. Up with you, all together!" . . . Are twenty of you no match for two?" The voice ended in a spasm of coughing but emerged. "One push, and you have them. . . . Then spur for Auvergne . . . and spread the news. . . . En avant!"

But, for a moment, the rush of the men, now gathered on the stairs, was delayed. Vibrant, racing, urgent, a trumpet call shattered through the building, drowning out de Norville's voice. It was the old rallying call of the companies, the desperate call of "To the standard!" It woke every echo in the house before dying away on a last note.

"It's that mad trumpeter of the King," someone explained. "He got away from us up one of the western turrets and barricaded himself in. Let him blow his lungs out for the good it will do him!"

"Brave Francisque!" said the King to Blaise. "Brave heart!" And, beneath his breath, "There was some talk of La Palisse."

"I sent word, Sire, but it failed. We can't count on the Marshal. Your Grace came a day too soon."

"The more fool I! Well let's be merry, Monsieur de Lallière! We have our own arms and a good fight to use them on. Here come the whoresons. Aim at their faces." He raised his voice to a shout that roared under the vaults of the stair well. "France! France!"

And as if the trumpeter in the turret could hear him, the brazen call sounded again and again, eclipsing the cry of "Bourbon!" as the upward rush began.

There was room on the stairs for three abreast. Standing at each side, the King and Blaise accounted for the first rank, with thrusts to the face, supplemented on the part of Blaise, with a downward shove of one leg against the cuirass of the man in the center. As the three toppled back against those behind them, a tangle ensued which delayed the attack for a moment.

"France!"

"To the standard!" racketed the trumpet.

A second push fared no better than the first. But a third carried to the landing, toppled back and forth, surged ahead.

"Back, Sire!" Blaise shouted, taking two swords on his blade and parrying another with his dagger. "Back! We'll hold them at the doorway."

But the King, for a moment surrounded, had some ado to break free. With the recklessness of a cornered lion, using all his drive and skill, he gained a space for himself and joined Blaise, his shirt torn, his right hand dripping.

"Your Grace is wounded?"

"A scratch only."

Then followed a pause, as the circle of men on the landing hesitated to close with the two dreaded swords. Blaise caught a glimpse of Anne, pinned against the wall in the background, her eyes wide, fixed on him. The clamor of the trumpet swelled louder. It was incredible that one pair of human lungs could raise such a din.

"To the standard!"

Blaise's heart gave a sudden leap. By God, it was not a single trumpet. Another was blaring in the entrance hall two floors below.

"Sire, you hear?"

"Hear! Sainte-Barbe! I'm neither deaf nor dead. Ho! You would, eh?"

A man dashed in. The circle closed. But now, as he fought, spending his last strength in the melée, Blaise listened; heard the clanging rush up the stairs below; the swelling of new voices. "France! France!"

Sweat blinded him. He hardly saw it happen. The attackers melted away; other faces surrounded him. A man in complete harness flicked up his vizor, dropped to one knee in front of the King.

"Thank God, Sire, we did not come too late! On my soul, Francisque's trumpet lifted us over the last quarter-league as if we had wings. Is all well with Your Grace?"

"The better for the sight of you, Monsieur le Maréchal. And thanks, gentlemen, to you all." Turning to Blaise, Francis gripped his shoulder. "As for you, Monsieur de Lallière, it is hardly fitting that the King of France should owe so much to one man."

Blaise drew a sleeve across his eyes. "My duty, Sire, but after all it was Pierre de la Barre who carried word of this to the Marshal and saved us both."

"Where is he? He has only to name his reward."

A shout went up for de la Barre. Someone ran in search of him, but he had disappeared.

Chapter 54

The fear which Renée had expressed haunted Pierre during his mission to Feurs. Upon his return, he immediately searched for her, instead of joining in the fight, which La Palisse's men-at-arms at once had well in hand. Finding no trace of her in the house, he went down to the spot where they had parted. There, at first relieved, then horror-stricken, he found her body close to the water's edge.

Perhaps she had run out here, when the fight began; perhaps she had fainted. He bent down, calling her name. She did not stir. Then, fearfully, he touched her and drew back his hand.

"Renée, darling! M'amour!"

Surely she could not be dead. In the moonlight, she looked only asleep.

At last, he accepted the incredible.

Finally, he carried her into the house in his arms. As someone who saw him declared afterwards, it was like the dead carrying the dead. He spoke, but it was not his voice. He asked merely for some room where he could take her; and, when he had been shown to a little turret chamber with a narrow cot, he laid her down, carefully arranging the white and silver folds of her dress. Having lighted the candles which were brought in, he placed them at her head and feet. Then, sinking down on a stool beside her, he gazed into emptiness.

He seemed unaware of those who entered, or of Blaise, who stood beside him, one hand on his shoulder, in a grief too bitter for words. He did not see La Palisse, who lingered to say a prayer. He did not know that the King had come and then withdrawn, his comfort and his rewards unspoken. He saw nothing beyond the world between the candles, his lost world.

It was startling at last when he looked up at Anne Russell, standing on the other side of the bed. She, too, seemed oblivious to anything but Renée's face peaceful in the light of the candles.

"Milady," he said, "I shall be forever beholden to you if you can find a veil for Mademoiselle my love such as brides wear. Would that be possible? It was a promise."

"Yes," said Anne, "I shall find it." And she left the room, her eyes empty like Pierre's.

Returning, after a time, she brought with her the length of lace which the King had praised last evening, the lace which a Venetian galley had carried from the East. Then tenderly placing it over Renée's head, with here and there a touch and thoughtful laying of the folds, she fashioned a bridal veil such as a royal princess might have worn.

"Does it please you, sir?"

He stood silent. Then he took Renée's hand.

"Is she not beautiful, Milady? Is she not beautiful?"

"Most beautiful."

He held Renée's hand, his lips moving; but Blaise could see that it was not in prayer. A whisper. "I, Pierre Louis . . ."

For a while longer, he kept her hand in his. Then, suddenly kneeling, he buried his face in his arms upon the bed.

And so they left him.

But downstairs, in another room, the King and La Palisse stood by the couch of the dying de Norville. Adroit to the last, he was escaping them; and their eyes were hard and their mouths bitter. He would not furnish an example of royal justice in the great square at Lyons. Death baffled them. But perhaps he would speak to some purpose before he died.

De Norville had sent away the chaplain attached to the château, who had been summoned to administer the last rites; for these, on the pain of mortal sin, could not be denied to the blackest villain.

"Nenni, Dom Thomas," he gasped, "don't bother. I may fool others, I do not fool myself."

And the King derived some comfort from this. After all, Hell was a substitute for the great square at Lyons and lasted longer. Now, with La Palisse beside him, he stared down at de Norville's face, which was still handsome except when spasms of pain convulsed it. The eyes were closed; a spume of blood showed now and then at the lips; he was sinking fast.

"Come!" growled La Palisse. "Have you nothing to tell us? What do you lose now by speaking the truth?" There was no answer. The Marshal added, "Devil take the luck!"

Then suddenly de Norville's eyes opened. His lips twitched. "What do I *gain?* That's the point, messieurs." But after a moment, he breathed, "I may have time to answer a question."

"Tell me," the King asked, "what part has Milady Russell had in this?"

"Yes." De Norville struggled an instant with the blood in his throat. "A letter to her . . . from Sir John . . . in my wallet. Her instructions." He managed to smile. "No forgery, this time. Quite damning!"

He indicated a side pocket. La Palisse drew out several papers, among them the letter, which he handed the King.

Francis spread it out hastily under the candlelight. His face grew darker.

"Indeed!" he said, when he had finished. "As much a Judas as you."

De Norville made a supreme effort. "We are so much alike. Between us, we could have attained . . . to great power in Europe. Raise me a little, Monsieur de la Palisse. I could speak better."

Grimly the Marshal supported him with his arm, thrust a pillow behind him, and stepped back.

"Grand merci," said de Norville, catching his breath. "Yes . . . a gifted woman . . . a cool brain. She laughed at . . . Your Grace's gullibility." His voice faded. " 'King Fool,' she used to say . . . 'King Fool.' . . ."

La Palisse raised his arm but Francis caught it. "No. Listen attentively. Remember what you hear."

A gleam showed in de Norville's eyes. He grimaced, whether with pain or triumph, it was hard to tell.

"She advised me in this plot. But I would not use poison . . . a woman's weapon . . . Perhaps I was wrong. I think . . . she fears the sight of blood. . . . Her one weakness." He shook with a fit of coughing, the red spume on his lips. "Give her my love."

La Palisse cut in. "Is this true, man? Remember, what you have said will bring her to the stake."

"My dying confession," whispered de Norville. "Be sure . . . to give her my love."

A convulsion took him. He fell to one side, plucking at the couch, then, after a moment, he lay still. When La Palisse turned him over, his distorted face was hideous to look at. Both men turned away, crossing themselves.

"A pity," murmured La Palisse, "that we could not learn more."

"We have learned enough," said the King. "By my soul, his corpse shall burn with her in the same fire."

Chapter 55

Louise de Savoie, accompanied by the Marquis de Vaulx, left Lyons as soon as the report of the King's headlong departure reached her. Riding hard until nightfall and starting again at dawn, she arrived at Chavan-la-Tour early next day. Fear lent wings. The news that de Norville had suggested this change of date to the King confirmed the suspicions of him and pointed to imminent danger. With her usual foresight, the Regent had seen to it that La Palisse should be in Feurs with a day to spare, but her entire plan was risky at best and left room for a good deal of suspense. Great, then, was the relief and triumph, when a horseman, sent on ahead to reconnoiter, returned with the tidings of last night's action, de Norville's death, and the King's safety. All had turned out to her wish, and she could dismount in the courtyard of the château with every reason for elation.

But neither she nor the Marquis was so tactless as to overplay their hand with the King. They found Francis in a chastened, sensitive mood, which required soothing rather than reproaches.

"Ma foi," he told them, "on an occasion like this, I would almost rather be surrounded by my enemies than my friends. And I ask your lordships most mercifully not to rub salt in the wounds. They smart enough without that."

It was plainly the cue both of his mother and his old minister to let well enough alone and to lay the entire blame on de Norville. His Majesty had not been the only one deceived by that arch-hypocrite and villain. Even the astute Chancellor Duprat had been completely bubbled, as well as most of the court. Nay, the Regent declared, it could be truly affirmed that said de Norville was in league with Satan himself. What wonder, then, that the King, for all his native shrewdness and insight, had been the victim of diabolic wiles, from which even the greatest saints were not secure?

But, perhaps, it was Denis de Surcy who most accurately epitomized de Norville. "He was, Your Majesty — I say it with sorrow — the most complete exemplar of our modern age whom it has been my ill fortune to know. He was all intelligence, without one grain of heart or faith. Beauty he loved, but found nothing divine in it. And this single-minded worship of intelligence and art is the creed which makes devils of men. Thank Heaven for those stupidities, if they are such, that incline us to fear of God and reverence of the past. For so are we guided to think less of ourselves — and of our trivial mortality."

Francis agreed. "You say well, Monsieur de Marquis, you say well. I shall bear it in mind. . . . But how to keep this wretched affair secret? It does not serve the public interest to let it be known that the King has been so cozened. We must avoid ridicule."

"I have taken order for that," put in the Regent. "Your visit to this place was incognito and will not be chronicled. Your gentlemen,

366

who were taken off guard last night and disarmed, have every reason to keep quiet about it. The Marshal vouches for his men-at-arms. The knaves who took part in the attack will be hanged at once. It will be well if Milady Russell is burned at Feurs or Montbrison on the charge of conspiracy and the attempted murder of Your Highness. We shall have no public gossip."

"I thank you, madame," the King approved. "You think of everything. I have sworn to have de Norville's body strapped with her to the same stake. And they shall be taken hence together in the same cart. They were so much alike, he said. 'Give her my love,' he said with his last breath. My word, they shall not be parted."

Louise gave her pinched smile. "A fitting judgment. Let her be associated in the public mind with him, not with Your Grace. She may demand a trial; but, as a foreign spy, she is outside the law. Does she know her sentence?"

"It shall be imposed at once." He directed a servant to inform her guards that the English woman, known as Anne Russell, was to be brought in.

"Do not weaken," cautioned the Regent, glancing sidelong at him.

The King flushed. "Madame, to have been bewitched is no crime, as Your Highness pointed out. But, believe me, the spell was soundly broken last night. And the witch shall burn."

Meanwhile, the royal decision with respect to Anne Russell had been generally reported, together with the dying de Norville's charges against her. The account of it reached Blaise from the very guard who had been stationed at de Norville's door and had witnessed the latter's death. His Grace, said the guard, was in hot rage against Mademoiselle de Russell, not only because of what had happened, but by reason of a letter which de Norville had communicated in proof of his statements. Worst of all was the charge that Milady would have used poison against His Majesty, had de Norville permitted it. And, to fill up the measure, she had laughed at the King for a fool.

The good man-at-arms who related this was only paying his court to Blaise as the hero of the moment and the new favorite. He happened to be one of the Marshal's lances who had been present at de Chamand's hunting lodge, and he knew of the trick which had all but cost Blaise his life. The present report could only be good news and a full vengeance. He marveled that Monsieur de Lallière took it so grimly.

As for de Norville's "confession," Blaise knew it at once for the last sting of a dying adder. The talk he had overheard in Anne's room explained it. But he had heard nothing about the letter. He wondered if she knew of it and, late though the hour was, sent a page to learn whether he might have word with her.

"I regret, monsieur," said the lad, returning, "Milady is now under guard, and no one may have speech with her, except by the King's order."

After that, worn out as he was, Blaise did not close his eyes during the night. The most envied man at Chavan-la-Tour, he could only regard his success as the bitterest irony. Because of it, Anne Russell, the woman he had come to love better than life itself, was doomed, unless, by some means, he contrived to save her. He had no illusions about the difficulty of the task. There was no lingering fondness on the King's part to help him. That infatuation had turned to gall. Every appearance — in part justified — was against her. She had used her charm to decoy the King into an ambush with a view to his capture. It was only a weak defense to plead that she did not intend his death and had acted a role which she hated because of her loyalty to the English Sovereign. Even so, she remained guilty in the eyes of the King.

As he tossed back and forth, nightmare pictures of the hideous death which had been decreed alternated in Blaise's mind with fantastic schemes of rescue too impractical for a moment's consideration. No, if Anne was to be saved, it must be by cleverness in speech rather than by force. He rehearsed one eloquent approach after the other, realizing that, when the time came, he would have to use his wits as the spirit moved him.

The arrival of the Marquis de Vaulx in the morning raised hopes of an ally, and he poured himself out to that nobleman as soon as he could get him aside. But de Surcy was in no sympathetic mood.

"Mon fils," he answered, "I can well understand that you're taken with this woman. Her fascination has been amply proved. It may be, too, that she's not as guilty as she seems. But the fact remains that she might have refused to bait de Norville's hook and did not. Being no fool, she must have known what sort of man she was dealing with. Consequently, it is little fault of hers that the King at this moment is not dead and the kingdom in such confusion that there would be little hope of saving it. The punishment of burning is terrible — I wish it did not exist — but still more dreadful punishments are inflicted on those guilty of practicing against the King's life. I can see no reason for sparing her when many another, far more innocent than she, has been sent to the stake. No, mon fils, it would need the tongue of the late de Norville himself to talk her free of this; and, God knows, he did what he could to seal her death warrant."

De Norville! A sudden light went up in Blaise's mind. How would de Norville have carried it in this case? Would he stickle over scruples and strain at gnats, if he wished to save her? Most certainly not. To ruin her, he had not refrained from adding lie to lie with his last breath. And, if it took a de Norville to plead her cause, Blaise must put on the dead man's shoes. Let de Norville save her from de Norville's vengeance. The burning hatred Blaise felt for him, alive or dead, found satisfaction in the thought.

Viewing the problem, then, from de Norville's standpoint, Blaise determined to make the most of his one great asset. He had saved the King's life at the risk of his own, not only once but repeatedly during last night's battle. The Prince's former suspicions had been so completely reversed that anything which Blaise now said would carry conviction. But he must have luck. He must play the de Norville role before the King had pronounced sentence on Anne and thus placed himself in a position from which he could not retreat without loss of dignity.

"Monseigneur," he begged of the Marquis, "will you at least do me the favor of suggesting to His Majesty that I should be grateful for a moment's audience before he renders final judgment on Milady Russell. There are some matters which I have not yet disclosed to him — or, indeed, to your lordship — which are pertinent to the case."

"I'll do that," agreed de Surcy, "But, my son, for God's sake, be careful. Your affairs are now most flourishing. Don't ruin them and yourself, too, out of foolish sentiment for a woman who does not deserve it."

"I shall be careful, indeed, monseigneur," Blaise answered.

Then, with de Norville very much in mind, he hurried off to make himself as presentable as possible. The villainous model he was copying was always well groomed. The King did not like shabby people. With the help of a couple of pages, who today would do anything for Monsieur de Lallière, Blaise shaved off his beard, had his hair trimmed and brushed, secured a new suit from the de Norville wardrobe, and achieved a proper degree of splendor.

If Anne, he worried, would only play up to him, when the time came! That was another risk. He would have given anything for a word with her. Accused of duplicity as she was, what he most feared now was her inherent honesty.

Then, hastening back to the Marquis again, in hope that the latter had secured him the wished-for audience, he found that his luck was out. The King had already given order that Milady Russell should be brought before him in the grande salle. He and the Regent had taken their places. No time remained for a private interview. The best that de Surcy had been able to manage was a cordial invitation to Blaise to be present when sentence was passed. "And, faith," the King had said, "I owe it to him."

Chapter 56

With his heart in his boots, Blaise entered the great room. Francis and the Regent sat at one end. La Palisse stood beside them. De la Guiche, de Bruges, and de Montpezat, looking properly dejected, were on duty. The Marshal's men-at-arms stood guard at the doors or were at intervals along the walls. To speak before such an audience required twice the boldness and address which Blaise would have needed if he could have talked with the King alone.

But the thought of de Norville steadied him. Would that scoundrel have been dashed by a roomful of people? He would have risen superbly to the occasion. He would have been simply more brazen and more assured. And what a villain could do, Blaise could do — all the more since he cared not a farthing what happened to him if he failed.

Catching sight of him and the Marquis, Francis beckoned. "Venez-ça, messieurs. It is only right that you, my good friends, should stand beside me at the close of this affair, in which you have played so honorable a part. I trust now to make some amends to you for — " the King hesitated — "for the annoyance you may have had in connection with it, by doing justice upon your enemy and mine."

Blaise made a bow to the King and the Regent, equal to de Norville's best.

Louise smiled at him. "Ha, Monsieur de Lallière! I hear great things of you. You have more than fulfilled my expectations. Be sure that I shall not forget it."

"And I," threw in the King pleasantly, "am delighted to see you restored after your labors of last night. Ma foi, you look transformed — "

He broke off as Monsieur de Luppé, at the door, announced the prisoner.

Smiles vanished. Faces stiffened. Between hard glances, in complete silence, Anne Russell advanced alone down the room toward her royal judges. Her face impassive, her head held high, she walked slowly, as if taking part in some state ceremony. She wore a long green mantle, which set off the bronze of her hair and added to her stature. Slender, fearless, queenly, she impressed even the hostile onlookers; and the hush deepened as she approached the King. Her bearing dignified the occasion. She was not merely a woman about to be condemned, but a great lady of a great kingdom. The House of Russell, the pride of England, was identified with her.

She stopped at some paces from the King and swept a low curtsy, such as good breeding required; but she did not kneel, and no one was petty enough to correct the omission.

A brief silence followed. How, thought Blaise desperately, was he to speak under these circumstances? What pretext could he find to gain a hearing in advance of the King's arraignment of Anne, to be followed by her sentence? Much depended on timing. Then his luck took an unexpected turn; for, instead of addressing Anne, Francis turned to him.

"Monsieur de Lallière, some time ago at Saint-Just, misled by the deceits of the villain whom you did me the service of killing last night, I condemned you to death in the presence of this woman, de Norville's ally and decoy. She triumphed then. It is only fitting that you should triumph now in the knowledge that her intrigues, which you did so much to foil, are to have their just payment. I congratulate you."

Blaise drew a long breath. He glanced at Anne, who was eying him inscrutably. She gave a faint smile.

"Your Grace," he answered in de Norville's best manner, "is the soul of kindness. It is by virtue of this that I dare entreat Your Majesty's permission to reveal a secret, which the pressure of events last night and today has given Your Grace no leisure to hear. I am

371

persuaded, Sire, that justice, as well as your royal pleasure, will be served by the intelligence which I beg leave to submit."

"Indeed?" stared the King. "Well, say on."

De Surcy pursed his lips and shook his head, but Blaise did not look at him.

"First, Sire, it is difficult to believe that Milady Russell was de Norville's ally, since she has been so heartily mine, as well as devoted to Your Majesty. Nor is this strange, since I have the honor to inform Your Grace that she is my promised wife."

If a bolt from the blue had struck suddenly in the center of the grand salle, its effect could not have been more startling. Astonishment expressed itself in a paralyzed silence. But, among them all, no one looked so amazed as Anne Russell herself. Her lips parted. Her eyes widened on Blaise in complete incomprehension.

"Your promised wife!" breathed Francis at last. "She was betrothed to de Norville."

Now that he had gained a foothold in the breach, Blaise determined to keep it at all costs. Pile lie on lie. Give his hearers no time to think. But, using the de Norville method, sprinkle in truth enough for plausibility.

"Yes, Sire, betrothed before she had ever met him — by her brother, Milord Russell, and the Cardinal of York. She proudly rejected such a betrothal and did me the honor of pledging herself to me."

"When was this?" snapped the Regent.

"Madame, if I had no strict regard for the truth, I should say on our ride to Geneva; for, indeed, we came to an understanding of our own sentiments at that time. But Milady was then in the service of her King; while I, of course, belonged to His Majesty of France. We agreed to await the end of her service before plighting our troth, so that we might feel free to act with a clear conscience in the interest of our several princes. And, faith, she did marvelously well for Henry of England. But, to be exact, madame, we exchanged our vows at Monsieur de Chamand's hunting lodge after she had tricked me during the ride from Nantua. For there she resolved that her service of England had come to an end. This, Sire" — he turned to Francis — "will explain why Milady Russell did not avoid arrest, in spite of my urging. She came to Lyons not to conspire against Your Majesty but to save my life."

372

"But, look you," the King protested, "she did nothing that I recall — "

"Sire, by your leave, she did everything. She procured my escape from Pierre-Scize." And, to give no room for troublesome questions, he plunged into an account of Maître Thibault and his bribe that muddied the water still more. As he talked, his glance slid around to Anne. She was regarding him with a quizzical expression that gave him no assurance. Ah, God, if she would only bear him out! She must see that, if she failed him, he was weaving a noose for his own neck. And being, at the moment on safe ground, he added, "Is it not true, Milady?"

"Yes," she nodded, to his vast relief. "That's true."

The King exclaimed: "Well, pardie, I thank her for it. But did she not act with de Norville in coming here to Chavan-la-Tour, pose as his fiancée, make herself agreeable to us, dissemble his conspiracy, and so abet him that we all but lost our life? Do you call that being true to you and devoted to us?"

Here was ice so thin that it looked like sheer water. Now let de Norville speak as he never spoke before.

"Sire, I beg Your Majesty to recall the devilish enchantments used by that archvillain, de Norville, to disguise himself to Your Majesty as an angel of light. They were such that not even Madame la Régente or Monseigneur de Vaulx could unseat him in Your Grace's esteem. Consider then the position of Milady, a prisoner, a confessed agent of England. Had she warned Your Highness of this hypocrite, would she have been believed? Would she not rather have deprived herself of the only means she had of serving Your Grace? No, Sire, she was forced, though against her will, to pluck a leaf from de Norville's book, and, while appearing to act with him, risk her very life for Your Majesty as, indeed, she showed plainly last night by throwing herself before his sword." Blaise glanced at the Regent. "How else could de Norville be exposed than by allowing him to expose himself? Do you not agree, madame?"

Louise de Savoie looked noncommittal. She had no wish to accept the blame for a plan so risky as the one she had sponsored. "Perhaps," she murmured.

"At least so Milady believed," Blaise went on. "When I arrived here, we at once conferred. I told her of Monseigneur the Marshal's presence at Feurs. What afterwards befell is wholly due to her management. If we were not allies in the service of Your Majesty, how

373

else should I have come to be concealed in her room? And, in that connection, it would be well to explain the lies with which de Norville at the moment of death sought to destroy her."

Blaise paused to heighten the suspense. The eyes of everyone in the room were fastened on him.

"Yes?" said the King. "Yes?"

"I overheard the last talk which Milady Russell and de Norville had. Then she unmasked herself to him, denounced his infamy, proclaimed herself the servant of Your Grace. Is it not so, Milady?"

"Yes, I spoke in those terms."

"And took a grave risk." Blaise pictured de Norville's rage and hatred. He would have stabbed her then if he had dared. As it was, he did worse by poisoning His Majesty's gracious mind against her, for which, Blaise devoutly hoped, he was now finding his just punishment.

"And so, good my lord," Blaise concluded, sinking to his knees before the King, "my betrothed and I throw ourselves upon Your Majesty's august mercy" (Blaise glanced appealingly at Anne. Why the devil didn't she kneel? But she stood straight as a lance.), "beseeching Your Grace to forgive any errors we may have committed in the past and to crown our happiness by looking with favor on our marriage."

A vast sigh went around the room. Francis gazed bewildered at the Regent, at La Palisse, at the Marquis.

"Grand Dieu!" he muttered. And then, appealing to Anne: "You have not spoken, Mademoiselle de Russell. Is this true?"

Blaise's heart stopped, as he waited for her answer.

"I will not deny it," she said.

"One moment," the Regent put in dryly. "It is the custom, when people exchange promises of marriage, to exchange pledges as well, and gentlemen are apt to wear these about their persons. May I ask to see hers, Monsieur de Lallière?"

Anne bit her lips, then looked up sharply as Blaise answered: "With all my heart, madame. It is a jewel most dear to those who have the honor of wearing it; and that Milady parted with it signifies not only her pledge to me but her allegiance to France." He had been fumbling at his neck and now disengaging a thin chain, he placed it with its pendant in the hand of the Duchess. "You will perceive, madame, that it is the Tudor Rose."

"Jesu bless us!" exclaimed Anne in English. Her face showed wonder, relief and amusement.

The Regent fingered the medal, and the eyes of everyone were on her. "It is indeed," she said, "the badge of the English King, much prized and worn only by his confidants. See," she held it out to Francis, who examined it in turn. "I believe that Monsieur de Lallière has told us the truth."

"But . . ." objected the King, "but . . ." Like a man teased by flies, one *but* assailed him after the other.

"I know," the Regent agreed, "I know. What Monsieur de Lallière has said is most *remarkable*." She gave him a sidelong look; her nose twitched. "But who can doubt a man of Monsieur de Lallière's proved integrity? As I view it, Sire, the facts are these. Milady Russell is now the affianced bride of that man whom all France today has every cause to honor. As such, she deserves esteem, aside from the eminent services which, on the testimony of Monsieur de Lallière, she has rendered to Your Majesty. We must therefore wish her happiness and thank her most heartily for assisting our good friend in his mission at Chavan-la-Tour."

She blinked slightly, with that indefinable look of the expert bar·gainer who sees a good opening.

"We are much indebted to Monsieur de Lallière, but, from the ardor with which he speaks, I make no doubt that he will hold us acquitted of any further reward if he obtains the hand of Milady Russell. Am I right, monsieur? Of course," she added, "in view of your services, I think we could promise the release of your father and the restitution of his lands."

"I shall never live long enough," Blaise glowed, "to express my thanks in words and in deeds to Your Highness and to His Majesty."

"Then, my lord," said Louise to the King, with the grand manner of one who bestows a benefit that costs nothing, "I think we should so decide."

The King turned to de Surcy. "What's your opinion, monsieur? For there is none I value so highly."

The Marquis controlled a smile, but he could not suppress the twinkle in his eyes.

"Far be it from me," he said, "to differ from Madame la Régente in any way. But if I may add a suggestion, it would be that Monsieur de Lallière and Mademoiselle de Russell should marry at once, and that he should be made answerable with his life, if by any chance, she relapses into the service of England."

"Well put," nodded Francis. "You hear, mon ami?"

"My life on it," Blaise repeated.

"You hear, Milady?"

She smiled. "Most excellently well, Your Grace."

"And I," said de Surcy, "shall be no less answerable for her myself. With Your Majesty's permission, I shall keep her fast a prisoner at Surcy-le-Château, when her husband returns to the army, as no doubt he will. And this is all the more fitting since, with Your Grace's permission, I have resolved to bequeath my estates to Monsieur de Lallière. It is only right then that he and Madame" — he bowed to Anne — "should accompany me to Touraine on their wedding journey."

"So be it." The King stood up. The tense room relaxed. "It is seldom," he said, "that the course of justice finds so pleasant an ending. You have heard your sentence, Milady Russell. This day before sundown you will be married to Monsieur de Lallière. Stand nearer."

She approached him with lowered eyes. He took her hand and gave it to Blaise.

"Be happy."

One by one, the Regent and then the gentlemen present congratulated them. But, singularly enough, the Marquis de Vaulx said nothing until, all the bows and compliments being over, Blaise and Anne withdrew to the petite salle, where a deep window recess looked out upon the lake. There he followed them and kissed them heartily. Then he said to Blaise: "Monsieur mon fils, I hope you took note of my remark about your return to the army."

"I did, monseigneur. With war upon us, it's only natural that I should rejoin my company and Monsieur de Bayard."

"It's more than natural, mon fils," said the other with mock solemnity, "it's urgent. After your wedding journey, the sooner you're back with Captain Bayard, the better."

"How so?" Blaise asked, startled. "Is there bad news?"

"The worst possible for you. Your soul is in danger. This career you've been following is not for you."

"But I have not failed."

"By no means. You have succeeded too well. I grieve to tell you that at moments during this last performance of yours before the

376

King, something in your voice and manner reminded me of the late Monsieur de Norville himself. Is it not so, Milady?"

Anne nodded. "Yes, I was shocked. *What* a liar!"

Blaise flushed. "I beg — "

"No use begging, my son," struck in de Surcy. "Get back to armor and hard knocks and honest company. That's your native air. Perhaps the corruption hasn't spread too far."

He burst out laughing, clapped Blaise on the shoulder, and left them.

At last they were alone. Blaise tried to smile, met Anne's severe gaze, felt red and helpless, looked at the floor.

"Villain!" she said finally.

He was too stricken for any sense of humor. "Milady," he burst out, "don't you understand? I couldn't do anything else. I thought . . . I hoped that you might — "

"Villain! And I believed you honest! We have an English saw about killing two birds with one stone. I never heard of three. But you save my life, propose to me, and compel me to marry you, all in one breath. I call that clever."

"Compel?" he repeated. "Milady, I know it has that appearance. I hoped, as I say, that you would not so regard it. God knows how much I . . . But there must be some way out . . ."

"No, Monsieur de Lallière, you have seen to that. There is no way out. Remember how Saint Paul says that it is better to marry than burn."

"Alas!"

She took pity on him so suddenly that he had no time to realize it until her lips were pressed to his.

"And I am burning now," she said, "and have been burning a long time for you, m'amour, a long, long time. So, there is no way out."

They stood lost in each other. The shimmering reflection on the water lay before them, then the circle of the woods; beyond that, the world, the years.

But someone has written that they who have once been happy have received life's tribute and made a conquest of time.

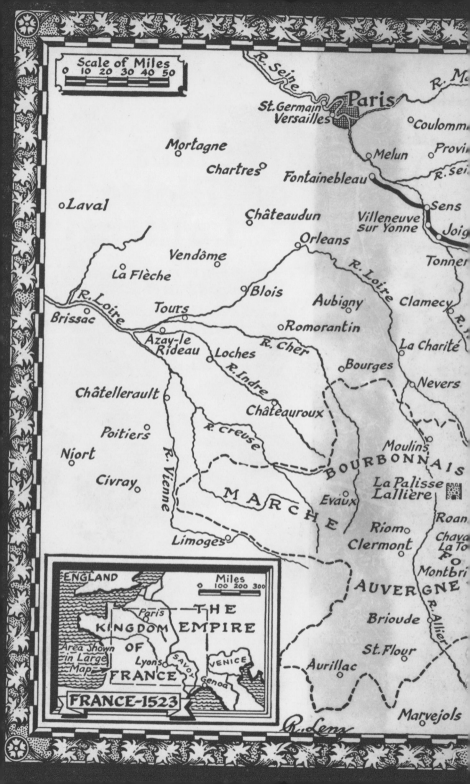